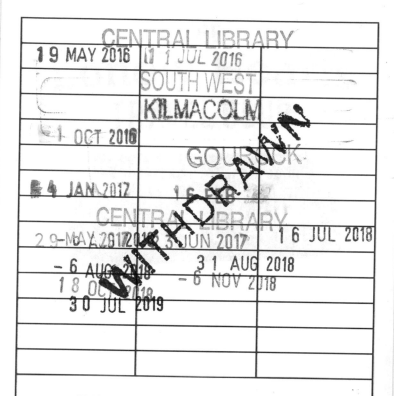

DESTINATION: THAILAND

Katy
Colins

CARINA

This edition is published by arrangement with Harlequin Books S.A. CARINA is a trademark of Harlequin Enterprises Limited, used under licence.

First Published in Great Britain 2016
by Carina, an imprint of HarperCollins*Publishers*
1 London Bridge Street, London, SE1 9GF

© 2016 Katy Colins

ISBN 978-0-263-92365-0

98-0115

Our policy is to use papers that are natural, renewable and recyclable products and made from wood grown in sustainable forests.
The logging and manufacturing processes conform to the legal environmental regulations of the country of origin.

Printed and bound by
CPI Group (UK) Ltd, Croydon, CR0 4YY

KATY COLINS

Katy completed her first novel *A Dogs Tale* at the age of 11 which received rave reviews . . . from her Grandad and English teacher. This was just the encouragement she needed to carry on writing.

As a qualified journalist with articles published in *Company* magazine and *The Daily Star* she crossed sides to work in Public Relations before selling all she owned to backpack solo around South East Asia, finally put her thoughts into words, writing as she travelled.

Katy currently lives by the sea in France where she is on a one-woman mission to educate the French about the necessity and technicalities of making a good cup of tea. When she is not writing about romance, travel and adventure, she loves travelling, catching up with family and friends and convincing herself that her croissant addiction isn't out of control – just yet.

You can find out more about Katy, her writing and her travels on her blog www.notwedordead.com or via twitter @notwedordead

Subscribe to her blog for your free quick guide to Thailand, inspired by *Destination Thailand*!

Available from
KATY COLINS

The Lonely Hearts Travel Club

Destination: Thailand

Destination: India

Destination: Chile

Gather ye rosebuds while ye may.

Grandad, this is for you.

CHAPTER 1

Wanderlust (n.) A strong desire or urge to wander or travel and explore the world

It was my wedding day. A day I'd been fantasising about since I was a little girl, a day I had spent the last twelve months planning and organising. It was going to be a rustic English country wedding, complete with homemade bunting strung from the beams of an outrageously expensive manor house and a billowing marquee set up in the perfectly manicured grounds. The harpist would pluck a simple but charming set as we glided into the grand reception room with our nearest and dearest cheering and clapping our arrival as Mr and Mrs Doherty. That was the part I was cacking myself about the most; all those people staring at me, expecting a radiant blushing bride, when really I was terrified I would go arse over tit on my train. Being the centre of attention made my stomach churn and my sweat glands go into overdrive, but I'd limited the numbers as much as I could and *technically* I was only half of the centre of attention.

I should be in my creamy, laced, fishtail gown by now. As I glanced at my watch, I realised the hand-tied bouquets of soft powder-blue forget-me-nots, complemented by the sweet scent of freesias, should have been delivered ten minutes ago. I should be preparing to sink into the plush chair at the pricy hairdresser's as they transformed my limp locks into a work of art.

Except that I was sat on an uncomfortable plastic sun lounger trying to hide the big fat tears falling down my slightly sunburnt face, as my best friend Marie passed me yet another dodgy watered-down sex on the beach punch from the all-inclusive pool bar.

In one hour's time I would have married my fiancé, Alex, but this had all changed fifteen days earlier when I was half-watching a re-run of *Don't Tell the Bride* whilst triple-checking the seating plan matched up to the 3D replica Alex's sister-in-law Francesca had loaned me. She was the one who'd been to school with Kate Middleton, and managed to bring it up in *every* conversation I'd ever had with her. Waiting for him to arrive home after yet *another* late shift at work, I had become so engrossed in the episode in which the henpecked husband-to-be had got it oh-so-wrong by choosing a size eight dress for his blatantly curvy size sixteen bride, that I hadn't realised Alex was standing in the doorframe chewing his fingernails and loosening his tie.

'We need to talk.' His voice sounded strangled and distant. His tie had an ink stain that no doubt I'd get chastised by his mother for not being able to scrub off. She'd pursed her lips many a time at my lack of domestic goddesstry. Alex had rebelled against it at the beginning, being the last single man in a family of smug married older brothers. I had been the breath of fresh air next to his Martha Stewart sisters-in-law. Five years later that sweet scent had soured into country air.

We'd met at a dodgy indie nightclub in Manchester, having been dragged there by our respective best friends one wet Saturday night. Bonding over cheap lager in plastic pint pots, chatting like long-lost friends to the strains of the Smiths and the Kaiser Chiefs, as our two 'besties' got off with each other. After sharing a deep appreciation of cholesterol-clogging cheesy chips in the taxi ride back home, and a mutual love for garlic mayo, I knew this was something special.

The years passed, the clubbing stopped as focusing on climbing the career ladder became a priority. After years of renting mould-filled hovels with dodgy landlords, we had saved up enough to buy our own home. Alex had proudly turned down his parents' offer of financial support, so we couldn't live in Millionaires' Row rubbing shoulders with WAGs like the rest of his family, but he'd revelled in our bohemian charm, even if it meant our neighbours were often more likely to be guests on Jeremy Kyle. I'd loved how steadfast he was to his morals, even if at times we could have done with a helping hand.

So it was inevitable when one wet June night Alex asked me to marry him. OK, so it wasn't the engagement of my dreams. He hadn't even got down on one knee, just passed the ring box over as we shared an Indian takeaway, both of us on our iPhones half-watching *Coronation Street*. He did leave me the last poppadum, so that was something, I guess. Of course, that wasn't the engagement story we told people. No, in that one he'd whisked me away unexpectedly, showered me with unconditional adorations of love and asked a nearby elderly couple to take our photo; me blubbing and him bursting with pride, shame that they couldn't use the camera properly, meaning we had no evidence of this. But real life isn't like a Disney film, is it?

However, with both a mortgage to pay and a wedding to save for we'd gone out less and less. So yeah, maybe life had got a little stale; routine ruled our world and I could recite the TV guide off by heart, but we were building a future together, that's what we both wanted, wasn't it?

Looking up at his tired face in the doorway, I didn't recognise the man who had bounded into the basement club years earlier asking me to dance. Then, looking down at myself in stained oversized pyjamas, I didn't recognise the fresh-faced girl who'd said yes.

'It's not working…I, I, can't marry you,' he stuttered, his thin fingers nervously twitching down his stained tie.

He'd met someone else, a girl from his work who he'd started to develop '*feelings*' for. He didn't want it to be like this but he had changed, we had changed. He didn't need to spell it out, but his mother was right, I just wasn't marriage material. As with the voluptuous bride on the TV in the too-tiny dress, I felt like I couldn't breathe. He packed his bag that night and left, as I sobbed, drank an old bottle of peach schnapps, spilling half onto Francesca's seating plan, and curled up in a ball, not believing my world was falling down around me.

'Come on, let it all out.' Marie rubbed my sun-heated back as tears plopped into my now warm glass. She had decided that we had to get away for what would have been the big day, so hastily booked us a week's last-minute holiday to the Aegean coast, dubbed the St Tropez of Turkey. This accolade had obviously come from someone who had never visited southern France, as the once-sleepy Turkish fishing village was now a prime party spot full of neon-lit bars, kebab shops and tattoo parlours. Not that we had hit the town – the past few nights had been spent playing cards on the balcony, downing a bottle or two of cheap white wine, Marie slagging Alex off, as I fluctuated between brutal put-downs and scared sob-fests that I wasn't strong enough to be alone.

'Thank you. It's just… Well, that's it…done.' I wiped sweaty strands of hair from my blotchy face, fixing my red-rimmed eyes on Marie's. She winced, not just at my appearance but because her idea of guaranteed sun, hot men and an all-inclusive bar being the perfect solution to my pain wasn't exactly going to plan.

She paused for a moment, rearranging her small bum on the hard seat. 'Think about it, Georgia, you're exactly right.' She paused. 'It is all in the past and now it's time to look to your future. And as we're both single ladies, the best way to get through today is to show Alex a big fat two fingers and have a wicked time together. So I'm taking charge and I rule we're going to the beach.' Marie jumped up, stuffed our things into an oversized Primark beach bag and put her extremely large floppy sun hat on.

'I guess,' I pathetically murmured, gulping the dregs of my drink.

'Come on! You can do this, I know you can. Let's work on our tans and then tonight we'll find a really cool place to go and have fun, just the two of us, like the old days.'

I nodded and scraped my chlorine-soaked hair up into a messy top knot and jogged to catch up with her, my cheap flip-flops loudly slapping against the wet tiles. Strolling down the small rocky path connecting the hotel to the busy beach, our eyes took in row upon row of full sun loungers.

'Bugger, it's a bit crowded isn't it?' Marie chewed her lips, clasping a hand over her eyes to see further, even though they were covered in oversized Jackie O sunglasses.

'Yeah, you could say that,' I sighed, my resolve slipping as I thought longingly of an afternoon snooze back in our room between crisp white sheets. The sound of laughter, cars tooting and music wafting out from the competing beach bars was making my head spin. *Why couldn't Marie just let me sleep today and wake me up once the church, the cake cutting and even the first dance had passed?*

'Come on, hun. Let's wander along a bit, I'm sure I overheard there's a little cove not too far away,' Marie said chirpily, acting like a Girl Guide off on an adventure, which belied the fact she had been expelled from Brownies for giving Tawny Owl food poisoning trying to get her cook badge.

Snaking down the sandy beach, past thick fragrant bushes, and successfully navigating rocky steps, we eventually arrived at a pristine horseshoe bay, which had just a smattering of sun loungers. I felt my bunched-up shoulders relax a little. We had found a small oasis of calm from the chaos of the Turkish town. With the quiet and unspoilt topaz blue bay glistening ahead of us I let my toes spread out on the sand, inhaling the balmy air which carried familiar smells of coconut sun cream and greasy chips.

We settled on two loungers and stripped off to reveal reddening skin. If she wasn't my best friend, I could really hate Marie. Her toned figure hid the fact that she had a son, Cole, who was the unexpected result of a jaeger-bombed night of passion with Mike, a guy whom she'd met down at her local. With long, fiery-red hair, which she only admitted to 'touching up', plus the dirtiest mind and most caring personality, she commanded the attention of any room she entered. I wished I were more like her; secretly I had always hoped that by hanging out together some of Marie's sparkle would rub off on me.

'Hello there, ladies. I'm Ali. Just the two beds is it?' A local man in his early thirties with a smiling, tanned face bounded over. He was topless, wearing just a necklace holding an animal tooth, which pointed to his six-pack, and his sculpted chest was adorned with faded tattoo script, which crept down into the waistband of his battered denim cut-offs.

'Yes please,' Marie smiled up at him.

'It's suddenly got very hot around here,' he winked, taking our money.

Marie's eyes followed his admittedly nice arse back to his beach cabin before turning to me grinning. 'Phwoarsome or what?'

I made a noise between a huff and a sigh. Members of the opposite sex were so far off my radar right now I needed to wear binoculars just to see them.

'Oh come on, Georgia. You can't pretend that a bit of eye candy doesn't stir something deep in those closed-off loins of yours?' Marie laughed as I rolled my eyes. 'You know what, I'm suddenly really thirsty, want a beer?'

'Strange that the bar is right next to his hut.'

'Maybe.' Marie ignored my raised eyebrow and delved into her bag, bringing out a pen and unscrunching a flyer that we'd been handed for a ladies-drink-free night. 'Anyway, while I'm gone I have a plan for you. I think it's time to make a list. I know how much you love them, plus my mum's always said, "if in doubt, write it out".' She paused with the pen lid pressed to her lips. 'I want you to make a list of everything you want to do and see in your life. Kind of like a bucket list, but with no terminal cancer spurring you on.' She passed me the pen, moist at the top, and the flyer, blank side up.

'I don't know what I want any more. I thought I knew. I had everything planned and sorted, but now I feel like I'm in some horrible limbo,' I whined. But I took the soggy pen since it was true, I did love a good list. There was something about the control you get from emptying your head by simply jotting your thoughts down, then the satisfaction when slicing through them with a big fat tick once completed.

'No. You've moped enough and now it's time to make changes and take action,' Marie said firmly, looking as if she was scoping out a nearby rock as a makeshift naughty step if I didn't play along. 'What's happened has been shit. Really shit. But think of it like this, at least you never have to see his demon mother again, never have to worry about fitting in on their ridiculous family getaways. No more putting up with their la-di-dah ways.' She pursed her lips and cupped her hand like the Queen waving – not a bad impression of Alex's mum, Ruth, to be honest. 'I wouldn't be surprised if all this time he's been taking that trust fund they offered him, but then playing the *I'm one of the common people* card. Bastard.'

I sniffed loudly.

'I know it's hard. But please try and think of the positives, hun. If you don't know what you do want, then maybe think about what you don't want.' She paused, adjusting her sunglasses as Ali waved to her from his beach cabin, tearing his eyes away from a nearby game of beach volleyball. 'You don't want to be with he-who-shall-not-be-named. You don't want to be living in my spare room for the rest of your life. You don't want to be some lonely boring cat-lady –'

'Only because of my allergies,' I returned.

'No. You don't just want to be someone's other half. You need to be a whole and we're going to get you back on track with a plan that's going to do that.' She smiled gently. 'Just give it a go, please.' She pecked me on the top of my head, tied on her sarong and headed off to buy us both a drink, sashaying effortlessly across the sand.

I glanced down at the blank paper, so creamy and fresh, scared to write anything down, as it felt like committing to achieving it. The problem was, I had always had a plan. But now? Now, all that lay ahead was an empty space, like this paper in my sweaty hands.

A family had taken the sun loungers next to ours and were chatting animatedly to one another in what sounded like fast Spanish, their foreign tones seeming so exotic compared to my broad Northern accent. I'd never learned another language, apart from my French GCSE thirteen years ago, but I could barely remember any of it. Maybe that's something I could do?

In fact, apart from this trip with Marie, I hadn't been abroad in years. What with saving for the wedding and the house, all of my summer leave was spent doing DIY or visiting Alex's family's second home in Edinburgh. When I was younger I had always dreamt that my salary would be spent on exotic trips, but my pitiful wage never seemed to stretch far enough. Even when I'd found a last-minute billy-bargain to Benidorm, Alex had scoffed that it would be like going on holiday with our neighbours, that only *those* types of people would go book a package deal then spend all week drinking English beer in an Irish bar. When I'd protested that by 'those sorts of people' he could have been describing my family he'd pulled me close and nibbled my neck. 'Oh Gigi, you know what I mean. I love your family, but maybe we need to think about the finances. My mum said Ed and Francesca are looking for someone to housesit their place in Devon for the week?'

To be fair, Alex had seen a lot of the world when he was growing up, so I had sacrificed my wanderlust dreams for him and his happiness, telling myself that one day I'd get some much-longed-for stamps in my passport. I could cringe at how lame that sounded.

The nearby family pulled out a picnic blanket and opened a cooler box full of things I hadn't seen before. Foods I didn't know the name of, had never tasted but which looked and smelled amazing. This is what I wanted to do. I wanted to be the girl who would *parlez* a new lingo effortlessly, who would cook up exotic recipes with ingredients I couldn't currently pronounce, who would have stories to share at dinner parties, '...oh, that reminds me of a time when I was doing a silent retreat in an Indian ashram', sharing facts and tales from far-flung locations, rather than grumbling about the rising property market or council tax brackets.

OK, I can do this. I started to write...

I want to eat the world. I want to explore, travel, learn and push my limits. I want to find myself. Mountains and oceans will be my best friends, the stars will guide me home at night and my tongue will be desperate to speak and share all I have seen. I want to travel.

Yikes. My pen kind of ran away with me there. I looked at the paper in my hand and tucked my legs underneath me. Apparently I wanted to become Michael Palin. OK, so how was I going to achieve all this? Just like before, the pen seemed to have a mind of its own.

Quit and go.

That simple, hey biro?

What's holding you back? No man, no children, soon to be no home. Just a crappy job where you constantly moan about feeling undervalued but stick it out as they have good maternity packages. Packages that you won't need now. Sell everything, buy a backpack and go.

OK, maybe the pen did have a point. My job as a PA at Fresh Air PR, a small but growing firm near Topshop on the high street, was where I'd stayed for the past five years, working my way up from post-room assistant to personal assistant to the Director of Marketing; same office, same faces, same printer problems. The thought of not having to worry if I'd chosen the right mug to brew up in, not to be forced to drink through the mundanity of the Christmas parties, to avoid listening to petty arguments over who had the best parking space and what Boots meal-deals were the best value for money sounded pretty good. I'd got too comfortable; like everything else in my life, agreeing to things I didn't want to please others and not pursuing my own dreams for fear of failure or embarrassment. The routine of cohabitation had come naturally with Alex, even if there were times when I looked at my chore list, my shopping list and our practically empty social calendar and despised the domestic drudgery.

But where would I go and what would I do? *Pen, don't let me down.* I closed my eyes, breathing in the salty sun lotion-filled air and started to write.

Go skinny dipping in the moonlit ocean
Dance all night under the stars
Taste incredible exotic food
Ride an elephant
Visit historic temples
Explore new beliefs
Climb a mountain
Make friends with different nationalities
Listen to the advice of a wise soul
Do something wild

My hand was aching but my head was whirring. Then I caught myself, as a mix of doubts and reality sliced into my thoughts. *How can you do this? It'll take months of planning, saving and organising. Where do you even start with a trip like this?! You'd never be brave enough to touch an elephant, let alone ride one. The last time you did any exercise you nearly passed out, so trekking up Everest is out of the equation, and you cried when you had your blood taken, so how are you going to manage something wild like getting a tattoo?* The wildest thing I'd done recently was sleep with my make-up on.

I much preferred the dreamy freedom of my pen than my stupid conscience.

Today is meant to be your wedding day, or have you forgotten that? It's absurd that you're sat here writing about a whole new life you intend to start when you know you're not strong enough to change anything, I scolded myself.

We'll see about that, said my pen.

CHAPTER 2

Drapetomania (n.) An overwhelming urge to run away

Two hours later my head was still fizzing with ideas that maybe, just maybe, I could actually see the world, become a backpacker and change my life. Leaving sunken footprints in the sand, letting the cooling water of the shore lick my sunburnt feet, I closed my eyes and breathed in the fresh sea breeze. Our wedding vows would have taken place by now. Our spoken promise to love, honour and cherish each other for as long as we both shall live. A single tear fell down my cheek but I shook myself. *Now it is the time for you*. To make a vow, a promise, an oath to myself that is just as life-changing, but one I have full control over: to be happy.

I half-jogged back up the hot sand to a snoring Marie. Thankfully Ali was nowhere to be seen otherwise her unsexy catching-flies impression might have blown her chances with him. Tucking my travel wish-list back in her beach bag under her *Heat* magazine and bottle of sun cream, I gave her a nudge before she spluttered to attention.

'What?…where?…who?' She threw herself upright, wiping the saliva from her mouth.

I smiled at Marie's sleepy face and matted hair. 'Hey, I'm going to head back to the hotel.'

'Great idea, pass me that bottle of water and we'll go. How long was I asleep? Did I miss anything?' she asked between gulps, wincing at the heat and combing her fingers through her hair.

'Nah, not much,' I said casually, deciding to give the list some more thought before I told her my radical ideas. 'So what happened with Baywatch boy?' I asked nodding towards Ali's cabin.

She huffed and flicked back her head. 'Turns out he's gay.'

I tried to stifle a laugh, 'What do you mean?'

'Well, I did my classic lean-over-the-bar-to-suggestively-pick-up-a-straw manoeuvre. I swear that technique has *never* failed before.'

'Isn't that how you ended up pregnant with Cole?' I teased.

She folded her arms across her chest. 'Exactly! See, I told you, it's a golden flirting style. Anyway, he didn't even flinch. It was like my cleavage sparked nothing in his underwear department.'

'So because of that you think he's gay?'

'No. But even when I licked my lips and walked over to him, Kim Kardashian-butt out and everything, he was too obsessed with watching these guys playing beach volleyball to notice!'

'Maybe he just really, really loves sport?' I suggested. She rolled her eyes, annoyed at having such a blot on her impeccable seduction record.

'Trust me, I know. Let's just say he was more interested in watching the guys grease up with sun lotion than keeping track of the score.'

'Ah, oh well. Hey, you know that I still love you.'

She smiled and shook her head. 'Sorry, Georgia. We came here to help sort you out, not for Turkish hotties to put me in a bad mood.' She stroked my arm. 'At least I know my straw technique still works, well for straight men anyway,' she laughed.

Listening to her talking it suddenly hit me that this was what I'd need to be doing now that I was single. Finding ways of attracting men's attention. If Marie found it hard, Lord knows how I was going to cope. I physically shuddered at being reminded that I was now flying solo. I was no longer someone's better half, fiancée or girlfriend. It was just me and soon I'd have to dive head-first into the ever-shrinking dating pool. Oh God.

'You OK, hun? You've gone a little pale under your sunburn.' Marie's voice brought me back to the present.

'Yeah, yeah. Just a little tired.'

'Right, well, let's head back, get some food and then we'll get ready to head out and see what nightlife this town has to offer. And I'm not taking no for an answer.'

It was our last night here, and even though I'd handled the day pretty well so far, who knew what a few more cocktails could do to my fragile resolve? However, in the spirit of making changes to what now seemed like a pathetic life, maybe being forced out of my pit and into the bright lights of bar street would be a good idea.

'Fine,' I nodded

'What?!' Marie leaned over and hugged me. 'I was convinced you'd say no.'

'Well, maybe I'm going to try saying yes to more things from now on,' I smiled.

'That's great, Georgia. See, I knew coming here would be the best thing for you. Tonight's going to be awesome, I can just feel it.'

*

Although being scrawny rather than slender, due to my recent loss of appetite – surely the only bonus in a breakup – looking at my reflection, I didn't recognise myself. Staring back was a glamorously made-up woman, her slightly acne-pocked skin camouflaged in heavy bronzer, her glossy brown blow-dried hair framing her almond-shaped eyes, and a slick of lipstick staining her angel-bud lips. Marie had insisted on giving me a makeover, so the face that shone in the glass was nothing like the old Georgia, and I wasn't sure I liked it. I felt self-conscious in my outfit. My hot-pink clutch bag matched the vertiginous stilettos that she'd pressured me into borrowing, ignoring my protests that I walked like a drunk Tina Turner in heels.

'We'll walk slowly, then.' She shushed me by shoving a pale-gold dress in my hands. It was the same one I'd bought on a whim a few years back, all hail Beyoncé. I'd never taken the tags off it after Alex had commented how it looked like I'd stolen it off a cheap hooker; I did have to admit that Queen Bey wasn't going to be quaking in her rhinestone-studded boots at the sight of me. Marie must have packed it in secret. I wished that I'd had time to change into the baggy linen trousers and safe blouse I had picked out before Marie had hidden them. That had been a fun game.

We eventually made it out into the balmy evening to the chirp of crickets and smell of petrol fumes and headed to the harbour, where fifty-foot masts swayed on the inky-blue water highlighted by white sugar-cube villas that shone from the hillside in the distance, their lights twinkling like fallen stars. This stunning setting was unfortunately butchered by the line of identical bars and nightclubs facing the water's edge. Every bar had A boards advertising fishbowls, free shots and buy-one-get-three-drinks-free offers in neon swirly handwriting. A girl wearing furry boots, tiny sequin hot pants and a bikini top that just covered her nipples danced over to us, wrapping her tanned arms around our shoulders, trying to steer us into the bar she was working for.

'All right, ladies! My name's Mel, you 'ere on ya hols? Well you've come to the right place. The cheapest and best drinks in town are right 'ere. I'll do ya three cheeky Vimtos for the price of one, any triple spirit an' a mixer for just a paaand and chuck in a couple of shots too!' The manic-eyed blonde half-screeched at us in a thick cockney accent without taking a breath. I glanced at Marie, who looked as uncomfortable as I felt at having this strange woman half-woven around us.

The bar she was adamantly pulling us into was deserted. A sad bucking bronco waited patiently to chuck overweight tourists around in the corner, and the bar staff were leaning on the bar smoking while pathetic strobe lights bounced off the empty tables.

'It's like waaaaay early, but trust me, this is *the* place to be. In a few hours you'll be wantin' to lezz up with me for nabbing you a table, as it's gonna be kerazy!' Manic Mel explained, looking at our half-terrified, half-disappointed faces.

A couple of other bar touts were peering over to see if she was going to get her catch or if they could have a go once we'd walked on. Seeing them eyeing us up like vultures, working out the commission they could get from us made me want to grab Marie's hand and run back to the safety and quiet of our hotel room.

'Yeah, go on then,' Marie said, instantly crushing my hopes for a speedy exit. *It's your last night here, don't be such a square, Georgia.*

'Awesome!' Manic Mel cracked her thick make-up into a fake smile. 'Follow me, ladiez!'

Back home the wedding guests would be dancing to 'Come on Eileen', hitting the free bar and trying to ignore Alex's arrogant best man Ryan wafting his willy about as he streaked round the marquee with his tie on his head Rambo-style. But here I was, trying to drown out the Freddie Mercury tribute act, listening to Marie being chatted up by a group of baby-faced lads wearing matching 'I got off my tits in Turkey' T-shirts, and feeling my shoulders throbbing from sunburn. I wasn't quite sure which was the lesser of two evils.

'Georgia! This is Rickaaaay!' Marie shouted over the music, doing her best Bianca Jackson impression as the lad she had her arm around looked on bemused. He was either too young or too drunk to know what the hell she was on about. 'Him and his mates are from Cardiff.'

'All right?' Ricky headed in for a peck on the cheek but stumbled and half head-butted my cheekbone. Once all this cheap alcohol wore off that was going to sting like a motherlover.

'Oww. Yeah fine,' I said, rubbing my face, messing up the make-up that Marie had carefully applied following a YouTube contouring video in our room. I went to head back to our table to grab some ice – Manic Mel was right, this place had livened up since we'd arrived – but Marie caught my arm.

'Come on, don't stop now!' she pleaded, her eyes alight with what was either happiness or a vodka-glaze before pulling me back out to the dance floor. 'This is bloody brilliant. It's so amazing to see you smiling again,' Marie shouted over a 'Bohemian Rhapsody' remix. 'Also I think you're well in there,' she sang in my ear, nodding her head towards Ricky, who seemed to have learnt his dance moves from the *Inbetweeners* film.

I scrunched up my face, 'I dunno.'

'I'm telling you, he's *gagging* for it!'

I winced. 'I really don't think I'm ready for that.'

'Maybe you just need to get it over with. Rip that plaster off?' she suggested as an enthusiastic dancer hip-bumped past us.

I stared at Marie, remembering the last time she had tried encouraging me to 'get it over with'. Memories of being fifteen and waiting in the cold bunker flooded back. Marie clocked my deadpan expression and wrapped her arms around me.

'Sorry, forgot I'm not the world's best cupid,' she said gingerly.

'It's fine, but I need to take it at my own pace. And I don't want to be rude but Ricky may still be a virgin.'

'You could be a cougar!' She burst out laughing. 'No, I understand, but hey, it's nice to know you've still got it. Plus, I read somewhere that if you don't use it then it'll seal back up,' she giggled before spinning me around.

As she was teaching Ricky and his mates our signature lawn-mower move there seemed to be some sort of commotion near the entrance. Expecting to see some Z-list Turkish reality TV star, Marie pulled us through the partygoers to get a better view. But where a fame-hungry wannabe should have stood was in fact a pretty woman wearing a long white dress, grinning and holding hands with a guy wearing a black suit. They were soon followed by energetic ladies all in matching sage-green prom-style dresses as it dawned on me…we were being joined by a wedding party.

You've got to be kidding me. I glared up at the sky. On the night when, by this time, I should have been slow dancing with Alex, I was now face to face with an actual wedding, in the company of the kind of fun hosts who got the wedding customs out of the way before hitting the clubs to really party together. Alex would have hated that.

Actually, Alex would have hated this entire trip, from the plastic sun loungers, to the karaoke bars, to the flashiness of the Turkish men. He probably would have looked down at what I was wearing and commented on how much slap I had on. Grabbing Marie's hand I led her to the ladies' room.

'OMG! Are you OK?' Marie asked with concerned wide eyes. 'I take it you saw the unwanted visitors. I can go and ask the bouncers to remove them if you like?' She began bouncing on the spot Rocky-style.

'No, it's OK. I might be a little bit sick, but that could also be the luminous fishbowl we drank.' I leaned onto the cold stone of the basin. 'Oh Marie, seeing them has made this feel so real.'

'What do you mean? Do you need to sit down?'

I shook my head. 'Did you see the look that groom was giving his new wife? Did you see that? God! I could sense the hormones from way over here. It's been years since Alex looked at me like that. Years! Maybe I've had a lucky escape, like you said. Maybe this is the perfect time for me to make some serious changes in my life. I've made a list like you asked.' Marie looked totally confused, forgetting her brainwave on the beach. I rooted around in my clutch bag, spilling half of the contents on the tiled floor, and thrust the paper at her.

'Read this. This is what I want to do with my life now. I'm sick of pining for what I probably never had anyway. I was so caught up in the wedding planning, making sure it would live up to the expectations of his mum and perfect Francesca, that I hadn't thought about the actual marriage. The vows were the last thing I had to write, even though I nagged him into writing his, as I found the words just didn't come,' I admitted for the first time ever.

Marie tried to focus her hazy, drunken eyes on the list.

'I'm terrified of what the future will hold, but it has to be better than sharing my lovely home with a cheating fiancé, working a job I hate to pay the bills and being in more debt because of how much the wedding had cost. This should be the time in my life when I'm out there exploring, seeing the world, learning new things and finding me.' I felt very passionate and might have been shouting slightly. God, those cocktails were lethal.

For a few seconds Marie didn't say anything. Then a huge grin broke out over her squiffy face. 'This is awesome, hun. I really think you should go for it. God, I'll miss you, but what better time to get out there than now? I'm so proud of how you've coped with everything and even seeing that couple tonight, you've done so bloody brilliantly.'

'Thank you, but honestly I couldn't have done any of it without you.'

'Yes you could. You're so amazing.' She was definitely slurring now.

'No, you're the amazing one.'

'No, *you* are!'

A girl with a humongous bouffant broke up our love fest as she barged past to dry her hands. 'I want whatever they're drinking,' she called out to one of her friends in the stalls as we fell into a fit of giggles. Looking up at the clock near the sinks I realised we were leaving this country in a few hours' time and we still hadn't packed.

'We need to be making a move, hun,' I said. From the way she was swaying I guessed she was ready to head off too.

'Aww, yeah, you're right. I've had such a good night! I know, you should come back here and get a job like lovely Mel, that could be a bit of travelling for you?' Marie slurred, taking my hand to move past the ever-growing queue for the ladies' toilets. The bride and groom had long since been swallowed up amongst young Turks on the packed dance floor.

'Err, yeah, maybe,' I absently replied.

We made it safely outside and out of the grip of commission-hungry touts. I could still hear snippets of a banging bass line and felt the buzz of adrenalin pumping through me. Under the bright light of the stars that were reflected in the pitch-black water lapping at the quayside I felt alive with excitement and anticipation at what my new future had in store. *If I could survive coming face to face with another bride on what should have been my wedding day, then surely I could survive anything.*

Back in the calm of our hotel room Marie was fast asleep in minutes after I stripped her off, tucked her in and turned up the air con. I took off my make-up, got into my cotton pyjamas and tied my hair into a low ponytail, letting the soft sheets wrap themselves around me. My head was spinning from the alcohol, the emotion, *and* the fact I'd survived coming face-to-face with a bridal party, tonight of all nights.

I should be lying with Alex in the marital suite at the country house after drinking champagne in the huge free-standing bubble bath, making love as Mr and Mrs and marvelling at how perfectly the day had gone. The day of my dreams. But that's the thing with dreams, they hardly ever become reality. No, what would have happened is this: the night would have ended in us rowing about why his mate Ryan had alluded to other women during the best man's speech. My embarrassing uncle Ron, who we only invited to avoid any family politics but actually none of us wanted there, would have started an impromptu and uncensored karaoke during the cake-cutting causing Alex's parents to have strong words with their son over why he had married into such an uncouth family. Alex and I would have been too tired to even run a bath, let alone drink any more booze and we'd have fallen into a drunken snoring state on either side of the huge bed still in our clothes. Why start making love now when we hadn't got jiggy in months? We'd settled into sluggishness and I'm positive that's not the name of a Kama Sutra move. I'd put Alex's lack of interest in me down to the stress and nerves of the wedding, or the fact that he was tired from working late again. I was so naïve! And to think he'd been getting it all along from someone else.

I looked fondly over to Marie; actually, lying slightly intoxicated next to my half-naked best mate in Turkey wasn't too shabby a way to spend tonight either. Right now I was happy to remember today not as the day I was supposed to get married, but the day I made a plan for my new life.

All I had to do now was put it into action.

CHAPTER 3

Hiraeth (n.) Homesickness for a home you can't return to, or that never was

Manchester welcomed us home in the way it knew best; grey drizzle kissed our shoulders as we stepped off the plane and it hadn't stopped raining since. But even the non-existent Indian summer that the weather presenters had predicted couldn't dampen my spirits. Our non-stop excited chatter on the flight home about where, how and when I'd be saying *au revoir* took my mind off the impending task ahead.

I still needed to move the rest of my things out of my old house to Marie's spare room, something I'd hoped magic fairies would have sorted for me whilst I was away. There was never an impish elf around when you needed one. Marie had tried to encourage me to stick to my guns and fight to stay in the house that I half-owned. 'Alex should be the one to leave, go live with whatever skank he has these *feelings* for,' she'd told me straight one evening over a game of chase the ace. She was probably right, but the thing was I couldn't bear the thought of living there on my own, going through the front door to an empty house where memories bled through every brick. I'd never lived on my own before and certainly wasn't strong enough to start now. Plus I didn't have the energy to fight, to confront him about it, I just wanted it to be sorted so I could move on. *Tomorrow. I'll do it tomorrow. Tonight was all about a bath, an early night and devouring the giant Toblerone that had somehow fallen into my shopping basket in duty free.*

We whizzed through customs and were soon outside Marie's flat as the surly cabbie chucked our bags onto the rain-soaked pavement, miraculously avoiding any puddles. Welcome home.

With Marie on the phone to Cole I pottered about turning up the heating, chucking out gone-off milk and putting the kettle on.

'OMG!' Marie burst into the room screeching, her hangover dramatically lifted. 'My agent just called telling me I've been offered a callback on the audition I did!'

'That's great news. Where, what, when?'

'I leave tomorrow. I have to be away for a few days as the director's filming on location but asked for me personally to come for the second audition. It's the one I tried out for *ages* ago – you know, the stuffy costume drama with an edgy twist?'

'Oh yeah.' I remembered that there was something she had been getting nervous about around the same time that I'd had to choose between having the DJ start straight after cutting the cake or move the speeches until later. It had been a stressful time for us both.

'They want to urbanise *Jane Eyre* and film it in Brixton, not the Lake District, or wherever it was the first time. I've just got a few lines, but my agent reckons if I get in with the director then it could lead to bigger things,' she said excitedly.

'That's brilliant news! Well done you.'

'The bad news is I won't get to see Cole for a few more days, which is killing me, but Mike said he'd keep hold of him, with his mum's help, till I get back so FaceTime chats will have to suffice till then,' Marie said sadly.

Considering Cole's dad, Mike, had just been a one-night stand, he really had manned up and between them he and Marie had childcare duties perfectly organised. I often caught Mike's longing look at Marie when he brought Cole back from a weekend at his house and wondered if they would ever make a go of it, doing the whole parent thing together. From the outside they seemed perfect for each other and both totally adored Cole, but whenever I questioned Marie she changed the subject saying that just one man in her life was all she needed.

'Well, fame comes at a price,' I smiled, 'but hey, it's not too much longer and imagine Cole's face when he gets to see his mum on the telly.' Marie shrugged, but secretly I knew how much this childhood dream of becoming an actress meant to her, especially as she had Cole to provide for. She had fallen into mobile hairdressing as a means to pay the bills, but her heart lay in drama and plots, not dye and perms.

She chewed her lip. 'So that means we need to get your things from Chez Prick this evening as I won't be able to help otherwise.' She was right. Damn it.

I couldn't ask my mum and dad to help, especially with my dad's back. I scrolled through my phone contacts list mentally calculating any possible candidates I could call to help move my boxes. Skimming past the names of Alex's friends, distant relations, old schoolmates with whom I hadn't had contact for years bar the annual Facebook happy birthday posts, I realised that there was nobody.

Nobody.

I had never been a popular child, but I had imagined that in my glamorous late twenties I would at least have a circle of friends so close-knit that they would make the cast of *Friends* look like they were sharing an awkward lift ride. Another thing to add to the travel wish-list – make more friends.

'Sorry, hun. Moving my paltry boxes is the last thing you need to be doing when you should be packing for your new role.'

'Nah, it's fine. I'll just chuck a few clean knickers into my case and I'm good to go,' she smiled. 'It's more important that we get you away from that knob. You ready to go now?'

It took all my strength to nod. I didn't want to go; I didn't want reminders, to see our small but sweet house, where the kitchen tap leaked unless you jammed a teaspoon under it, the floorboards which squeaked if you stepped on them in certain places and the comforting sound of the central heating when it whirred into action. I wasn't ready to say goodbye to the house. But it wasn't my home any more. It couldn't be. As much as I wished that none of this had happened, something deep down in me knew I wasn't going to be the wailing woman scorned, begging for him to take me back. My parents raised me better than that. No, I needed to go grab my stuff and move on with my new life plan. Baby steps and all that.

It was dark outside when we pulled up. I held the front-door key in my unsteady hand as Marie guided me to the door, swearing as she stumbled over a wonky paving slab. No one was home. We walked from room to room in silence. I smelt *our* smell and felt my resolve slipping.

'So where do you reckon he's piled up your stuff?' Marie broke my pathetic thoughts.

'Probably the spare room and under the stairs,' I guessed. They were always the two places we would dump stuff we didn't need any more.

It's just bricks and stone, Georgia, get a grip. The house represents all the lies that he has spun. The future you can't have and don't want any more. Nothing more.

I opened the door to the box room, surprised to find neatly stacked and packed cardboard boxes labelled with my things. 'Winter clothes, books, CDs, other,' Marie read with a similar shocked expression. Alex was messy, disorganised and allergic to cleaning. I'd expected my possessions to be stuffed into bin bags, but this? This was new.

'I'll get these in the car, you carry on looking around,' she instructed.

The smell of bleach and lemon hit me as I slowly walked into the master bedroom. The bed was made, an empty glass lined the dust-free bedside table, and without my things – jewellery strung over the mirror, shoes lined up against the wall and books piled on the floor – it looked bigger and barer. No pink pyjamas on the creased pillow, no used make-up wipes in the bin and no magazines dropped on the floor.

'I think he's put your joint things down here, hun,' Marie called up.

She was stood in the doorway of the large cupboard under the stairs holding out a scribbled note that Alex had tacked to the door. 'Here's most of the joint stuff I thought you'd want. The bigger items like the fridge and bed I'll leave to you to decide ownership of. Alex.'

I looked around at unwanted Christmas presents, board games and garden furniture that had been piled up in the far corner next to the ironing board and hoover. It was depressing to see what five years of a relationship looked like: a cracked photo frame, potato masher and an expensive but hardly used smoothie maker. Was that it? I felt my eyes prick with tears. I didn't want to sort out *ownership*, to saw things down the middle. I just wanted to be out of here.

'I'm not sure I can get all that in the car, hun,' Marie said softly.

'I don't want it. Any of it. I'll buy new things. Things that are just mine, with my own money.' I roughly wiped my eyes.

'OK…if you're sure.' Marie stroked my arm protectively. I nodded before placing my house key on top of the kitchen counter, the *spotless* kitchen counter. I didn't leave a note. I had nothing more to say.

I started crying as soon as we shut the front door. Sadness that I'd never watch TV settled on the comfy sofa or use the oven to cook again. Stupid small things. Shutting that door felt more symbolic than it should have done. I felt exhausted, even though I knew it was the right thing to have a fresh start and let him live here with the joint memories taunting him, it still felt like a heart-wrenching big step into my new life. A life that I had no idea how to function in.

CHAPTER 4

Epiphany (n.) A moment of sudden revelation

The city centre was full of harassed office workers and early-morning shoppers. Three strangers had almost collided with us on the busy street already, their eyes glued to their phone screens, including a huge stocky man who barged into me, almost knocking me to the ground.

'Where did your parents say they were meeting us?' Marie asked.

'Err, Kendal's,' I said absently, rubbing my shoulder.

'Ah, should have known. Remember when your mum used to take us there as kids? We felt so posh! Desperate to spot a Corrie star before drowning ourselves in the perfume samples. Look, there they are!' Marie shouted, waving excitedly up the street.

My smiling but tired-looking dad waved back, my mum had her hands full gripping her handbag to her chest, warily glancing at a *Big Issue* seller huddled under a nearby shopfront.

'Morning. Sorry we're late.'

'Oh there you are, lazy bones. You never were an early riser, I said that to your dad, didn't I, Len?' My mum clucked, not letting her husband answer before she busied past, giving me a peck on the cheek and shooting a look of suspicion to the seller.

'Morning love, good to have you back.' My dad hugged me, enveloping me in his familiar smell of soap and washing powder.

'So, what's this about you going off to be a huge star!' My mum turned to Marie.

Marie laughed. 'Ah not just yet, Sheila, it's more Hackney than Hollywood, but don't worry, you'll all be invited to the premiere,' she smiled, before pulling out a fiver for the *Big Issue* seller who wandered off grinning.

'Oh I hope so. Isn't that exciting, Georgia?' She didn't let me answer before she was off again. 'I bet your mum must be so proud. Who would have thought all those years ago when Georgia brought home the new girl in class with a southern accent and an allergy to chips and gravy that she would transform into a successful movie star! It's a shame we haven't got long as I want to hear all about it. But Len has an appointment in town for his back. It's been giving him gyp again,' my mum said, linking Marie's arm.

Ten minutes later we were settled on squishy sofas with a tray of cappuccinos and shortbread biscuits laid out in front of us. As my mum had a mouthful of coffee and Marie had nipped to the loo, my dad was able to start the conversation.

'So pet, how've you been? You've caught the sun a little. Weather must've been good,' he grinned, pointing at my peeling nose.

'It was great, but just being back it already feels like a distant memory,' I said sadly, still unable to shake this cloud that had settled around me since last night. I'd cried all the way back to Marie's after leaving my old house. Then tortured myself even more by opening the few boxes we had packed in her car. Under neatly folded clothes, CDs and Harry Potter books was a shoebox filled with ticket stubs and bottle caps from our first dates, blurry Polaroid photographs and pages torn from magazines with exotic beaches, advice on booking a couples' trip and places you must see before you die. I'd tipped it all into the wastepaper bin along with my travel wish-list scrunched up at the bottom of my case. Who was I kidding?

'Ah, holiday blues,' he sighed. 'That's totally normal, especially after everything you've been through.'

'So, did Marie have you dancing around till the small hours with attractive Turkish men?' my mum asked. My dad cleared his throat and shifted on his seat.

'Not really, you know it was never going to be one of those kinds of holidays.'

'Well, probably for the best. I've read so many awful articles about women parading down foreign streets wearing hardly anything and drinking too much, then waking up missing an organ, or worse.' She raised a thin eyebrow. 'So what was Turkey like? Was your hotel nice? Was it clean?'

'It was lovely, beautiful in fact.' I took a gulp of my latte. 'It gave me a lot of time to think.'

'Ah, so you've told them about your globetrotting plans then, eh?' Marie plopped on the sofa, downing her coffee as if it held the elixir of life.

'What's that supposed to mean?' my mum swiftly turned her head, sparrow-like, at me. I picked up my cup to stall for time. She scoffed at stories of confused women grabbing their passport to 'find themselves'. She viewed them as irresponsible and selfish with heads full of hippy mumbo-jumbo.

I took a deep breath. 'Well, not quite. When we were away Marie encouraged me to make a little list of the countries I'd like to see and the things I'd like to experience.'

She let out a shrill laugh. 'Oh our Georgia has always been one for daydreaming, hasn't she, Len? Remember that time when she decided to run off to join a convent after watching *The Sound of Music* on repeat? She was convinced the bus at the end of the road would take her to Austria but only managed to do the town circuit before we found her with a plastic bag full of Tesco strudels by the church hall.'

My dad smiled at the memory before clocking my flustered face. 'I'm afraid you got your sense of direction from me, pet.'

'It's lucky you've got me around as otherwise Lord knows where you and your dad would end up,' my mum cooed.

'Actually, Sheila, Georgia was serious about this trip,' Marie piped up.

The room stood still for a moment. 'Oh, for goodness' sake. I do hope you are joking?' My mum was death-staring me out.

I let out a small fake laugh: 'Yeah, yeah. Just a joke, wasn't it, Marie?'

Marie looked confused. 'You said you wanted to get out there and explore more. It wasn't just a silly game,' she mumbled into her mug.

'Hmm. Well, we're just glad to have you both back in one piece. I couldn't cope over there with that foreign food and UV factors. No, much better to stick with what you know.' My mum shook her head, looking queasy at the thought of a dodgy dim sum.

'I don't know, love,' my dad turned to my mum. 'They say travelling is a great soul-enricher.'

'Ha,' she snorted, 'a soul-enricher! Well, you tell me that when she's lying in some third world hospital after eating a steak that turned out to be a rabid dog. The muggings, the rapes, the murders. Oh no, I'm much happier she's staying here. She couldn't cope with all that.' She wafted her hand around.

It was as if those things didn't happen in the UK – well, maybe not the dog steak – although the kebab shop by Marie's did smell a little dodgy at times. 'Is that what you think of me?' I mumbled.

'Oh Georgia,' she sighed, 'you've been in a pickle here, but you can't just up and leave. What about your job, your friends…us? I think you're being ridiculous. You're twenty-eight years old and have had a bit of a shock, that's all. But that doesn't mean running away and leaving everyone else to pick up the pieces.' She looked appalled at the thought.

We sat in an awkward silence. Thankfully Marie understood that situations like these were not the time or the place for a heated disagreement, no matter how much she was chomping at the bit to stick up for me.

'Well, I think it's a cracking idea, love,' my dad grinned, breaking the stifling atmosphere. 'Before I met your mother, me and a couple of mates had a lot of fun interrailing around Europe. May not seem that exotic now, but we got up to some right adventures on that trip.' He sighed wistfully, lost in a faded memory. Before he could get any more nostalgic, my mum swiftly dug a sharp elbow into his arm that signalled him to stop encouraging their daughter.

'Well, it was just that. A silly idea, so don't worry.' I stared pleadingly at Marie to move the conversation on before my mum collapsed, but she was fiddling with a sachet of sugar, no doubt sulking that I'd ridiculed her travel wish-list plan. 'So, how did you spend Saturday?' I asked as breezily as I could, knowing that Alex hadn't just hurt me when he'd called off our wedding. My mum had been bragging about it for months to anyone and everyone we knew. There's going to be a chocolate fountain, a harpist and even rumours that Kate Middleton's going to show up, I mean can you imagine?!

'We just had a quiet day; the weather was very poor so we pottered around the house. The photos would've been awful with the grey skies, love,' my dad said.

'I guess. Did Marie tell you I gave him back my key last night? Well, not to him personally. I don't even want to think about hearing from him again,' I babbled, feeling that ache in my stomach at leaving our house last night claw at me.

My parents quickly fixed their gaze deep into the bottom of their cups, my mum shifted uncomfortably in her seat. 'What?' I asked, as confusion rose in my voice.

Her pale-blue eyes filled with tears. 'We need to give you this letter, Georgia. It's from him.' My mum slowly pulled a sealed envelope out of her handbag. 'Your dad... well, he sort of asked him to write it.'

I rubbed at my forehead. 'What? I don't understand. Why would you be speaking to him? When did you speak to him?' Marie looked as clueless as I did. My dad was tearing up pieces of the paper napkin under his shortbread, avoiding my stare, getting buttery fingers and crumbs everywhere.

'Your dad found out some news that's...quite upsetting. We only discovered this after you left to go to Turkey and we didn't want to ruin your week away by telling you,' my mum said, blinking quickly.

Something was scratching my throat, my mouth had gone really dry but I'd already finished my cup of coffee. 'Mum, you're scaring me now.'

'OK, well please don't get too upset. So, your dad was picking up a few bits for tea from Morrison's – you know we usually go to Asda, but it was on his way back from that new Homebase they've built down Larkberry Lane so he decided to stop there.'

'OK...' I willed her to speed things along, knowing it was unlikely given that her normal conversations involved describing things in inane detail, usually to do with a friend of a friend that I'd never met or heard of even though my mum was adamant I knew them.

'Well, as he hadn't been to this store before he wasn't sure of the layout, and whilst walking down one of the aisles looking for blueberries for a flan I was making for the church fete, he saw Alex…and that tart.' She pursed her lips as if someone had just passed wind.

The thought of them doing mundane things like food shopping made my stomach drop. So they were together then. It wasn't just 'feelings' he had developed or a drunken quickie. That explained why our, no probably their, house was so spotless. There must have been a new woman's touch to the place. My stomach clenched like it did when I tried on skinny jeans in the January sales, squeezing in that extra roll of flab from devouring a whole tin of Quality Street.

My mum leaned over the coffee table and lowered her voice. 'The other thing is they were stood in the baby care aisle looking at…nappies.'

I heard Marie take a sharp intake of breath. It took a moment for this all to click.

'She's pregnant, Georgia,' my dad said sadly.

His words swam around me; I felt like I was in that stage between dreaming and waking, where you kind of know where you are, but everything doesn't feel real. I could hear them loudly whispering to each other.

'I knew we should have told her earlier.' 'No, you said to keep it quiet until the baby was born.' 'What the actual fuck?' (That last one was Marie, who looked as gobsmacked as I must have done, ignoring my mum's shock at her potty mouth.)

'How…how pregnant is she?' I eventually managed to spit out.

'Well, your dad's no expert and I haven't seen her, but Denise Williams, who works on reception at the doctors, said she'd seen her recently and she looked about five or six months gone,' my mum said gripping my hands, which were now shaking.

The receptionist at Alex's work, Stephanie something or other, for whom he had ended our relationship, was pregnant.

'Wait, what's in that letter?' I was suddenly horribly aware of other diners staring at us. My dad prised the letter out of my mum's grip and leaned forward, placing his hand on my knee and passing it to me.

'I didn't know what to do. I was so angry at him, after all these years treating him as part of the family and to do this to you. I just lost my rag. I marched over to him demanding answers and he started to make excuses and moved her out of the way. So I…swung for him.'

I gaped open-mouthed like a guppy fish. My dad punched someone! Not just someone, but my ex-fiancé! My dad, the kindest, softest man I knew, had a hidden feisty Rocky Balboa inside his calm shell. I didn't know what was more surprising.

'I'm not proud of it and violence is never an answer but I just saw red.' He looked at the floor, shamefaced. 'This spotty security guard saw the commotion and marched me out of the store as Alex ran over to apologise and explain to the jumped-up teenager that he didn't want to go to the police. It was there that I told him in no uncertain terms that I wanted the house paperwork to be fast-tracked, that he would make sure you received your share quickly and that it was highly favourable to you. I want him out of your life and thought by getting everything ready it would help. He's nothing but trouble and I truly believe you've had a lucky escape.' He paused for breath, having worked himself up retelling this tale.

'Go Len!' Marie shouted, almost high-fiving him.

I opened the envelope in a daze. Official bank and mortgage forms tumbled out. In a formal letter stating which document I needed to sign in order for Alex to buy me out, money I guessed that would be coming from the bank of his mum and dad, he added how sorry he was, but it was for the best that we not contact each other again. I didn't know what to say.

'He also sent us a copy so I could see what you were coming back to and that he didn't try to get you back. He's made his bed and now he needs to lie in it. I've looked over the bank's terms on the house and the money you'll get back is above the price you should have got. I just tried to protect you. I'm so sorry, Georgie.' My dad looked like he was close to tears. Marie just sat there grinning, shaking her head in disbelief that someone had finally punched Alex. I let the news sink in as my mum rushed to the ladies' room in a fluster. The sudden silence was filled with the dulcet tones of James Blunt playing out of the speakers above our heads.

I was suddenly reminded of an out-of-the-ordinary night a few months ago. Alex had taken me to dinner in this new restaurant in town, he'd just received a bonus at work and wanted to treat me, something that hadn't happened in ages. We drank cocktails in a bar which overlooked the whole of the city, ate melt-in-your-mouth steaks with all the trimmings, followed by the best tiramisu I'd ever tasted. Embarrassingly, I'd even considered running to the kitchen to persuade the chef to let me have the recipe so that I could pass it to our wedding caterers. The wine flowed and we'd actually had a few non-wedding-related conversations as he uncharacteristically showered me with clunky compliments. I remembered that his phone had seemed to buzz more than usual as it lay on the white linen tablecloth, but he took my hand and dismissed it as a problem with work, not even glancing to look at the persistent caller before placing it back in his pocket.

The alcohol had affected my thinking; Alex works for an accountancy firm, which doesn't open at weekends, let alone 9.30pm on a Saturday night. It must have been her. Maybe she had just taken the test; maybe those two blue positive lines had just appeared. The start of a new life and, little did I know, the end of ours.

I massaged my temples as my mum reappeared. Glancing down at her watch she gave her husband a sympathetic look: 'We have to be going soon to get your dad to this appointment. They fine you if you're late.'

'Oh OK.' I looked at their faces, creased with worry and pain for their only child. I remembered when Alex and I had got engaged (retelling the fake story, of course); smiles all round, Cava corks popping and wedding chatter over the dinner table. They were so pleased that I was settling down and was being taken care of by a good man from a wealthy family. As parents they couldn't have wished for more for their only daughter, even if I knew at times that they felt inferior compared to the very different social circles that his parents mixed in. My dad had shrugged it off, telling me they didn't need to be bezzie mates with my in-laws, just as long as I was happy, and that hopefully longed-for grandchildren wouldn't be far behind. Another disappointment.

'You going to be OK, pet?' my dad asked.

I shook myself together and plastered on a pathetic smile. 'Sure. I'm fine. Like you've all said, I've had a lucky escape. Better to be a jilted bride than a divorcee at twenty-eight, eh?' My joke fell flat as my dad gave me another bear hug.

'You deserve better than him. This will be the making of you, I'm sure of it. Look after yourself, kid,' he whispered as tears pricked my eyes.

'I will, Dad. Good luck at your appointment. I'll call you later.' I waved them off, my mum's heels clacking on the tiled floor as she brushed the crumbs from the sleeve of my dad's jumper.

'Shit, I can't believe it, what a bloody bombshell.' Marie shook her head, flicking through Alex's official papers which now had coffee-ring stains on them. 'Still, imagine his mum's face when he comes clean about an illegitimate grandchild, they certainly won't like that at the polo club.' She looked up at my pale face. 'Sorry. But you have to admit Ruthless Ruth will be having kittens at this. Right, I'm going to get a later train as we need a drink, or retail therapy or both.'

I let out a deep sigh. 'No, no, don't do that. You can't be late for your new role, as much as a vat of vodka has my name on it I'm not going to be jumping off into the nearest canal or anything. Have a safe journey and call me when you get there, OK?'

Marie nodded uncertainly. 'You sure? I really don't want to leave you after that.'

'Positive. He's managed to screw up enough things and your acting career is not going to be one of them.'

'You sure you don't want to track him down and give him a piece of your mind?' she asked, looking fired up for a fight. When we were in Turkey she'd tried to teach me how to master snappy comebacks and fierce confrontation, an area that I was useless at. I'd always leave a fight kicking myself over the things that I should have said. Marie had even written down a list of blush-inducing insults, telling me I needed to be confident, stay calm, and that above all 'If you hesitate, you lose. Think like Eminem in his *8 Mile* rap battle.' She'd gone into acting-teacher mode, telling me to see confrontation as an invite to play then walk away with dignity, firmly instructing me that under no circumstances was I ever to repeat what the other person had said in a funny voice.

I'd tried coming up with my own putdowns, including the corker: 'Have you been on holiday to Greece, as you're so greasy,' but even I could tell that wasn't going to be a classic. She'd even made me download the word-a-day app, hoping to extend my vocabulary with feisty retorts. But I was nowhere near ready to go all Slim Shady on Alex's ass, my thoughts were too twisted up to be able to condense what I wanted to say to him into an eloquent putdown. Realising what a lost cause I was Marie had changed tactics, asking, 'What's the most powerful way of getting a man's attention or driving him wild?'

I looked at her blankly.

'Ignoring him. Moving on. Silent but deadly,' she said wisely, ignoring my protests that that was also the name of a fart. Unfortunately, I had to agree with her. Realising that if Alex was getting on with his life then I had to get on with mine, I suddenly knew exactly where I needed to go.

CHAPTER 5

Lobally (adj.) Lout, stupid, rude or awkward person

'Totally Awesome Adventours' travel agent was just opposite Kendal's. Its bright lights beamed like a beacon of sunshine nestled next to a drab charity shop and boarded up pharmacy. The cluttered, colourful window display of a tropical beach scene complete with wooden deckchairs, hats with corks hanging from the rim carelessly tossed onto the striped fabric alongside a blow-up kangaroo, looked out of place on the grey Manchester street. *'Learn Spanish in Argentina'*, *'Peace out at the Taj Mahal in India'*, *'Trek the Inca Trail in Peru'*, *'Go raving in Thailand'*, an array of signs called out, each promising a new experience and adventure. I wistfully thought back to sitting in the sun writing out my travel wish-list, then finding my memory box full of trips I'd wanted to take for so long. This shop offered me the chance to go and see these places for real, and now I had the money to do it.

Taking a deep breath I pushed open the door.

Two guys in their early twenties wearing matching neon orange T-shirts looked up from computers on their kidney-shaped desks, took one glance at me then quickly looked back down again. Huge comfy-looking acid-yellow and lime-green beanbags were scattered in the corner next to a packed bookcase with stacks of glossy travel brochures, each containing hidden gems, exotic cultures and new worlds. I felt a shiver of excitement – until I took in the rest of the room, which made me feel ancient, out of touch and out of place. There was a map of the world with flags where customers could pin the countries they had been and their top tips. I could only add a sad flag to Portugal; my mum had found a cheap deal one year, but moaned constantly that it was too foreign. There had also been nauseating ferry trips to France, which my dad promised would be culturally enlightening but actually turned out to be a quick booze cruise to sell on nice bottles of plonk at mates' rates in the local pub car park.

Music I vaguely remembered blasting out from the bedlam of bars in Turkey played with an irritating repetitive beat. Tacked to the colourful walls were photos of nubile-looking women with wet hair excitedly waving to the camera, bar tout Manic Mel could easily have been one of them. My determination vanished as fast as those bikini babes' morals. Maybe this was a stupid idea; these sorts of places were for carefree students, baby-faced backpackers sharing a manky hostel dorm, not a nearly-thirty-year-old career woman, if you could even call me that. Without Marie's unwavering support I suddenly felt foolish being in here; maybe I'd have a look online first from the safety of my bedroom, or maybe this was just an idiotic thing to do in the first place. I tried to sidle my way to the door but it was too late to walk out of the empty shop without going unnoticed.

'All right?' A guy with gelled-back ginger hair, oversized ironic black geek glasses and barely-there stubble beckoned me to take a seat on the Perspex chair opposite his desk. His name badge pinned to his skin-tight T-shirt read: '*Ask me about Awesomeness*'. The other guy was engrossed in his laptop.

'Welcome to Totally Awesome Adventours, where our motto is "Escape, Explore, Evolve" or Triple E as we like to call it,' he said in a deep monotone as if reading a script. His smile didn't quite make it to his eyes, which looked sleep-deprived and bloodshot. I couldn't help but think 'Triple E' sounded like some dodgy drug found in the underbelly of secret raves that my mum had warned me about after recently reading an article in *The Daily Mail*, her newspaper of choice after spotting a copy at Alex's parents' house one time.

'My name's Rick. What can I do for you today?' He pronounced the 'ick' part of his name as if licking the strawberry sauce off the top of a Mr Whippy. I shuddered slightly and shifted in the trendy but uncomfortable seat. What could he do for me today?

'Well…I'm…erm.'

'Sorry, can you speak up?' he bellowed, making me jump.

'I want to quit my job and go travelling,' I blurted out surprising myself.

'Don't we all, luv,' he sniggered, rolling his eyes. 'So, where do you want to go as part of this *radical* plan?' He signified speech marks with his fingers, looking pleased with himself, shaking his head in silent mirth.

I felt his eyes take in my practical ponytail, flowered blouse and straight-legged light denim jeans. I thought it was quite a nice look, but it just echoed the rest of my bland and dull wardrobe, a bit like the owner. I'd never been into fashion, always wanting to blend in rather than stand out. Alex had said he preferred it that way, saying it was less hassle having a girlfriend who didn't stick out like a sore thumb, but sat here I felt like I stood out a mile.

'Well, I'd like to experience different cultures, taste exotic food and maybe learn a new language?' I replied, self-consciously tucking a strand of hair behind my ear.

'Sounds all right, that, but where's the adrenalin? The excitement? Got some cracking bungee jumps in Oz or white water rafting in New Zealand I could book you on?'

It felt as though he was taking the piss out of me as his colleague had turned his attention to our discussion, providing Rick with an audience. God. What was I doing here? I didn't know how to travel, how to live out of an uber-sized backpack or share a dorm room with strangers. I wasn't ready to hang out with the 'R-icks' of this world. I'd fantasised about travelling without thinking about any of the practicalities and how difficult the reality might actually be.

'Um…no…that's not really my sort of thing,' I muttered dejectedly.

'Listen darlin', I like your spirit an' all that, but you may want to try "Tasteful Travels" down the road; they do a lovely two-week package to Spain that would be more your scene,' he laughed.

'Um…OK…well, thanks for your time.' I got up from my seat and turned to the door feeling humiliated and pathetic. Of course I couldn't just swan off to some meditation retreat in India, who was I kidding?

As I was about to leave I overheard the two guys talking together: 'God! Talk about a mood killer. Can you imagine her at a full moon rave? It'd be like taking your mum–nah, your nan.' They both burst out laughing.

'I'm sorry?'

'Nothing for you to worry about. Enjoy Costa Bianca,' Rick smirked, waving his pen and pointing to the exit. I stood still, staring at his pudgy grinning face.

In that moment a tide of fury rose in my stomach. I don't know if it was the realisation that Alex was starting a new life and family without me, that my wedding dream was over or hearing my mum's instant dismissal of my travel dreams, but my body tensed and my veins fizzed with anger. I couldn't remember even one of the snappy put-downs Marie had taught me, so I did the most grown-up and mature thing I could have done; I scooped a pile of brochures into my arms, knocked over a glitter ball that was artfully balanced on a side table and, with a loud thud, sent a life-sized cardboard figure of bikini-clad babes doing the peace sign to the floor. The two men just sat open-mouthed gawping at me.

'And it's Costa Blanca, *not* Costa Bianca, you idiot!' I yelled, stalking out as fast as my sensible flats would take me, slamming the door behind me, causing an inflatable beach ball to drop from the ceiling, adding to the destruction I'd left behind.

My legs were shaking, my chest was pounding and I felt like I might be sick. Running down the street I heaved the heavy brochures into the nearest bin before gripping onto it to catch my breath.

'Hey!' a guy's voice shouted out. I froze. What if R-ick had called the police? What prison time came with brochure stealing? I've seen *Orange is the New Black* and I wouldn't last a minute locked up. I forced myself to look up but it wasn't the stern face of the law peering down on me. No. It was much, much worse.

Stood just feet away was Alex.

'Georgia, are you OK?' he asked coming closer, wincing at how sweaty I was. He looked different; he was walking taller and was wearing clothes I didn't recognise. *Why, oh why, did I have to bump into him today?*

'I don't want to talk to you.' I tried desperately not to cry and willed my heart rate to slow down. My voice sounded weird. I was gulping at smelly bin air.

'I know. But – are you sure you're OK?' He pointed to the overflowing bin and the scrambled egg-like vomit I was unwittingly standing in.

I shook my head as if I could make him vanish. My legs had frozen to the spot, my knuckles had turned white, and I was gripping the bin hard for support. This was not how I had *ever* imagined seeing him again; in those daydreams I was confident and dressed to kill, not perspiring and panicking.

'There's nothing left to say. I never want to see you again,' I forced myself to spit out defiantly, hoping that he couldn't see my trembling chin and bottom lip.

'OK, OK.' He spoke like a negotiator would to a hostage taker, rubbing the back of his neck. He had had his hair cut shorter, neater, more grown up. He looked like his dad. Or maybe just like *a* dad. My confused and humiliated brain couldn't focus.

'Did you get your things from the house yet? I've not been back for a few days. I'm staying at…err…a friend's place for the moment.'

I nodded, trying to swallow down a burp of bile scorching my throat. I knew exactly which *friend* he was talking about.

'Thanks, appreciate it. Both gotta move on and all that. Maybe it'll be good that you don't have to rely on me so much now.'

I couldn't believe this! He'd relied on *me*. I'd tried my hardest to fit the role of homemaker that every woman in his family neatly slotted into, and I'd done it all to make him happy. For cooking, cleaning, planning our diary, reminding him of when his mum's birthday was and then buying her presents that she always cast aside once one of her other daughters-in-law presented some artisanal made-with-the-blood-of-a-virgin-unicorn thingymajiggy. My gift card to Next never stood a chance. But that was all I was to him; a lousy maid, chef and Filofax. I stared at him open-mouthed, cheeks flaming in embarrassment at the attempt to leave my life here in search of a new one, only to come face to face with my past.

'I can't believe you! I–' I stopped mid-sentence as a woman with highlighted blonde hair and a neat freckled nose had joined us. Stephanie. Seeing her doll-like features I instantly remembered her. She'd asked to borrow my hairbrush in the ladies' toilets at Alex's work Christmas party last year. Bitch. She was pretty. Of course she was. She looked down at me through long lashes, her green eyes flicking between me and Alex as if working out how he had traded up so dramatically. I could almost hear her thinking, *This was his ex? This bin lady?*

'Oh hi, erm OK, you ready to go?' Alex said stumbling in between us both and taking the shopping bag from her hands, not before I noticed the slight bump under her tight striped jumper. 'Anyway, I'll leave you and er...the bin to it. Take care.' Alex waved bashfully and headed off down the street, steering Stephanie forward without a backwards glance.

My head was suddenly filled with snapshots of them, perfectly filtered Instagram photos of their new life together. Her with her lithe body that would no doubt snap back to pre-pregnancy skinny jeans an hour after giving birth, an adventurous vixen in the bedroom, a domestic goddess in the kitchen, funny, intelligent and BFF's with his mum Ruth. I pictured them laughing about me, at the state of me, at what I'd become, how Alex would shake his head trying to remember what had attracted him to me in the first place, how he'd had a lucky escape calling off our wedding. My face burned with shame.

My legs gave way as soon as Alex and Stephanie were lost in the crowd. I knocked over an empty can of lager as I slumped onto a cold step, holding my head in my hands. *Breathe, just breathe.*

'Here ya go, luv.' Someone chucked a few coins at my feet. 'Get yourself a decent meal.'

I looked up mortified. 'No I'm not a tramp, I'm just...' I faded out looking down at the bin stains on my jeans, the dodgy sticky residue on my hands, and the tangy smell of vomit at my feet then nodded slowly. 'Cheers.'

'All the single ladies, all the single ladies.' The jazzy tones of Queen B started blaring out of my handbag, which had narrowly avoided falling into an open kebab box. Marie had changed the ringtone when we were away, shoved a Hula Hoop crisp on my ring finger and spun me around the hotel bedroom trying to perfect her twerking skills. I snatched my phone out of my bag, not seeing the funny side any more.

'Hello?'

'Georgia. Catrina,' said my boss sharply.

I mentally ran through the week in my head. I was definitely due back at work tomorrow, not today. What the hell was she calling me for?

'Oh hi, erm, everything OK?'

'As a matter of fact, no, it isn't.' She paused as if collecting her thoughts.

My stomach did that funny clawing feeling you get when you know that as soon as they mutter the next few words everything could change. Catrina was never one to beat around the bush but also lacked the tact to pull off any emotional conversations.

'When you were off *gallivanting* on holiday you seemed to forget that a memory stick containing some sort of "mood" board was left on your desk,' she seethed.

My mouth went dry. I had selected a few photos – OK, maybe a hundred – that I liked from the internet as inspiration to show to the wedding venue before the final checks were made. And yes, maybe I did turn it into a live mood board with special effects – and, oh yep, even a backing track. I'd grabbed a work USB stick and quickly copied everything across, before Catrina came back from a meeting and clocked me wasting work time again, but I must have forgotten to put it in my handbag to take home.

'Unluckily for you, the temp covering your work, that stuck-up cow Dawn, found this stick whilst you were tanning yourself on holiday and got it mixed it up with her own USB for the presentation at today's pitch meeting. So instead of bloody pie charts and graphs the overseas clients and the whole of the Board, *including* Mr Rivers, have seen frothy bridal images and Lionel bloody Ritchie blasting out.'

Crap. This wasn't good.

I knew how slightly over the top I'd gone with the wedding montage, if you would call adding *The Best of Lionel* a little excessive. Looking at personal things in work time was bad, especially when this was the second time it had happened. I just found myself getting lost in wedding blogs on my lunch hour, losing track of the time until Catrina was stood watching over me, suffocating me in her heavy perfume, glowering at me with a furious scrunched-up face. I'd been given a verbal warning for this already but that time it had just affected Catrina, not the whole of the Board. Nope, really not good.

'Oh God. I'm…I'm sure we can explain it all,' I stuttered in shock.

'Georgia – did all that cheap booze last week affect your brain cells?' Catrina seethed.

My stomach lurched. I felt light-headed, the smell of a stranger's vomit burnt my nostrils. 'Catrina, I don't know what to say. I am *so* sorry. Maybe if I speak to Mr Rivers and explain it was all my fault. I've been under a lot of stress planning the wedding, which didn't actually happen, and–'

She let out a deep sigh crossed between boredom and amusement at hearing me begging for my job. 'Georgia, it's not going to be possible, I've given you enough chances to buck up your ideas and each time you throw them back in my face. So, you leave me no choice but to tell you that you're fired.'

'No, wait I...' I babbled, desperately trying not to cry.

Then it dawned on me: I could try my hardest to apologise, get off this step and storm into the office, bin juice and all, demanding a chance to make this right and possibly keep my job. Or...what if I let fate work its magic, giving me a shove to freedom and into the unknown? The face of 'R-ick' laughing at my boring spirit flashed in front of my eyes; my mum's voice entered my head telling me I could never be so adventurous and Alex's patronising smile made my cheeks heat up.

Sat on that beach in Turkey I'd planned to quit my job anyway, so, yeah, this wasn't anything like the scenes I'd imagined in which I'd leave to rapturous applause from my colleagues for my bravery and courage, not for unwittingly pitching 1001 Ways to Improve Your Wedding to important clients.

'Georgia. Did you hear me?' she shouted down the phone.

I made my decision.

'Yep. Loud and clear. OK, well thanks for everything.' My voice sounded high-pitched and wobbly.

'OK?' She paused, taken aback by my quick acceptance and lack of fight. 'Well, right, good. So that's that then. I'll get your things couriered to your address.'

I hung up before I had the chance to tell her I no longer lived at my old address. Oh well, looks like Alex and Stephanie would be getting a bittersweet housewarming gift of post-it notes and some naff logo merchandise.

I pushed myself onto my feet and wandered down the busy high street buzzing with adrenalin, which lasted as far as Superdrug, where suddenly the reality of what I'd done dawned on me. The reliable side of my conscience had a panic attack, shocked, as my other hidden, risky side looked on smirking. I was unemployed. I'd wreaked havoc in the travel agent's, my ex was going to become a daddy *and* I stank of some stranger's vomit. What had my life become?

CHAPTER 6

Serendipity (n.) The chance occurrence of events in a beneficial way

I stumbled into a nearby Weatherspoon's, ordered a pint of fruity cider and immediately dialled Marie's number.

'I can't frigging believe it,' Marie kept repeating as I filled her in on what had happened in the brat pack travel agency, Alex and Stephanie finding me in a compromising position with the council's bins and how Lionel Ritchie had got me the sack.

'It was mortifying.' I closed my eyes, willing it from my brain before downing the rest of my glass, the super-sweet bubbles slipping down my throat way too easily for a Monday lunchtime.

'You were clinging onto a rubbish bin? Oh God, Georgia.'

'I know! I should never have gone into that stupid travel agent's. I don't even know what came over me in there. I just felt like I was sick of people laughing at me, like *"Oh there she goes, that stupid jilted bride who says she wants to change her life but doesn't have the faintest idea how to do anything right. Oh, here she is, boring Georgia who didn't even know her ex got some slapper up the duff. Oh wait, Miss Green, isn't that the bridezilla with a penchant for Lionel Ritchie?"'* If there hadn't been a queue of people behind me I would have face-slapped the bar.

'Oh stop it. No one will think that,' Marie tutted. 'So what was it like seeing Sir Knob of Knobsville? I don't know how you could have even looked at him.'

I sighed. 'It still hasn't really sunk in, I guess. I was too paralysed with shock and shame to react properly. But the weird thing was, as unprepared as I was to see him, I didn't get a rush of loving emotions – just a rush of humiliation at the situation. I didn't really feel *anything* for him.'

'That's good, Georgia. You don't need him and yeah, well, meeting your ex whilst draped over a stinking bin probably didn't give off the clearest "I'm over you, my life is fabulous" message, but you're just a bit lost, that's all. Nobody's life goes to plan, especially not one they found in a stupid magazine quiz.'

I smiled, I knew exactly what quiz she was talking about. *One warm Summer day back when we were teens, weeks before the nightmare bunker incident, Marie and I were lying on the cool stubbly grass in her back garden, scribbling our answers to a trashy 'What kind of life will you have?' quiz I'd found in an old copy of my mum's* Woman's Weekly *magazine.*

'But this is stupid,' Marie had moaned as I'd asked her about her dreams and aspirations, 'I'm going to marry Ricky Martin; he just doesn't know it yet.'

'OK,' I sighed, 'so you run off to Puerto Rico to find him – then what?'

Marie rolled over to her back and shaded her eyes from the sun. 'Well, I want to be married by the time I'm twenty-two and have had my first child by at least twenty-four.' We both shuddered at how ancient that sounded. 'After that, I'll become a world-famous actress and we'll live in Hollywood with our three model-looking children.'

'You'd better start paying attention in your Spanish classes then,' I teased, picking dirt out of my fingernails.

'Nah, we'll speak the language of lurve,' she smiled before pulling the quiz away roughly. 'Right then, Miss Green, what's your life plan going to be?'

My eyes lit up as I spoke: 'I want to travel, to see more of life than what's on our doorstep. Oh, and also to write. Being a travel journalist would be pretty cool. Imagine waking up in a different country every day and getting paid to tell the world what you're seeing, eating and doing?'

'Then you can write better quizzes than what's in here,' Marie smirked, whacking me with the rolled up mag.

'Look what happened to my plan!' Marie exclaimed. 'I never did get round to marrying Ricky Martin and *definitely* never thought I'd be a single mum, but even though Cole wasn't part of my original plan, I couldn't imagine how my life could be any better without him.'

'To be fair, I don't think you're Ricky's type.' She laughed. 'Well, I never got to be the next Judith Chalmers,' I sighed, thinking of my unloved passport. 'I guess I hadn't realised how fast life passes you by. One minute you're fresh-faced, taking the first job you're offered, convinced it will be a springboard for better things to come, then the next, you're older, settled and saggy,' I said sadly, just as an unshaved old man waddled past holding a pint of bitter before hacking up a load of phlegm into a mucky handkerchief.

'It's easily done, babe.' Marie paused. 'OK, I'm going to be real with you for a second, and don't get mad. I hadn't wanted to say anything because, you know, the whole not getting married thing, but actually, hun, you've changed. Going away with you last week reminded me what the real Georgia was like. Not the one who fusses over Alex, who stresses about table runners and ruddy place mats. Not the one who checks the weather to see if they can put their washing out rather than if it's hot enough to head to a beer garden, not the one who pretends to enjoy eating kale and drinking pomegranate juice. You never used to be like that, but over time you've changed. So maybe you did get lost along the way, but now it's like you've been given a ticket to start again, to reinvent yourself and do exactly what you want. Not go along with what Alex likes, or follow Catrina's direction, but actually think: what does Georgia Green want to do?'

'I guess,' I mumbled tearing the moist edges of the beer mats in front of me. She was right, about all of it. Kale is bloody nasty.

'I'm serious, hun, if I was in your situation, but obviously minus a child, then I'd be out of here faster than when Big Claire orders her kebab at closing time. The world is your oyster. Go and grab it by the pearly balls!'

*

'Oh hello, I'll be with you in just one tic. Oh you silly bugger just work!' A woman was wrestling with an ancient printer almost half her petite size. Papers were strewn everywhere and a strange gurgling noise was blaring from the knackered machine. 'This is why I write everything down. Don't trust these impetuous things. You know where you are with a paper and pen.' She ran a wrinkled hand through her grey hair, flattening down loose strands that had formed a halo in the dust-particled light streaming through the window.

I'd taken Marie's advice and left the pub having Googled nearby travel agents, one I hopefully wouldn't be humiliated in. 'Have you changed the ink recently?' I suggested, stepping over documents flung on the floor to get a closer look. 'We used to have the same model at work and all it needed was a good whack. Like this.' Without thinking I thumped down hard on the lid. It wheezed to life then began churning out copies like brand new.

'Oh my days. Thank you so much. Do you know how long I've been faffing with this? Turning it on and off again, trying different paper and I never once thought to do that.' She beamed a genuine heartfelt smile at me.

'No problem. Glad to be of service.'

'So now that's working, I can properly introduce myself and make you a cup of tea – it's the least I can do for saving my sanity!' She wiped her hands on her trousers and came round from behind the desk, cautiously placing her pale-pink court shoes amongst the carpet of paper between us. 'Welcome to Making Memories. Owner, explorer and technology-phobe Trisha at your service! How can I help you?' She stuck her ink-splatted hand out to me.

This small, slightly sweating woman was a world away from the intimidating chimps at the other travel agency. Trisha was more like someone's grandma. In fact, how had she not yet retired? Her cotton wool-coloured hair was loosely pulled into a low chignon and gold necklaces jangled against her crinkly tanned neck. She was wearing a smart trouser suit with a name badge and smelled like incense and sun lotion.

I shook Trisha's hand and smiled down at her. 'Hi. Georgia. Wannabe backpacker, gherkin-hater and printer-fixer who would *love* a brew,' I said gratefully.

'Coming right up! Eurgh I hate gherkins too, why ruin a perfectly good burger by plonking slimy bogey-coloured strips on the top?'

'Exactly!'

Trisha smiled. 'Oh, and please excuse the mess, usually there are two of us here but Deidre's had to take some time off. To be honest I'm not sure if she's coming back. Her son's just had a baby you see, a little girl, so now it's babies rather than brochures,' she chuckled. 'I'm so pleased for her but I could probably do with another pair of hands around the place, especially where modern technology is involved.' She laughed lightly, awkwardly hiding some dirty mugs behind a framed picture of a handsome young man grinning by the Empire State Building. 'I guess it's good to keep busy though. Right, now for tea.'

Even though this shop had a prime position just off the packed high street, I'd walked past it every day not giving it a glance. It was a beautiful old room. I remember my dad telling me that there used to be an old bank on this street, I guess a few of these smaller shops must have been born from spare bank rooms when it moved location. Looking past the messy stacks of paper, a striking ornate marble fireplace drew my eyes, my feet sank into the faded, thick plum-coloured rug that partially covered decorative floor tiles, and large lanterns hung from the high ceiling that was iced with gilt trim carvings. So grand for such a small travel agent's.

Apart from the stacks of bright, glossy brochures the rest of the room was dark, muted colours with a weathered world map above the fireplace and an ancient-looking globe standing proudly in the corner. A melodic tune emanated from some hidden speakers; it sounded aboriginal and enchanting.

Trisha noticed me tilting my head to listen. 'It's from a remote Botswanan tribe I stumbled across when I visited the country many years ago. The bushmen from the Kalahari Desert performed at this tiny camp I was sleeping in for the night and their voices, rhythms and unusual dance moves were nothing like you would find down the local discotheque back home. I just fell into a trance and persuaded the tribesmen to let me tape them on my Dictaphone. It's not the best quality, but it takes me back.'

'I've never heard anything like it,' I admitted, as Trisha returned to making the tea, humming along.

Brochures on a walnut bookcase were meticulously separated into areas – exactly how I would have placed them, with European breaks at the top followed by Russia, China, Asia, Africa, the Americas, Australia and New Zealand and even Antarctic brochures. Trisha had the whole world covered here. My fingers reached out instantly to a South East Asia brochure. I lazily flicked through pages of colour from Indonesia, Malaysia and Thailand, each exotic image drawing me in.

'You take milk and sugar, love?' Trisha called out, making me pop the brochure back on the shelf nervously.

'Just milk please.'

'Ah, sweet enough, are you?' She smiled, repeating my dad's favourite catchphrase.

'Yeah, something like that,' I grinned and padded over to the far wall, which was covered in postcards from all over the world. Must be from happy clients, I thought, absently picking one that had dropped to the floor and turning it over. *'Greetings from Uganda! You were right Trish, the tilapia is incredible here. Who knew I'd be choosing fish over greasy kebabs, how things have changed hey! Having an incredible time. It's hard work getting around this beautiful country, especially in the heat, but it is so worthwhile. Hope all is good with you and you're following the doctors' orders? Love Stevie x'*

'Ah, most of those are from Stevie, he's such an adventurer,' Trisha said warmly. I quickly put the card back on the wall, flushed from reading her personal messages. Who was Stevie and why did Trisha need to be following doctors' orders? I thought she seemed quite sprightly, albeit a little tired-looking.

A liver-spotted hand passed over a cup of tea, breaking my thoughts. Beckoning me to sit on the sofa with her, Trisha explained that she'd picked up the beautiful emerald-green teacups in Iran eighteen years earlier. Sat close up Trisha didn't look like your typical explorer; there were no stuffed animals hung on the walls, none of those round brown hats you imagine adventurers wearing or rifle guns proudly displayed. She looked like she would be more at home watching *Bargain Hunt* rather than bartering for crockery in an exotic eastern market.

'Your shop's beautiful, how long have you had this place?' I waved my hand around the mysterious room, taking in the heavy aubergine velvet drapes hung majestically at the windows and a large sumptuous chandelier casting droplets of golden light from its vertical glass shards. It was a mix of safari meets Moroccan boudoir.

'Ah, this is my baby,' Trisha beamed as if seeing the room for the first time. 'Never got round to having children of my own as me and my wonderful late husband Fred spent most of our time globetrotting. When we finally settled in Manchester I'd unfortunately missed that boat. His health wasn't in the best condition back then so we used every penny we had to buy this place and focused our energies here.'

'It's a stunning space; you must actually enjoy coming to work here every day?' It's a world away from my nondescript desk in the ugly grey office building I *used* to work at.

'I truly love it and have been very blessed to have loyal clients help me, but I'm not getting any younger and the day will soon come when all this gets passed on to my godson, Stevie.' She nodded towards the collection of postcards. 'He's about your age and just one of the few family members I have left.' She rubbed her neck, wincing slightly. 'He's always sending me postcards from the countries he travels to, mostly on work trips. We have a lot of itchy feet in our family, if you know what I mean!'

'Athlete's foot?' I asked.

Trisha let out a long chuckle. 'No dear, I mean that our feet itch to be on the move. To travel. That's why sometimes I worry that when my time is up Stevie will struggle to cope with staying in one place indefinitely. Don't get me wrong, he's a good boy, but exactly like his mother was when she was his age, always looking for the next challenge and country to discover. I don't think he's lived in one town for longer than a year, keeps you on your toes, our Stevie!'

God, this guy sounded like the polar opposite of Alex, who wouldn't have moved to turn off the television if he'd lost the remote. Imagine leading such an exciting and fun life, always on the road, travelling all over the world. I could understand why the poor lad didn't want to come rushing to Manchester to help his godmother's business, it would be such a comedown.

'I saw you earlier actually, running with a handful of brochures from those idiots up the road. I wanted to open my door and shout out for you to come in here as I was certain you wouldn't find what you were looking for in that noisy, childish place. They should be ashamed, being so dismissive of anyone who isn't eighteen years old, doesn't look like them or is only clutching pocketful's of Daddy's money on some sort of enriching gap year,' Trisha said before breaking into a laugh. 'Ha! The only thing those kids will be learning is how to get out of a Bali jail after being caught with marijuana on them. They think that traveling is just risking their lives, livers and futures for a jaunt around Asia with their eyes completely closed to the beauty and hospitality that receives them. But you – you remind me of me when I was your age.'

I spilled a little of my tea. 'Oh, erm, really?'

'Now, of course I don't know you, but I don't think *you* do either. That can be confusing, scary but also exhilarating.' *She had a point.* 'Over the years I've become pretty adept at understanding others; you need to, if you want to see the world. You also have to understand that *everyone* has a story and many of those stay hidden unless you really look for them.' She sipped her tea. 'So, have you just finished work for the day?'

'I got fired.' The words tasted bitter in my mouth.

'Ah, I see. I've also noticed you're not wearing a ring on an important finger and I look into your eyes and see a sadness, so I'm guessing there has been some recent mess-up in the love department?' I fidgeted slightly, almost getting swallowed up on this cloud of a sofa. 'You want to make changes in your life, but are scared of what these will mean, both to you and others around you.'

'Yeah, something like that.' She was right, of course. After I gave Trisha a much-shortened story, as apparently I was sat with 'Mystic Meg', she rose and handed me the South East Asia brochure – the one I'd previously picked up myself.

'It sounds like you're new at this game, so I don't want to fling you in some Outer Mongolian goat shed. Not just yet, anyway,' she smiled, taken back to some distant memory. By the look on her face I thought maybe.I did want to stay in some stinky goat shed.

'I think Thailand would be perfect for you. They mostly speak English; it's a country full of joy, charm and smiles. Just what you need to be around at the moment. It has beaches, jungles, metropolitan cities and the capital, Bangkok, is a place I'd advise anyone to go at least once in their life.'

'That does sound pretty great.' I thought back to my travel wish-list that I'd hastily unscrunched from my wastepaper bin, mentally checking things off: ride an elephant, laze on white sandy beaches, get some culture and visit temples. The images shining from the sleek pages were so tempting. Suddenly my mum's shrill tones clanged in my head: *Who would help me if I got sick? What if someone tried to drug me, or even worse, force me to become a drugs mule?*

Trisha must have sensed my hesitation: 'For the first-time traveller it can all feel a bit overwhelming, so why don't we look at joining you onto a tour group? That way you'll be with people in similar situations to yours; maybe first-timers or nervous about solo travel, but you also have the safety and ease of the trip being planned for you?'

I hadn't even thought about that as an option. 'Yeah, I reckon that could work,' I smiled, giving Trisha the date I wanted to leave – basically as soon as possible – and she began tapping at a clunky keyboard.

'Let me see… I think all my popular Thailand tours are booked up as it's so last-minute. Looking at your dates of travel and discounting geriatric retirees, the only one I could book you on is this one.' Her printer spluttered into life, acting as if it had always been so efficient. 'It's a family-owned business and will hopefully open your eyes to the world.'

The itinerary consisted of Bangkok, Chiang Mai, Kanchanaburi and island-hopping, with organised visits to temples, street markets, cooking classes, language school and paradise beaches. 'It sounds perfect,' I breathed, noticing the uneasy look on Trisha's face as she chewed her bottom lip. 'What's wrong with it?'

'Nothing, nothing. The accommodation isn't going to be five-star luxury and at times it may feel far from home, especially after everything you've told me you've been through. My advice would be to keep your mind open and if it all gets too much then you *must* head to the Blue Butterfly Huts on this island here.' She pointed to an ant-sized speck in the ocean off the larger Koh Phangan island called Koh Lanta. 'They'll look after you.'

An hour, nearly a full pack of biscuits and a few more cups of tea later, we had everything finalised; I was booked onto the six-week tour leaving in ten days! I didn't want to worry about what I'd do once that was over and I was back here again. *Stop trying to make plans for the future and just, for once, go with the flow.* Trisha helped me apply for a fast-tracked Thai visa, sorted my travel insurance, booked me in for a few immunisations and gave me a list of all the things I needed to buy and pack. My cheeks were hurting from smiling; there was no going back now.

OM effing G! Georgia Green was going travelling.

CHAPTER 7

Eleutheromania (n.) An intense and irresistible desire for freedom

This evening was my leaving party, and also the first time I'd seen my mum since our slight disagreement over the phone last week when I'd come clean about my travel plans.

'Georgia Louise Green.' Oh God. She'd full-named me. 'Why, when I called your work phone, did some rude woman tell me you'd been fired?'

I was transported back to being eleven years old, to when I'd accidently broken two of my mum's china dogs that stood proudly on each end of the mantelpiece. I'd been dancing slightly too energetically to the Spice Girls album, trying to perfect Sporty Spice's high kick, when my heel took out the left dog. In an effort to hide the evidence, I figured my mum would be less likely to notice if both were smashed and hidden in the bin. Genius logic. What I forgot was that my mum has the nose of a bloodhound sniffing out any change in her surroundings. I'd been grounded for a week and had to save a month's worth of pocket money to replace them.

'I haven't been fired, no I, erm, quit,' I replied, hoping she was sat down. OK so that was only a half-truth but I needed to rein in some control over this messy situation called my life.

'What?!' My mum's shrill tones screamed down the line, forcing me to hold the phone away from my ear.

'I need to have a change of scene and get out of Manchester for a while. You know I wasn't happy in my job and it wasn't going anywhere, so I quit.' I felt like I was being interrogated over the china dogs all over again. Where did you put its right paw? What happened to its left ear?

'I'd hoped this hoity-toity lady was wrong and this was all a misunderstanding.' She paused, collecting her thoughts. 'So what are you going to do? Please tell me you have another job lined up?'

'I'm going to travel.' I didn't wait for her reaction as I continued, feeling braver with every word. 'I've bought a plane ticket to Thailand. I'm going to go and see the world, Mum.' There was silence on the other end of the phone, punctuated by a deep sigh.

'Oh, Georgia. I thought you said all that was just a silly game you played with Marie, not that you were going to go and actually do it! I understand you've been through the wringer, but gallivanting off is not the answer. You can't run away from the past. It will always find you.'

'Mum, I'm not running from but running to. I'm changing my life. Surely you want me to be happy? And I really think by going out there to see the world, I will be,' I said, full of confidence and a little bit of fear, having never been so forward with her before.

'But…but how on earth will you survive? You've never done anything on your own!'

I flinched at that comment. It was one hundred percent true, of course, but it still stung that I hadn't been more independent in my twenty-eight years. I'd never have been accepted into Destiny's Child, I was a let-down as a Spice Girls fan. 'I'll be fine, Mum. People say you should treat strangers as friends you haven't met yet.' I tried to ignore the thought of the pulsating vein on the left side of her temple that would be throbbing at this conversation.

'Yes, but they also say one in three murder victims know their killer,' she blustered. 'You know this world is a dangerous place and all me and your father have ever wanted was to keep you safe. We can't do that from the other side of the world. I'll not be able to sleep a wink every night you're away – have you thought about that?'

'Actually, Mum, I want to think about myself. Just me, for once in my life.' There was silence on the line. Immediately I regretted biting her head off.

'Well…well, OK then. I just hope for your sake you don't end up regretting this silly holiday. Anyway, I need to go.' With that she hung up, leaving me breathless, staring into the white noise in shock.

I hadn't heard from her since then, but my dad had been sending me the odd secretive supportive text message. #DON'T WORRY ABOUT YOUR MUM. YOU GO FOR IT KIDDO. LOL. He clearly didn't know what a hashtag was but the thought was there, in all its shouty glory.

'You nervous about tomorrow then?' Marie asked in the taxi as we made our way to the Chinese restaurant.

'Yeah.' I pulled a face. 'A little! Although I think I'm more excited than terrified.'

'I bet! Excited about all the hot men you're going to meet?' She winked and passed Cole his Sophie the giraffe toy he'd chucked on the floor.

'Is that all you think about?' I rolled my eyes. I don't know what was with Marie, but at the moment she was like a dog on heat, more obsessed with men than I'd ever seen her before.

'Not *all* I think about.' She stuck her tongue out, which made Cole laugh. 'But you must have imagined the tanned hunks, from all over the world, that will be backpacking too? You have to admit that there's something sexy about a guy going off to explore the world, to face the unknown, unafraid of challenges and obstacles in his path,' she sighed. 'So manly and adventurous.'

'Like Stevie,' I said before clapping my hand to my mouth, stopping myself. Where had that come from?!

'Stevie?' Marie turned to face me. 'Who's Stevie?' Her eyes were glowing with excitement.

I shook my head quickly. 'Forget I said it.' I blushed.

'Err, come on! Out with it, if you're keeping some man gossip from me, Miss Green, I swear I'll make you walk the rest of the way there.'

'OK, OK! But listen, I'm sorry to disappoint you but there's no gossip. I don't even know anything about him.' She looked confused.

'OMG, wait, are you online dating! Swiping left on Tinder?' she gushed excitedly, getting her phone out of her handbag.

'No!' I shuddered at the thought. 'Stevie's the godson of Trisha, you know the lovely lady I booked my tour with?' Marie nodded. 'Anyway, in her shop I'd seen these postcards from, like, all over the world and I read one.'

Marie looked visibly deflated. 'Postcards?'

'Yeah, from all these cool places. Anyway, I read one by accident and he just sounded so lovely and, like you said, adventurous, caring, kind, exciting.' I pulled myself to a stop and cleared my throat. Marie was now staring quizzically at me with a sly smile on her bright fuchsia-pink lips. 'I just have this image in my head of the type of man this Stevie is. The type of guy that I guess in the future, I'd like to be with.' I closed my eyes wincing, waiting for the moment that she burst into a fit of laughter, but she stayed silent. Squinting one eye open Marie was looking at me, but not with a what-a-ridiculous-stupid-idea type look but more an understanding yeah-I-get-it type look. 'It's crazy isn't it?'

Marie shook her head, her recently-tonged vibrant red curls dancing about. 'No, not crazy. Inspiring. It's good that you're thinking about the future, about guys again – '

'Loooooooonnnnnng into the future,' I interrupted her.

'Yeah, OK, long into the future. But still, this is a positive sign, hun.' I smiled, realising this was one of many reasons she was my best friend. Having a crush – was that what this was? –on a guy I'd never met, wasn't that strange to her. 'And you never know, maybe you'll bump into this Stevie when you're away, get married on some exotic beach, have a ton of kids and live happily ever after.'

I scoffed. 'Yeah and maybe one day you'll realise that Mike is the one for you.'

She busied herself with Cole's car seat straps, ignoring my teasing. 'Mmm. Right. Here we are.' Saved by the bell or what.

'Err, you don't get out of it that easy, Marie. One day you're going to realise that I'm right and I don't want you to be heartbroken if that day's too late for Mike to still be waiting for you,' I said. Maybe a bit harsh but true.

'Georgia. I'm fine.' She patted her hand on mine. 'Like I've told you a million times before, me and Mike just won't work. We had Cole, had some fun, but that's it. I'm having way too much fun being single for all that anyway.' She wafted her hand away. 'You'll see!' She took a note out of her purse to pay the driver. I knew her well enough to know when she was telling the truth but kidding herself at the same time. Maybe that was what all this sudden infatuation with other men was about, she didn't want to admit her true feelings for the father of her child. 'Now come on, we've got a leaving party to enjoy!'

Since arriving at the almost empty restaurant neither myself nor my parents had mentioned the argument, an unspoken ceasefire had been called for my last night with them all. Marie had surprised me with a pair of sunglasses, a cheap wind-up torch and a hand-drawn card from Cole that my parents cooed over. Mum and Dad gave me an envelope stuffed with Thai baht and a rape alarm which, when they had tested it prior to arriving here, had almost given my mum a heart attack. I guessed that this was their olive branch.

'I also wanted to give you this, pet.' My dad rummaged into his jeans pocket, bringing out a small brown envelope and passing it over to me.

'You've all given me enough. I honestly didn't expect any presents.'

'I think you'll like this,' he grinned. I tipped the contents of the package into my hand and out fell a thin silver chain with an engraved solid disc in the centre. 'It's a St Christopher, the Patron Saint of Travellers,' he explained. 'My father gave it to me when I went off for my brief travels. It's meant to give the wearer good luck and protection.'

'Wow…thanks.' I squeezed his hand as Marie leaned over to fix the clasp around my neck.

My dad winked, before clearing his throat. 'It suits you, Georgie. I know you've promised us you'll be safe but this is just a little extra protection,' he sniffed.

'Thank you. Dad, this is a good thing, a start of something new. I promise I'll be careful and as soon as I can, I'll be in touch. You won't even notice I've gone.'

He ruffled my hair: 'You know we love you so much. We're very proud of you and just want you to have the time of your life. Lord knows, if I was your age I'd be doing exactly the same.'

'Now, now, that's enough emotion,' my mum cut in briskly. 'Ooh, look! Fortune cookies.'

The smiling waitress placed a small bowl of strawberry ice cream in front of Cole with four cookies wrapped in shiny plastic for the adults. We each picked one and tore off the berry-red foil.

'"May the sun shine to light your way,"' Marie read out, impersonating 'Mystic Meg'. 'Well I hope so, as I wouldn't see a bloody thing in the dark.'

'Oh, like those poor Norwegians,' my mum said sympathetically.

'No dear, they can still walk about, it's just that in the north in winter they have less sunlight than us,' my dad corrected her, laughing. 'Who even writes these stupid sayings? Right – "Be bold, for those who have valour will fight to victory." Well, it has been a very tough battle with my clematis bush…but I think I may have won,' he smiled.

One of the few things that Dad seemed to have found enjoyment in since taking early retirement was pottering around in his small but impeccable garden. Every time I visited he would pop on his yellow crocs, which my mum had picked up from the market, convinced they were très chic, and proudly show me his newly-laid flower beds, or organic fertiliser that they'd splashed out on at Homebase when it had been on special offer. 'That'll make all the difference,' he'd said, pointing his head towards the bag of manure, nodding wisely.

'My turn.' My mum had torn off the wrapper and put her reading glasses on to squint at the tiny letters. '"A bad word uttered once will always be repeated twice." Oh, I bet that means Viv from number twenty-three has been gossiping about my hanging baskets again. She even has her eye on my hydrangeas, but I swore I'd never reveal my secret for their growth.'

'Right, your go,' Marie said wiping Cole's mouth. She gave me a look that said move on from this green-fingered conversation before she jabbed a fork in her eye. I smiled and carefully pulled out the crisp cookie and snapped it in two.

But it was empty.

I dug my fingernails into each crevice and then smashed it completely, just in case the paper strip had become lodged in the side. But there was nothing...I had no fortune.

'Oh my God. I have no fortune, no future! This cannot be a good omen, seeing as I'm getting on that flight tomorrow.' I felt like I was hyperventilating. My dad rummaged through the crumbs, my mum shot evil looks at him for having booked this restaurant and told me to calm down. Marie was trying to catch the waiter's attention for another cookie, or the bill, or a strong drink, whichever arrived first.

'Don't panic. I'm sure there was just a mistake in the manufacturing. Isn't that right, Len?' my mum snapped at my dad, who offered to give me his fortune cookie before Cole grasped his pink chubby fingers around the paper slip.

'It's all a load of nonsense anyway. Don't get worked up about it, pet,' he said pulling the paper from Cole's mouth, causing him to cry grumpily. I was still trying to find my breath when a shot of something clear and pungent was placed in front of me by a smiling waitress, who was completely unaware of the drama that had occurred.

'Drink this,' Marie ordered. I downed the acrid-tasting alcohol in one. As the liquid burned my throat, I started to relax. Maybe they were right; it was just a cock-up in the production line. It wasn't as if anyone had taken it out before they gave it to me. We each picked our own cookie. But I knew I was trying to think positively when I glanced at their worried faces as the bill arrived.

Crap. I have no fortune.

If I could have gone back in time, I would have asked the waitress for another cookie, because what really lay in store for me couldn't have been thought up in some Chinese fortune cookie factory.

*

Having never flown anywhere on my own before, a mixture of excitement, fear and hope grew in my stomach. Everything was a novelty – from the complimentary drinks, to the ridiculous number of films to choose from on the small screen in the seatback in front, to the scratchy, free blanket and cotton eye mask. I arrived in Dubai six hours later where I had a couple of hours to kill before transferring to the next flight on to Bangkok. Following the throng of passengers through this gigantic airport was overwhelming; this place was off-the-scale huge. I felt like Macaulay Culkin in *Home Alone 2*, gallivanting through this big and busy airport with my bag on my back and a skip in my step. My senses were assaulted by expensive smells from the designer shops and my ears caught snippets of conversation, all spoken in foreign tongues.

Not having any free space in my bulging smaller backpack to go shopping, I spotted a free computer area where I could pass some time with a final check of Facebook. There were a few well wishes from distant family members who had heard the news about my trip from my parents. I was surprised that Mum and Dad had told anyone, imagining their shame at having to change their story. Now they would be boasting that I had transformed from a jilted bride to Dora the Explorer. None of us had mentioned Fortune Cookiegate when they dropped me at the airport early this morning, too many tears, hugs and complaints about the daylight robbery car parking prices.

A Tannoy flight announcement shrieked loudly as I clicked on my emails. In amongst adverts for Gala Bingo and Candy Crush requests there was one from Alex's mum. Confused I clicked it open.

Dear Georgia,

Please call me as soon as you receive this message. I understand you may not want word from me or my family but I do have some pressing information that I need to share with you.

Regards,

Ruth Doherty

I read and re-read the email three times. What the hell was Alex's mum doing emailing me and what was she talking about? We had never really bonded and she'd never contacted me directly, apart from forwarding on emails about her other sons' weddings, pricy contacts and suppliers we needed to use (who didn't come with mates' rates). We were hardly pen pals.

Another Tannoy announcement caught my attention. My flight was now boarding. Passengers filed towards the smiling, perfectly made-up flight attendants at the doors just ahead. I hastily began to reply, struggling to think about how to start a message to the mother of my ex-fiancé when another announcement rang out instructing a few late passengers, including me, to report to the gate immediately.

I decided whatever it was must be over-the-top drama. I deleted my draft reply and logged off, running towards the now-frowning flight attendant who grabbed my boarding card and swiftly glanced at my passport as she shoo'ed me down the passenger tunnel towards the plane. I raced through the doors, boarded the plane, only to be greeted by pissed-off looks from the other seated passengers. I fumbled my way to my seat and secured my seatbelt.

Half listening to the safety announcement, I forced myself to forget about it. I had to look to the future from now on.

Next stop, Bangkok.

CHAPTER 8

*Dépaysement (n.) The disorientation felt in a foreign
country or culture, the sense of being a fish out of water*

'Georgia Green? Are you Georgia Green?' A small Thai
guy was pulling at my creased sleeve in the three-man-deep
arrivals hall in Bangkok Airport.

'Yes, that's me,' I said, relieved that I didn't have to try
and decipher the badly scrawled handwriting on the sea of
homemade placards in front of me. 'Are you…er…Kit?' I
asked, fumbling for my 'welcome' information.

'Yes, me, Kit and you, Miss Green.' He stuck a bony
finger into his thin chest and then jabbed me in the arm.
'Follow me.' I nodded and lugged my backpack onto my
shoulders, immediately shortening my height by a few
inches because of the weight of it. Even with Marie's
military-precision packing, it still felt like a small
stowaway could have crawled in there.

We stepped out of the air-conditioned space into a much
stickier heat as Kit led the way to the transfer car. When I
clapped eyes on the heap of rust in front of me, I assumed
that this was Thai humour and the actual air-conditioned
people carrier would be hidden just behind it.

No such luck.

'You get in. Give me bag,' he ordered, opening a door
that yelped on its hinges. The smell of dog and stale fags

instantly hit my nose. Gold plastic Buddhas blu-tacked onto the dusty dashboard were barely visible in the cloudy fug. Kit had surprising strength for such a weedy man, hoisting my bag off me in one fell swoop, relieving my aching neck and shoulders. Before I could grumble about the stink-mobile, Kit jumped into the front of the car, turned up the radio and beckoned me in with his thin hands and long brown fingernails.

'I'm not sure how safe this looks. I was expecting something a bit newer and…erm…cooler?' I shouted over the music, fanning my face with my passport. After a sixteen-hour journey to get here I was not in the mood for jokes.

'This very good car!' Kit struggled to wind down his windows. 'This air con,' he smiled crookedly.

I bit my lip, unsure of what to do. I'd only been here less than an hour and already I felt my courage slipping.

'*Mai pen rai!*' he barked.

I had no idea what he was saying, but realising there wasn't another option, I grabbed hold of the loose grey seatbelt marked with dodgy-looking stains and climbed in. Black dog hair stuck to my cotton pants and crisp packets rustled at my feet.

Welcome to Thailand.

'So, erm, where are the others on the tour?' I shouted as we set off, the sound of the ancient engine now competing with the warbling singer on the radio.

'You meet in hotel. You stay Bangkok two night then we go. Very nice hotel. Very nice girl,' he replied licking his lips. God knows how he managed to avoid careering into a large truck as he gazed at my breasts through the rear-view mirror, covered in cobwebbed wooden beads. I quickly shut my eyes and gripped the sticky armrest.

He didn't even flinch.

To take my mind off the queasiness I felt at Kit's awful driving, I stared out the grimy window. Huge sleek skyscrapers loomed ahead as scraps of deserted wasteland stood between us and the centre of the capital. Large road signs with photos of the King and adverts for soft drinks written in Thai peppered the modern highway. Our speed slowed slightly as we approached an expressway toll booth. Kit told me I needed to give him 400 baht for the toll charge, which seemed suspiciously higher than the 150 baht I'd seen quoted in the guide books I'd devoured before arriving. Feeling too hot and bothered to question it, I pulled out the soft crumpled notes and took a look at my chauffeur. He was older than I had imagined, easily in his late forties and could have been a distant relation to Mr Burns from the Simpsons, with receding black hair, wrinkled tanned skin and exceptionally large nostrils.

Well, at least it won't be all-night raves, and with age comes wisdom.

A little while later and we had swapped motorways for bustling streets. My senses were freaking out at the cacophony of horns, shouting, brightly coloured shop fronts, greasy fried food smells, ragged-looking street children and shining silver tower blocks. This place really was a mix of rustic and modern, poor and rich, proud heritage and sleazy sex shows. We travelled down a few quieter streets, driving past a McDonald's and a Subway. The backpackers' ghetto we pulled up at could have easily been back home, except for the language and deep-fried insects, which I'd never seen on offer at the local market next to the Bury black-pudding stall.

The hotel was called 'Happy Endings'. Wasn't that a euphemism for receiving a…ahem…present from a prostitute? I was certain I'd overheard Alex's best mate, Ryan, laughing about this when they were chatting about

Alex's stag do in Amsterdam. My hen party had been a sedate affair, Francesca had insisted on organising it all as is 'family tradition' much to Marie's disgust. We'd spent the day relaxing at an eye-wateringly expensive spa in Cheshire, not a blow-up willy or L plate in sight. Fran and Ruth, who was more like an outlaw than a mother-in-law, spent the entire time bitching about other guests as I tried to explain to Marie why punching them wasn't going to make the day go any quicker. I could cringe, thinking about how dull and lacklustre that supposed last night of freedom was. Well, no more boring Georgia.

Nestled between a convenience store called '7/11' and a graffiti-covered alleyway, the hotel was in desperate need of some TLC. I followed Kit into the sparse foyer, where a bored-looking Thai teenager played with his phone, unaware of our arrival until Kit cleared his throat and the kid bolted upright, plastering a fake smile on his young face.

'Welcome to Happy Endings,' he parroted as Kit rolled his eyes and barked at him in fast Thai.

'You go room and later we meet at 8pm for welcome dinner. No be late,' Kit said rapidly.

He passed over my room key as the scrawny teen effortlessly lolloped off with my bag slung over one shoulder. I quickly nodded my understanding to Kit and chased the young lad down the dark, but cool, corridors. I worked out that I had time for a quick nap and, looking down at my pasty white arms where a sheen of sweat and dirt from the journey was clearly visible, a much-needed shower. The shared bedroom had a faint smell of sick lingering in the clammy air that was being moved around by an ancient air-conditioning unit huffing on the wall. There was one single bed and two bunk beds with a small, scuffed mahogany bedside table between them. On the paisley orange sheets sat a duck, fashioned from stained white towels, proudly surveying the scene, its drooped beak facing the small yellowing window opposite, where metal bars looked out onto a brick wall. Faint car horns and shouting floated in through broken slats. Trisha was right, luxury this wasn't.

Sitting on the bed, trying to ignore a couple having a screaming match outside the window, I pulled my knees up to my chin and shut my eyes. I was in Bangkok. It didn't feel real that I was here. So, it wasn't the Hilton and that Kit guy seemed a bit sketchy, but I had done what I said I was going to do; for the first time in my life I'd had the balls to make a decision and stick to it. A mixture of excitement and apprehension fizzed over me.

'Here. Look, Room six.'

'No, the key says Room nine.'

'You're holding it upside down, you moron.'

'I'm not. Just push it!'

High-pitched female voices floated under the door from the corridor, pulling me back to the present. The door suddenly swung open and two of the most attractive women I had ever seen tumbled in. Long milky-white hair on slender pale shoulders for one and auburn waves on the other.

'God, does maintenance mean nothing to these people?!' The one with auburn hair scowled at the door before registering I was in the room. 'Oh, hi,' she said with all the enthusiasm of going to a smear test.

'Hi, hello, erm, I'm Georgia. I guess we're roommates!' I said, way too over-excitedly, awkwardly walking over to shake her hand. Obviously all that coffee I necked on the journey here was kicking in.

She flicked her slender wrist unenthusiastically towards her chest ignoring my outstretched hand: 'Amelie' then pointed to her friend, 'Luna' she drawled in a Canadian accent, who at least managed a half smile before they wheeled their bulging suitcases into the room, knocking over my bag.

'Right, I call shotgun.' Amelie flopped onto the bed I'd been sitting on. Her patterned maxi dress billowed around her slim frame, covering my hand luggage bag.

'Oh, I–'

'Cool, bunk beds,' Luna interrupted me and pushed past to climb up the stained wooden frame and bellyflopped on the top bunk as if she was seven years old at a sleepover.

'I'm not sure how secure...' Before I could finish there was a loud creak and ping of springs. Luna's pale body sandwiched in on itself.

'Arghhhh!' she screamed.

Amelie howled with laughter. 'Oh my gawd, I can't take you anywhere.'

'Help me! Don't just laugh. Georgina, do something,' Luna called out, muffled slightly by the dirty duvets swallowing her whole. The bed had dipped so low it was almost touching the bottom bunk.

'It's Georgia, but never mind,' I muttered, quickly climbing the ladder as Amelie had half rolled onto the floor clutching her sides laughing.

'Whatever, just help me!' Luna flailed about like a ladybird on its back. I grabbed her almost translucent hand and yanked her forward. She leapt up to her feet and began brushing off fluff and dust from her pale-blue capri trousers and floaty sheer top. 'If I have any serious injuries I am totally suing them for everything!' she huffed, flouncing off to the bathroom, stepping over Amelie still doubled up in mirth.

'Don't even think about asking to share my bed,' Amelie called out behind her. 'Georgina, you're going to have to do the honours.'

'It's Georgia,' I said quietly. 'So you two already know each other?'

Amelie was bent over her suitcase, struggling to unzip it. 'Yeah. Unfortunately.'

'Hey! You mean fortunately,' Luna called from inside the bathroom. 'And there is no way I'm sharing with anyone.'

I took a look at the destroyed bed that was beyond repair. 'Maybe we should ask at reception to change rooms?'

'Are you joking?! They'll bill us for that, and God knows what else on top. Before you know it, we will all be paying for a full renovation of this hellhole.'

'Well, technically it was Luna who broke the bed,' I said quietly, not wanting to pay for the damage caused by her overexcited bellyflop. I was on a budget after all. The room went silent, I felt my cheeks heat up as Amelie narrowed her eyes at me.

'Georgina, when you share a room you share everything. There is no I in team.'

I nodded quickly, fixing my gaze to my dusty-covered feet. 'Yeah, course.'

'We'll just say it was like that when we arrived. OK?' Amelie snapped before continuing to rummage through the mountain of clothes in her case.

I chewed my fingernails as Luna emerged from the bathroom rolling her eyes at the destruction she had caused. 'It's not our fault they make such rubbish furniture here.'

'OK, Georgina?' Amelie pushed, glaring at me.

Why was I being such a goody two shoes? It went against my nature to be dishonest, but I clearly wasn't going to be making any friends with that attitude. 'OK,' I said quietly.

*

After the world's longest shower, due to the insanely slow, cold drips of water, I felt cleaner, more awake and ready to meet the rest of the tour group. The two girls had called shotgun on the shower, got changed thankfully without causing any more damage and headed off to find the Wi-Fi code without me. I'd changed into black linen trousers, a slouchy grey vest top and black-thonged sandals to show off my newly-painted toenails. My hair hung to one side in a simple braid and I applied a small amount of make-up, feeling as white as the pillows.

I forced myself to walk confidently into reception, even though inside I was nearly peeing my pants, terrified of who I'd be meeting. Trisha had said it would be a mix of men and women, aged between eighteen and forty, who wanted to experience Thai culture and make memories that would last a lifetime. The problem was, I'd never been good when meeting strangers, always too worried that my handshake wasn't firm enough, or my eye contact wasn't strong enough, meaning that I vice-gripped and eyeballed to overcompensate.

A large group of other equally unsure-looking people were sat on the beige sofas near to the main doors, watched over by Kit ticking off information on a clipboard. I did some lame hand movement somewhere between a wave and a 'howdy'. Loser. Amelie and Luna were absorbed in their mobile phones, repeatedly swiping their screens and ignoring the people sat around them.

'People – this Miss Georgia. She on tour too.' Kit waved his thin arm as if wafting away a fly; I smiled awkwardly and sat in the spare chair. 'You late. So now we do get to know the other. Everyone stand up and say your name, where you from and why you here.' He scowled at me.

First to stand up were three strapping lads wearing fluro vests and board shorts more suited to Ibiza shores than a Thai hotel lobby, built like rugby players with cauliflower ears and scars on their matching shaved heads.

'Jay, Sean and Magnet,' boomed a deep voice, proudly banging on their respective arms as an introduction.

'Magnet?' Kit asked.

'Yeah, 'cos he's so good with the ladies – just attracts 'em all, eh lads?!' They fell into fits of manly laughter. 'We're all twenty-one, from Essex and here to get on the lash, bang some birds and basically just 'av it large! Yeah boi.'

Oh... My... God.

They chest bumped each other then flopped back on the sofa. Luna stood up next and had to pull at Amelie's wrist to get her off her phone and get involved. She sighed and stood up as if it took all the effort in the world, ignoring the three lads unsubtly checking her out as she did. A mixture of fear and boredom crossed their blemish-free faces. They really were like real-life Elsa and Anna from *Frozen* and just as frosty. 'Luna and Amelie. We're both nineteen, from Edmonton in Canada and here 'cos we want to, you know, see the world.' Luna yawned as the teenaged receptionist wobbled over to the group, carrying a tray of bright-orange drinks adorned with little umbrellas, much to the delight of the three lads.

'Here you go.' A thin arm passed me a glass before its owner stood up next.

'Thanks.' I took the strong-smelling fruity cocktail from the guy. His features were small and dormouse-like with thin, wire glasses that minimised his slight features; the rugby trio could snap him like a twig.

'Not a problem, although I'm not sure if it is safe to drink,' he replied with a heavy French accent, running a napkin round the rim of the glass before cautiously taking a sip. The girl to his right, who also looked like a timid mouse, reached into her bag and pulled out a bottle of sanitising hand gel. She squirted a dollop onto his pale veiny hands which he graciously accepted by giving her a peck on the cheek and stood up.

'Hello, everyone. My name's Pierre, or Peter, for you English. I'm twenty and this is my girlfriend, Clare, she's nineteen.' Clare smiled and waved, causing a delicate silver charm bracelet to jangle. 'We are here to have a bit of light relief as you say, before I start a very serious new job.'

'OK, last girl – you go,' Kit said glaring at me, interrupting Pierre who brushed some fluff away from the sagging cushion before rigidly sitting down.

I took a deep breath and stood up: 'Er...hi, my name's Georgia. Erm...I'm twenty-eight from Manchester, England,' I half whispered, trying not to be fazed by Amelie and Luna looking me up and down. 'I'm here because I'd like to meet new people, have new experiences and just live a little–'.

'OK, very good,' Kit cut me off so I quickly slunk back into my seat, feeling like an awkward parent rocking up early to their teen's house party. I hadn't even thought about the fact that I could be the oldest one on the tour. 'First we go dinner in very nice place then we go Khao San Road.' His words were muffled by the lads smashing down their empty glasses onto the sticky coffee table and making howling noises. 'Tomorrow we have day in Bangkok. Very busy. Then we go train to island. No be late.' He turned away as the group got ready to leave.

I sprang out of my seat to catch up with him. 'Excuse me, Kit, you said something about an island? I thought we were heading to Chiang Mai first.'

'Yes, that right,' he said flicking a small yellow grain from his stained teeth with a toothpick.

'But the islands are in the south of Thailand and Chiang Mai is in the north?'

'Yes, we go there first, then back,' he snapped, keen to end the conversation and clock off for the night.

'But, I was given a different itinerary.' My breath quickened as the itinerary I thought I'd be following dissolved in front of my eyes.

'Plan change. We go, new plan. New plan very good. *Mai pen rai.*' Kit turned, breathing stale cigarettes in my face then walked off scratching his balls, leaving me to stare pleadingly at the teenager behind the desk.

'Do you know why it's changed?' I tried to remain calm and pulled out the printed itinerary from my back pocket that Trisha had given me, which listed temples and cooking courses, holding it in my unsteady hands. 'And what does "My Pen Rye" mean?'

'*Mai pen rai* means no problem. He's telling you not to worry.' The young lad studied the crumpled plan and replied in perfect English. 'I'm sorry, but this looks like an old plan. Kit took over the family business and has been making a lot of changes to the tour.'

'But…but…do you know what we'll be doing each day?' I'd memorised the plan by heart in an effort to calm down my nerves. I know I sounded high-pitched and needy but being so far away from home, not knowing anyone or what we would be doing each day made my stomach lurch with anxiety.

'Please, don't worry. I'm sure it'll still be lots of fun, but Kit is a difficult person to reason with. If I were you,

I'd just make the most of the new tour and our beautiful country, even if it may not be what you had hoped.' His apologetic smile did little to calm me down.

Realising that the group were heading out of the door, I thanked him and told myself that I'd get in touch with Trisha the following morning to figure this out before hurriedly joining the others, not wanting to be left behind.

I'd sat between Pierre and Clare making polite small talk over dinner in a nearby touristy Thai restaurant, trying not to make eye contact with Magnet, Jay and Sean, who'd stuck chopsticks up their noses and made walrus noises for every painfully slow course. The only person Luna and Amelie spoke to had been the sour-faced waitress to give their order before going back to their phone screens. It's the first night, everyone is a little tired and nervous, I told myself, thinking how hard the next six weeks would be if every meal was as awkward as this. The restaurant was slap bang in the middle of Khao San Road, which we ventured into after splitting the bill.

On the original itinerary, a visit to this backpacker mecca was planned during the day, which suited me just fine. I hadn't really wanted to be here after dark. The gaudy strip of flashing neon lights stung my jet-lagged eyes; a cacophony of different songs blared from each bar in some sort of torture experiment and smells of noodles, greasy fried chicken and sweet, sickly cocktails filled my nose. Lady boys strolled past winking at the guys in the group and grubby street children ran around sticking their dirty hands out for coins.

'I'm gonna get smashed!' Magnet cried, banging his vein-pumped chest. He started to make monkey noises – perhaps over here it was some kind of wild mating call – as plenty of bar girls in glittery Stetsons draped over fat Western men with handlebar moustaches turned round seductively. Pierre and Clare looked like they were regretting not packing white sterile masks to avoid inhaling any of this debauchery. Luna, with her Milkybar blonde hair, stood out like a beacon in the dark and dirty street. I imagined Amelie's shocked expression was mirroring my own.

'We're going back now.' Clare clung to Pierre like a child on their first day of school, not wanting to mix with all these strange faces.

They were already halfway down the street before I'd replied. 'Oh, OK.' I wanted someone to cling onto as well.

'Screw this! We're leaving too.' Amelie and Luna stormed off after a drunk Rasta guy started to lick Luna's arm.

'Erm…I think I may head back as well,' I said to Jay, who was currently being hassled by an old beggar woman trying to sell a wooden frog that made a croaking noise if you rubbed a dirty stick across its back.

'Nah, you can stay for one, can't you? We're in fookin' Bangkok baby!' He grabbed my arm and swiped the woman away with the other, causing her to mutter something under her breath. The old woman hobbled off, spitting on the litter-strewn floor. The dizzying lights, nameless faces and continuous movement was disorientating.

Well, I guess there's safety in numbers and the guys must be as exhausted as I am. One drink couldn't hurt.

Could it?

CHAPTER 9

Bibulous (adj.) Fond of alcoholic beverages

Someone had decided to play fist drums on the bedroom door, my head was banging in time to the incessant pounding of the unwanted alarm clock. A hot pain seared through my chest as I pulled myself off the floor. Amelie and Luna had already taken the beds when I staggered in at whatever time in the morning, meaning I'd had to pull down the duvet and sleep on the floor with a towel as a blanket.

Fuck. I stubbed my toe against the wastepaper bin and fell backwards onto Amelie's empty and unmade bed. Hobbling to the door I opened it to Kit's angry wrinkled face.

'What??'

'You late! You come breakfast and we go,' he barked, keeping eye contact for a second before dropping his vision a few inches lower, a slow smile appearing on his thin lips.

'OK, OK, I'll be down in ten minutes.' I quickly shut the door and shuffled back inside wondering why the girls hadn't woken me to go to breakfast together, catching my reflection in the mirror on the way. I had an attractive pillow crease down my right cheek and hair that could house a family of starlings. A few buttons had awkwardly popped open on my vest top showing my greying bra. *Great. Just what I didn't need, to add to Pervy Kit's wank bank.* Changing my top for a cleaner one, a quick blast of deodorant, a pair of khaki shorts and sturdy travel sandals that made me look like I should be in an over-50s hiking group, and I was ready to go and meet the others.

'Morning,' I croaked, my sunglasses doing nothing to help with the glaring light of the breakfast room.

'Finally. We've been waiting for you, you know,' Amelie scolded through a mouthful of scrambled eggs. 'You should probably eat something then we can go.' She looked fresh in a patterned T-shirt and denim cut-offs, her hair perfectly braided down her back, wafting a freshly showered apple scent towards me. Judging by her wincing face I wasn't the only one who could smell how musky I must be – that quick spritz of deodorant had only masked my slept-in odour.

'I can't face anything more than toast,' I groaned, before carefully pouring a cup of warm coffee from the buffet table and slowly sitting down. None of the rest of the tour group said hello. Or even looked at me.

'Oh, here she is,' smirked Sean, leaning back in his plastic chair.

'How's your nip?' The guy to his right, that one was definitely Jay, said pinching his nipple.

'What?' I tried to clear the raspiness from my throat and for a split second feared actual vomit might follow through. Man, I felt rough.

'Last time you take us on, eh?' they jeered as the others at the table fixed their gaze into their half-finished continental breakfasts.

'What're you talking about?' The lads melted into peals of laughter. 'Fine, whatever.' I gently shook my head telling myself to ignore them.

Luna nudged me, her eyes as wide as ashtrays. 'You really don't remember?' Her voice was even more floaty and away with the fairies than normal.

'No...what? I'm getting a bit freaked out now.'

'Everyone was talking about it before you arrived. Apparently, you got quite drunk last night.'

'I didn't realise how strong Thai beer is until I wanted to rip open my skull and take out my withered brain this morning. I hardly remember anything.'

'Well, maybe that's a good thing. The others seem to think you got friendly with that lot over there,' Amelie jumped in and pointed to the three monkeys at the end of the table.

'Oh God! Please tell me I didn't do something with one of them,' I moaned, cursing the shots in that friendly karaoke bar which happened to be the last thing I remembered.

'No, I think even comatose you had the sense to keep your knickers on, especially around those morons. But you did make a bet with them and according to the others, you lost,' Amelie said, pursing her lips.

'What was the bet? What did I lose?' As I willed my brain to remember, my stomach sank. Snippets of the night were coming back in Technicolor surround sound.

Dancing badly to Karma Club with a balding man who may have been American, judging by his slurring voice as he gyrated his chubby hips towards mine; getting up on a rickety stage holding an inflatable dolphin as a backing dancer to the three jocks who were murdering an Oasis song; pretty bar girls yawning on rickety stools, jutting their fake breasts out while playing Connect Four; sat on the pavement with a grazed knee which must have been from an ungracious fall off the aforementioned stage; having a heart to heart with a slim Thai boy, or girl (or both?) who offered to sell me Viagra. I shut my eyes, forcing myself to remember more. I'd never felt this hungover and had never blacked out before. Then, as slowly as I could manage to move my head, it all flooded back. I had challenged one of the jocks, Sean possibly, to a drinking game. Obviously powered by shots and emboldened by some horrendous cheap cocktails full of E-numbers, I'd thought I could win, forgetting that he'd boasted he was a star drinker for his uni rugby team.

'The bet was that if you won, he'd get his nipple pierced and if he won...' Amelie faded out as I self-consciously felt the padding in my bra '...you'd get yours pierced,' she finished with an expression that was either deeply worried or seriously amused.

I rushed to the ladies' room; bloodshot eyes stared back at me in the grubby mirror. Slamming closed the door of a toilet stall, I tugged off my vest top and gently lowered my bra, hoping Amelie had got it wrong.

Nope.

The nipple on my small, milky left breast was inflamed, the puckered skin angry and red around a shiny silver bar. *Oh My Holy Everything.*

Now the alcohol and shock was wearing off my nipple started to sting. It was too sore to touch and oozing slightly. God knows what the hygiene levels had been like in the piercing parlour. I sat on the toilet lid and pressed my face onto the cool tiles, not worried about catching any more infections. Shame would kill me first. I'd barely arrived in Bangkok and already had my nipple pierced. If this was just the start of the trip, who knew what else was going to happen.

'What am I going to do?' I pleaded to Luna, who had joined me in the bathroom with a tube of antiseptic cream.

'Don't touch it, unless you want it to scar. I've got a scar on my knee when I fell off a donkey at school that's still there because I picked the scab too much. Here, put this on. Then Kit said you need to hurry up – everyone's waiting.'

'Thanks.' I took the cream. 'Erm…donkey?'

She whipped her slender leg onto the sink to point out a barely visible silvery line. 'Yeah, I was six, and it was the nativity play. It wasn't a real donkey, just a huge cut out of one but still it really hurt falling off it.' I was starting to get the impression she was clumsier than I was.

'What was I thinking?' The cold cream made me wince.

'It looks like you weren't. Now come on.'

*

Late night Khao San Road revellers were sleeping off their regret, something I wished I could be doing, but the streets were starting to fill up with tourists, workers and tuk tuk drivers erratically beeping their horns. I'd previously prepared myself for a day visiting the temples of Bangkok, of which there were over four hundred, including the largest temple, Wat Pho, the main tourist trap due to its chilled-out, reclining golden Buddha reaching over fifteen metres high. At least I'd finally be able to tick something off my wish-list. Instead, Kit told us we would be trying authentic Thai food then taking a cruise down the Chaophraya river. Food and fresh air was definitely what I needed to clear my head.

We strolled down Yaowarat Road in the Samphanthawong district that makes up China Town, the oldest district in Bangkok where trashy bleeping electronics, stuffed toys and a dense concentration of blingtastic gold shops sparkled in the hazy sunlight. Forced to stay close together to navigate the winding alleys, it was difficult not to step on people selling their wares on brightly patterned blankets littering the dusty ground. Locals weaved through the throng determinedly, used to their territory being filled with wandering souls.

My mouth watered passing street stalls selling fresh plump noodles, roasted chicken on wooden skewers, spicy soups and pad Thai. My hangover needed grease and pronto.

'You know, these carts are a breeding ground for really serious diseases,' Pierre said disdainfully, seeing me practically drooling. 'The hygiene levels are non-existent.'

'Actually, superbrain, it's better for you to eat the food from these stalls as they're cooked fresh. Just look at the turnover.' Amelie pointed to the large queue of Thai people waiting to be served, rolling her eyes at Pierre's ignorance. 'The food in the restaurants or hotels could have been sat there sweating on a hot plate for hours.'

'But at least it would be a clean place to eat. Clare and I have the intelligence not to risk our health for a quick snack, don't we?' He shot a warning look at his girlfriend, her face immediately transformed from 'get in my belly' to 'get me a rabies jab'.

'*Oui*,' she said unconvincingly.

Kit, however, continued to walk past the busy stalls to the end of the street, heading further away from the yummy smells, stepping over uneven kerbstones and litter. Stray dogs roamed past and a flock of gulls scavenged for fallen extras. I looked back up the street and said a silent sad farewell to the delicious dishes, trying not to lick my lips. I hoped Kit was going to impress us with his local knowledge.

He must know all the hidden gems and probably wants to give us an authentic Thai lunch, the best in the city.

But I was slowly learning that Kit over-promised and under-delivered, especially when we stopped at the designated 'lunch spot'. It *was* a street cart and it *was* full of local delicacies. The only problem was that they were all crispy, creepy-crawlies.

'Eurgh,' Clare and Luna squealed in unison. I swallowed down the bile that scorched my dry throat.

'This is lunch? No, surely not?!' Pierre paled in an instant.

Kit nodded. 'Best food in Bangkok. Very nice. Good for bodies.'

'Well, we're not going to take that chance,' Pierre said, quickly pulling out a bottle of antibacterial hand gel and squirting a blob onto his and Clare's hands.

'This is epic. Wait till the lads back home hear about this,' Magnet boomed over Pierre, his eyes alight as he watched the bugs being threaded onto wooden sticks. The three guys wasted no time in munching on them as nonplussed as if demolishing a KFC family bucket.

'There is no way I am putting *that* into my mouth,' Luna cried, fanning herself with a pocket mirror.

'I've got something you can put into your mouth that tastes a lot better, if you like?' Sean winked as a piece of insect bristle flew out of his gob.

Luna looked even more disgusted at Sean's suggestion than the bugs in front of her. 'In your dreams.'

Sean looked faux offended. 'What? It's just a bit of flanter. Cheer up, luv.'

The rest of the group stared at him for an explanation. 'You know, flirty banter – flanter? Whatevs. You're just a cock tease anyway,' he grunted.

Luna grimaced before striding off to stand near to the French couple, who were cowering in a doorway as if even being near the insects would contaminate them.

'So, you goin' to man up or what?' Jay licked his greasy fingers, nodding at me. I'd found a concrete ledge to sit for a moment in the shade, taking deep breaths so as not to spew everywhere. Heat, hunger and hangover was a nightmare combination.

'Tsk. Course we are.' Amelie rolled her eyes and grabbed my arm. 'Come on, Georgina.'

'Err...wait – what?'

Amelie was a woman on a mission, pulling me towards the cart whether I wanted to join her or not. 'This'll show them.' Her eyes were afire with excitement. 'Can you sub me the cash for them? I'll pay you back later.'

'Err – yeah, sure.' I fished in my bag for change. 'You know, I'm going to skip this.'

'What? No you're not. Don't be such a wimp. I thought you said you came here to try new adventures? Don't play the prude now when your nipple jewellery tells a different story.' She flicked her hair back and looked at me sceptically.

'I *really* can't do this.'

'You can and you will. We want cockroaches on sticks please.' One lazy eye of the stallholder crinkled in delight that she had some business. 'Right. Stop procrastinating and pay the woman.'

I paid and picked up two skewers of cockroaches laced between what looked like dung beetles. Covered in an orange crispy coating I tried to imagine they were just smaller chicken wings.

'You're joking, no?!' Pierre jerked his head back in disgust at what we were holding.

Amelie smiled sweetly and brought the kebab up to her full lips. 'Ready? Three, two, one–'

I closed my eyes and crunched down on the little blighters, not wanting my ounce of courage to fail. I had to choke back the tough, chewy insides as I bit into their hardened legs and shell, and swallow the rubbery body as fast as I could. Bloody hell, I'd just eaten an insect. Ant and Dec should be springing out from behind a bush telling me how many stars I'd won for camp. I opened my eyes to see Pierre looking as if he wanted to squirt hand gel into my mouth. Amelie and the three guys were laughing and pointing at me, and in Amelie's outstretched hand was her untouched stick of cockroaches.

'You didn't do it!' I cried, and my stomach gurgled loudly, causing Jay, Sean and Magnet to laugh harder.

Amelie changed her face to mock innocence, her green eyes wide and eyebrows raised. 'Sorry Georgina, I guess I lost my appetite.'

I didn't have time to reply as Kit clapped his hands to get our attention. He was smoking a rolled-up cigarette and chatted animatedly to a balding Thai man who was sweating profusely whilst he swatted flies with a stained newspaper.

'OK. Yes very funny. Very good. Now you meet Pravat – he drive boat for boat party.' Kit pointed to the man next to him, who waved a chunky scab-covered hand at us.

'Did I just hear him say boat party?' I asked Pierre weakly, thinking about how much of a beating I'd given my poor liver last night, and now my poor stomach had a deep-fried cockroach swirling around inside it. I couldn't believe Amelie had tricked me like that, I was so bloody gullible. His nod confirmed my fears; so long relaxing, tranquil river cruise – hello Ibiza thumping party boat. Tears filled my tired eyes, but I blinked them back telling myself that I'd come on this trip to try new things, even if my desk outside of Catrina's office had never seemed so inviting right now.

CHAPTER 10

Crepehanger (adj.) Killjoy

Fluro wristbands were tied round our wrists and plastic cups filled with neon-pink liquid forced into our hands. The strong scent of the Calpol-coloured liquor made my stomach sway in the opposite direction to the knackered boat. A mix of heavy petrol fumes, fishy sea water, sickly alcoholic scents and bobbing up and down would only end in one thing. Vom.

Which is exactly what happened roughly thirteen minutes later.

We'd set off at a snail's pace down the Chaophraya river, getting the dirtiest of looks from locals and sightseers, understandably annoyed that our DJ was blaring out 'Gangnam Style', butchering this peaceful place, before my stomach jerked and my mouth filled with saliva. I didn't know where the nearest bathroom was so I leant over the chipped iron railings and spewed last night's fishbowl cocktails as discreetly as I could down the side of the boat. Thankfully Clare was by my side within seconds holding a bottle of water and a packet of tissues, failing to hide the repulsion on her face at the sight of me.

'This has been the worst twenty-four hours of my life,' I groaned, wiping my stinging eyes. 'How long until we reach dry land?'

She scrunched up her nose and passed me a mint. 'I have no idea but I just heard someone say there's going to be drinking games soon.'

'Oh please no.' We could have been extras in one of those *Malia: Uncovered* type programmes. Marie and I used to be transfixed by those trashy shows, laughing as the voice-over would sarcastically comment, 'Becki from Leeds has told her unwitting parents that she's spending her first girls' holiday with her mate's family in Portugal.' Well, if Becki's parents were into late-night trashy TV, they would be more than a little disgusted with their angel daughter, who was attempting to get a free shot by simulating sex moves with a stranger.

'Why don't you get us a drink and I'll go find Pierre and grab us somewhere to sit,' Clare shouted over the beat before getting lost in the crowd, quickly swerving past an inebriated skinny guy with painful-looking sunburn having a wee over the deck. Looking at some teen wearing braces and another acne-marked couple snogging to my right I felt like I'd interrupted some nature programme about fresh-faced gap year travellers 'finding themselves' but really just finding chlamydia and remorse.

A crackly voice boomed out from an ancient microphone. 'OK now, everyone on the tables and hands in air! This is about to go *off*!'

People scrabbled to stand on the sticky tables with their arms raised, pumping the warm air. It was a sea of limbs, voices and alcohol sprayed over my head. A grinning guy waved a large camera around causing girls to flash their pale breasts, standing out like guiding lights against their dark tans, which led to more jeers and whistles from the men on board. Jay, Sean and Magnet were in their element heckling two girls taking part in a wet T-shirt competition.

Luna and Amelie were unsurprisingly the centre of attention, getting pawed and stroked by spotty teens who gazed at the two beauties as if they were in the presence of actual supermodels. Which wasn't far off, to be fair. The two girls were lapping it up, posing for selfies, reminding me of that bikini-clad life-sized cardboard cut-out I'd toppled over in rage at Totally Awesome Adventours. Peace signs and everything.

The barman insisted there were no soft drinks on board: 'Hell no h2O' and all that, so I made my way over to an aghast-looking Clare and Pierre clutching plastic glasses of watered-down vodka and orange mixer. My path was suddenly blocked by a guy with a greasy man bun who bounced over and planted himself in front of me.

'You gotta down that now,' he declared, unsteady on his feet. The smell of BO and stale cigarettes that accompanied him was stomach-churning.

'No, you're all right,' I said.

'Come on, Grandma – you gotta down it,' he shouted over the bass line, causing others to stare.

'No thanks.' I turned my back on him, irritated and embarrassed.

'Oi! Lads. She ain't gonna down it.' He stepped in front of me again. 'Them's the rules, you know.' He pulled another glassy-eyed guy into the mix.

'What rules?'

'Left-hand rules,' he boomed, 'you got a full drink in yer left hand, then yer gotta down it.' This was followed by a series of 'Down it! Down it! Down it!' cries.

'No thank you,' I said more forcefully, wishing he would just fuck the fuck off…

'Oooh! She said no.'

I could have sworn that the music stopped and everyone turned to look at me.

People started to boo. I was being booed by a group of strangers for not following the rules of a drinking game I didn't know existed. Boo. An eager crowd had gathered, their eyes and peer pressure suffocating me. Feeling like I had no other option, I chugged my drink, ignoring the saliva rushing into my mouth and I slammed the empty glass down onto the table as the audience cheered.

'You've still got it, luv!' BO boy, who'd initiated the dare, slapped my back before taking his crew to find the next victim. I sank into the hard beer-soaked seat opposite Clare, my cheeks flaming red and stomach spasming.

'I thought you were hungover?' Pierre asked with a sly smile, taking a sip from his cup after sanitising the rim.

'I am,' I groaned, massaging my temples, hearing more cheers from the back of the deck. Another left-handed rookie mistake. What the hell am I doing here?!

Pierre was talking to Clare in fast French – I guessed about me, judging by the sympathetic glances Clare kept giving me. Hearing their incomprehensible words float around me, mixed with the blaring Rhianna remix, only heightened how alone I felt. Trisha had said this tour would be full of first-time solo travellers like me, not that I'd be the third wheel to everyone else already coupled up.

When Pierre went to find the toilet Clare shimmied up the bench closer to me.

'Look how beautiful the sky is!' she gasped.

I pulled my head up and looked at where she was pointing. She was spot on, we had front row seats to the pretty spectacular finale of the sun clocking off for the day. The sky was lit up with wisps of pale-peach and burnt-orange streaks. The colours haphazardly washed across the darkening canvas, fading until the sun was swallowed up into the ocean and disappeared off the horizon. No one else on board had noticed.

'Wow, that's one highlight on this boat trip,' I said with all the energy I had left.

Clare nodded in agreement. 'So, you said you were from Manchester? I've always wanted to visit there. Is it near London? We went there on a school trip once and we had to try this hot brown sauce. I can't remember the name but it was nothing like I've ever eaten in France before.' Her words toppled out through her small mouth, which was in a tight grimace at the memory of this sauce.

I was about to explain the joys of gravy when I felt like I'd been punched in the chest. My ears pricked up at what the DJ was currently playing. Our song. Our first dance. It had been playing the night we met. Alex had known every word, I'd pretended to sing along but only knew the chorus. As his deep brown eyes crinkled with laughter I'd tried to style it out making up new lyrics that had us both in fits of laughter. He'd pulled me close, shouting over the music that no one had ever made him laugh to a Smiths song before.

I felt my eyes fill with tears, so quickly grabbed my sunglasses to put on. The anguish and sorrow of the song, which is actually pretty depressing and all about death anyway, eventually broke into the heavy house blaring horns remix, thankfully ruining the nostalgic sadness gnawing at my chest.

'Georgia, are you OK?' Clare asked worriedly. 'You've gone very white.' I nodded and swallowed down the saliva that had filled my throat. 'I'm sorry. The sauce wasn't so bad. Maybe it was one of those things you need to get accustomed to.'

Looking at her tense face, hearing our song getting slaughtered by an electro beat and earpiercing whistles, I wiped my eyes roughly with the base of my thumb and laughed. 'It's gravy – the sauce. And yeah, it does take some getting used to.'

The rest of the boat crossing went by, thankfully, without any more tears or vomit, but in a blur of football anthems, water fights and shots that were mandatory for everyone to down.

With their left hands, of course.

CHAPTER 11

Solitude (n.) A state of seclusion or isolation

'Hurry up! We're going to miss the train!' Amelie shouted across the packed station concourse. She and Luna were dragging their cases across the tiled floor receiving dirty looks from the groups of people they unapologetically cut through.

'I told you we should have got backpacks,' Luna whined, narrowly missing running over the feet of a young boy gawping at the colourful pair in their matching harem pants.

'Have you seen how special the rest of the group look weighed down by those ugly things? Anyway shut up and hurry up,' Amelie replied huffing.

I ran as fast as humanly possible, with 15kg of 'special' backpack weighing heavy on my shoulders, to join the others on the crowded platform. Squeezing down the small aisles of the train that must have been in service since the 1960s, we made it to our carriage, thankfully passing the cramped, cheaper bench-seats where ruddy-cheeked men held wooden crates with squawking chickens inside and old women balanced large plastic bags of mangos on their laps. A smiling train conductor transformed our seats into bunk beds with the swift moves of a magician, pulling out starched white sheets and mint-green blankets to tuck as tight as they would go, just as we were pulling away from the station. We'd made it with seconds to spare.

We'd all slept in late after stumbling back from the boat party at stupid o'clock this morning. Kit hadn't told us what time to be up and ready to catch our train so it was a manic rush of wolfing down some food, packing up our bags and making our way to the station all at the last minute. It was the first time I'd seen him break a sweat as he barked orders at the group, who all seemed to be suffering from the after effects of the nightmare boat party. Tender and hungover were an understatement.

Speaking of tender, my new nipple jewellery still looked extremely angry, but until I could face touching it to take it out all I could do was smear on thick layers of antiseptic cream, hoping that it wouldn't turn gangrenous. I felt horrendous. I didn't even have the energy to complain when Kit spilt his glass of orange juice over me at breakfast, forked out for some mysterious 'traveller room tax' at checkout without questioning it and bit my lip when Magnet pushed in front of me, stepping on my toes to jump in the taxi.

Amelie had eyed me warily as we checked out, waiting to see if I would own up about the damage to our room. I just nodded politely as the young teen cheerfully asked if everything had been OK with our stay. He was doing a good job of avoiding Kit's snarling expression – which seemed to imply that our tardiness was all this guy's fault, like Kit wasn't to blame for the disorganised tour. Amelie's slow smile showed me her approval for keeping my mouth shut. *There's no I in team.*

Everything felt like a challenge, my emotions were all over the place from a lack of sleep, too much alcohol and feeling like the tour-group raspberry. Not helped by sleeping on a lumpy duvet on the floor for the past two nights, trying to ignore Luna's sleep-talking gobbledygook. My normal hangover cure usually consisted of binge-watching Netflix, snuggled up in soft pjs and unashamedly eating Nutella straight out of the jar, not being herded around a crazy, foreign capital city in the blazing heat by a grumpy Thai Mr Burns.

This was going to be the longest train journey I'd ever been on but I was actually looking forward to having a proper bed – well, converted train bunk – time to write in my travel journal and switch off from the rest of the group.

'Georgia. You go here,' Kit instructed, pointing a long dirty finger at the top bunk.

'Careful you don't break it,' Amelie said, causing me to blush. Kit looked puzzled, then walked off down the carriage past me struggling to lift my bag, to show the others to their bunks.

'Only jokin', Jeez, lighten up.' She rolled her eyes at me before hip-bumping Luna out of the way from the bottom bunk opposite.

I clambered up and pulled the thin nylon curtain closed, blocking out Luna's moans that her blanket smelt of old peoples' feet. Breathing a sigh of relief that I could have some alone time, I quickly pulled out my iPod that Marie had updated for me. No Smiths songs on here. But as I pressed the small button the menacing black half-eaten apple appeared. No battery. *Damn it!* OK, well I'll write in my travel journal, practise those Kate Adie journalism skills I had so longed to try, I thought. Only the pen had leaked in my bag, and now sticky blue ink stained my fingertips. *Really?!*

So in between trying not to sleep on my tender left breast, and not to drink too much water for fear of having to ungracefully clamber down onto some poor Thai person's head sleeping in the bunk underneath to get to the toilet, I cried. My head swam with homesickness; my body clenched with a deep ache for my previous life. I wanted to be gossiping with Marie, drinking tea and eating cakes in my parents' new conservatory, watching my dad pottering in his greenhouse.

I knew no one here; Clare had been the only one to act as a friend in the loosest possible sense of the term, but judging by the looks I often found Pierre giving me I wasn't welcome into their crew. I almost wanted to laugh at how wrong Marie and I were thinking about the type of backpackers we thought I'd be surrounded by. No hunky adventurous Stevie types to be seen anywhere. Stevie, hah! What was I even doing still thinking about him? I was kidding myself that a man, like the fantasy I'd built up in my mind about Stevie, even existed, and if he did then why would he be interested in me?

How was it possible to feel so lonely when surrounded by so many people? This trip was supposed to have been different, fewer screw-ups and more smiles. In the darkness of the carriage amongst snippets of hushed whispers and grunting snores I let the tears fall. How had I ended up here? I'd had it all back home. A lovely house, a man I thought loved me, a supportive family, and independence with my job. My life had been filled with people who knew me and liked me. Why did I give all that up to come here? But I didn't give it up. It had all been snatched away from me, a small voice spoke in my ear. You thought you had control and everything was following some plan that you thought you needed to achieve – man, house, career, wedding, babies etc. But actually you can't control anything. I couldn't control whether Alex thought with his brain or his you-know-what, I couldn't control that my boss had never liked me and had got rid of me at the first opportunity, I couldn't control our friends deserting me and siding with Alex when we broke up. I couldn't even control the itinerary of this tour.

Or could I? Should I have done more? What could I have done? *Oh, who was I kidding?* Being here wasn't going to solve anything. I wondered what Alex was doing right now. My brain just couldn't compute that he had a new girlfriend, that he was going to be a dad. I pictured him hunched over the PlayStation console in his slouchy grey jogging bottoms, the ones that no one else ever saw him in but me. He would stroke my leg as I sprawled on the couch next to him reading, he would leave a game halfway through saying I was too much of a distraction, dramatically throwing the console pad on the floor and gently pulling me at the ankles until I was on my back giggling. He would nuzzle my neck and make stupid animal noises pretending to claw off my clothes. We had so much history together. We could have those moments together again. Surely.

I'd tried to be this strong woman of the world, convinced that I could do better than stay with a guy who would do this to me. But actually that was just an act. I was weak, needy and missed him. I thought back to the email his mum had sent me. What if the important message she urgently wanted to tell me was that it had all been a mistake, that Stephanie had never been pregnant, that they hadn't been anything more than just friends, that he wanted me back?! A whirlwind of anxiety fluttered around me. I clung onto my dad's St Christopher, rubbing its dull face as if I could magic some sort of power or strength from it and made my decision.

Once we arrived at the islands I'd talk to Kit and tell him I was going to return home. I'd probably lose the money I'd paid for this trip, which made me feel a little sick at just how much I had paid upfront for this *experience*, but making things right comes at a price. If I could make any sort of amends and re-establish the life I had back in Manchester then I needed to try. My mum was right, swanning off and thinking I could do this wasn't the answer. I needed to be back at home and make it all better. I wiped my eyes and snuggled under the itchy blanket. At least I'd tried backpacking; it just wasn't for me. As the ancient train rocked its way forward, eventually sleep found me.

*

Seven hours on the rickety train, a four-and-a-half hour wait at a tiny train station in the middle of nowhere at the crack of dawn thanks to another Kit screw-up, and a two-hour ferry journey later and we had arrived.

However, I felt my tensions dissolve just by taking in the picture-postcard view of the sandy white shores of Koh Pa Sai. Drooping palm trees provided shade over sprawling beach bums who were lying on bright, tie-dye sarongs, as others swam in the turquoise ocean. The only sounds were the gentle lapping of waves and the long-tailed fishing boats with their diesel engines spluttering away.

Welcome to Paradise.

Even our hostel was an upgrade compared to the prison cell we'd stayed in in Bangkok. This place was total luxury with Amelie, Luna and me each getting our own single bed. Not a grimy bar on the window to be seen, plus it had a balcony facing the inviting waters. OK, so it was more like a rickety raised shelf – which any health and safety bod back home would immediately shut down – with a broken plastic chair and a full-to-bursting ashtray... But still a balcony! I could touch palm trees leaves with my hands and smell the charred remnants of a recent beach barbecue. The warm breeze that wafted through the small room seemed to lift some of the worries and homesickness that had clouded me on the train journey here. Some but not all. I still needed to tell Kit I was leaving. Even though that decision seemed a lot shakier now we had made it out of Bangkok and into this utopia.

'Kit said we needed to meet him at one of the beach restaurants for lunch. Apparently some new person is joining our tour today,' Luna said distantly, struggling to switch on the air conditioning.

'If he's fit then I call shotgun. If not, then Georgina you can take him.' Amelie let out a cackle and roughly slapped my back in jest.

'Thanks, but I'm not really looking for anyone,' I said, flinching at the sting her palm had left behind. I'd given up correcting them about my name.

'Wait. You're not a lesbian are you?' Luna narrowed her eyes as if I'd suddenly pounce on her.

'No. It's just not been long since my last breakup.' Why was I even telling them this? I'd be leaving by tomorrow. Maybe that was why, what did it matter?

Amelie looked up from unpacking her bag. Her interest piqued by some possible gossip. 'Oh really?' She put down the many bikinis she was clutching and tilted her head to one side. 'What happened? You can tell us.'

I bit my lip and took a deep breath. This was actually the first time either of them had shown any interest in getting to know me. 'Well, I was meant to be getting married, had everything booked and paid for, you know, the works?' They nodded along. I cleared my throat, slightly unnerved at the two of them staring at me so intently. 'But then erm... just two weeks before the big day he called it off. I found out he'd been cheating on me.' I paused, watching their reaction. Luna winced but Amelie remained impassive. 'Then I lost my job so I – well, with the help of my best friend – decided to go travelling for a bit. It sounds stupid, but I have this list that I need to tick things off.'

'A list?' Amelie leaned back against the wall.

'Yeah, of the things I want to see and do whilst I'm away.'

'What's on it?'

'A mixture of things really. Like, I want to ride an elephant, do something crazy and, I don't know, sort of find myself.' I winced slightly; saying it out loud made it sound petty and childish.

'Cool.' She said it in a way that made it sound like the most uncool thing she'd ever heard. 'If that's what you like. I prefer to let life dictate things – just go with the flow, you know?'

I nodded, embarrassed. 'Erm, yeah, I guess. So how about you? How did you two end up here?' I wanted to change the conversation, Alex had stormed my thoughts for the past twenty-four hours and I needed to focus on something else.

Amelie let out a long sigh and closed her eyes: 'Like I said, we let life do what it wants and just go along with it. Don't we, Luna?'

Luna looked up from figuring out the grubby air conditioning remote control and nodded, absent-mindedly.

'So, is this the first time you've both been backpacking?' I asked.

'Yeah. We do everything back home together, can't get rid of her,' Amelie said bitchily, not letting Luna reply before continuing. 'But this tour is just the first in a big backpacking trip we've got planned. We're going off afterwards by ourselves. Going to Cambodia, Bali, might spend some time in an Indian ashram, then heading to Oz, or Fiji, or something cool like that.'

'Wow. That sounds incredible. So how come you joined this tour if you're off on your own later?' I questioned gently.

A brief flash of annoyance shadowed Amelie's face as she propped herself onto her elbows. 'Well, some people back home don't agree with my – I mean our – life choices. We like to live for the moment, you know?' Luna was only half listening to this conversation but still nodded along with what Amelie was saying. 'So I – I mean we – decided to come on this tour to please our families, to show them that we would be safe and knew what we were doing. We don't need to be here, being child-minded – especially not with this group of losers. No offence.' She glanced at me as if baiting me to react. I remained impassive. 'But you can't win every battle,' she huffed, letting her resting bitch face settle on her pretty features.

I didn't fully understand what she meant, but even though we were here for different reasons, I was relieved that I wasn't the only one not loving every second of this tour. 'No offence taken. It wasn't what I had in mind either.'

'I mean, what is *with* this group? That weird French couple with more drama than a theatre group – and don't get me started on *those* brain-dead apes.'

Her honest opinion of everyone shocked me. Yeah, so the guys in the group wouldn't be entering *University Challenge* any time soon, but they seemed harmless enough. And as for Clare, she was the only one who had made any effort with me, who had tried to get to know me.

She raised a thick Cara Delevingne-inspired eyebrow. 'You don't agree with me?'

'Erm, well, I guess I wouldn't pick them to be my friends back home,' I replied as tactfully as I could, even though I'd never been popular enough to 'pick' friends.

This response seemed to be good enough for Amelie who shrugged and continued to sort through her clothes before snapping at Luna about a Victoria's Secret vest top that had been borrowed. Conversation time over.

CHAPTER 12

Lackadaisical (adj.) Without interest, vigour or determination

We were finally ready to leave our room, after having sat through three of Luna's outfit changes before she eventually decided to wear the very first look. I reminded Amelie to unplug her hair straighteners and went for a safety wee before we could go to join the rest of the group. Earlier, Luna had gone to find out the Wi-Fi code, but the internet in the hostel was as sketchy as Kit, intermittently cutting out so I couldn't FaceTime my parents like I wanted to. I'd taught them how to do video calling before I left, listening to them huffing and puffing that the stupid camera didn't work on the trial run we'd had, and trying not to laugh when they'd realised my dad's finger had been blocking the viewfinder.

I'd hoped to see their faces, to tell them that this tour wasn't for me and that I'd be coming home as soon as I could. However, without being able to get online I didn't know when that might be, so I sent them a quick text to let them know that I'd arrived safely, was fine (omitting the part about my nipple bling, obvs) and that I'd see them soon.

We meandered down winding paths, dodging tuk tuks driven by perving men unable to keep their eyes *off* Amelie and Luna and *on* the crumbling roads before arriving at a small open-air restaurant on the beach to meet the new tour-goer who couldn't join us in Bangkok. I tried to grab Kit's attention to explain I needed to talk to him urgently, but each time he suddenly had to make a phone call or see one of his business contacts he'd spotted wandering the beach. So, I ordered my food along with everyone else. Might as well make the last supper a good one. Just as a plateful of Thai green curry had been served, whispered squeals floated down the table coming from Amelie and Luna. Judging by their girlish giggles the new addition to our tour had arrived.

'This Dillon. He join you now.' Kit stopped chatting to the newcomer and presented him, with what seemed to be a sly grin on his face.

My eyes widened in shock as he sat down. The new recruit was gorgeous! Short, dirty-blond hair framed his strong cheekbones and freckles peppered his tanned nose. He nodded 'hello' to the rest of the table as Kit lamely did the introductions. Amelie and Luna both sat up a little straighter and flicked back their hair, whilst suggestively sipping their drinks, which only made Jay, Sean and Magnet grunt in annoyance. There was a new wolf in the pack. Knowing I was going to be leaving soon, I didn't have the energy to go through the whole pleasantries thing with another stranger, even one as fit as Dillon, so I smiled briefly at him and continued to tuck into my dinner. Although, I had to admit, it was refreshing to have some eye candy nearby.

I'd just shoved a forkful of curry into my mouth when this tanned hunk of a man caught my eye and flashed an ovary-clenching smile, causing me to nearly spit grains of rice all over the table.

'Can you pass the salt, please?' his deep, smooth voice asked me.

'Sure, here you go.' I tried to swallow as fast as I could and passed the salt, spilling some on the patterned table cloth.

'Whoops. That's bad luck, you know, if you're into superstitions.' He threw a few grains over his shoulder, grinning. 'It's Georgia, isn't it?'

'Yep, and you are …?' I paused, trying to look like I could remember his name, stalling for time whilst I gulped my drink to wash down the rice. Of course, I remembered it the moment he'd arrived.

'Dillon.' He smiled, focusing his hazel-coloured eyes on mine. Strong, masculine intrepid-explorer, heart-breaker, Dillon. *Marie would be beside herself if she were here.*

'So, how long have you been with this motley crew?' he asked, as I struggled to remember that we were surrounded by other people. I swore I heard the Canadian girls huff because he had deigned to start talking to me before them.

'Um, just a few days. I think there was a mix-up with the tour I'd booked to go on. What about you?'

'I've kind of been on a sabbatical for the past few months, taking in South East Asia and, you know, finding myself.' He used his fingers to indicate air quotes and laughed, revealing a perfect set of straight white teeth. 'I'm returning back home soon and just figured, after spending most of this trip by myself, it'd be nice to be around others, before I have to face that level of normality back home.'

I was about to say that it was a shame I couldn't talk more as I was leaving tomorrow, but something inside glared at me to keep quiet. As the conversation flowed, more naturally than I thought possible with such a good-looking guy staring intently at me, into the usual comfortable territory of careers (plumber for his dad's company), place he calls home (Bristol), best place he had seen so far on this trip (sunrise over Angkor Wat in Cambodia), age (twenty-eight) and so on, I hadn't noticed that we were the only ones still sat on the floor of the restaurant.

'Oh, I guess we should probably move, to let them clean up.' I looked around blushing.

'Yeah, you're probably right. Fancy a quick dip?' He stretched his muscular arms over his head.

'Err, yeah OK.' I looked at the inviting turquoise waters just behind us and then spotted Amelie applying sun lotion to Luna's slim back as if it was massage oil. *Of course he wants to go and find the others, the poor guy is probably sick of me chewing his ear off for the past goodness knows how long. What red-blooded male wouldn't want sun cream rubbed on his body in such a suggestive way by those two beauties?*

Amelie put down the factor fifteen and waved as if she hadn't realised Dillon was watching. 'Oh, not there,' he said, nodding at the *Frozen* sisters and returning his intense gaze to me. 'I've got a better idea.' My heart lifted and suddenly all thoughts of finding Kit to tell him I was leaving vanished from my mind.

*

Dillon effortlessly bartered with the guy in the motorbike shop and was soon steering out a large, red motorbike, passing me a helmet.

'You've been on a bike before, haven't you?' he asked uncertainly.

'Yeah,' I lied. *How hard could this be?*

'Cool, well put this on and hold on tight. The roads leave a lot to be desired, but I'll look after you, don't worry,' he winked.

I swung my leg over onto the warm leather seat, silently praying that my travel insurance would cover me

if anything went wrong. Alex had never been interested
in bikes or cars, his favourite hobby was lazing on the
sofa watching footie on the TV or in the local pub. From
nowhere I suddenly wondered if Stevie ever donned a pair
of leathers and biked his way across far-flung lands. *Focus,
Georgia! Focus on not dying.* Dillon grasped my arms and
placed them tightly against his hot skin.

'Hold on, babe,' he shouted through his visor.

We tore off down dirt tracks, rushing past lush green
fields, swaying palm trees and laughing local school
children wandering aimlessly. In the warm breeze, my
nose was filled with sun lotion, the tang of Dillon's sweat
and the petrol fumes. It was intoxicating. After driving for
twenty minutes we pulled up near to where a smattering
of restaurants, a small shop and a sleek hotel shone
against the dusty, red ground. Sweat beaded down Dillon's
beautiful, rugged face as he offered me a bottle of water. I
took lady-like sips, even though I wanted to gulp it down
greedily.

'We've made it. Leave your helmet here and let's check
it out.'

'Great, can't wait.' I passed the warm bottle back to him,
feeling a tingle as our fingers touched. *Why am I feeling
so attracted to this guy I don't even know?* Dillon took my
hand as if it was the most natural thing in the world, my
small, pale hand in his large rough palm, and led us into
the plush foyer of the hotel.

'Oh. It's kind of posher than I expected.' I was suddenly
extremely conscious of my mud-splattered beach dress,
helmet hair and the slightly damp patches under my arms.
But I didn't want to let go of his hand to try and fix myself
up.

'Relax, you look great,' Dillon smiled, as the women on
the spotless reception desk gazed at him gooey-eyed. 'It's

through here.' He nodded hello and then pushed open a heavy, brown door.

'Oh wow,' I breathed. Behind the door was a jaw-dropping view of the whole island, the sparkling sea and overlooking the edge, as if seemingly dropping off the side, was an inviting infinity pool. Dotted around were white padded sun loungers shaded by parasols and covered with soft, pale lavender-coloured cushions. Relaxing house music was playing and smiling bar staff waved, not showing any concern about the way we were dressed. Dillon dropped my hand and dumped our beach bags onto the nearest sunbed.

'Pretty cool, huh? Get yourself comfy and I'll grab us a drink,' he grinned, then bounded over to the bar, shaking hands and clapping the barman's back.

I sucked in my stomach and stripped off quickly, trying to lie in what I thought was a seductive pose on the sun lounger, wondering which side – if any – was my best.

'You OK? You look like you've got cramp,' Dillon frowned, walking over to me.

'No, no, just err...stretching.' I shifted with embarrassment.

'Right, well – here, I got you a beer.' He passed over a cool bottle, crossed his arms to reveal bulging biceps, and pulled his thin black T-shirt over his head in one swift motion. He was already wearing board shorts and when he smiled I took a deep breath and sucked in my stomach, embarrassed at how my pale body practically glowed next to his golden tan. 'Come on. That water looks too good to be sat here.'

I padded across the warm tiles, pleased he was in front of me and therefore unable to see my cellulite. We plunged in, enjoying the freshness of the instantly cooling water on our hot skin.

'So, I know we covered the basics before, Georgia, but why not tell me why you're *really* here? You don't strike me as the normal type of female backpacker I've met on this trip.'

'What do you mean?' I asked treading water.

'Well, you haven't got any dreadlocks; you haven't stockpiled cheap anklets or stacks of bracelets running up your wrist; I can't see any visible Buddhist-script tattoos and your Barbie beach towel doesn't scream "Round the World Explorer". No offence.'

'It's Ariel, not Barbie, and I'm just late to the party, I guess,' I said, cringing, 'but I suppose you're right, being such a "newbie" is hard to hide.'

'Well, it's refreshing to see.' He winked and pushed his face underwater, not spotting my huge grin and scarlet cheeks.

No one has ever called me refreshing before. Especially no one as god-like as him.

Smiling to myself, I stared at the magnificent view. 'I've never been somewhere so stunning before.'

'That's outrageous. I don't want to speak out of turn but you look like the kind of girl who deserves to be surrounded by impressive places.'

I knew he was being really cheesy and if I relayed this conversation to Marie, she would be gagging into her wine glass, but something felt different about him. It felt like he wasn't trotting out the well-worn chat up lines, like he was honestly surprised.

I smiled weakly: 'I think this sea air's affecting your thinking.'

'I'm serious, Georgia. Like I said, you're really refreshing.' He fixed his deep eyes on mine so firmly that I blinked and looked away, taken aback by the intensity of his gaze. 'You don't like it when I give you compliments?'

'It's not that I don't like it. It's just that I'm not used to it and don't think I deserve them, especially not coming from you,' I said, before I could stop myself. He smiled warmly then kissed my pruned fingertips gently.

'You deserve a whole lot more than me, I'm sure.'

I smiled, remaining quiet. The little seduction knowledge I had told me that pouring your heart out to a fit guy about being a jilted bride would only make him dive off the edge of this pool, desperate to escape the obsessed bridezilla. *I mean, what man wants to know that you have an unused wedding dress hanging up at home waiting for its big day? It's like you're ready at a moment's notice to say 'I do'.*

'You want to catch some rays?' He nodded to the sunbeds. 'Yeah, next to you I feel like Casper the ghost.' He laughed.

Climbing out of the pool, leaving a trail of water around our feet, we padded back to the sun loungers. 'So, who told you about this place?' I asked, sinking onto the squidgy mattress.

'Erm…I overheard two guys talking about it last night at some bar I was in and just thought I had to check it out. Back home I'm a bit of a petrol head, but the daily commute is nothing compared to driving through Paradise,' he replied, roughly rubbing a towel over his face.

He really was the most beautiful man I'd ever seen, the odd scar on his defined body adding to his rugged charm. Alex seemed like Mr Dull compared to him. The next few hours passed quickly in a blur of compliments, dips and relaxing on the super-soft sun loungers.

We were back on the bike as the sun started to set. However, we seemed to be taking a different route back to the town. 'Are we lost?' I shouted over the sound of the wind rushing past my helmet.

'Relax,' he shouted, revving up faster.

I tried to put the nerves building and gnawing at my chest out of my mind. Everything's fine, he seems totally relaxed and knows where he's going. Then he pulled to a stop, glanced around frowning and sped off up a different road before I could ask him what was going on. Oh shit. This was it. I was being dragged to some Thai trafficking ring. I'd seen *Taken* a million times so why did I agree to go off with a guy, clearly out of my league, miles from anywhere and anyone I knew? My mum was right. I was going to die. Dillon speeded up, causing me to grip his waist tighter; we went off-road through a patch of skinny trees and slowly pulled to a stop in a sun-dappled clearing.

OK, all I needed to do was leave a trail behind me, Hansel and Gretel-style. As Dillon propped the bike up I sneaked my bottle of sun cream from my beach bag and squeezed out blobs of creamy lotion on the ground.

He turned round to face me, wiping the sweat from his forehead. 'OK, follow me, but it's a surprise.'

'Oh…OK.' Oh God.

'Georgia, I think your sun cream's leaking?' He took the bottle from me and placed a thick hand over my eyes before I could protest.

'I'm quite clumsy, so maybe it's better if I see where I'm going?' I said breezily. I'd seen enough episodes of *Criminal Minds* to understand that you should always go along with what the serial killer wants, lure them into a false sense of security to waste time before the gorgeous FBI agents save the day. *Ooh…I wonder who'd play me in this episode?* Something scratched my foot, bringing me back to the moment and the danger I was in.

'I've got you. I promise.' He sounded so laid back it was unnerving. With one sense down, the sound of bird song was deafening. I could smell chlorine and coconut oil from his fingers and felt large palm tree leaves being pushed out of the way, before Dillon stopped suddenly.

'Here we are,' he whispered, removing his hand, the sweet smell of his breath tickling my neck. 'Open your eyes, Georgia.'

Here we go... What was it going to be? An open grave? The rest of the tour group blindfolded and frozen in fear? A hangman's noose?

I slowly inched my eyes open and dropped my jaw at what I saw.

We were much higher up now. The infinity pool and hotel were just a small dot to our right; ahead lay the deep blue of the ocean and at its centre was the most incredible sunset I'd ever seen. Forget the one from the party boat, this was an entirely unobstructed panorama, and its beauty gave me a shiver of happiness. Apricot hues, blood-orange reds and wisps of gold lit up the darkening sky.

'Wow.' Thank goodness! He didn't want to sell me, he wanted to surprise me. There wasn't a shovel, rope or gun in sight.

Dillon squeezed my shoulders gently. 'We couldn't leave before a quick look at this, eh?' He was staring more at me than the stunning scene in front of us. I shook my head, not wanting to miss a second. The sky seemed to be having a paintball fight; the colours were so striking. It lasted just a few minutes until the sunset of nectarine ice cream seemed to melt into the ocean, causing me to shiver slightly.

'That was amazing.' I felt so foolish for doubting him. Drama queen or what?!

'Good. I'm glad you liked it,' he grinned, rubbing my arms. 'Come on, let's get you back – you need to get warmed up.'

Katy Colins

Taking a last look at the incredible sky, we pushed back through the undergrowth to the bike and snaked our way back down to earth.

'See you soon, then?' Dillon said, as he pulled up outside my hostel.

'Are you not staying here too?'

'Nah, there was a cock-up with my reservation, so they placed me somewhere else,' he said, getting off the bike and taking my helmet. 'I've had such a great day with you, Georgia.'

'Me too.' I gazed at the floor hoping he wouldn't see the blush on my cheeks.

'Listen, if you don't have any plans tomorrow, I'd love to take you out again?'

Butterflies started dancing Gangnam-style in my stomach. 'No, no plans.'

'Perfect. Well, I'll pick you up at 11am?'

'I'll look forward to it,' I grinned.

He gently pushed my hair behind my ears and cupped my face. With the slightest of nods he unexpectedly pulled me close, wrapping his thick arms around my waist.

And kissed me.

CHAPTER 13

Tenderfoot (n.) A raw, inexperienced person; novice

From: GGreen@hotmail.co.uk
To: SassyM@ymail.com
Subject: You'll never believe it!!
Hey hun,

How is everything? I have so much to tell you! The tour started off worse than my singing voice and we both know how bad that is. Seriously, you will not believe what I've been through. But, it's got a whole lot better as I've met a guy!! I know, I know, I said I wasn't even looking but there's just something about him. He's called Dillon, is SO freaking hot (I still don't know why he's showing an interest in me) but we had such a magical date yesterday AND he's going to be picking me up in a few minutes for another date! Got a good feeling about this one. You would love him!

How's the filming going? I'll try calling you soon, as miss your voice. Better go, give a huge sloppy kiss to Cole from me.
Love you,
Georgia xx

I woke up this morning to find that either Amelie or Luna had unplugged my iPhone, which I'd purposely left charging overnight. I'd tried to give it as much of a charge as I could whilst I was getting ready this morning, mainly so I could message Marie to share the goss about Dillon. The electricity here was haphazard enough without those two interfering. I minimised the email app on my phone and placed it in my beach bag when I heard Dillon's bike pull up then raced outside, my flip-flops slapping on the marble floor of the hostel lobby. My stomach flipped excitedly at the sight of him, immediately taking me back to our kiss. His tongue knew just what to do; his lips had tasted of salt and faintly of beer. He was dominating and forceful, but in a good way. He was obviously used to being in control, something that Alex had never got the hang of. It had been years since I'd been kissed like that, his tongue wanting more, his breathing growing faster and his large hands pawing at my waist.

'Morning,' I chimed.

'Hey. You look as lovely as ever. So – you ready?'

'Yep. Let's go!' I hopped on the bike like a pro and quickly relaxed into his back, enjoying the warm breeze on my face that was currently drying my hair. It wasn't long before Dillon pulled up outside a beach hut in full view of the sparkling Andaman Sea. Small ripples seemed to flash silver as they broke away from the calm, jade-green ocean.

'Are we spending the day on the beach?' I asked getting off the bike, trying to pull my bikini bottoms out of my arse cheeks without him noticing.

'Not quite,' Dillon smirked and headed into the ramshackle hut, where a white Rasta guy high-fived him. The Bob Marley wannabee came around the counter to scoop me into a big hug.

'Hey there, little lady,' he drawled in an accent which was more Birmingham than Jamaican. 'I'm Nige and I'll be your guide for the day.' He pressed a hand to his chest.

'Ooh, what's the tour? He hasn't told me anything.' I gently elbowed Dillon, who laughed, rubbing his ribs.

'Hey. Just wait and see. I promised you a surprise and Nige is just the guy to help us out.'

Intrigued, I followed Nige to another hut, where he unlocked a door to reveal rows of wetsuits, snorkelling gear, diving masks, fins and other terrifying-looking dive kit.

We were going scuba diving.

I felt faint. Being so deep underwater, breathing unnaturally and not being able to touch the bottom was not high on my list of things to do. I wasn't scared of water per se, but I'd always been a big fan of having my feet firmly on the ground. Obviously my silence wasn't the reaction Dillon had hoped for.

'Hey, are you OK? You've gone really pale, babe.' He pulled me to sit on the sandy floor of the hut as Nige, oblivious to the look of horror on my face, carried on selecting what we would need. 'You're not scared are you?'

My stomach clenched at the rows of rubber. Was it hot in here or just me? 'No, no. I'm fine, just need some food, I think,' I lied.

'OK, good idea. Let's go grab some breakfast as my man here gets us sorted. See you in five, mate.' Nige made the peace sign back.

In a nearby bamboo beach café I picked at the edges of a blueberry pancake washed down with a cup of strong coffee as Dillon animatedly explained how much he loved scuba diving and the world we were about to see. Hearing him so passionate about it all made me desperate to impress him, even though I was so far out of my comfort zone I could hardly see myself. I knew he could have picked beautiful Amelie and Luna as dive buddies rather than dumpy old me.

Come on, Georgia. You can do this. Stop putting yourself down. Maybe he does actually like you.

I ate as slowly as I could, chewing every last mouthful, but I knew that I couldn't put off the inevitable; we were going scuba diving and I had to man up.

What's the worst that could happen? OK, drowning was pretty high on that list, as well as making a total fool of myself in front of Dillon so that he would run away faster than one of Amelie's mood swings. I tried to push those dramatic thoughts out of my mind as Nige helped me struggle into a clingy wetsuit, silently scolding myself for picking carbs over fruit as I sucked in my stomach. I looked over at Dillon, whose body seemed to be made for a second skin of black neoprene, as he nonchalantly tied the sleeves round his toned, tanned waist.

A small swimming pool was hidden behind tropical bushes as Nige, a trained scuba diving instructor, talked me through the basic steps. Meanwhile, over at a nearby wooden bench Dillon chatted to two girls who looked as though they had just stepped off a catwalk and, of course, were also coming for the dive. I felt like a child being taught how to swim and flushed with embarrassment as every never-ending minute slowly ticked by. I tried to concentrate on what Nige was saying, I really did. But all I could hear was Dillon's 'Awesome', 'Rad' and other surfer expressions, which the supermodels lapped up, laughing and touching his biceps. Every so often Dillon would wave at me, the girls following his gaze until they broke out into peals of laughter at the newbie beached whale in the kid's pool.

This is mortifying.

'Georgia…earth to Georgia. Did you hear what I said about this?' Nige was pointing to a black button on the side of the gas mask – whoops, I mean dive mask.

'Sorry, yep. I heard you,' I lied, 'you know, I just remembered I have done this before.' Nige looked like he didn't believe me. 'Yeah, yeah it suddenly started coming back to me when you put this, erm, thing on the, erm, belt thing. So really this quick recap will be fine.' Another lie.

I was just desperate to get out of the shallow end and figured this whole scuba diving lark couldn't be too difficult. Nige would control my large tank and do most of the legwork, and I didn't want to leave Dillon alone for too long. This must be how Victoria Beckham feels when David is away, I thought. Nige glanced over to where I'd fixed a steely glare on the two girls, as I hoped to use mind tricks to move the beauties away.

'Hey, so are you and Dillon like, a thing then?' he asked, tightening a belt around the large heavy tank now attached to my back, pulling my waist further into the water.

'Um no, not really. I don't know.' I looked up at his kind leathery face. His sun-kissed dreads were roughly tied into a ponytail with a tatty piece of string.

'Well listen, chica, you going to be hanging round with that dude, then you just gotta accept that you won't be the only one. Seems everyone loves Dillon and you need to be prepared to share your toys.' I tried to make sense of what he was saying, but all I could picture was the stoned turtle from *Finding Nemo* giving me life advice. 'You gotta chill, girl. He's a sound dude, but guys like that always have an eye for the surf babes, you catch my drift?'

'Erm, yeah I guess. So, how well do you know –'

Just then Dillon dived into the pool and lazily swam over to us, making the gaggle of girls giggle.

'You all ready to go?' he interrupted my question to Nige, pushing his wet hair back as beads of water dripped from his torso.

'Yep, as ready as I will ever be.' I had to show him, and those girls, that I could totally do this.

The plan would have worked if I'd been paying attention to anything that Nige had explained to me.

We were soon on Nige's battered boat, which stank of fish and petrol, surrounded by inky water into which we would soon be diving, so dark I could definitely not see the nice familiar bottom. The two scuba divas had an iPhone out and were giggling to one another. 'Hey, so can we, like, get a selfie together?' The one with an anchor tattoo on each of her bony hips asked Dillon.

He looked genuinely surprised. 'Err yeah. Cool. Why not?'

The tattooed one squealed like she was front row at a Justin Bieber concert. 'Sick!' She thrust her phone at me and put her arms round Dillon and her mate, posing with her best duck pout. 'We are so on fleek today. Say cheese!'

I gritted my teeth, took their photo and handed back the phone.

'Oh my God! I look so minging in that one! Take another!' Her mate moaned, even though there wasn't a hair out of place. Trust me, I was looking for it. The iPhone was back in my hands again as Dillon gave me a sorry-about-this-goodness-isn't-it-exhausting-having-these-hot-women-want-another-photo look. I sighed.

'Say cheese,' I said dryly, although all this selfie taking was prolonging the moment of our descent into the ocean, so maybe that was a good thing. This photo must have pleased them as they passed the phone round, taking turns staring at it and zooming in and out.

'Georgia, your turn now,' Dillon winked, catching me off guard.

'Oh, erm, OK.' The two women scowled at me slightly and put their phone quickly back in their bag.

'You got your phone on you?' Dillon asked. I nodded and rooted in my bag. 'You don't mind do you, girls?' he asked them nicely. The tattooed one took my phone and wobbled to her feet, trying to balance herself on the rocking deck, simpering at Dillon that she didn't mind at all. She minded.

'OK. Three, two,' she stepped further back. 'One, arrgggghhhh!!' She screamed as she lost her footing, slipping on a puddle of sea water that had collected from all the spray as we'd zoomed out here. Her right leg swung up in the air, her arms outstretched like a new-born baby. Trying to cushion her fall she gripped onto the side of the boat, planted her tiny bum on the wooden bench with a crack and let go of my iPhone. I watched it in slow motion arc through the air and plop into the water behind us.

'Nooooo!!!' I screamed, ignoring her swearing about how much her arse hurt, and quickly peered over the side of the boat searching for my precious phone. It was nowhere to be seen, sunk to the depths of the blasted water. 'My phone's my life!' I turned to face the others, panic-stricken. Their faces didn't register how much of a big deal this was.

'But you've got travel insurance, right? You can claim for another one?' Dillon said, biting his lip.

'Yeah, but how long's that going to take! I'll have lost so many photos, texts, phone numbers.' My heart was racing at the realisation. 'And I've still got five weeks here without a phone!'

Tattoo girl looked embarrassed but didn't apologise. 'It was an accident.' She huffed as she suggestively rubbed her arse cheeks.

'Yeah, it was just an accident, babe,' Dillon said trying to calm me down. 'Maybe, it will be a good thing. Phones connect us to the world back home, but when you're backpacking you need to be free from distractions of that life you've left behind. Ain't that right, Nige?'

Nige was smoking what looked suspiciously like a spliff, oblivious to what had just happened. 'Yeah, man! Leave it all behind. One love!'

Dillon turned to face me, nodding in agreement as if Nige had just delivered an Oscar-winning speech. 'I lost my phone when I was hitchhiking through Vietnam. It's hard at first but trust me, you won't even notice it's gone in a few days.' I shrugged slowly, not sure if I believed him. 'You ready to go for a dive, babe? It'll take your mind off your phone,' Dillon grinned. I did feel stupid for having gone so mental about just a tiny thing. Hadn't I lost more important things – my fiancé, my job – in the last few weeks? Plus, I was a backpacker now so I guess Nige was right, I did need to be in the moment more. 'You're going to love it. Trust me.'

'Mmm,' was all I could muster as I concentrated on my breathing so I wouldn't pass out. In, two three four, out, two three four.

Lining our fins up, Dillon grabbed my hand as we sploshed into the water together. I hoped that those girls had seen him take my hand and that he didn't pull away at how sweaty it was. Once in the ocean Nige motioned for me to start using the face contraption by pointing downwards to submerge. The weight of the metal tank dragged me down faster than I was prepared for. The rest of the group were now fully immersed.

The pressure of the water sucked the mask tight, cutting into my cheekbones. Waves splashed at my face. All I could see was the hull of the boat and dark ominous water.

Oh God. I'm going to die. On a so-called date.

Bubbles sprayed from my mask, the unnatural breathing in and out under water was causing me to pant faster and faster, as I was pulled deeper and deeper. I wanted to tear my mask off, clamber to the surface, and breathe in actual real air, but Nige was behind lowering me down and he couldn't see how frantic I was becoming. I could just make out Dillon ahead of me, as a blonde-haired mermaid swam effortlessly next to him pointing out fish that I couldn't see through all the bubbles of my panic and the steamed-up mask.

I was being starved of air. Don't people realise how unnatural it is to breathe under water? I had to get out. And quickly. With a huge amount of effort I kicked my heavy, uncomfortable fins towards Nige, who moved round to face me, his eyes growing wide as he finally understood my panic. I jabbed my finger towards the surface, trying to break free from the hold he had on me.

Why was he taking so long to get me out of this torturous nightmare?

Then I remembered the only piece of information that my brain had picked up, which wasn't concerned with trying to spot cellulite on the two models. If you come to the surface too quickly then your lungs can pop and you can *die*.

Shit. And people do this for fun?

Every second felt like a minute, black spots appeared in my vision. Eventually, after a lifetime, we broke the surface. Nige snapped off my mask, propping me up whilst treading water and reaching for a rope from the boat.

'Dude, what happened?' He looked pale and worried as he pulled off my fins and half-pushed me up a thin rusty ladder to get on board. I gulped the fresh air, not able to speak before collapsing on the warm deck.

'You had a major freak-out down there. Never seen anything like that before. Here, drink this and munch on these.' He passed me a bottle of water and a pack of sugary biscuits as I lay on the rocking floor of the boat, spitting out salty water, thankful to be alive, no longer caring about my lost phone.

'I thought you were just taking your time to submerge, I didn't realise that you hated it. I thought you said you'd done this before?'

'I lied. I just wanted to impress Dillon. Please don't tell him. I already feel like a complete idiot,' I wailed, feeling so embarrassed at being the worst date ever. Saying that, where was Dillon? – and why didn't he stay by my side more? Even though I'd told him I'd done it before, he could see I was nervous.

'That's not cool, man. You don't lie about this kinda stuff, it can be proper serious for newbies who think they know how to dive.' I didn't think Nige could look this stern. Within seconds his frown relaxed into a look of sympathy. 'Don't worry, I'll tell him that there was a problem with one of your tank straps and I forgot to pack the spare. But listen, you seem like a cool girl, why do you want to impress someone and not just be you?'

I shrugged sadly, wishing I had an answer. I'd never tried this hard to get someone to like me before. I wasn't even sure what this was, but I knew I'd never felt instant chemistry like this before.

'You want me to go and grab Dill for you? I promise I'll keep what happened between us two, but seriously, girl, you need to be with a dude that likes you for you.' He was a wise old turtle after all.

'No, it's OK. I don't want to ruin the dive for everyone else.' Nige looked at me anxiously before nodding.

Dillon was apologetic on the boat ride back that he had swum off too soon, thinking I was right behind him and how sorry he was that I didn't get to complete the dive that was so 'freakin' amazing'. 'It's a bummer. Nige is all booked up, otherwise we could have tried again tomorrow.'

'Yeah, it's a shame, but maybe some other time?' I said plastering on a fake smile, shuddering at the thought of willingly going into that death trap again. The glam girls were swapping stories of what sea life they'd seen and how 'dope' it had been, before throwing me faux pitiful looks and laughing. Dillon acted unaware of their catty behaviour and joined in exclaiming how great the dive had been.

Once our boat finally reached solid ground I offered to help Nige carry all the wet, salty equipment back to the hut. As the girls paraded off to find a shower, I noticed Dillon look on wistfully as their barely there arses bobbed along the sand.

He eventually pulled his gaze back to me: 'So, what do you want to do for the rest of the afternoon? Heard some people talking about this epic rock we could try and climb?'

I sighed inwardly. What was I getting myself into?

CHAPTER 14

Twitterpated (adj.) Excited; overcome by romantic feelings; smitten

The last few days had been one big adrenalin blur. Kit had sheepishly told our group that we had four days of free time; in other words, he couldn't be arsed to arrange any activities, meaning we were able to do what we liked. For Dillon it was the more active the better. We had climbed rocks, zip-wired off a decidedly crumbling ledge and even rented a pedalo – this last one was my lame suggestion, but honestly I just needed a break from thinking I was going to die *all the blooming time*. Being the girl that Dillon wanted was seriously exhausting. However, even though my stomach dropped each time he mentioned a new activity, I had gone through with them all, no matter how death-defying and terrifying they were. Mostly, because when it was finally over, he kissed me like he had on our first 'date'. The desire I felt for him was so strong, I was convinced he could sense it.

'You know what, I think it's about time we have an afternoon lazing about. Watch some crap Thai TV and chillax?' he said, looking up from a torn map. If we hadn't been just feet away from a sheer rock face I would have jumped for joy.

It was the first time I'd visited his hostel, but nothing prepared me for what I walked into. His enormous, private bedroom had a view of the glistening ocean through floor-to-ceiling glass windows; tasteful bright art popped out from the pale-grey walls and a modern flat screen TV loomed over the perfectly made up king-size bed; he wasn't travelling like any backpacker I'd met.

'Wow! Dillon, so *this* is the replacement room you got after Kit screwed up your booking?' The words spilled from my mouth as I gawped around in shock.

He smiled and pulled me towards him: 'I just got lucky, I guess,' he began nibbling at my neck.

I didn't care how he could afford such a luxurious room, how he seemed to know everyone on the island and how much both girls and guys loved him. All that mattered was that he was here with *me*, kissing and stroking *me*. He took off my sundress, letting it fall to the stone floor and picked me up and carried me to the bed. His fingers laced into the edges of my bikini bottoms as I thumbed the waistband of his board shorts, feeling the soft hair running down from his navel. A chill ran through me as I realised that he was about to see me naked; the first man since Alex, months ago, but even that was a fumble in the dark, completing our normal routine. This room was bathed in soft early evening sunlight; my hidden white bits fresh and vulnerable to his salty lips and roaming hands. I panicked that my lumpy cellulite would gross him out, that the varnish on my toenails had chipped and that my bikini line wasn't completely hair-free, but I was *desperate* to feel his touch.

'You're beautiful, Georgia,' Dillon breathed, as if reading my worried mind before he kissed me hard, full of want and need. I kissed him back in the same way, our bodies moving and turning to feel and explore each other. As he gently removed my bikini top, my pierced and now practically healed nipple glinted in the light.

'Wow. You do surprise me,' he smiled and let his lips trail down my breasts. I released a moan. I wanted and needed him *now*. I felt high with the desire pulsating through me. He pulled away to hurriedly grab a condom.

A while later, we lay back, hands entwined and legs crossed over each other as the air con blew on our hot, sweaty bodies. He turned to face me, kissing my hand and pushing back a stray hair from my flushed face.

'Well, I especially enjoyed all the Thai words I've just learnt,' he teased.

I sighed. 'If only learning a language was always that fun.'

'I'd have aced my A-Levels if they were,' Dillon grinned, kissed my forehead and jumped up to turn on the shower. He cracked open a can of Pepsi, now sitting in a pool of water, passing one to me: 'I hope you're going to join me, Georgia?' He took a swig, winked, and confidently sauntered to the bathroom.

I heaved myself up, trying not to glance in the mirror on the way and quickly followed after him. My bare feet left imprints on the cold tiled floor. He was standing under a rain shower inside the tastefully decorated steamy room, lathering up his body with spicy-smelling foam. I boldly stepped in, accepting a dollop of expensive-looking shower gel that he squirted on my outstretched hands.

'Mmm, before was lovely.' He kissed me softly as blobs of bubbles fell to the floor, immediately squashing all the fears rushing into my post-coital mind that I wasn't as experienced in the bedroom as he'd seemed to be.

'Yes, it was,' I sighed happily.

As Dillon turned around to place the bottle of shower gel back on the rack, I spotted an intricate swirling tattoo on the smooth whiter skin below his left hip bone, just above his peachy arse, that I hadn't noticed during our lovemaking. A date in italic-style font was almost hidden among the line work; it was August 16th of last year.

I stroked it gently. 'What's this?'

He looked flustered for a moment. 'Oh, that was a stupid dare that me and the lads had on a recent holiday. You know, the lightweight gets a tattoo. You going to tell me the story of your nipple jewellery?' He smiled, looking down at my naked pale breasts, diverting the attention away from his tattoo.

'Ha. Similar kind of story, actually.' I blushed, acting like it was totally normal that the hot guy I'd spilt salt over just a few days ago was now chatting about my nipple as we stood fully nude in his swanky shower.

'I knew there was more to you than meets the eye.' He slowly bit his lower lip looking me up and down, drinking me in. 'Come here, you.'

At least this was one activity we could share without me feeling like I was going to die.

CHAPTER 15

Audacious (adj.) Reckless, daring

Little wooden crates were adorned with tea lights, creating romantic makeshift tables that were sunk into the soft sand. People from every nationality sat on cushions and patterned mats, relaxing to reggae music under the dark veil of stars. Luna and Amelie hadn't waited for me when I'd returned from Dillon's to get changed so I hurried up the still-warm sand to join the rest of the group. I hoped my post-coital glow wouldn't be so visible in the inky evening light.

I scanned the chilled-out bodies and spotted Kit's scrawny arm waving me over to where he was sitting at the head of the group. I edged my way over to him, taking care not to step on limbs, or outstretched flip-flop-covered feet. Dillon spotted me and mouthed something to Kit, who sneered before punctuating the air with a throaty, dirty laugh. Luna and Amelie were sitting next to Dillon, looking at him with puppy-dog eyes and throwing daggers in my direction. I wanted to saunter up, grab Dillon's stubbled jaw and kiss him in the way I had earlier, but I'd never do something so bold in front of the others. Besides, there was no space for me to sit down, so I had to settle at the other end of the group, nestled on large tie-dye cushions next to Clare, who kept fiddling with a charm bracelet that glinted in the soft light. Pierre looked bored rigid, ignoring whatever Clare was telling him, staring at the energetic fire show just feet away.

Nimble, lithe Thai men danced, throwing flames across their bodies, tossing large sticks in the air to an electro beat, performing acrobatics for the audience, which was in awe of the heat from the flames licking their torsos. Dillon waved and smiled at me a few times, but was always pulled back into conversation by the two girls to his right, who seemingly found every single thing he said the most hilarious thing *ever*, judging by the way they threw their heads back and screamed with laughter.

'They seem to be pretty comfortable over there,' Clare whispered, nodding towards the other end of the table. My stomach dropped as Luna placed her thin arm around Dillon's shoulders for a selfie. I felt a sudden rage in my stomach at the fact I couldn't pose for photos with Dillon, make people back home jealous when I posted the perfectly filtered snap on Facebook, all because of some clumsy scuba diva. I still reckon she did it on purpose.

'Mmm,' was all I could reply.

'Have you been with Dillon for the past few days? I was worried I hadn't seen you,' Clare said, as the glow from the fire show reflected in the lenses of her glasses.

'Yeah. Did Amelie and Luna not tell you? I asked them to let the rest of the group know what we were up to.' As soon as I'd said it I knew they were obviously punishing me for being picked by Dillon when they'd called shotgun. Eurgh.

Clare shook her head. 'No. Well it's nice to see you now.' She smiled and went to pat my hand but spotted Pierre looking over at us so continued to play with her bracelet instead.

'You too,' I smiled. I was about to ask her what she'd been up to when Amelie's high-pitched laugh pierced the air, instantly making my stomach clench.

Focus on the fire show, I told myself, which was getting more dangerous by the second. The trained athletes had stopped parading about and were now standing on upturned buckets holding huge hula-hoops wrapped in petrol-soaked rags that had been set alight.

The ring of fire.

A long queue of drunken revellers waited their turn to roll, jump or get thrown through it.

'*Mon dieu!* Look at *them*,' Pierre scoffed. My head automatically twisted towards the end of the table before realising that Pierre was staring at a group of girls who had launched themselves through the ring, tumbling onto the sand laughing. As dangerous as it seemed, it did look like they were having fun.

'You don't fancy it then?' I took a sip of my drink, teasing him.

'Oh yeah, I'll give it a go right before I find some rusty syringe to stick in my arm,' Pierre said sarcastically. 'Do you not understand how dangerous it is?! I bet not many travel insurers would cover you if – sorry, I mean when – something goes wrong. I wouldn't be surprised if half of these idiots wake up without their eyebrows tomorrow.'

Clare quickly rolled her eyes at him when he wasn't looking, making me laugh. 'It does look very adventurous, though, doesn't it?' she said quietly.

They were both right. It was utterly stupid but also stupidly adventurous. And I knew exactly who loved adventure. I looked from Clare, now staring in awe at the brave participants, over to Dillon being pawed by Amelie and Luna, before my subconscious kicked in. *I could never do something as daring as that. What if my hair caught fire, or I fell and really hurt or embarrassed myself?*

On second thoughts, maybe I *should* challenge myself more. It could be ticked off my travel wish-list as 'something wild' and I knew that it would impress Dillon, and make the *Frozen* friends look boring, compared with daredevil Georgia.

Daredevil Georgia. Who would have thought it?

I jumped to my feet and stomped over to the burning ring, not looking back, not wanting this new-found bravery and confidence to desert me, barely aware of Clare calling something out behind me.

'New girl, you go next.' A young Thai guy with soot on his chest and a small goatee beard pulled me into the line. Closer up, I quickly realised how stupid this might be. I was the least flexible, least co-ordinated person you could meet and I was about to run and jump through a burning hula hoop. Oh my God. I moved to back out, but beard-boy blocked my way. A guy in front of me landed perfectly on his feet, pumping his arms in the air, meaning I was next.

'Don't be scared. Take a running jump and go for it. If you hesitate, you burn,' the Thai man shouted.

What was I doing?

My feet became leaden. The noise of the party, the music and the cheers faded out as I psyched myself up to do this. Seconds later, I was half jogging, half sprinting to the raised ring, instinctively diving when I got close enough. Then I was falling, hurtling through the hoop as flames and heat licked my arms and legs. It couldn't have been longer than a few seconds, but it felt like minutes until I roughly half-rolled to the ground and crowd noise filled my ears once more. I got to my feet, wiping sand from my legs. The hoop was behind me and thin arms were shoving a shot glass into my trembling hands.

'Not bad,' a tall guy with spiky ginger hair said, chinking his glass to mine, our prize for having survived. The aniseed-flavoured heat slipped down my throat. 'Wanna go again?'

'Once was enough, thanks.' I shook my head laughing, watching him bound off to rejoin the line.

I don't want to brag, but I did it! I did it!!

I couldn't wait to see the looks on Amelie, Luna and Dillon's faces when they'd have to admit that they'd underestimated me.

Hell. I'd underestimated myself.

Only, I didn't get the chance to boast as when I padded back up the sand I realised our table was now missing three people: Dillon and the two Canadian girls had left. Sean saw me looking around and sauntered over.

'Sorry, Nip, but looks like two beats one. What a lucky sod, to be taking those two worldies home for a good time. I know if I got just one of them in my bed they'd be screaming for more.' He started air-slapping an imaginary woman from behind.

'You don't know what you're talking about.' My cheeks heated up, all my confidence from surviving the ring of fire plummeting as quickly as an *X Factor* winner's career.

'Oh really? Well, how come I saw them all leave together? Looked pretty cosy to me. Hey, don't worry, even if lover boy's left you, you can still come and feel the good old Sean lovin'.' He put a thick, hairy arm over my shoulders, nearly gassing me with his BO.

'Get off me!' I pushed him away as the rest of his posse laughed and high-fived each other.

Not knowing where Dillon had gone and not wanting to make small talk with the French couple, I walked back to my room, tears sliding down my face. I felt sick. I'd seen how Dillon looked at me, how his lips had tasted against mine, how he'd stared into my eyes as we'd made love.

Yes, this must all be a misunderstanding. Sean is just winding me up. But unfortunately, my instincts betrayed me. All I could picture was Dillon's beautiful face; those deep, dark eyes, long lashes and grabbable arse being touched by Amelie and Luna. After spending the past few days with this demi-god, desperate to impress him, only to be tossed aside, well, it stung. *Maybe I should have been more forward? More adventurous in bed? Maybe I should have told him how he made me feel? Maybe – maybe – maybe.*

This was the reason holiday romances didn't last. It takes time to build up trust; it doesn't happen after a few days in a paradise setting, I scolded myself. I roughly dried my eyes, angry that I was letting yet another man make me feel so low. A man I hardly knew. Had being jilted by Alex not taught me a single bloody thing? I needed to wrap my heart back up in bubble wrap, not leave it open and vulnerable to the charms of out-of-my-league strangers. There was a reason I'd relied on my rational head over my heart for so long, it was safer that way.

CHAPTER 16

Atrabilious (adj.) Gloomy; melancholy; miserable

I'd spent the night tossing and turning, my mind whirring with doubts, fears and humiliation. I was still struggling to accept that Dillon had only wanted me for sex and nothing more but obviously that was all this was. I must have eventually dropped off to sleep as when I woke Amelie and Luna's beds were empty but slept in. I'd never even heard them come back. But their sheets crumpled at the end of their beds instantly brought back that sick feeling of seeing their empty seats at the fire show.

Judging by the stuffy churned air in the room I must have slept for hours. Feeling dozy from the heat I ran an ice-cold shower and pottered about getting changed. It was nice to have the room to myself for the first time. This must be what it feels like to have sisters, I thought grumpily, picking up discarded clothes and skimpy used underwear.

I scooped up lipsticks with their lids nowhere to be seen, foundation brushes caked in make-up and tangle teasers with wiry stray hairs wrapped around them that had been cluttering the rickety shelf in the bathroom. I wrung out my washbag that had been tossed onto the soaked floor – did they not have shower curtains in Canada?

I needed to keep busy to stop my head filling with X-rated shots of Dillon being centre of a ménage à trois with my roommates. I told myself to squish those niggling doubts still fluttering in my head, but it wasn't even like Dillon could WhatsApp me and let me know what exactly happened with Amelie and Luna since the scuba diva had launched my phone into the sea. I took a shower that instantly made me feel a little brighter, and piled everything from the floor that wasn't mine onto Luna and Amelie's messy beds so at least I could walk around without breaking my ankle over a pair of Amelie's gladiator heels. After a while my stomach grumbled for food, and taking a satisfying look around the cleaner room I padded out of the door to grab something to eat.

I couldn't see anyone else from the tour in the small hostel restaurant but looking at the flies dancing around the opened butter and leftover continental breakfast from hours ago I swiftly decided to head outside to the small café under a blue tarpaulin. My flip-flops slapped on the tiles of the reception area as I headed to the main doors. I stopped suddenly, seeing Dillon sat on a bench outside. How long had he been waiting here? A smile started to develop on my lips watching him hunched over, his hand nervously scratching the back of his neck. He jumped up as soon as he spotted me. I felt a slight flutter building in my stomach. I knew it, it had all been a big misunderstanding, my traitorous heart shrieked.

'You came. I wasn't sure you would.' He shuffled his feet in the dusty pebbles.

'What do you mean?' I asked cautiously.

'Didn't you get my message? I asked the receptionist to put a note through your door asking you to meet me, so I could explain everything. I thought you were punishing me by making me wait.'

'I didn't see any note.'

'Ah, well listen, I'm so sorry I had to leave suddenly last night. Amelie told me that her mate, er...Luna, had her bag pinched whilst she was chatting to some Swedish guys by the toilets. So I helped try to sort it out. It took longer than we'd hoped, as we had to go to the police station and make a formal statement and all that. She was pretty shook up about it all, so I couldn't just leave her, even though all I wanted to do was be back with you. I really hope you understand, babe.' His words tumbled out.

Having never had a guy as hot as him interested in me, I wasn't going to blow it over some stupid mix-up, even if I did have to shush the prickling feeling at the back of my brain that something wasn't quite right. But when he looked at me like that all my sense went straight out of the window.

'Oh no, I hope they're OK. That was really sweet of you to help them out.'

He shrugged bashfully. 'Have you, erm, not spoken to them today then?'

I shook my head. 'No, I was fast asleep when they left. I was actually on my way for some food. I can't believe what time it is already.'

His eyes lit up. 'Oh, well if you want company I could murder some pad Thai.'

I laughed. 'Don't most men prefer fry ups and pints of lager?'

'We're in Thailand, baby!' He winked, setting off butterflies once more. 'Come on, my treat. I know this great little place not far from here.'

I'd been so silly last night. Of course it was all a mistake. I can't believe I'd listened to Sean, when actually Dillon had gone to help those girls. He was more of a hero than a whore. I took his outstretched hand, unable to stop smiling as he squeezed it, leading the way.

The restaurant didn't look like anything special from the outside. Two cracked plant pots holding wilting green leaves clinging onto the sides marked out the dark burgundy-red chipped door where the name of the restaurant had been hand-painted many years ago. I must have pulled back, unsure about this unloved-looking place he was heading into, since all the other little restaurants we'd passed were full of life and laughter, but Dillon seemed unaware and strode down the shabby path and pushed the creaking door open.

Inside fared no better. Small, dark wooden tables were dotted around the badly lit room, which was empty apart from two fat old Thai men in the corner. If this does the best food in Thailand then it was definitely a well-guarded secret.

By the way he confidently led me here I'd been expecting to be met with mouth-watering smells and freshly cooked food simmering away in the background, not a place as dead as a working men's social club. The clicking of a plastic gold wall clock turning a grinning dragon past each second highlighted how eerily silent this place was.

'You're going to love it in here, babe,' Dillon grinned, unaware of my reservations and eagerly thumbing through the sticky, stained plastic menu we'd been handed.

'So you've been here before?' I asked, giving up on trying to understand the swirly tiny Thai writing in front of me.

He studied the menu before answering. 'No, I was just told by one of my mates who came last year.' Then he went back to acting like he could understand all that was written in front of him, and I felt stupid admitting it was all gibberish to me.

'Wow, there's, er, so much choice.'

'How about I order what I think you'll like? Do you trust me?' For a second the mood darkened as his stare laser-beamed into me.

I nodded. 'Of course.'

'Perfect.' He jumped up to order at a black-lacquered table where a young waitress was sat reading a book. She changed her bored expression to that of a wanton sex goddess within seconds of him leaning on the pile of menus next to her. This is relentless, everywhere we go women fawn over him and I feel like this uncultured slug in the background. Well not tonight. I will prove that I am worthy of sharing a dinner table with him.

Soon the table was a mess of delicate china bowls, cutlery, chipped plates and small dishes filled with orange, green and clear watery sauces. Moist golden noodles, sticky puffed rice, glazed chicken breast and what looked like crispy duck were spread out in front of us.

'Wasabi mayonnaise, prawn dumplings, tom kha soup, Thai red curry, and my fave jungle curry.' He licked his lips, pointing things out with a chopstick.

'Wow, are you sure you didn't invite anyone else to join us?' I glanced at the full table, feeling slightly overwhelmed.

'I kinda got a mix of everything that's amazing.' He offered me a fork and a spoon.

The flavours were strong and competing, each wanting to pack a punch with no care for my timid Western taste buds. Limes, sugar, shallots, chillies, all battling it out to overpower my taste buds. The first mouthful was heavenly, then the taste grew in intensity and heat, and by the third mouthful I was breaking out into a sweat, silently trying to blow air on my tongue. Dillon munched on, unaware of the fire show in my throat that would make a vindaloo seem as bland as baby food. He gave me a thumbs up, and I smiled weakly, grimacing in pain.

'Mathew would have loved it here,' he said pouring soy sauce into a plastic dish.

'Ah, who's that?' I asked, pleased to have a pause from eating.

'My brother, the one I told you about. Don't you remember?' He looked up at me, his brown eyes dim in this dingy light.

I shook my head. 'I thought you were an only child, like me?' I was certain that's what he'd said when we first met.

He paused for a moment, looking as if he was weighing things up in his head. 'No, I said I was like an only child now. He died.'

A flush heated my face. 'Oh, I'm positive you didn't tell me that, I would have remembered,' I stuttered. 'I am so sorry.'

'Thanks. Yeah, he died three years ago. Kind of the reason I took this trip to be honest. He always wanted to get out and see the world but never got the chance. He died in a car crash coming off a slip road just before Christmas. Roads hadn't been gritted, he never stood a chance,' he said, his voice cracking slightly.

I blinked back tears. 'That's so tragic. How old was he?'

Dillon cleared his throat. 'Twenty-eight, same as me now. He was my older brother, you see, I thought the sun shone out of him. I just hope he's proud of me.' He took a large gulp of his lager. It seemed he didn't share this story often.

I leaned over the table, narrowly missing catching my elbow in a bowl of noodles, to stroke his tense arm. 'I'm sure he is,' I said softly.

He smiled back. 'Right, enough of that, you have to try this.' He spooned a pile of bean sprouts in a neon-green sauce onto a fork and fed it to me.

My taste buds were being assaulted. Garlic, lemongrass, ginger and peanuts were alternating between delicious tang and delirious searing heat. I choked, unable to speak.

'How's it going down?' he asked through a mouthful.

'It's a…a…a bit hot,' I admitted, wafting my mouth with my hand. Hot? More like burning lava.

He laughed. 'I thought you northern girls were made of stronger stuff than this, I bet this is nothing compared to what you get on curry mile.'

'Yeah, I guess,' I said, not wanting to admit that I'd only ever ordered bland chicken korma and boiled rice when I went for an Indian.

The aftertaste was literally karate-chopping my epiglottis. I guzzled down my glass of water and felt my stomach contract as my head swum with the intensity of the heat, this claustrophobic room and the foreign flavours. Dillon barely registered what real pain I was in, instead he was filling up his plate, giving a thumbs up to the waitress, who hadn't taken her eyes off him since we'd arrived.

'Here you go, try this one. I know you'll love it.' He began spooning some neon-orange sauce onto my plate.

I didn't know what to do. Part of me wanted to be all Nigella-like and purr over how mouth-watering the food was, as if I ate this level of spice every day. I didn't want him to think I was this timid northern girl whose taste buds were better suited to black pudding and pies. But on the other hand I was getting dangerously close to feeling like I might pass out or spew it back up, and if either of those things happened then worrying if I looked cultured or enough of a foodie for him would go out the window.

'I think I need to get some air.' My chair made an ear-burning scraping noise as I hurriedly left the table, causing the two fat men to tut.

'You OK, babe?' He frowned but by that point I didn't care if I had half my dinner all over my face, I just needed to get out of there.

'Yep, never better,' I called out as I fled the small room, breathing in deep lungfuls of air and fanning my mouth as I made it outside. Dropping down to sit on a cool stone bench I threw my head in my hands. I didn't know what burned more, the chillies still lodged in my throat or the embarrassment of running out on a date as I couldn't handle the heat.

Within minutes Dillon heaved himself down next to me awkwardly. 'Are you sure you're OK?' he asked, unsure of how to deal with the *worst date ever*. I sniffed and wiped my mouth, which only seemed to aggravate the spicy residue on my lips.

'I'm so sorry, I just needed some air. I'm not really used to spicy food like that.'

He nodded slowly. 'You should have said. I could have gone for the mild menu instead.' He kicked dirt around with his flip-flops. His closed-off body language made me feel stupid and immature, and all I wanted was a hug, to be told it didn't matter and a gallon of cold water or natural yogurt to gulp down. Dillon provided none of this but continued to scuff his feet and sigh. After what felt like a lifetime he pulled himself to his feet and placed his hands behind his head, looking at a group of giggling girls that wandered past.

'Sorry for being a rubbish date. First I suck at scuba diving and now I can't control my taste buds,' I said weakly, wanting to break the silence, hoping for reassurance.

'You're not a rubbish date. Not at all.' He crouched down to my level and moved a strand of hair from my face, which I hoped had returned to its normal colour. 'I'm just annoyed with myself for bringing you here–'

'It's my fault, I should have said I–'

He shook his head, interrupting me. '– I really wanted to treat you, to make up for last night but the thing is,' he took a deep breath, 'I can't actually afford it.'

I hesitated, what did he mean? It certainly wasn't the Ritz, I doubt they give you a key to use a locked stinking toilet in there, even with all the things we – no, he – had ordered it couldn't cost that much. 'Oh right, well I can pay. Don't worry.'

His shoulders relaxed. 'I feel awful making you do that, babe.'

'It's fine. It can't be that expensive.' I let out a little laugh. He seemed so uptight about something so silly. We were in the twenty-first century – women accepted paying their way now. 'Come on, let's settle up then head back, didn't Kit say we had to be up early for the jungle trek tomorrow? I've never been into a jungle before, well, apart from the jungle gym which we took Cole to once, which was full of knackered-looking parents, inflatable slides and ball pools – let me tell you, indoor play centres are the one place to avoid if you're hungover – so I'm guessing this will be a little different,' I babbled, smiling at the memory.

Dillon stopped walking and folded his arms across his chest. 'I didn't know how to tell you this…but I'm not going to be there tomorrow.'

'What? Why not? It's part of the tour,' I gasped.

'Well, I don't want to worry you or anything, but the thing is, I don't have any cash left. Not to pay for this dinner, not to pay for the jungle trek, not to pay for anything.' He paused, running his hand through his hair and sighing: 'There's been a massive cock-up at my bank in England and the cash I'd put aside hasn't transferred over. Kit went mental at me last night as he hadn't received my payment for this tour. So going off on the trip tomorrow is out of the question.'

'No! He can't do that. It's not your fault the bank has messed up.'

He kicked his feet into the dusty ground. 'He doesn't seem to understand that. It's just been one of those days today, I'm getting kicked out of my hostel tomorrow for unpaid bills too. I just really wanted this night to be special together even if I was kidding myself that I could justify the cost.'

'But where will you sleep?'

'I got chatting to a guy in a bar earlier who said I could crash at his for a while. My mate back home has said he's wiring me some cash to tide me over 'til it's all worked out, but until it comes through I'm going to have to sofa surf,' he said quietly.

Oh balls. Things really were bad. I felt doubly bad at how I'd behaved in the restaurant now and was desperate to help him. I hated seeing him this way, his cheeky grin faded into worry and doubt.

'I can lend you some money,' I offered, before even knowing for sure whether I had enough spare cash to help.

'I don't know, babe.' He winced, then gazed around uncomfortably.

'Seriously, how much do you need? It would be a loan, of course, but I can lend you a bit, at least for you to stay in your own room, not on the floor somewhere.' I took his hand that was clenched in a tight fist by his side.

'Well, thing is, I'd need a couple of hundred.' He looked down at his dusty feet.

'No probs! I've got that on me.' I rootled into my bag.

'I mean pounds. A couple of hundred pounds, not baht.'

'A couple of hundred pounds?!' I parroted back in shock. Thailand was a cheap country.

'I know.' He flinched, checking to see if people walking past were listening to our conversation. 'It's not just the room, I haven't got any cash for food and even though I can't come with you to the jungle, unless I give Kit something to get him off my back I'll have to leave the tour group entirely.'

My stomach clenched at the very mention of him not being here, and I made my decision. 'OK,' I said. This must be killing his pride.

'Seriously?' I nodded. 'You're amazing, Georgia – you know that?' He kissed me hard on my forehead then let out a relaxed sigh.

'But can you not give some cash to Kit so you can come on the jungle tour too? It's really strange he's asking you to pay extra for that as it was included in the price of my entire trip.'

'I guess as I joined late I didn't pay upfront for everything like the rest of you did, meaning I have a load of add-ons. I kinda wish I had paid a lump sum as I wouldn't be in this mess now.' He let out a light laugh before a serious expression formed. 'I really don't reckon I'll be able to make it tomorrow, even with the cash you can help me out with. I've just got too many other debts to sort out first. But it's only two nights apart and I'll be here waiting for you to hear all about it when you get back.'

'Oh, right, OK,' I said sadly.

'Hey, don't be like that. If I could I would, babe.'

I nodded. 'I know.' I'd just hoped that after the mix-up at the beach fire show I would get to spend more time with him. And, I was feeling silly at how I had overreacted.

'Georgia, I really do appreciate this, you know.' He gently moved and tilted my jaw to kiss me softly before taking my hand and leading me inside to pay our bill.

'It's nothing,' I said, fishing into my bag for my bank card. I hoped.

CHAPTER 17

Mollify (v.) To soften in feeling or temper, as a person; pacify; appease

Amelie and Luna were standing in front of the mirror as I got back to our room. 'Oh look who's finally returned,' Amelie said, dabbing fuchsia-pink lip gloss on her pursed lips.

'I'm not late am I?' I asked, pulling out something clean to wear from my backpack. I'd spent the night with Dillon – after giving him the cash for his room bill it seemed a waste not to get some use out of it. Lying in bed, our bodies entwined together, I hadn't wanted the moment to end. I was scared of my feelings, scared of saying something stupid, scared of reading too much into his words and scared of getting hurt. Did he just see this as a holiday romance, or was there more to this? In my heart I felt like I had so much more to say and more to know, but the questions hung heavily on my lips as Dillon relaxed into a deep, calm sleep next to me.

'Well, you missed breakfast and the gossip that was served with it. Apparently Clare's bracelet was stolen at the fire show. That charm bracelet – you know, the one she's always fiddling with?' Luna piped up braiding her icy-blonde hair into a fishtail plait.

'No, really?'

'Yeah, wouldn't stop crying. Was pretty sad actually,' Luna added, walking into the bathroom.

'I haven't seen you since your bag went missing, did you get everything sorted OK?' I asked pulling on a pale-blue T-shirt after making sure it passed the sniff test. Amelie looked at me out of the corner of her eye. 'Did they understand English so they could help you?' It looked like it took a moment for her to register what I was asking. 'At the police station, I mean.'

'Oh, yeah, it's all fine. Just Luna leaving our things lying around for people to steal, normal idiotic behaviour isn't it?' she answered quickly. 'Speaking of things lying around, who said you could touch my stuff?'

She meant from when I'd done a spontaneous spring clean in our pig sty of a room. 'Sorry, but it was a real mess in here.' So, that 'there's no I in team' attitude obviously had an expiry date.

'You know that's what the cleaners are for?' she said, looking at me like an idiot.

'Yeah, but if they can't even get into the room how can they clean?' I said ignoring her scowl.

'Well next time, ask first. I don't want anyone touching my things.' I heard her mutter under her breath, 'Don't touch what you can't afford.'

I ignored her and went into the bathroom that Luna had left as if a tornado had travelled through whilst I'd been out. Brushing my teeth, trying to rise above the irritation at the time I'd wasted in tidying things up, I thought how weird it was that Clare's bracelet had gone missing as well as Luna's bag. This island didn't seem to be a hotspot for crime, but our small group had been targeted twice. All since Dillon joined, I heard a quiet voice in my head pipe up. But he was with Luna and Amelie that night, and yeah he might be having cash flow problems at the moment but that doesn't make him a thief, the rational side of my brain replied.

Twenty minutes later, our tour group boarded a creaking old red bus to take us up the rocky roads for a two-day jungle trek. Kit was deep in conversation with the bus driver, a dark frown knitting his brow. All the other seats were taken so I sat down next to Jay opposite Clare and Pierre, childishly upset that Dillon wasn't here to sit next to.

'So, where's lover boy? Off finding new friends with benefits? Sean said he was getting it on with them two the other night?' Jay pointed a fat finger at Amelie and Luna as the bus lurched forward.

'That was a lie. It was just a misunderstanding,' I huffed.

'Oh right. Soz.'

As we careered over another pothole I noticed Clare subconsciously feeling around her bare wrist. 'Do you know if they found her bracelet?' I asked Jay quietly.

'Nope. But they had the biggest row over breakfast. Summat about how expensive the thing was. Pretty awks if you ask me.'

'That's awful, she must feel devastated.' I stroked my dad's necklace, catching Jay looking at me from the corner of his eye. 'It must have been the same guy that stole Luna's bag.'

'What?' He turned in his seat, banging me with his thick arm as he did.

'Dillon said her bag was nicked that night too. That was why he went off to help them, not to get it on with them.' By the confused look on his face this wasn't public knowledge.

Jay straightened up in his seat: 'No it weren't.'

'Sorry?'

'Her bag – Luna's the one with the bigger tits, right? – it didn't get stolen too. Heard them two chatting about it this morning, they were defo saying something about bags together.'

'Oh, well maybe Dillon got it wrong.' Did he get it mixed up?

'Sounds like you need to have another word with yer man,' Jay sighed, closing his eyes.

Putting it out of my mind, I looked out of the window, noticing that the dusty streets and beachy landscape had changed to lush green towering trees and wobbly tin huts. Not long after, the bus dropped us off on the edge of an unpaved dirt road where a smiling, muscular Thai man was standing and waving. After introducing Stone, our trek guide, Kit stayed behind as we set off.

'Don't worry, he isn't really cut out for the jungle lifestyle, so he'll be meeting us when we return. Lazy bastard,' Stone grinned, speaking in perfect English before breaking into a run to get to the front of the group. The jocks sized him up and decided that he was cool enough to be accepted into their gang. Lucky him.

It was a difficult walk beneath the ceiling of thick leaves that shut out nearly all of the sunlight; the crackling sounds of crickets and cicadas were deafening. The sounds of the jungle were only inaudible when sliced by Amelie and Luna's regular squeals, swatting flies and screaming when large bugs flew too close to their faces. The air was so thick I could have been back in my dad's greenhouse, inhaling the heady scent of his tomato plants in the humid heat. Sweat dripped off me; as soon as I wiped it off, more moist beads would appear. I paused at a babbling stream, where crystal-clear water ran over smooth pebbles and burnt-orange rocks and, cupping my hands together, I splashed ice-cold water onto my hot face. God, it felt good. We continued to amble forward, taking in the surroundings, as Pierre and Clare lagged at the back having what sounded like an argument, bickering in French. Pierre quickened his pace and walked ahead, leaving Clare quietly sobbing.

'What's going on? Are you OK?' I passed her a piece of toilet roll from my side pocket.

'I just want to go home. I don't know what to do any more,' Clare sniffed, wiping her eyes.

'Is it about your bracelet?' I asked gently.

The rest of the group were striding ahead, out of earshot, with Stone lopping down jutting-out bamboo sticks to clear our path in the dense undergrowth.

'A little. He's so angry that I lost it, saying I didn't take care of it enough. But I did. He was the one who told me to stop messing with it at the fire show. So I took it off and put it in my bag and I had my bag with me all night. When we got back to our room, I realised it had gone.' She paused to wipe her nose. 'Also, I thought if we went to see the world together, we would be so much happier than we are back at home. I was wrong. All he does is say how much he misses France; the food isn't good enough here; the place is dirty and he thinks we should leave.'

'Maybe he just isn't adjusting to the culture; it can be quite a shock.' I thought back to the first few days of this tour, pre-Dillon, and shuddered at how desperate I had been to escape too. I couldn't believe I had been so close to quitting, I'd never have met Dillon if I had, and whatever Jay said about him I knew he was a genuine guy.

'No, it's not the country – that's just part of the problem – it's us. I'd wanted to go backpacking for so long and he eventually agreed that we could go for six weeks, but we had to come on a tour as he didn't trust my navigation skills. Once we return home, we're moving to the north of France for his work, where I know no one. I don't want to leave here, or my life back home, but if I don't, then he will leave me – and I love him.' Clare's tears mixed with her sweat, glistening in the heat.

'I'm sure things will be fine, maybe…' I stopped, thinking who was I to give relationship advice?

'No, I'm happy really,' Clare said unconvincingly, 'I just wish things were different. I wish I could find my bracelet; that would show him at least one thing wasn't my fault.'

'I'm sure it'll turn up soon.' I stroked her thin arm, realising she hadn't rubbed in her high factor sun cream that now glooped to my palm.

Clare glanced at me shyly. 'I heard that Dillon left quickly at the fire show…'

'Well, yeah, but he was with Amelie and Luna…' I stuttered, not sure if Clare was accusing Dillon, or me.

Clare nodded and paused: 'But it is strange that he said Luna's bag had been taken when it hadn't.'

'I don't know. I must have misunderstood him,' I said quickly, telling myself never to confide in Jay again. Who said men didn't gossip?

'Oi, you lot! Hurry up,' Stone shouted, his voice sounding louder in the stillness of the jungle.

'Coming.' Clare slapped on a fake smile that didn't meet her red, crinkled eyes.

*

A few hours of sweating, huffing, puffing and complaining later we made it to our camp. We silently trudged past mud huts and farm animals to enter this remote rustic village. As we explored, Stone explained that the locals mostly survived through tourism, but that they limited the numbers passing through, only working with selected guides to minimise exposure to the outside world, as it were.

If our group was one of only a few examples of the outside world that they got to see, no wonder these villagers preferred to live off the grid. The three lads had brought a bottle of cheap whisky with them and were determined to loudly sing every football chant they knew. Dinner was served in a clouded fug of mozzie spray as Amelie and Luna insisted they could hear a buzzing every five minutes, then Pierre refused to eat out of the handmade clay bowls the stew was served in, complaining that it was unhygienic, before Magnet 'accidently' smashed his dish, covering my tired legs in sticky, meaty froth.

'That's it. Enough,' Stone seethed. Looking exasperated he put down the battered guitar he had started playing in the vain hope of trying to salvage what was left of this chaotic evening. 'Time for bed.'

I stood up, wiping pieces of diced carrot from my shins and headed to chat to Amelie. I needed to just check that I wasn't going crazy, that Luna's bag had been stolen.

'Amelie, have you got a minute?'

She turned to face me. 'What?'

I felt myself wavering under her cold stare. 'Erm, I was just wondering about something.' She crossed her arms, waiting for me to spit it out. 'Luna's bag, whereabouts did you last have it? You know, before it was stolen?'

What looked like a sly grin broke out on her face, but half illuminated by the inky night sky it was hard to tell. 'What? You don't believe Prince Dillon's story?'

'No, I just, I...'

'Look, if you're having relationship problems then don't you think you should be sorting your shit out with him instead of accusing me?' She strutted off, kicking someone's walking boot out of the way.

I was about to forget it when I spotted Luna coming back from the hole-in-the-ground toilet, rubbing her hands with antibacterial gel and swearing under her breath as she side-stepped large mounds of animal poo. This was the first time I'd seen her on her own. I had to get this sorted once and for all.

'Hey, Luna.' I jogged over to her. 'So you braved the loo then.'

'Eurgh, I'm not drinking anything else, no way am I going back in there again.'

'Yeah, pretty rustic. So hey, I was wondering something. Which bag was it that got stolen at the fire show?'

She looked at me blankly. 'What? My bag didn't get stolen.'

'Oh.' My stomach dropped. So Dillon – and Amelie – had lied.

'Well actually, I thought it had been stolen – that purple one with the tassels – but turns out I'd just left it in our room the whole time,' she said matter of factly, making me feel foolish for having asked the question. 'Why?'

'Oh, nothing – I just got things mixed up, that's all.'

Stone had told us, in no uncertain terms, that if we made any sound we would be kicked out of the large bamboo hut we were all sharing, sleeping on thin mattresses covered by mosquito nets, and made to sleep by the pig pen instead. As I climbed into my sleeping bag, getting a whiff of beef juice that floated from my legs every so often, I tried to make sense of what Amelie and Luna had told me. I was certain that Dillon had said that Luna's bag had been stolen. I closed my eyes and tried not to think about it, even if it wasn't really clear why he had gone off to help them. Maybe it was a ploy by them to get him alone; but he came back to me, I thought smugly, before finally drifting off to sleep.

CHAPTER 18

Veridical (adj.) Truthful; veracious

Bright morning sunlight streamed onto the veranda where the rest of the group were chatting, eating or getting packed up for whatever today held in store. I was slowly stuffing my things into my rucksack; every slight stretch or movement hurt and my body was aching all over from the lumpy mattress on the floor. I'd had such a bad night's sleep and felt extremely grouchy. The three guys had competed in some snoreathon during the cool night, each subconsciously trying to outdo the other with their raspy, heavy breaths and gurgling snorts. I was stomping around the room grumbling to myself that Amelie and Luna had ignored Stone's pleas to leave the room tidy and pack up their things before breakfast; they hadn't even bothered to clear their beds away, so I decided just to do it myself. As I rolled up Amelie's sleeping bag I heard something land with a thump on the sheets.

I clapped my hand to my mouth with shock at what I saw. Clare's charm bracelet glinted up at me. *Amelie was the thief!* I swallowed back the acidic taste of bile in my mouth. Stone's deep voice floated into the room – he wanted everyone to congregate outside immediately. Panicking I scooped the delicate bracelet up, put it in the front pocket of my rucksack and rushed to join the others, my heart beating so loudly I was convinced it would drown out the chirping crickets.

'Guys please, listen. OK, so today we've got a shorter trek to cover, and we'll be stopping off at a local elephant sanctuary on the way to the new camp for tonight. So, if you could all grab your things and meet me out the front, we'll get going,' Stone shouted.

I stayed back and watched as Amelie returned to her bed.

'Luna, did you clear this away?' she called out, eyes darting around the room. I froze. I couldn't admit that I'd done it or else she would know that I knew her secret.

'What?' Luna asked, her dreamy voice echoing in the bare room.

'Never mind,' Amelie snapped and stalked off back outside to join a harassed-looking Stone, desperate to leave these angry-faced villagers in peace.

The walk was actually easier downhill, especially as it was still extremely early, and the cover of the jungle meant it was refreshingly cool. Not having braved the outdoor shower near to the pig pen, I appreciated the cooling droplets cascading down from the wide, dark-green leaves, freshening me up. I was very aware that I was wearing the same pair of knickers from the day before.

I'd been formulating in my mind what I was going to say to Amelie, running through opening lines that were a mixture of concern for her stealing problem and outrage at her crime. This was what all my training with Marie had been for, finally a confrontation. After my appalling attempt when I'd bumped into Alex I was determined not to fail this time. First, I had to work out what to say, and when. At least it took my mind off Dillon. I couldn't believe that I'd ever considered him as the thief.

After a few hours of slow trekking, we followed a wide, sandy path with images of elephants hand-painted on driftwood signs dotted along the lane, finally reaching a large overhead board which said: 'Elephantastic Conservation Centre'. A river wound through parched fields under a backdrop of hilly mountains. Elephants of differing heights were scratching, trundling around and being washed in the gently flowing water.

A smiling man wearing a 'Save the Elephants' polo shirt bounded over to greet our group. 'Hello, everyone. My name's Chris,' he said in a soft, faint Welsh accent. 'Welcome to Elephantastic, a sanctuary and rescue centre for elephants. We pride ourselves on providing the best care and treatment for distressed or orphaned elephants that have been rescued, as well as helping to contribute to the local community. Local villagers also find work here, whether it's selling hand-made products in our gift shop, or by spreading the word about the work we do. Our aim is not only to protect this wonderful endangered species, but also to educate tourists and locals alike.'

He had mud in his fingernails, tatty denim shorts and a sheen of sweat at his shaved hairline. He looked like a Welsh action man, desperate to save the world of elephants from the bad guys. I sensed the women swooning over him, as the men in the group bristled. I was so excited to get up close to elephants for the very first time, wanting to feel how leathery their skin was *and* experience washing one. It was another thing to tick off my travel wish-list, something I had barely given a thought to recently.

'I came here when I was backpacking – just like you guys – and never really left. We have elephants here that are blind or injured, due to being abused as working animals, especially as a tourist trap for begging.' He dipped his eyes, choking back what looked like actual tears. He made Ryan Gosling cuddling a kitten whilst tending to a sick orphan look cold-hearted.

'When we goin' to ride one?' Magnet shouted over Chris's passionate and heartfelt welcome speech, snapping those with vaginas out of their heart-eyed daydream.

Chris replied sharply, 'We have thirty-eight elephants here in this huge 250-acre park. We promote sustainable tourism, *not* cheap thrills that can harm the elephants. This is a sanctuary, *not* a circus.' Magnet looked away sullenly as Luna shot him a '*you're a heartless turd*' look.

'However, we would love to invite you to help us with feeding time and also to get hands-on with washing them in the river.' The jocks yawned and said that they would 'catch up on some kip' as they headed to a large, shady tree. Pierre had snuck off to find refuge in the small café, grumbling at the hygiene standards. 'Right, well, that's four down.' Chris looked relieved. 'I'll go and sort out overalls for everyone else.' He strode off to a large locker room containing special outfits that we needed to put on over our clothes to get into the river with the mammals.

Amelie eventually looked up from pouting for Snapchat photos, having missed most of what Chris was saying. 'Where's Mr Sexy gone?'

Luna nudged her. 'I'm not sure. I think he's gone to get some outfit or something we have to put on.'

'Are you joking me? It's not enough that I have to get into the stinking water with those beasts let alone look like a retard whilst I'm doing it?' As much as she enjoyed Chris's philanthropic attitude and sexy good looks, she wasn't the type willing to risk breaking a fingernail to help others. Her eyes widened when Luna didn't instantly agree with her. 'Have you not seen how gross that water looks? I swear this country thinks cleaning is just spit and polish. I never knew how third world Thailand was. Well, he can forget about bringing potato sacks out for us two, we're going to sunbathe. Come on, Luna, hurry up I'm being eaten alive by mozzies here.' Amelie didn't seem to care or realise that Stone was standing only metres away, hearing his country being described in such a thoughtless way.

Luna turned her head between the lake of elephants to the sun spot Amelie was pointing to, visibly torn between doing something exciting and being separated from the shadow of Amelie. 'Erm, actually I think I'm going to do this,' she half whispered, her body tense, poised for Amelie's backlash.

Amelie stopped walking and spun on her heel. 'What? You actually want to go into that disease-ridden water?' She grimaced. 'I can't believe I'm saying this, but for the first time I have to admit that *that* germ-phobe freak has some common sense.' She jabbed her finger in the direction of Pierre, who was currently using wet-wipes to clean a spot on the picnic bench so he could sit down.

'He's not a germ-phobe freak, he's just got a lot of allergies,' Clare piped up, sticking up for her boyfriend, her soft voice barely audible over the squeals of delight from other backpackers, thigh-deep in the water, as the elephants they were trying to wash sprayed them, splashing about and enjoying the attention.

Amelie threw back her head laughing. 'Allergies? Is that what he sold it to you as? The only thing that pathetic excuse of a boyfriend of yours is allergic to is a sense of humour. Although he might want to get his eyesight tested, judging by his choice of girlfriend material.' Clare's cheeks flamed up, an itchy looking flush spreading across her milky freckled skin. 'Come on, Luna,' Amelie spat.

Luna seemed to wince as she spotted Clare blink away tears. 'Amelie, I told you I really wanted to do this. I've never seen an elephant up close before,' she said, her lower lip jutted out like a toddler learning to stand its ground.

'Fine. Hang with your new friends. See if I care. I didn't even want to come here with you, only your mum forced me to. She actually paid for my ticket as she knew you couldn't do any of this by yourself. Why else do you think she gave you permission to come here? I swear if your brain was made of ketchup it wouldn't fit into one of those fiddly sachets,' Amelie said, her eyes blazing.

That hit a nerve. Luna clenched a fist. 'Don't talk about my mum like that,' she said through gritted teeth.

'Ha ha or what?!'

I was waiting for Luna to stand up for herself, to scream at her fake friend for bringing her mum into this. Or at least get some 'yo mamma's so fat' jokes into the mix. But Luna just looked like a deflated party balloon, all the air being squeezed out of her. She practically withered and nodded. 'You're right, sorry,' she mumbled.

With that I couldn't take it any more. Luna was apologising to Amelie? No way. I marched over to the two girls, my hands balled into fists at my side. Clare nervously jumped out of the way, wiping her eyes under her glasses.

'Luna, you can do what you like, don't let her stop you.'

'Oh here she goes, the grandma of the group.' Amelie wafted me away with her hand. 'Back off, Georgina. Just because you haven't got Dillon to follow after like some pathetic puppy doesn't mean you need to get involved here.' Something inside me snapped. I'd had enough of her petty comments, moans and putting Luna down, who, OK, probably wasn't the brightest spark in the fireworks box, but she didn't need to be so damn mean to her. I'd have loved to have been here with Marie, didn't she know how lucky she was sharing this experience with one of her best friends? Even if they were toxic together.

'No. You're not the boss of her, of anyone.' She seemed stunned that I had the nerve to answer back to her. 'Do the voices in your head encourage you to act like such a bitch?'

'What did you say, Grandma?'

This was it. The moment I brought her down for being such an uber mean-girl. Taking a deep breath, I shouted: 'I know that you stole Clare's bracelet.'

Amelie flinched for just a moment then pulled herself taller, squaring up to me. 'You have no idea what you're talking about. Be careful, two can play at this game,' she snarled.

'Georgia?' Clare had stopped wiping her red-tipped nose and was staring up at me. 'What…what did you say?'

'I said, she has your bracelet. I found it this morning in her bedsheets. She stole it from you, Clare.'

'Is this true?' Clare turned to Amelie, her lower lip wobbling. Amelie's eyes flicked between us both; like a lion trapped in a cage she was looking for a way out.

She snapped her head towards me, ignoring Clare's hurt eyes. 'So, where is this magical bracelet then, Georgina?'

The rest of the group were staring at us, their heads pinging between us as if watching a game of tennis.

'It's Georgia. And it's in my rucksack as – '

'– oh it's in *your* rucksack?! Yours. How convenient. Wait a minute, so you're threatening me, accusing me, when all along this bracelet is safely hidden away in your rucksack?' She paused as if she was a lawyer in some made-for-TV afternoon courtroom drama. 'So how do *we* know that *you* didn't take it, have had it all this time and are now using it as revenge?'

'I didn't…I wouldn't,' I stuttered. 'What do you mean revenge?'

She tilted her head to the side, now looking like she was enjoying the show. 'Well, you obviously want to get back at me for what happened at the fire show.'

My stomach dropped. 'What?'

'Oh come on. You've not worked it out by now? The oldest trick in the book – act the damsel in distress and men come flocking!' Amelie looked wide-eyed and helpless before breaking into a bitchy sneer: 'Luna *didn't* lose her bag and neither was it stolen, but it didn't take much to separate Dillon from whatever spell you put on him, so he could be with the type of girl he *really* deserves.'

I shook my head. 'You don't know what you're talking about.'

'Oh come on, you didn't actually think he *liked* you, did you?' Amelie folded her arms and raised an eyebrow. 'Oh my God. She *did*. That's hilarious.'

'Just shut up! Shut up!'

'And, Clare. Don't be thinking Georgia here is such a saint. She told us that she doesn't really like you and that she would *never* in a million years be your friend if we weren't all stuck here together.' What a bitch! She was twisting my words from back when we'd first met. Clare looked from Amelie to me, devastation etched on her features.

'I didn't mean that, I –'

'Georgia.' Stone had bounded over to the female stand-off. His blunt tone warned me to calm down, to put an end to the commotion and the fact that everyone in this sanctuary was staring at us more than the elephants. I could sense the guys getting out their phones to film what they hoped was going to turn into a cat fight. Stone looked at me. I braced myself for a bollocking for causing such a scene. Maybe he would escort me from the park, off the tour and send me home. What I didn't expect was when he got closer, his dark eyes caught mine and a slight smile danced on his lips. 'Bucket,' he mouthed. I looked over to see where he was nodding his head; there was a bucket of slop near the wooden gate to one of the compounds.

Without thinking of the consequences I crouched down, picked it up, staggered forward a few steps and heaved the contents over Amelie's head. I swear my parents back home could have heard her screams.

'What the fuck! You mental bitch. Did you see what she just did to me?' Amelie screeched, her body tense, arms raised in the air like a new-born baby's falling reflex, her face was a picture. I wished my phone wasn't lost at sea as a selfie right now would be priceless. I was about to ask Clare for her phone, but thought better of it when Amelie scowled at me from under the murky olive-green slime. 'You're going to pay for that!'

The others were all gawping at me, like a silent choir, their mouths forming perfect 'o's. Stone was desperately trying not to laugh. Then Chris raced over, covered in elephant spit and river water. 'What the hell's going on here? I was waiting for you by the river. I heard all this noise and thought someone had opened the elephant enclosure, not that it was you lot.' His tanned face had contorted from blissed-out backpacker to ballistic boss.

Stone stepped forward, his palms outstretched, a professional sombre look on his face. 'I'm so sorry, we just had an accident with –'

'An accident! That cow did this to me,' Amelie screeched. Magnet quickly jumped in front of her, holding her back, secretly thrilled to be so close to her even if she was leaving flubber-green gloop on his T-shirt.

Chris put his hand up. 'Shut up! Stop it! I don't care who did what. I've never had such a group of unruly, disruptive, chavvy backpackers. Now leave immediately. The tour is banned from coming here *ever* again.'

Stone suddenly saw the serious side. As much as he had enjoyed watching Amelie get her comeuppance he would get in serious trouble if Kit found out about this. 'No listen mate, we can sort this out. I apologise for our behaviour but banning us is a little over the top.'

Chris shook his head so violently I thought it might flick off. 'You can tell that Kit this is the last time *any* of his business is welcome here. Now get out of the park before I have to call the police. I mean it.'

Close by to where the stand-off was taking place was a large enclosure, full of adorable baby elephants scampering around. The young elephants seemed to have decided that this was an opportune moment to take a dump and our ears were filled with the loud thump of faeces hitting the ground. On that note Chris stormed off, leaving a cloud of chalky red dust in his wake. Stone jogged after him to try and talk him round.

Amelie pushed Magnet off her and barged past yelling behind her: 'This is all your fault, Luna.'

Luna's shoulders sunk. She mouthed 'Sorry.' Then dashed after her *friend.*

I shook my head in disbelief at the pair of them. Turning around to apologise for ruining the day's activity, I was surprised to see the rest of the group grinning.

'That was incredible.' 'Very nicely done.' 'Not bad, Nip,' Sean winked.

I blushed. 'I honestly didn't mean to do that. I…' I paused. 'Clare, I wasn't lying, I've got your bracelet in my bag but I didn't take it.'

She pulled me into an awkward bony hug. 'Do you really think I'd believe her over you? Thank you for getting it back to me. Also, I'm sure she's lying about Dillon, probably just wanting to wind you up.'

'Thanks Clare, I hope you're right.' Even when I said it my stomach flipped at the possibility that she might not be.

The bus driver forced Amelie to hose herself down in an outdoor shower before she could get on board and even then she had to sit on an oil-stained rough towel, which was ironic after everything she had said about the Thais being dirty. Neither of the girls looked at me as I moved past to sit on the back row with Clare and Pierre. I'd fished out Clare's bracelet and returned it to her, though Amelie was still denying that she'd had anything to do with it.

'Do you want to go to the police?' I asked Clare.

Clare shook her head. 'No, I've got it back safe. That was the main thing and I think Amelie has learnt her lesson. Nice work on spotting that bucket of gunge.'

After the drama of the day I leant back in my seat exhausted. Stone had pulled me to one side to tell me not to worry about Chris or Kit, he'd managed to smooth it all over. At first I panicked that the others would be furious with me that I'd cut this jungle trek short and we'd all missed out on the opportunity to get close to the elephants, but to be honest they seemed pleased to be heading back to the modern world – namely Wi-Fi and a proper bed. We eventually traipsed off the bus, dog-tired and dreaming of hot showers and clean clothes, some of us more than others. As everyone plodded inside I hung back, desperate to go and find Dillon and put my mind at rest.

CHAPTER 19

Protean (adj.) Readily assuming different forms or characters

The receptionist at Dillon's hostel wouldn't give me any information about where he was. Client confidentiality and all that. So I wandered over to Nige's beach hut to see if he'd seen him, plus the longer I spent away from Amelie the more I hoped she would calm down. Part of me was convinced that when I returned to my room all of my things would have been trashed. With my flip-flops in one hand my bare feet sank into the warm sand as I padded to Nige's hut. My stomach clenched at the sight of the small locker room full of scuba diving equipment. Never, ever again.

'Hey there,' Nige beamed and scooped me up into a hug. 'Didn't think I'd be seeing you back here. You ready to try again?'

His face fell when I explained that I was actually looking for Dillon, and that although he was an excellent teacher, me and oceans just didn't mix.

'Ah cool, cool. Yeah, actually I'm meant to be meeting him for a beer later. He came round earlier looking for a place to store his stuff.'

'So he's been kicked out of his room?'

He look puzzled. 'Dunno about that. No, he wanted to store his guitar and amps. Pretty sweet set of equipment, if you ask me.'

Dillon never told me he could play the guitar and I never saw any musical instruments in his plush hotel room. I tried not to let my face show my confusion. 'Oh right. Yeah. So where was it you were going to meet? I might swing by early to see if I can catch him.'

Nige scratched his head thinking, making his thick dreadlocks dance together. 'Karma Club. You know the one just opposite the bank? It's full of wannabes and travellers who are up their own arseholes in there, but the beer's not too pricy and they have some sweet DJ sets. Anyway, let Dillon know I'll finish up here and join him in an hour or so.'

I nodded. 'Will do, thanks Nige.'

*

In the fancy beach club filled with white sofas, tall church candles and relaxing house music, I couldn't see Dillon anywhere. I figured I'd have to come back later when Nige had finished his shift. I was just turning to leave and feeling dejected, as I was desperate to finally get the truth, when I heard what sounded like Dillon's deep laugh coming from behind a bamboo wall.

Peering around it there was a large comfy-looking sofa with a stunning slim woman laughing at what the guy next to her was saying. Her tanned arm was stroking his muscular thighs.

'Dillon?' I asked hesitantly.

He took his arm away from the girl's exposed shoulders and turned to face me as if a firework had gone off up his bum. 'Oh Georgia. You're, er, you're back early. Kit said you guys were heading straight to Koh Phangan for the full moon party after the trek.' I didn't explain that it was because of me – and indirectly him – that our trip got cut

short. 'I was planning to meet you all there. So what's...
what's up?' The words tumbled out, and he looked
flustered. The woman, sensing the mood, decided to
quietly slip away. He didn't make a move to stop her.

'What's up? Well, let me think.' I paused, glaring at him.
'Nige said you're starting a band and Amelie ended up
with elephant poo all over her because of you.'

Silence. Oh wait, I'd got that all mixed up, the words
knotting together like a collection of cheap necklaces.

'What? Are you OK? You're not making any sense.' He
frowned at me.

'No, wait. You talk first, who was that girl?'

'That?' He laughed. 'No one. Come on babe, why don't
you sit down and have a drink, you're acting all weird. Did
you have a good trek?'

'No, Dillon, I need to know that what Amelie was
spouting off about was just vicious lies.'

'OK, OK. I didn't think she would actually tell you.' He
rolled his eyes at the annoyance of it all, which only fired
up my anger even more. He took a sip of his drink before
continuing. 'Right, so, I've known Kit for a few years. He's
a friend of a friend, as they say.'

Wait. Why was he chattering on about Kit?! This was
about him and Amelie, wasn't it?

'That's why I was staying in different digs to yours;
I just tagged along with your group so I could catch up
with Kit...and spend time with you,' he added as an
afterthought.

I gripped onto the precarious tall table on my right.
It all hit me like a tonne of bricks; he wasn't just passing
through, he was actually living here. He knew everyone on
this island, had used his contacts to impress me on dates,
making me think he liked me, so that I wouldn't hesitate to
give him money to help him out. My money had obviously

paid for his luxurious hotel room, and all along, I was just a girl for this week until the next boatload arrived. Bastard! Hot, angry tears threatened to fall. I willed my shaking legs to hold me up.

'So you made me think you were just like me? Is this your plan – to stay in Thailand and chat up fresh-meat backpackers that your mates have rounded up, telling you which are easy pickings or good targets?! Console that broken-hearted one; give compliments to that fat one and have sex with that ugly one?' I shouted. I'd had enough of being lied to, of being naïve, of trusting and then being taken for a fool. Just like Alex had done to me.

'It's not like that,' he coughed, aware of others staring over at us.

'So you were with Amelie at the beach fire show?' My heart was pounding against my ribcage. Please say no, please say no.

'She told you then.' I felt my stomach drop. I'd let him into my heart, my head and my knickers, convinced that he had felt the same. I felt disgusted at myself for falling for it all.

'You lying scumbag.'

'Hey! I never said we were exclusive. You women are all the same. Listen, good luck with the rest of your trip and all that. Oh, and thanks for the money,' he said spitefully, stomping off.

I spun round and fled the bar, letting frustrated tears streak down my face. I was angry, upset and humiliated that I thought I'd met someone really special. I sank onto a bench down the street, taking some deep breaths, willing my heart to stop beating so fast. I didn't feel strong enough for all of this.

Maybe Dillon was right: I had decided to go travelling to find myself, experience carefree living, to challenge myself and to stand on my own two feet. Instead, I'd fallen head over heels for a lying pig, followed Kit's stupid rules and terrible itinerary, nearly drowned, eaten a cockroach, vomited over the side of a party boat, got my nipple pierced, and suffered through too many hangovers to count. Back in Turkey I hadn't envisaged any of this when I wrote my travel wish-list. I was expecting culture, not carnage.

I was desperate to speak to Marie or my parents, to hear a comforting voice or the sound of home, but with my phone as fish food at the bottom of the sea it was out of the question. I somehow stumbled my way from the beach club back to my hostel. I remembered seeing a small internet café nearby and entered in a daze.

Inside the gloomy room were two teenaged boys squeezed together in a booth, both playing some noisy computer game. The woman at the counter just rolled her eyes at their occasional calls to kill it quickly, and pointed to a computer I could use, far enough away from the monster hunters that I might be able to make a call. I logged onto Skype and dialled Marie. Dusk was drawing in here, meaning it was nearly midnight back at home. I hoped she hadn't gone to bed just yet.

Closing my eyes, hearing the ring tone try to connect us I felt like I was back in that bunker in the park near my parents' house. Embarrassment, shame and humiliation stabbed at my heart, the same way it had fifteen years ago. I was immediately taken back to that night.

It was dark and smelled like stale wee. I wasn't sure I even wanted to be in this abandoned war bunker in our local park. This wasn't the setting I'd ever imagined for my first time. Virgin was a dirty word at our school. Everyone else had done it. I was the last in my class, possibly in the whole school, and would be mad to miss giving this unwanted gift to Dean Summers. His parents were loaded; he smelt of Cool Water, wore Kickers and for some unknown reason had shown a speck of interest in me. Yeah, so he was arrogant, spoke with his mouth full and always had a flake of ear wax nestled in his slightly sticking-out ears, but he was popular and Marie was desperate for us to double-date with Dean's best – and better-looking – mate, with whom she had had sex at least twice. Looking around the damp, mouldy space, sat on a concrete ledge stained in piss, graffiti and cheap cider, I tried to tell myself that it could be worse. I'm not sure how much worse, but surely it could?

I bet Dean's done it with loads of girls already, even with his obvious ear wax, I thought. What if he expects me to lick it seductively or something? Worry and doubt filled my Bacardi Breezer-clouded mind. What if I wasn't good enough? What if I did it wrong? Did I even really want to do it? 'You're well fit, Georgia,' he had slurred earlier, giving me a face full of fags and body spray fumes, before telling me to go and wait for him down here. That had been almost an hour ago.

Kicking over an old, empty bottle of rum, the tiniest worm of fear swam into my head that maybe this was just one big joke. Dean hung around with Lisa and Heather, the two prettiest and bitchiest girls in the year who had never liked me. I'd had a series of bad luck whenever they were around; my gym kit went missing meaning I had to borrow a netball kit from the smelly lost-property bin, then prank calls were made to my house, and finally somehow I managed to sit on the only broken chair in the lunch hall last week.

What if they were in on this?

Suddenly the sound of heavy running footsteps filled the cavernous space. My heart lifted. I knew he would come! I quickly sat up straighter, pulled my skirt up shorter and my top down lower, like I'd seen Marie do. But it wasn't Dean that ran in, it was Marie.

'What are you doing? Dean's going to be here in a minute, you can't be here.'

She doubled over, trying to catch her breath. 'He's... he's not coming, Georgia. It's a joke, they set you up,' she panted, wrinkling her nose up at the smell. 'It's all my fault. I thought he genuinely liked you. I'd never have told you to come here if I'd known.'

'What? What do you mean?' I asked slowly, trying to ignore the wave of saliva that had rushed into my mouth.

Tears shone in her wide eyes. 'Oh Georgia. It was just a dare. I heard them laughing about you when I came out of the loo. I ran here as fast as I could but these stupid shoes slowed me down. They're all waiting for you!'

'Who? Where?' I slumped onto the ledge, trying to calm my erratic breathing down.

'Everyone,' she said sadly, blinking away her tears. 'They are all outside. Come on, we need to get you out of here, get it over with. Just walk out of here laughing. Like you knew it was a joke all along. We can do this.'

I grabbed my pointless clutch bag, containing a single untouched condom, before letting her take my trembling hand. An hour ago I thought I would be emerging from this cave a woman, not the mortified butt of a joke. Everything seemed to happen in slow motion. I blinked, adjusting to the street lights, to be met with a roar of laughter, pointing and cat calling. It was a wall of noise that Marie was desperately trying to pull me through, protecting me, but she couldn't shield me from their vicious taunts. 'Frigid,' 'Freak,' 'Loser,' 'As if he'd be interested in you,' Lisa boasted, her arm wrapped around Dean's skinny waist. I started to shake uncontrollably, my pale bony shoulders juddering in the half light, tears spilling down my face and cheap glitter stinging my lips.

Since that awful night I'd vowed a hundred times never to be so weak and foolish when it came to men. I could kick myself at how I'd ignored my own words of wisdom, not once but twice. I slammed my hand onto the desk. Why the hell wasn't Marie answering? I needed to speak to her now more than ever. She would understand, I needed to hear her voice, needed her to tell me what to do. The problem was she wasn't online, no one was. I couldn't worry my parents, my mum would have me booked on the first plane back to Manchester. Thinking about it, maybe that was what I should do. Just give up and go home, I'd tried at least. I needed to lick my wounds in private.

I'd pre-paid for the tour back in Trisha's shop so had budgeted myself a thrifty daily amount for food, drinks and general stuff I might want to treat myself to. But with Dillon taking two hundred pounds, and the extras that magically popped up whenever Kit was around, I was running very low. He'd never give me any of my money back if I left early. I scrolled through my emails looking for my return flight information to see if I could change my booking and how much it would sting my rapidly depleting travel fund.

In my list of unread messages was one from my dad telling me about the weather, how he'd won the beer and darts night at his local and an article my mum wanted me to read about a woman who'd travelled the world and returned home to start her own business, becoming a millionaire overnight because of some travel app invention. Marie had sent me some photos of Cole dressed as a goat for his upcoming nursery play and moaned about an unsuccessful date she'd been on. Apparently if the bathroom window in the cheap restaurant had been large enough she would have left right then and there.

Reading their words, I realised that life back home had been going on as usual, that even though they sounded like they missed me, nothing had changed. If I left now I knew what I'd be going back to. That was my safe, comfortable and normal reality – except in it I would still be homeless, single and unemployed. The thought didn't fill me with an intense desire to pack my case and leave, but I also knew I couldn't stay with this tour group, not with Dillon, Kit and Amelie.

I was about to draft a message to Marie, explaining everything and asking for her advice, when an email that Trisha had sent me with the original itinerary for the tour caught my eye. Scrolling through her detailed notes I realised there was an attachment I hadn't opened before. It was a hand-drawn map that she had scanned in, with instructions of where to go in Koh Lanta. To get to the Blue Butterfly. The place she had told me to go if it all got too difficult with the tour.

Suddenly I knew what I needed to do. I seemed to have forgotten that I was a PA for a living and if I could organise Catrina's diary, plan a wedding and learn how to be the perfect daughter-in-law, then surely I had the knowledge and brains to go travelling alone. If there was one thing I'd be thankful to Dillon for, it was giving me the wake-up call that I desperately needed. I was used to routine, to having a plan and following instructions – well this time, it would be on my terms. I could get myself cheaply to the Blue Butterfly, maybe negotiate a discount rate to stay, then spend the rest of my time there before flying home as planned.

I deleted my draft email to Marie and instead told her and my parents that I was off to explore a new island, that there was a change of plan with my tour, that I'd found the courage to spend some time on my own for a bit, they didn't need to worry, I missed them and I would see them soon. I added the contact details for the Blue Butterfly in case they needed to get hold of me as I'd lost my phone and logged out.

As I went to pay I nearly jumped out of my skin as the two young teens cheered and high-fived each other. They had won their battle. I smiled, feeling exactly the same.

*

My next challenge was how to get to Blue Butterfly the cheapest way possible. If I could get there by myself, then I could do anything. I left the internet café, a printout of Trisha's map clutched firmly in my sweaty hand, and walked towards the harbour, ready to use the car-boot haggling techniques that my mum had instilled in me from a young age. There was no way we'd pay a penny more for that used Girl Talk game than we had to.

Looking around for some sort of tourist information centre I noticed groups of backpackers sat around on the tiled floor of a large open-plan hut just feet from the many boats of different sizes gently bobbing on the waves. Cautiously I headed over to see if this was where I could source a ticket to get me off this island. Inside at the far end were two booths where semi-orderly queues snaked back from each tiny window. Harassed-looking Thai women wearing tight cream shirts sat inside barking replies to stressed-looking travellers. Backpackers and locals shuffled towards what I gathered was the ticket office at a snail's pace. This was clearly going to take a while. So I did what any well-mannered Brit does and joined the end of one of the lines, fanning my face as the sweat poured down my neck. Despite being late in the day the hut was full of people milling around, babies screaming, dogs barking and indecipherable Tannoy announcements.

I had wanted a taste of what it was like to travel solo, well this was it. Stressed, hot, flustered and confused, I didn't even know if I was even in the right line for what I wanted. I hadn't had to worry about booking tickets or making my own travel arrangements before as that had all been sorted on the tour. Ironically, it actually made me appreciate Kit's job. I couldn't believe how pampered I had been, how thoughtless I had been when shielded from the hard graft involved with getting from A to B in a foreign country.

My legs ached from standing up, sweat was dripping off me and my throat was as dry as sawdust; I hadn't even thought ahead enough to bring a bottle of water with me. I couldn't leave the queue to nip to the small shop and buy one just in case I lost my place. The two German guys behind me had scowled at me enough times for not shuffling into the minute gap in front of me when the line jolted forward a touch, I didn't want to ask them to watch my space for me.

Eventually, after what must have been over an hour, I made it to the counter. The two booths were cluttered with peeling stickers, posters and flyers for beach parties, full moon trips and scuba diving courses. A tight-mouthed Thai woman with dark circles under her eyes and a frizzy grey bob glared at me expectantly.

'Oh, hi. I'm not sure if I'm in the right place. I wondered if you could help me, you see I'm looking to find the next boat over to Koh Lanta, I wasn't sure if it was here or –'

She held a hand up to stop the apologetic drivel spewing out from my parched mouth. 'Koh Lanta. Boat leaves two hours.'

I let out a sigh of relief. 'Fantastic. Can I please book a ticket, just one? How much is it?' I rushed to get my purse out. That would give me time to quickly nip back to the hostel, pack my things up and make it back here to leave. This plan was going to work! I could be at the Blue Butterfly in just a few hours.

'5500 baht,' she snapped.

'Wait, what?' I reeled back in shock. That was over £100, just for one boat trip. I simply didn't have that much money – well, I did, but it would mean I wouldn't be able to eat for the rest of my stay. A hungry Georgia is a miserable Georgia.

The ticket office woman nodded her head sharply causing flakes of dandruff to flutter out like confetti.

'I…I…I can't afford that.' She rolled her eyes irritated. 'Is there another option, a cheaper boat?'

'5500 baht boat leaves today. Or you pay advance ticket, only 2000 baht, for boat that goes in three days.'

Three days! I couldn't stay here that long, not knowing Dillon was king of the island. Flustered, I could hear the German men mumbling behind me, annoyed that I was holding up the queue. I was desperate to leave, and it had felt so close, the Blue Butterfly had seemed within my grasp. I'd been so fired up to do this by myself, but the reality was that I couldn't even organise a simple boat ticket. Thanks to Dillon, I just couldn't afford it.

'You pay?' ticket office woman demanded.

I shook my head slowly. 'No. No thanks, no money.'

'Next!!' she barked over me as the German men roughly barged past, pushing me out of their way. I stumbled to the side, muttering under my breath and stumbled back out into the hazy evening.

What was I going to do now?

I felt very alone and very sad. Counting out my change I bought a bottle of water and a bag of crisps from a gummy-toothed old man out of the chipped blue cart that he was struggling to wheel around.

'Don't worry. Be happy!' His brown lips slapped together as he laughed. Looking at his wrinkled face, the load he had to carry at his age and how happy he seemed I couldn't help but smile sadly.

'Thanks, you too.'

'Don't worry, be happy!' he repeated.

I nodded and went to sit on one of the harbour walls. He did a little shimmy and wheeled his cart off ringing the bell and telling everyone around us not to worry and to be happy. Here I was thinking he was giving me some personalised advice. Resting my legs and gulping my water I spotted a smaller hut that I must have walked past earlier. A group of men were hunched on a gnarled bench, smoking, talking or sleeping. A couple of stray dogs cocked their legs up the sides of the cabin to take a leak before one of the men shooed them away with a folded-up newspaper. A few moments later all the men nudged one another awake, put their cigarette butts out and trudged over to a small fishing boat that had just docked. Hundreds of gulls swarmed round the dirty boat, squawking excitedly at the heavy scent of fish floating through the air.

The men called out to one another and started tugging at ropes and heaving large stained sacks over their muscular arms. I was mesmerised by the synchronised way they were all working: one would bend, the other lift, the next pull and the last push. It was quite extraordinary to see their precise team work and within a matter of minutes the bounty of freshly caught fish had been bagged up, taken off the boat and dumped into a waiting trailer.

I was about to get up and head back to my hostel, ready to climb into bed and feeling very sorry for myself when I spotted something painted on the side of the fishing boat. The letters were scuffed but it definitely said 'Koh Lanta'.

Jumping to my feet I jogged over to the couple of guys who were still on board.

'Hi! Hello!' I called out, waving my arms above my head. One man with thick black shaggy hair glanced up at me. 'Hi! Do you speak English?' He passed a look between him and the two other men on board and nodded. 'Fantastic! Do you sail to Koh Lanta?' He nodded, my heart lifted. 'When are you going there next?'

He wiped his oil-stained hands on his thighs and jumped up to the side of the boat and over onto the swaying pontoon where I was standing. 'Tomorrow morning. Why?' He eyed me suspiciously.

'Is there any chance, any chance at all, that I could come with you?' I breathed, not really thinking through this spur-of-the-moment decision, but feeling a glorious rush of adrenalin and confidence.

A look of confusion crossed his weathered face, he had a slight scar running through his left bushy eyebrow. 'You know how to fish?'

'Yep,' I replied as confidently as I could. OK, so my dad had tried to take me fishing a few times when I was younger but I'd got too bored to sit and patiently wait for a catch and begged to be taken home. How I regret that now.

He looked me over, sizing me up to see if I was telling the truth. 'OK. Tomorrow. Six o'clock.'

'Oh my God, thank you!'

'Don't be late. We won't wait for you.'

'I won't, I promise. How much do you want me to pay?' I winced, desperately hoping he wouldn't rip me off.

He laughed. 'You pay in fish. Pull your weight, catch us something, and we take you to Koh Lanta.'

'Oh right. Yep, OK. Well great, thanks again. See you bright and early tomorrow!' He nodded and jumped back on board, leaving me on the swaying pontoon both terrified and excited. All I needed to do was catch some fish and I'd be at the Blue Butterfly tomorrow, proud of myself for going it alone *and* going off the beaten track. I scoffed at the bustling ticket office, and the gullible travellers who were forking out a small fortune. Who needed to follow a Lonely Planet guide book when you had guts and determination?

Sadly, that smugness only lasted a few hours.

CHAPTER 20

Absquatulate (v.) To flee

In my haste to leave I'd quickly packed up my bags, amazed that Amelie hadn't sabotaged my things, and left a note for Kit to tell him that I'd quit the tour. The receptionist was too busy playing Candy Crush to look up, but grunted his assent when I asked him to pass it on to Kit when he saw him the next day. I'd hoped I would be able to say goodbye to Clare, but I wanted to avoid Amelie and Luna, and I certainly didn't want to hang around and face whatever reaction Kit would have.

Heaving my backpack on, wrapping my ugly money belt around my waist and rushing out of reception before anyone could stop me and charge me for some 'leaving the tour' tax, I staggered my way back towards the harbour, stopping for a quick bowl of pad Thai noodles for my dinner from a street cart on the way. I needed to find a closer hostel that I could sleep in just for the night, so my early morning start wouldn't be too much of a killer. It was slim pickings around here as most of the guesthouses, hotels and hostels were built along the dreamy beach. The only view from here was the dull and dreary harbour, half full of grimy boats bobbing on the litter-strewn waves. Sighing, I plodded to the first of the two dilapidated hostels opposite, telling myself that it was just for one night. I wouldn't see the view when I was asleep, plus the security of being able to sleep soundly without being worried that Amelie was going to throttle me with a coat hanger would be worth it.

Needing to hurry up as darkness was inching closer and still not knowing whether there was even a bed available, I chose the nicer-looking of the two hostels. A tired-looking man in his late thirties looked up from his computer screen as I entered. The reception desk was just a small white table propped in the corner of a bright room filled with couches, a huge fridge stocked with beer, and a football match playing on the flat screen TV. Not so shabby, I can totally do this.

Although apparently I couldn't as there were no beds left. Not the night before the full moon party as many backpackers planned ahead and reserved their place so they could easily get from the harbour over to Koh Phangan. Foolishly, I'd thought I was the only clever traveller, that I could just waltz in and get a bed. Right, one hostel down, one to go.

Entering the small reception in the unloved second hostel I felt like I'd stepped back in time. Garish paisley-print wallpaper was covering every tilting wall, the dusty old reception desk was made of heavy, dark brown wood and took up nearly all of the space. It smelled like a charity shop.

'Hello?' I called out, my optimism dropping.

A few minutes later a Weeble wobbled over. Well, near enough. The old woman was as round as she was tall, her little bare feet pattered on the stained wooden floor as she came up to me. Her grey hair was tied back in a low bun and she peered at me over half-moon glasses, frowning at me as if I'd just walked in on her on the loo.

'Yes?' she barked.

'Erm, hi, erm. I wondered if you have any beds for the night. For tonight?'

Mrs Weeble wobbled behind the giant desk. I could barely see the top of her head but I heard her rustling through papers. She emerged back in front of me with a key on a stupidly large wooden keychain and dangled it at me.

'Thousand baht.' I gawped at her. That was nearly twenty pounds. I'd only be in my bed for about seven hours. 'Own room. Double bed. Breakfast.'

'Oh erm, I don't know if…' I trailed off. I was torn. I couldn't face trekking back to the beach and going through the rigmarole of trying one hostel after the other looking for a bed. What if I bumped into anyone from the tour? Or Dillon? 'Erm, do you have anything cheaper?'

She tutted and mumbled something under her breath before heading round behind the desk again. 'Two hundred baht.' Less than a fiver.

'Wow, great, and that's a private room?' What was the catch?

She laughed, a sort of tinkly ringing chuckle. 'No! Bed. Dorm room. No breakfast.'

Oh.

Come on, it's cheap as chips (almost literally) and if I wanted to try this solo backpacking thing on a budget then I'd need to share with strangers. It might be like the dorms in Harry Potter, a fun sleepover with people who would become your best mates. 'OK.'

She put her palm out, which was the size of a child's, and waited for me to pay before passing over a key. 'Dorm two. Bed eleven.' Eleven! Jesus, how many of us would be in there? 'You leave at 10am. Pay extra if you don't go.'

'Oh, I'll be leaving early, probably around six as I've got a boat…' She'd already shuffled away. I mumbled thanks

and walked down the dimly lit corridor to find my bed for
the night.

The interior designer in this place must have been
having a laugh. As soon as I'd fumbled the key in the lock
and given the door a hard shove to open it, I could have
either burst into hysterics or sobbed on the filthy floor.
The dorm room was tiny, black metal bunk beds stacked
three high were laid out in rows almost touching the other.
There wasn't an inch of privacy. I counted fifteen beds.
Rusty lockers, most of which had their doors coming off
their hinges, lined the far wall from floor to ceiling. Two
pathetic ceiling fans panted warm air around the room,
which smelled of garlic and beer.

I located bed number eleven, a middle bunk with the
bed unmade. The beds above and below me appeared to
have been slept in but not cleaned. I said hello to the three
men in the bunk beds on either side of mine, but only one
bothered to look up and acknowledge me.

'They've been on a bender for six days. Probably won't
get any sense out of them anyway.' A girl who looked
like she was in her early twenties with dyed blue hair and
fifty pence piece-sized wooden plugs in her ear lobes said.
'How long you here for?'

'Oh, just tonight.'

'Lucky. We ran out of cash so gotta stay here till we
earn some more. The fat cow on reception has us doing
all sort of bollocks jobs to pay our bill. It's a dump.
No amount of cleaning's gonna make any difference.
You can't polish a turd, am I right?' It seemed to be
a rhetorical question as she was off again, curling her
legs under her, pleased to have an audience. I heard one
of the guys groaning. I didn't know if he wanted her to
shut up or if he was actually dying from sleeping in this
room for the past however many nights. 'It's all bullshit

this backpacking lark anyway. You leave home wanting to be free, to leave all the crap behind but you end up on the other side of the world working for pennies in a total dump like some prisoner on death row. Some freedom that is,' she scoffed. Once upon a time I could imagine her eyes were probably full of sparkle and light but now they just looked dim and soulless. I nodded as if I knew exactly what she was talking about.

'Is every bed full?' I nervously peered around the room.

'Yeah. Full of wankers.' She paused then broke into a raspy coughing fit/laugh. 'Nah, they're not all bad. Just don't leave anything on the floor as Kai, he's on bed nine, is a lazy bugger, always pissing over his bed cause he can't be arsed to get up to go to the loo.' *What the hell?* 'You seen the toilets yet?'

I shook my head, horrified that I might be urinated on by a total stranger as I slept. Maybe I should have stayed with Amelie and Luna after all. *You asked for this, Miss I-can-do-this-by-myself solo backpacker*, a voice in my head chirruped.

'Nah, well. I don't blame him.'

'Oh right. Well, you know, I'm probably just going to try and get some sleep. Got a big day tomorrow,' I said, rummaging through my bag for my pyjamas then deciding I'd rather sleep in my clothes.

'Oh yeah, cool. Listen, if you wanna hang out tomorrow I'll be here. Wasting away.'

I gave her a short smile. Oh God, how depressing was this?

A yellowing bed sheet, dubiously stained pillow case and what looked like a threadbare towel sat limply on my dipping mattress. I took a deep breath and told myself that it was just one night. One night. I made the bed, and got in, tucking the fishy-smelling sheet up as far as it would go, wondering if it would protect me at all from Kai's rain shower in the night.

I don't think I got more than twenty minutes of shuteye. What with the group of six hammered, shrieking women stumbling back in around three, guttural snores seemingly bouncing off the walls and the horns of the boats just after dawn. I felt like an extra in *The Walking Dead*. When I crept out of my bunk – difficult to do as the springs creaked under every slight movement – everyone was fast asleep. Sitting up and quietly putting my shoes on, determined I would never repeat this experience ever again, I got a whiff of strong tangy ammonia. Seems Kai had been at it again. My right flip-flop was sopping wet. For fuck's sake.

Racing out of the room and running my soggy flip-flop under the tap in the revoltingly filthy bathroom, I had never been so pleased to have left a place before. Dropping my key at reception, I squelched down the road to find the fishing boat that was going to get me far far away from here.

The shaggy-haired man spotted me at once and gave me a short but friendly wave, the other men on board looked at me with a mixture of disgust and smirks. I took a deep breath and wobbled down the pontoon to the grimy boat.

Yes, you could say I was running away, but I was sick of putting up with things that weren't making me happy. I'd stayed with Alex, telling myself that things would improve; I'd continued to work for Catrina, holding onto her empty promises of promotion and had stuck with a tour group that I hated. Nope. I was going to stand on my own two feet and move on alone.

'Throw your bag in there, I'm Wayne by the way,' the shaggy-haired man grunted.

'Wayne?' I asked stifling a laugh at the same time as unglamorously clambering on board.

'Yeah,' he replied straight-faced, as if Wayne was a perfectly common Thai name.

'Right, well thanks, I'm Georgia.' I quickly followed his directions and placed my bags on top of a box in the small cockpit room. An overweight man with thinning hair who stood peering at the dials next to the steering wheel grunted at me.

'Hello,' I smiled at him. The man grunted back.

'This is our captain. He doesn't speak any English,' Wayne explained as he walked into the room. 'No one else does except me. But, you won't have time for chatting as you're here to work.'

He chucked a pair of heavy rubber boots, three sizes too big, at my flip-flop-covered feet. 'It gets pretty wet, don't want you slipping overboard. Put this on too.' A stained extra-large T-shirt came hurtling at my head. I didn't catch it in time and heard the captain huff as I gingerly picked it up from the floor. 'We leave in five minutes.' With that, Wayne said something in Thai to the grumpy captain who followed him out, leaving me alone.

I probably should have felt more vulnerable being at sea on a boat with four male strangers. My mum would be clutching her chest in horror if she knew what situation I had put myself in, all to save some money. But the thing was, as random – and perhaps dangerous – as this experience was, I felt like I had to prove myself.

I used to hate sports day at school, hated the pressure, the competitiveness from naturally athletic students pitted against ones like me who couldn't swing a bat or cross country race to save my life. I knew my dad was just being kind when I came last every time, my face flamed in shame as other students laughed at me. He would tell me I was more a creative type, that not everyone could be the next Linford Christie. The world needed a mix of those who would boast and brag about their glory and those who quietly got on with the job. Well, I was sick of being the one who lost out to the bolder, mouthier types. I was going to prove to myself that I could be just as good as them.

I quickly pulled on the boots and the T-shirt, trying not to gag at the fishy fumes, and hurried out to meet the rest of the crew. While the men were uncurling an enormous fishing net onto the slippery deck, I held onto the rails as we picked up our speed. The small boat fought its way through the waves, slicing its path through the dark ocean, turbulently smashing up and down upon the froth. I gulped back the sickly feeling that the motion was causing my stomach. I was determined not to be sea sick and embarrass myself in front of these guys. I bet they all thought Wayne was crazy for letting a female backpacker onto their territory. I gingerly leant down to help them uncurl the heavy net but quickly regained my balance and clung onto the metal bars when we jerked over another wave.

They were talking to one another in fast Thai before jabbing their fingers at me. Wayne called my name. 'You need to get off that and come and help. Do some work, this is not a free ride.'

I nodded and tried to balance myself over to them all, shuffling my way slowly in these enormous boots he'd made me wear. I noticed that no one else was wearing them. A few of the men sniggered when I approached.

'Erm, Wayne?' I asked quietly, ignoring the others. Wayne jerked his head up from the rope he was working on and stared at me, waiting for me to speak. 'Erm, I just wondered if you maybe had any life jackets?'

Wayne must have translated what I said to the rest of the crew as everyone started laughing. 'No, you're a fisherwoman now. You'll be fine. Now hurry up and help pull this rope as we get the net over.' I blushed and did what I was told.

It took three men to heave the net over the side, where it quickly plunged into the water. I felt the rope in my hand burn my palms as it became taut. 'Now, whatever you do, don't let go.' Wayne looked extremely serious and for the first time I felt intimidated. *OK, easy. Don't let go. I can do this.*

The early morning sun was beating down on me and despite wearing a T-shirt made for an elephant I could feel the bright rays warming my skin. I wished I'd worn a hat and maybe applied more sun cream, but I couldn't let go of the rope to rummage in my bag, especially as sun safety didn't seem to be the number one concern amongst the rest of the crew, who were now smoking roll-ups and lying topless on the deck.

My arms started to feel heavy, my legs were getting sore from keeping balance and standing up for so long. I didn't dare ask how long I was expected to stay like this. I tried to ignore my suspicions that Wayne was making me stand here just for a laugh, like Catrina had done my first week working for her when I'd spent all morning running around Manchester looking for some white ink for the printer and left-handed teaspoons. I'd just been so desperate to impress her, not realising how gullible I'd been and how much she'd taken advantage of my eagerness to please.

I was just about to tell Wayne that the joke was up when suddenly the rope I was holding threatened to be pulled into the water, taking me with it. It was jerking so violently I struggled to keep my grip.

'Wayne!' I cried out, planting my feet firmly on the floor and taking two hands to hold on. I thought we must have caught a shark it was tugging so manically. My shouts alerted the rest of the crew, who raced over to where I was standing. Within seconds the boat was a scene of frenzied action, Wayne was yelling at me not to let go and swiftly took the end of the rope that was trailing on the wet deck and gripped it.

'Georgia, when I say go, we pull.' Wait, what? 'Pull!' he shouted.

Everyone was leaning over the side of the boat and pulling at whatever rope they could find. It was bone-achingly painful.

'I can't do it!' I cried, my palms on fire, my breathing erratic and head dizzy.

'You can! Now heave!' Wayne boomed back at me over the commotion from the other men shouting to one another. I shook my head, tears running down my sweaty face. I couldn't do any more. I couldn't physically carry on.

'I can't,' I half-sobbed half-wheezed. This was hell, no, worse than hell. Get me back on Kit's tour immediately, I prayed. I continued to struggle, pulling the rope, my hands burning at the rough frayed edges. My whole body was clenched, suffering, muscles shaking in areas that weren't meant to shake. I wanted to cave in so badly.

'You're just going to give up? Is that what you're going to do? Just because it hurts a little bit?' Wayne taunted me, obviously regretting his decision to let a girl on board. I couldn't answer him, my throat was clogged up with tears. 'You have to finish what you started, Georgia. You're in control, just pull harder,' he shouted.

I was about to let go of the rope, convinced I couldn't take a second more when Wayne's words hit me like a punch to the gut. I started thinking about everything I've started and not finished, every small goal I've set myself and given up, every Zumba class Marie dragged me to that I never went back to, every holiday I'd wanted to book but didn't make happen, every awful restaurant dinner I didn't have the courage to complain about, every sarky comment that Alex's mum made when she thought I couldn't hear that I'd let pass – hell, I couldn't even get a guy to marry me! *Don't quit. Don't be that girl*, a voice shouted in my head.

'Come on, Georgia!' Wayne yelled.

For the last few pulls I fought hard. I refused to be that girl, the quitter. I forced my arms to heave the ropes faster, harder. Sweat was dripping down my nose, my face scrunched in determination. I was making weird grunting noises that made it sound like I was in labour, but I didn't even care. I had to get this net up. This pain, this determination and frustration was for all the failure I'd willingly endured in my life, knowing Wayne was staring intently at me, feeling the other crew members waiting to see if I would crumble only pushed me harder. I wheezed and pulled, grunted and pulled, swore like a trooper and pulled.

And then we were done. The net toppled over the edge onto the soaked deck, my feet gave way and I collapsed in a crumpled lump surrounded by slippery flapping fish. I was a mess. I started laughing manically, amazed at myself that I'd done it, I'd persevered. I'd pulled in a huge haul of fish in the middle of the Andaman Sea, with a group of burly fishermen, all on my own!

I looked around at the other men, expecting the rest of the crew to have been on this emotional, spiritual and physical journey with me, but to my surprise everyone else was busy grabbing fish and filling bright-orange buckets. Just doing their daily work as usual. Ignoring the howling English banshee in the corner.

One of the men, a guy with a straggly black beard and hand-inked tattoos on his arms, barked something in Thai at me. 'Georgia, you're not finished yet, come on!' Wayne translated, giving me a look that was a little anxious about the mentally disturbed cargo he had allowed on board.

I scrabbled to my knees and began grabbing at the fish, not even wincing at how gross they felt between my fingers. Slimy, soft and wet. I scooped up as many as I could and chucked them into the orange bins. Ten minutes later and the net was empty once more.

'Good work. Now, we clean and then we arrive in Koh Lanta,' Wayne smiled quickly. After all the egotistical drama I'd forgotten that I was on this boat for a reason, not just to test my limits but because I was heading towards my new destination alone. I nodded and wiped my face on the edge of my T-shirt, before scrubbing the salty deck with a coarse brush I'd been thrown.

Every muscle moaned and writhed in pain, the adrenalin was still coursing through me and I couldn't stop grinning as we slowly made our way to Koh Lanta harbour. I was so proud of myself, a feeling that didn't happen often enough. As the rest of the crew snapped into their perfectly synchronised routine of getting the fish off the boat and onto trailers to be weighed and sold Wayne stepped over to me and slapped a rough hand on my back.

'You've made it. It wasn't that hard hey?'

I scoffed. 'Hard? More like torture!'

Wayne's scowl disappeared for a second as a friendly smile danced on his tight lips. 'You did good.' I beamed, bending down to collect my bags and rummaged for some cash to give him. 'No. I said you pay in fish, which you did. You can keep the T-shirt too.'

I shouted my thanks as he nodded and jumped over the edge onto the pontoon. Leaving the boots on the deck, I did the same, well not as easily as he made it look, and waved goodbye to the crew, who flicked their heads at me. Still wearing the baggy T-shirt with pride I wobbled on my sea legs to the street and looked down at Trisha's hand-drawn map. Next stop the Blue Butterfly.

CHAPTER 21

Foolhardy (adj.) Impetuous, rash

So, I'd made it to Koh Lanta but the only slight problem was that Wayne and his crew had dropped me off somewhere that wasn't even signposted on Trisha's map. Blocking the sun from my eyes with my smelly, fishy hand I looked around nervously. The harbour was much smaller than the one at Koh Pa Sai, not a ticket office or restaurant in sight. Ahead of me, just past the bobbing boats, was a dusty, empty road that forked to the left and right. The right fork seemed to be the busiest option, as a handful of trailers full of the day's catch were being slowly wheeled in that direction, whereas I'd only seen one tuk tuk drive down the left fork. I chewed my bottom lip. There was no one around to ask. Wayne had disappeared and the sound of the waves and the worry in my head was all I could hear.

Hmm. Now what? I didn't want to start walking down one road in case the Blue Butterfly huts turned out to be in the opposite direction. My body hurt too much from the fisherman's workout routine – coming to all good gyms next year, I was sure – to be lugging my heavy backpack too far. I hadn't even thought about how to find this place once I arrived. I guess I'd assumed it would be right by the harbour. Now all I had was a tatty map that had fish juice all over it. Thinking back to what Trisha had said in her office about the Blue Butterfly she definitely mentioned something about it being remote, hence why she drew me a map, but I didn't expect it to be so well hidden. Originally I'd been excited, feeling like Leo in *The Beach* going off in search of paradise, kept secret from the tourist crowd. But now I was here, stranded in the middle of nowhere, dripping in sweat, hungry, tired and very, very sore. My high from pulling that heavy net in had faded as fast as Marie's fake tan. They never showed this part of Leo's journey in the film.

OK, think practically, Georgia. I needed to find someone who could look at the map and at least maybe recognise in which direction it might be, catch a tuk tuk to go that way and hope it wasn't as off the beaten track as Trisha made it out to be. Feeling reinvigorated, I got ready to leave. Only I couldn't bend my sore legs to attempt putting my backpack on standing up, so I left it on the dusty ground and half lay on it before snapping the straps together and trying to roll up, ladybird style. It took me three attempts before I was back up on my feet, my thighs roaring in pain. Taking tentative steps, hoping that once I got moving I'd loosen up a bit, I set off. I chose the road on the right.

I had to stop every ten minutes to catch my breath, wiggle my shoulders under straps that were soaked with sweat and take deep breaths before I could continue. I wished I had someone to talk to, someone to take my mind off the agony my whole body was feeling, someone to help me find my way. *You wanted to try solo travel, well here you go,* a voice piped up in my head. *Oh, piss off.*

Eventually I made it to what looked like a cluster of dilapidated huts, with sunlight bouncing off the corrugated iron roofs that made my eyes water. A young boy, a little older than Cole and wearing a dusty Manchester United T-shirt ran around outside chasing a mangy-looking chicken, half of its feathers lying on the recently swept floor. A woman with a sheet of black hair down to her tiny bum was hanging up washing and scolding the excited boy, whose bottom lip wobbled until she rolled her eyes and he continued to race about.

'Hello, do you speak English?' My voice sounded hoarse and quiet, so I coughed to clear my throat, catching their attention.

She just stared at me. I guessed that was a no then. My hand was being tugged by the little boy. He'd lost his two front teeth so his smile was not dissimilar from yesterday's gummy water seller who'd told me 'don't worry, be happy'. 'Hello,' I smiled back at him, immediately picturing Cole and Marie. I missed them so much. 'I'm sorry, I'm lost and wondered if you could help me.' Again I tried talking to the woman who I presumed was his mother. She remained mute. Now what was I supposed to do? I could keep going until I found someone who maybe spoke English and could help me, but these were the first people I'd laid eyes on since I started walking and my back screamed at me to stop punishing it.

The little Manchester United fan was holding my hand and swinging my arm gently. 'Wait a minute,' I said, releasing my hand from his tiny grip to rummage in my shorts pocket for the map. He carefully watched what I was doing but soon lost interest when I didn't pull any sweets out. Unfolding the crumpled paper I hesitantly stepped towards his mum holding it out. 'Blue Butterfly?' I pointed to the map. She looked down at the creased drawing but stayed silent. This was so hard! I took a deep breath and then began wafting my arms to my sides and flapping around in my best butterfly impression, pointing to the blue of my backpack. The boy found this hilarious and started copying me, giggling at the strange lady, and soon the two of us were floating around the empty road.

Finally, his mum took another look at the map and said something in Thai to the child, who ran into the hut. She probably wanted to protect him from the crazy Westerner, well that was that then, I felt my shoulders slump as I prepared myself to keep on walking.

'Brooom broooom.' The little boy whizzed out making car noises. I glanced up at his mother, who nodded and beckoned me to walk down a side path with her. Nervously I followed, the little boy driving around us both. At the end of the path was a man snoozing in a hammock, and next to him was a bright green tuk tuk. She understood! She tried to gently nudge the snoozing driver awake before the little boy decided his own technique of just clambering on his legs and banging the man's head with his chubby fists would be more efficient. It worked. The sleepy man spluttered awake and scooped the child up in his arms, planting a wet kiss on his forehead, which the boy scrunched up his nose at and rubbed off. The woman pointed at me and spoke to him, he nodded, yawned and got into his vehicle.

'Blue Butterfly? You know it?' The woman nodded and smiled. 'Oh my goodness, thank you so much!' I rummaged in my bag and pulled out a couple of soft crumpled notes but they shook their heads. Wanting to give them something for their trouble, I found the dishevelled-looking bag of crisps I'd bought yesterday and not eaten and I handed it to the boy. His mother's face broke into a wide smile of approval, nodding at me before the boy raced up and wrapped his chubby arms around my legs. I winced at how bristly and sweaty they were under his soft touch, my heart melting at how genuinely thrilled he was to have just a bag of crisps.

'Ah, thank you,' I said, hugging him back. The driver clapped his hands and nodded his head towards the tuk tuk.

'Take care, and thank you again!' I called out, even though they hadn't the faintest idea of what I was saying, and climbed into the back seat. I let out a sigh of relief; I was on my way.

This island was a lot greener than Koh Pa Sai, if that was even possible. Luscious foliage, exotic bright flowers and thick, deep greenery zoomed past as my driver silently sped down empty roads, dirt tracks and winding paths. I still couldn't relax completely; being on my own I needed to have my wits about me but it seemed my now-wide-awake chauffeur knew exactly where he was headed. I just hoped it was where I wanted to go.

After about twenty minutes (driving down the road that forked to the left off the harbour) zipping up lanes that appeared not to be vehicle-worthy and didn't show up on Trisha's map, my driver pulled to a stop under the shade of a low-hanging palm tree. He nodded at me to get out, which I did with as much difficulty as I'd clambered in, and hoisted my backpack roughly to the floor. He smiled and dipped his slightly balding head low then pointed to a path ahead that was caked in dried mud and certainly wasn't fit for any cars, not even his tiny tuk tuk.

'Is that the way to Blue Butterfly?' I asked. It looked like I was about to hike into the jungle, alone.

He continued to smile and bowed again before jumping into the driver's seat and nipping off, back to the road we'd just driven down without even a backwards glance at me. *Deep breath.* I was now stranded in a bloody rainforest, the sun was starting to set and night was beginning to draw in. Pulling out Trisha's map I tried to trace a slightly trembling finger around her drawing but couldn't make out a thing. The driver must have dropped me here for a reason so I put my faith in the kindness of strangers, ladybird-style got my backpack back on and blotting out the pain in my neck and shoulders I levered myself up from the ground and set off down the narrow path. *Whose stupid idea was it to come here? Why didn't I just tough it out on Kit's tour?* Grumbling thoughts kept me company as I put one foot in front of the other, trying to watch where I stepped over boulders and crumbling rocks blocking the route. Under the canopy of thick leaves it was practically dark already.

After numerous swearwords, a few almost-tumbles and a near-snapped ankle, I realised that the air had a different quality about it compared to the humid jungle heat. It felt cleaner, clearer and was thick with sea salt, scented flowers and the sound of lazy crickets. I swear I could hear the sounds of crashing waves. Stumbling through the thick leaves of an overgrown path, I saw a peeling wooden sign hanging from a gnarled wooden post that read 'Blue Butterfly' and indicated which direction I should go. *Get in!!!* Quickening my pace and flattening overhanging palm tree leaves that slapped me in the face, I eventually emerged into paradise.

The calm, turquoise sea just metres away seemed to be dip-dyed, glistening a pale jade before seamlessly changing to a deeper, royal blue further out. It licked the sandy coved beach, secluded from the rest of the small island. Dotted along the edge of the hazy sunset-bathed shore were ten or so dark brown bamboo beach huts, each with its own tiny veranda strung with fairy lights and flower leys. Painted-on butterflies adorned the sides of each hut in varying colours and sizes and sweet incense filled my nose. It was heaven.

My feet sank into velvety sand that resembled the colour of creamy writing paper. Holding my hand up to my eyes, taken aback by the beauty and tranquillity of where I'd found myself, I didn't notice a smiling young Thai woman walk up to me holding a coconut with a pale-pink straw sticking out of it.

'*Sawasdee Ka.*' She placed her palms together under her chin and nodded graciously. 'Welcome to the Blue Butterfly. I take it you are Georgia?'

'Hi. Yes, er, that's me.' If I stank of fish half as pungently as I imagined, she didn't let on.

'My name is Thidarat. Most people call me Dara. It's a pleasure to welcome you. I've been expecting you.' My confused expression prompted her to continue: 'Trisha has had your hut waiting for you. Are you alone?'

I nodded, unsure if that was the right answer. When Trisha recommended this place I wasn't expecting her to have actually *reserved* something. Why did Trisha think I would be here with someone else? Dillon? A tight lump formed in my throat as I thought about him, about the person I'd thought he was. *Forget him – that's in the past.*

'You don't know how happy I am to be here.' I wiped the sweat dripping from my eyebrows and graciously accepted the drink. 'You keep this place pretty well hidden.'

She laughed softly. 'Yes, but you'll soon see it's worth the journey. Come on, I'll show you to your new home and if there's *anything* I can do, please don't hesitate to ask.' She seemed to glide me over to my hut. I half expected birds to place a ribbon in her hair and a fawn to skip past as she sang a lullaby.

'That sounds perfect.'

*

The hut was as beautiful on the inside as it was from the outside. Pastel-coloured cushions nestled on top of pale duck-egg-blue sheets stretched over the squishy double bed, the rustic wooden furniture looked handmade and rugs the colour of the ocean were dotted around the white-washed floor.

I took my time unpacking my things, wincing at the smell of some of my sweat and sunscreen-stained clothes. If this tiny place had a launderette then I needed to find it pronto. Finding hand-written notes dotted around the room, I smiled as I made myself at home. In the en-suite bathroom there was a note tied on with raffia to the pearly lavender soap telling me to *wash off my worries*, a small china cup and saucer explained that *tea solves everything* and on the full-length mirror just next to the round window someone had artistically written *you look beautiful*.

Reading these mini affirmations helped cheer up my knackered body and bruised ego. Resisting the urge to climb into the fresh sheets I listened to my growling stomach and forced myself to head to the Blue Butterfly restaurant. Billowing sheets were tied to thick wooden beams, creating a sort of open tent filled with patterned beanbags, handcrafted stools and rickety tables. It was Pinterest-worthy adorable. Inside, a smiling Thai man was busy cooking at a barbecue that had been fashioned out of a huge beer barrel. My mouth watered at the smells of spicy fresh fish and charcoaled plump chickens that turned lazily on a spit.

An older lady sat on a wooden stool, using a paisley cloth-covered box as a makeshift table for her tarot cards and was laughing animatedly with a man opposite her. Two guys lying in hammocks played cards, clinking their heavy-bottomed beer bottles together and next to them, surrounded by colorful cushions, sat a group of three women around my age chatting and drinking cocktails. I was too nervous to go over and introduce myself. I wasn't sure that I had the strength to meet a whole new set of people, going through the motions of pleasantries and niceties. So I slipped through a gap in the seating and headed towards the makeshift bar: a picnic table that held an assortment of glasses and bottles. I searched for the bartender – the thought of a drink, dinner and an early night sounded like all I could cope with tonight especially after today's epic adventure to get here.

'Hey, you can just help yourself, you know,' said an older woman with deep laughter lines and a pack of tarot cards clutched to her chest. 'They're very trusting around here.'

'Oh, thanks. Er...well I'll just grab a beer.' I hesitantly opened a heavy fridge door and cautiously pulled out a cold bottle.

'Take two! I don't think I've seen your face around here before?' she asked peering at me.

'Oh, no. Well I've just arrived,' I said, taking a sip of my beer and feeling a wave of tiredness wash over me.

'Astrid, you ready?!' a guy with a bald head called out, raising a hand to wave at me. I gingerly waved back.

'Sorry, I better go. Promised him I'd give him a reading ages ago. He's like an elephant that one – never forgets,' she chuckled. 'You'll have to stick around after dinner so I can introduce you to everyone else.' I nodded. 'Excuse me, luvvie.' She waddled off leaving me and my bottle of beer.

The rest of the room looked deep in conversation, and feeling like I could shut my eyes and fall asleep I quickly ate my dinner, wishing I'd brought a book to read, and snuck off back to my hut. I hoped I'd made the right decision to come here alone.

CHAPTER 22

Heliolatry (n.) Worship of the sun

My whole body ached. I felt like someone had run into my hut during the night and replaced my muscles with rocks. Slowly heaving myself out of the bed after such a great sleep – I'd literally nodded off the moment my head thumped against the soft cotton pillow – I smiled to myself that I was here. No Amelie or Luna sharing this room, gassing me with their heavy perfumes or incessant bitching to each other, no strange men weeing on your flip-flops and no depressing hippy traveller bringing me down; it was so worth the pain in my tendons.

Wincing I stood up and took a shower, changing into my bikini and a plain T-shirt and shorts before pulling out my travel wallet and counting what little cash I had left. It wasn't just the strain in my abs that made my stomach lurch. I was skint. I needed to go and find Dara as soon as possible to work out some sort of deal for me to stay here, either that or find an internet café to transfer some cash over from my separate account that should by now have been replenished with the money that Alex was meant to have paid in for my share of the house. I'd hoped my dad's stern warning in Morrison's was enough to make him pay up.

I padded along the sand, which seemed to melt under my step, flinching at the strain I felt in my tight thighs and arse. No wonder most backpackers looked like they could do with a good meal, they burned a stupid amount of calories just getting places. Dara was humming to herself as she tapped away at an old computer in the reception area. Well, it was more a partitioned-off space at the back of the restaurant with a map of Koh Lanta, well-thumbed novels other backpackers had left and a small wire rack containing a couple of postcards that had faded over time.

I smiled to myself looking at the pictures that perfectly captured the colours of the sea, women with large containers on their heads grinning to the camera and wide palm tree leaves that almost touched the ground; they could all have been taken on this beach. Picking one up that had curled over the top corners I grinned to myself. Trisha had asked me to send her a postcard to add to the wall in her shop, the wall where much of the space was taken over by cards sent from her godson Stevie. I hadn't thought about him since meeting Dillon but standing here now he was at the forefront of my mind. Had he been travelling alone, body sore and spirit tested? Where did he find these cards, mementos of his trips? With most things online these days, postcards really were relics of the past and hard to track down. Where had he sat when penning his short but sweet messages to his godmother? Worrying about her health, her business and life back home. I didn't even know where he called home or what he did that allowed him to see so much of the world but something fluttered in my tummy that told me I wanted to find out.

'Morning,' Dara said, once she got off the phone, pulling me from my thoughts. 'How did you sleep?'

'Hi, like a log thanks.'

'Ah, that's good. It's still a little early but I can see if Chef is around to get you some breakfast sorted if you like?' She sounded like a worried mum.

'No, don't worry I'll wait thanks. I actually wanted to speak to you about, erm, money.' Why were conversations involving the green stuff always so bloody difficult for us Brits?

'Money?' she asked looking confused.

'Yeah, to pay for my hut. You see, I was hoping to stay a while and wondered if that would be OK and also if maybe we could, erm, come to some sort of agreement on the price?' I winced.

Her dark eyes narrowed as if she was thinking about something, then she shook her head and smiled. 'Georgia, your hut is paid for. Trisha sorted that when she reserved it.'

'Oh right, erm, wow. Great. So it's OK to stay then?' I felt like an idiot. Maybe Trisha had overcharged me for the tour and paid for this place with that? I hadn't brought my receipts with me so couldn't check, but she wouldn't have paid out of her own pocket, would she?

Dara rubbed my arm, her skin as soft as my favourite onesie. 'You can stay as long as you like. Any friend of Trisha's a friend of mine too. Make yourself at home and just enjoy yourself.'

'Thanks, although you may be regretting that when you have to physically kick me out of my hut, I don't think I ever want to leave.' I felt like I'd won the jackpot. Leaving the tour group, being brave enough to make my own way here had already paid off.

'You'll know when it's time to go,' she laughed.

'Oh hi, you're up early,' The guy with the bald head who'd had his tarot reading last night smiled up at me as I left Dara and padded over the satiny sand to the handful of sun loungers, feet from the shore. 'I'm Phil, by the way.' He had a relaxing deep American accent.

'Hi. Georgia.' I shook his hand and smiled.

'Well, welcome to the club, Georgia. Always nice to see a new face. You're going to love it here.'

'Thanks, do you mind if I sit here?'

He shook his head. 'Be my guest!' I settled on the sun lounger next to him. There was a soft morning haze across the water, like looking at the sea through steamed-up glasses.

'So where're you from, Georgia?'

'Manchester in England.'

'Ah yes the Red Devils,' he laughed. 'I reckon everyone in the world knows about Man United and I don't even follow soccer.'

'Yeah, I guess. So judging from your accent I'm guessing you're American?'

'No. Russian,' he said, looking annoyed. Great, two minutes into meeting him and I'd already insulted him.

'Oh sorry, accents aren't my strong point,' I quickly apologised.

His stern look broke into a wide grin. 'Ha, I'm just fooling around. Yep, I'm from the US of A.' I let out a breath and laughed with him. 'Not far from New York. You ever been?'

I shook my head. 'No, but it looks incredible. It's definitely a place on my future bucket list.'

'A future one?'

'Yeah, I'm working through a pretty major one at the moment but I figure that once I achieve everything I'll need to start again!' I explained about my travel wish-list, which reminded me how little I'd ticked off since I'd been here. Well that was going to get addressed now I was free from the nightmare tour. Phil nodded along enthusiastically as I spoke. I reckoned he was around forty; he had a wedding ring on and skin so pale it made Pierre look like he'd been tangoed.

'This is my favourite part of the day. Just as things start to heat up, I like to get my sun in early before this pale skin gets frazzled. Come lunchtime, I'm like Dracula hiding in the shade hugging the air con.'

'I hope you've slathered yourself in a high factor?' I asked, concerned for his milk-bottle hue.

'Only the thickest gloop I can get my hands on.' He twisted his body to pick up a bottle of factor fifty to show me. As his slender waist turned to the side, I noticed a small tattoo running across his ribs.

'You've got a tattoo?' I asked nosily, trying to peer closer. As he lifted up his pink, freckled arm I felt very confused.

I've seen this design before.

'Oh, *this*? I got it years ago. It was when my wife and I got married; we had our honeymoon here in Thailand. That's kind of the reason I wanted to return as I remembered how tranquil this place was, full of special memories between us. It's faded quite a bit since then; I forget I have it as I don't see it all the time.'

'Oh, is your wife here?' I said looking around the empty beach.

'Ah no, we're having a few problems.' I must have winced, embarrassed at how I'd gone and put my foot in it. He quickly added: 'Don't worry, it's all been my fault. My mom died unexpectedly and I just wasn't prepared to deal with the grief that hit me. Instead of talking to my wife, and allowing her in, I bottled up all my emotions, hit the drink and let myself go.' He kicked the sand with his feet, uncomfortable reliving this time. 'My wife gave me an ultimatum to sort myself out. So I booked a ticket here, have been going for morning runs on the beach, cut out the booze and been doing a lot of thinking and talking, thanks to these guys.' He waved his hands around, indicating the huts with the guests fast asleep inside. 'They've been incredible, listening to me moan, helping me with my problems. It's been like free therapy with an awesome view,' he grinned, taking a sip of his orange juice.

'Oh right, well I hope you get it sorted.'

He nodded. 'Yesterday I called my wife for the first time in thirteen days and we've decided that we'll meet up in Singapore to give it another go. I guess sometimes we're too quick to judge the actions of others without fully letting ourselves take some part of the blame,' he finished with a bright, beaming smile.

'Wow, yeah I guess.' I felt the urge to clap and give him a cuddle. I was never good with people who overshared their problems, but he had such an honest face it didn't feel weird him pouring his heart out after we'd only just met.

'Thank you. So anyway, sorry I went off on a bit of a tangent there.' He sat up to face me. 'So my tattoo, now don't laugh, as it might seem a bit cheesy, but this is what you do when you're loved up – and probably doped up,' he whispered behind his hand. 'We both had it done at this tiny tattoo parlour on the other side of the island. It's the Thai symbol for marriage, love and eternity or something like that. I was just worried it meant "chow fried chicken", or something, but we asked a few honest Thai people afterwards, who confirmed the meaning. Phew.'

I laughed. 'Is it a common tattoo?'

'Not really, it's only inked on the skin of someone who's married, usually with the date of the wedding in there somewhere, but we missed that bit out.' He smiled at the memory.

I couldn't take my eyes off the thin lines and swirls; even though the ink had faded to a bluey-black it was identical to the one I had seen.

On Dillon.

'Are you sure you have to be married to get it?' I stuttered.

'Positive. The Thais take pride in their traditions, so there's no way they'd ink this on just anyone. It can be quite a sacred ceremony to tattoo a newly-married couple.' His voice faded out as I thought back to being lathered up in the shower when I saw this under Dillon's left hip. He had never explained the meaning behind it, but still allowed me to gently kiss the pale skin. Dillon was married. Not only was he a giant player, but he had conned me out of money *and* had a wife back home! That made me the other woman. I was the Stephanie to his Alex!

'Are you OK, Georgia?' Phil asked, pulling me back into the present.

I nodded sadly: 'I've just been a massive fool. This guy I really liked, well, thought I liked, had the same tattoo.'

He winced. 'Oh. I'm guessing he didn't tell you about its meaning? I'm sorry.'

'It's fine.' I brushed off the knot in my stomach. 'Let's just say there have been a *lot* of life lessons learnt on this trip.'

'I can imagine. That's what travel and backpacking is about, learning and adapting, so you're better prepared for the future.' I didn't know if he was giving me advice, or thinking about his own situation.

'Well, from now on I just want the simple life,' I sighed, lying back on the lounger.

'Nah, that's overrated.'

I must have dozed off as the next thing I heard was a cacophony of whispered giggles coming from my right. Lazily opening one eye I saw that Phil's sun lounger was empty. I groggily turned over to face the noise. A very pretty blonde girl's face was just inches away from mine. I could have counted the freckles on her small nose, she was so close.

'Argh!' I screamed, almost falling onto the sand.

She jumped back. 'Sorry! We were trying to work out if you were asleep or not. I wanted to try and pull the parasol over your legs as they are turning a very bright shade of pink,' she babbled in a husky Australian accent. There were two other girls behind her wrestling with a heavy parasol made of bamboo.

'Oh right. Thanks.' I quickly took a sip of my stale coffee, desperate to wash the slept-in taste from my dry mouth.

'I got really badly burned when I arrived here and I wouldn't wish that on my worst enemy,' the woman by my – admittedly pink – feet said, wincing at the memory.

'I'm Shelley, by the way,' the blonde freckled girl who'd given me such a start said. She had cropped blonde hair and a tattoo of a compass on her left wrist. 'This is Emily, we call her Little Em.' She pointed to the petite woman with the sunburn scare story. Both were wearing baggy, paisley-print cotton trousers that finished just above tanned ankles adorned with braided charms. Little Em nodded 'hiya!', revealing small plaits in her matted sun-lightened, blonde hair. She must have been four foot nothing, and I wondered if there was a Big Em around somewhere.

'And I'm Lou,' waved a pretty, black lady to my right, her almond-shaped eyes creasing as she grinned at me.

'I'm Georgia.'

'We noticed you last night, but you'd disappeared by the time we came to find you,' Lou said, finally fixing the parasol and coming to sit on Phil's empty sunbed.

'Yeah, I was pretty wiped out from travelling here.' Even seeing their smiling faces, I was still apprehensive, worried that they might be like the crazy collection of tour-goers I had just left.

'So, you here alone?' Little Em asked, propping her tiny frame up on her elbow.

'Yep, just me.'

'Wow! That's *so* brave. We were just saying, we'd love to have the guts to do this alone, but I guess fear gets to you – and we had wanted to travel together one day, anyway,' Lou smiled, playing with her jet-black braids.

'So you all already know each other?' I asked, feeling a sinking sense of déjà-vu.

'Well, me and Little Em have known each other for a while; we worked together back in Birmingham and then we met the lovely Shelley and her mate, Hannah, here a few days ago,' Lou said.

'Well, technically I'm now on my own, seeing as how Hannah has hooked up with Jake,' Shelley turned to me. 'He's out here working in a bar and they've been inseparable ever since. She's even moved into his dingy flat and she tells me she's going to extend her visa to get a job too.' Shelley rolled her eyes. 'The joy of holiday romances hey.' She let out a throaty laugh. 'I was worried about being on my own but these guys invited me over for drinks one night, and you know how it goes, a glass turns into two, which turns into a bottle and before you know it you've all become best friends for life.'

'Only because now we know all your secrets,' Little Em winked. 'Saying that, you know all mine too.' She started laughing.

I couldn't believe they had only just met each other, they seemed so at ease in each other's company. I had a sudden pang of homesickness for Marie, she would have loved to have been here.

'So Georgia. We're off to explore this waterfall that Dara's told us about. You fancy coming? Phil's having a siesta and Lord knows where Astrid has wandered off to,' Lou said.

'Probably doing some downward-facing dog move in her hut,' Little Em grinned. 'She's like the mum of our group, I'm sure you'll get to meet her later.' I thought back to the friendly busty woman who I briefly spoke to last night, and guessed she was Astrid. I had a hard time keeping up with all these new smiling faces and names, but as they were all being so welcoming – a far cry from the reception I'd received from Kit's tour group – I wanted to try my hardest to remember.

'Oh, yeah OK. If you don't mind,' I replied, forgetting about the ache in my muscles.

'You might want to put some sun cream on first,' Little Em pointed out. 'Ain't nothing sexy about peeling shins!'

CHAPTER 23

Genesis (n.) An origin, creation, or beginning

'Are you sure it's up here?' I clung onto the sides of the vehicle as my bum bounced high, landing with a crack on the split leather seat. Shelley, Little Em, Lou and I were navigating our way along narrow, dusty tracks in the back of a bright yellow and green tuk tuk. A bobbing Buddha head nodded manically and there was a repetitive clacking noise of wooden beads hanging from the rear-view mirror as we jolted over every bump in the road.

'Dara said it was past the large red house and then down a road like this, until we see a pale-blue church,' Little Em shouted.

My teeth chattered with every large stone and crater we thumped over. Suspension was obviously not such a big thing over here. 'Church! Church! Over there,' I pointed excitedly, happy to soon be getting out of this bone shaker. Our patient driver pulled up in a cloud of dust outside the church. We paid him, arranged for our return trip later, and grabbed the beach bag which Chef, a large jolly man with honest eyes and a shiny bald head, and Dara had kindly helped pack full of yummy picnic food and drink. Shelley wiped her glistening forehead with the back of her hand, scanning around the church.

'What a journey! That's gotta be one way to help with cellulite. Right, according to Dara's route, we turn right past the church and there should be a path we need to walk down,' she grinned.

We followed her lead, pushing our way through heavy ferns and stepping over cracked bamboo sticks.

'Wow, we're here,' Little Em exclaimed breathlessly, holding open thick leaves to peek inside. The '*here*' she was referring to was a natural waterfall – not a roaring, gushing one, but more of a gentle flow over large boulders into a pool that was the brightest green I'd ever seen. There wasn't a soul about. The lush trees provided shade until you looked to the right, where a ledge had naturally formed in the grassy rocks as a sort of sunbathing place. It was stunning.

After awkwardly climbing up to sit on the ledge, we quickly dug into the picnic. Passing round icy bottles of mineral water and small bottles of lager, we peeled the lids off tiny plastic boxes to reveal plump prawns and papaya salad, cold noodles in a zingy lime and chilli dressing with sweet-smelling coconut sticky rice and mango for dessert.

'This tastes amazing,' Shelley said through a mouthful of food, getting a fork in each box.

'Do you do much cooking back home, Georgia?' Little Em asked, peeling a prawn.

I thought back to the weekly food rota I'd had with Alex – every day with a set meal – including the Sunday roasts that I always stressed over getting just right and which he would always complain never tasted as good as when his mum made them.

'A little, yeah. I guess you could say I got stuck in a rut. I'd love to be able to whip up a meal like this, though. You?'

'Well, I don't want to beat my own drum, but I can make a mean scrambled egg,' she said proudly as I laughed.

Lou rolled her eyes. 'Do you want to tell her about the time you cooked a McCain's pizza still in its plastic wrapper or should I?' she teased.

Little Em scrunched up her tanned face. 'OK OK, that was one time! I have a more exotic palate nowadays anyway,' she grinned munching on a prawn.

Shelley leaned forward. 'You want to talk about exotic food? You should have seen the things they sell in Bangkok.' She turned to face me. 'Did you know you can try cockroaches and spiders on sticks over there?' She shook her head in disbelief.

'Yep, I actually tried one,' I said quietly.

'Eurgh, no way! You're braver than I am.'

I laughed. 'It wasn't really through choice, and definitely not something I want to experience again.'

'So how come you're out here? Doesn't have anything to do with a man, does it?' Shelley asked. I sighed deeply and nodded. 'How did I know!' Shelley slid her arm around me and squeezed. Considering that I'd only just met these girls, the simple movement felt surprisingly natural. 'Welcome to the club.' She raised her bottle high in the air and the sunlight caused the amber liquid to glint like a polished ruby.

I smiled weakly. 'What club's that?'

'Well, we haven't figured out a specific name, but new members are always welcome. I like to refer to it as "*those who have lost their way and been screwed over by men club*", but that title isn't too catchy,' Shelley chuckled.

'Yeah, and it's not just women, Phil's an honorary member too,' Lou said raising her hand.

'OK, OK, so the name needs a bit of working out, but basically, we've all been hurt in love and come out here to…I don't know – find ourselves. But not as cheesy as that,' Shelley quickly added. 'We won't be running off to find a new faith à la *Eat, Pray, Love*, unless Astrid talks you into it.'

'I thought I was the only one,' I said slowly, realising that I wasn't the first and would no doubt not be the last jilted bride who'd grabbed a backpack and gone in search of a new life.

Shelley tilted her head: 'Sorry, babe, but there's a whole bloody group of us.' She reminded me of Marie, who always filled a room with her personality.

'Me and Little Em came travelling because we've both had a few complicated breakups; it seems we always choose the wrong type of men. You know, those brooding, sexy, bad boys that your family hate, but you seem to fall under their spell?' Lou said. I nodded, imagining what my parents would have thought about Dillon.

'Well, we fall for that charm and then wonder why we're left sobbing in our pjs, stalking them on Facebook, having not showered for a week, when they inevitably leave. I guess for me personally, I needed to get away to prove to myself that I'm capable of getting around the world without the help of a man. I just wanted to improve my self-confidence and self-worth. Then, when I do meet the next guy, I'll have more to bring to the relationship *and* will be stronger if it doesn't work out.' Lou smiled and Little Em nodded in agreement.

'I can't talk about any of this with my friends back home. They didn't really understand my reasons for coming travelling and just kept telling me I was running away, that I should stay and work out my problems with my ex. But I knew that I wasn't happy. I was never a jealous person before, but I turned into this neurotic mess constantly checking up on him, convinced he was going to cheat again,' Little Em admitted. 'He promised me it was a mistake, that he'd changed. I guess even though I said I forgave him, I hadn't forgiven myself for sticking with a guy in such a toxic relationship.'

'Sometimes just letting it all out with strangers who won't judge you can help clear your mind. My mates are the same – all settled down and my social diary has gone from nights out to attending christenings, baby showers and weddings. I am *always* the single one who they try to match-make, convinced that their friend-of-a-friend is perfect for me. They think I must be sad and depressed living a life on my own, but truthfully, I was so hurt in my previous relationship, I didn't want to let anyone else in. I want to see the world and to find out who *I am* before I meet someone who I want to share my life with. You only get one chance on this crazy planet, so I think you might as well make sure you're happy rather than putting up with someone just because it's easier,' Shelley smiled.

It felt so cathartic sitting around with complete strangers, discussing everybody's failed love lives. Opening up to people who I didn't know and who I might never see again felt so liberating; it was as if I could be whoever I wanted to be.

'Right, enough of this deep chat. Who fancies a dip?' Shelley asked, stretching.

'Good idea. If I sit here cooking any longer I'll melt into this rock,' Lou said, rubbing her bum.

'Now that would be a tourist attraction,' Little Em teased.

We stood up, stripped off to our bikinis and took a few steps to the edge. The platform provided the perfect diving spot. I grinned at them and counted to three before we all instinctively jumped forward into the cold, crisp water, causing a large splash, leaving peaceful ripples to settle between us.

'Jeeeeezus, it's freezing!' Little Em spluttered.

'I nearly lost my bikini top. Doesn't take much for these bad boys to escape,' Lou laughed, checking her boobs had stayed hidden away.

'Girls, you all need to lie back, it's amazing,' Shelley shouted, changing her stroke to a starfish shape. The canopy of trees over the small lake formed a sort of heart shape, allowing beams of sunlight to shard around us. 'Nothing like any man could make,' she said in awe.

'Wow. It's just incredible,' I breathed. I felt weightless, gently letting the water run between my splayed-out fingers, unable to hide the big grin on my face as I listened to the constant churning of water falling beside us. We swam gently over to the waterfall and ducked through the glittering water curtain to the shelter of the dripping rock below. Hidden from the world we found a small protruding rock to sit on.

'Right, new girl, your turn.' Shelley winked before flicking back her hair, spraying droplets of clear water into the rainbow light of the waterfall and smiled.

So, I filled them in on all that had happened to me, starting from my non-wedding and the list in Turkey. We talked for so long my fingertips pruned up.

'So, this Dillon geezer, he just totally screwed with you?' Shelley gasped. 'He's such a prick there should be a species of cactus named after him!'

'What a slimeball. We could totally go and reap revenge you know.' Lou rubbed her hands together gleefully. I shook my head: what good would that do to my already-bruised ego?

'No, the '*Lost Souls Who Wander Club*' doesn't condone violence. We're here to forgive and move on, *not* get banged up for teaching useless men a lesson,' Little Em said. 'Nah, that name doesn't work either,' she frowned. We paused, trying to think of a catchier name.

'I know! "*Travelling Towards A Better Future*" Lou suggested, before being comedy-booed by everyone. 'Yeah, it wasn't my best idea.' '*Broken Backpackers*', '*Heartbroken Hippies*' and '*Wanderlust Warriors*' were all also vetoed.

'What about '*The Lonely Hearts Travel Club*?' I said quietly, not wanting to be laughed at and kicked out of this new fun group. Silence settled as they thought about my suggestion.

'Bloody perfect,' Shelley cried and raised her hand in the air as if making a toast: 'To Georgia! To us! To the Lonely Hearts Travel Club!'

CHAPTER 24

Admonition (n.) Counsel, advice or caution

'Hello, deary. Goodness that sun is awfully hot.' The older woman I'd seen giving tarot card readings the other night had wandered over to my sun lounger. I was watching Dara talking animatedly to some fishermen who had moored on the beach; I'd been trying to see if I could spot shaggy-haired Wayne and his crew.

The many rings on each of her chubby fingers glinted in the sunlight as she reached into her bag for a bottle of water. She had an unexpectedly posh, clipped accent. 'We didn't get to properly introduce ourselves the other night. I have overheard that your name is Georgia? Mine is Astrid. Nice to meet you.' She offered a clammy hand with a firm grip.

'Hi, nice to meet you too.'

Her pale blue eyes were warm and creased with laughter lines. 'So what brings you to this neck of the woods?'

'Well, I came here on a whim, actually. I was travelling in Thailand with a tour group, but it wasn't what I'd expected, so I cut loose and ended up here.' Saying those words felt like someone else was speaking, someone braver, someone more independent and more courageous than Georgia Green.

'I've been coming back here for the past fifteen years. Wonderful, wonderful place. How did you find out about it? Most of us like to keep this place hidden, stops it getting too touristy, you know?'

'Well actually, it was the lady in the travel agent's where I booked my trip. Trisha practically insisted I come here.' I still thought it was odd that she'd reserved a hut here for me, I needed to remember to thank her.

'Trisha? From Manchester? Making Memories?' I nodded. 'Heavens above. What a small world. What an angel that woman is. She was the one who told me about this gem all those years ago; we were introduced by a friend of a friend and have been great chums ever since. How is she?' she asked, taking a large slurp, dribbling water from her lower lip onto her oversized embroidered beach dress.

'Yep, fine I think.' I thought back to the chaotic mess of her beautiful shop.

'Oh well, say "hello" from me. Such a wonderful woman, so strong – especially after her husband passed. Awful news about her business though.'

I looked at her kind eyes. 'What do you mean?'

'Well, she isn't getting any younger and that job takes up so much of her energy. I have tried to persuade her to sell it many a time, but she's adamant that it needs to go to the right person, who will love it as much as she does. She has mentioned some distant family member a few times who's set to take it over, but by all accounts he is off jet-setting too. Must be something in their genes.' The soft scrawls of Stevie's handwriting flooded my mind. I wondered what he was up to now. Where in the world was he?

'Hopefully she'll find someone to help.'

Astrid put her water bottle back in her colourful beach bag. 'Let's hope. Anyway, as I was saying, you can really find yourself here, you know.'

'Is that what you've done?'

'Heavens, no. I'm still learning. But that's the essence of travel, my dear. It makes you see the world – not just exotic beaches and remote tribal villages – but you see yourself and your world back home in a way you didn't view it before. It's like someone has turned all the lights on when you didn't realise they were switched off.'

I lay back on the sun lounger. 'I can't even think about going home just yet.' After being away from the tour group for just a few days I already felt like a weight I didn't realise I was carrying had lifted.

'You're a wandering nomad just like us now,' Astrid chuckled. 'Only other backpackers will understand what it's like to leave home to follow your dreams. Those pals back home will nod along, listening to your travel tales, but for them it's just words and pretty pictures. For you, everything has changed and you look around feeling like an alien in the most foreign place you have visited: home. That's why it's called a travel bug – you literally get bitten with this desire inside you to keep moving and keep exploring, as the life you had back home isn't enough any more and may not ever be enough again.' She shifted in her seat and hoisted up her bikini top holding her very large breasts. 'Of course, you get some who return seamlessly to their lives. Their memories fade as fast as their tans, and the monotony and safety of a routine welcomes them back once more. But for others, they share the intensity of the trip, unless you change when you return and find something that will make you as happy as you would be globetrotting.'

'It's going to have to be something pretty awesome to compete with this paradise.' I swept my hand around the secluded, perfect beach.

'You'll be fine, I'm sure,' she smiled. 'If you will excuse me, I'm off for a quick dip. Was a pleasure talking to you.

Oh, and you must come to my moon-chanting session tomorrow evening.'

'A what, now?'

'It's where we ask the heavenly moon and stars for their advice. Very therapeutic and good for stretching those vocal cords.' She winked. Inching herself off the wooden bench, Astrid strode out from under the shade towards the ocean, stripping off her dress and tossing it onto the sand as she moved. I was about to head back to my hut when Shelley caught up with me.

'Hello, you,' I smiled at her warmly.

'OM freaking G, I've just bumped into Phil, he told me about Dillon being married.' Shelley's eyes were as wide as a parasol in shock. I nodded, confirming it all. 'Bastard. How're you feeling?'

I sighed: 'Tired. Sad. Angry. Embarrassed.'

She rubbed my arm: 'Yep, well I'd feel exactly the same, don't worry. So, I've got an idea that will hopefully cheer you up.'

'Have you got a time machine hidden in your beach bag?' I laughed.

'No, but you have.'

She's lost the plot. I stared at her blankly.

'That travel list that you told us about? We can go back in time to when you wrote it and none of this bad stuff had happened. It'll be like you're starting your travel adventure from fresh, but this time we're going to actually get things ticked off!'

I shook my head. 'Now that I'm here maybe I should just ditch it. It was just a silly thing that my best friend Marie suggested I write.' I had been so busy trying to survive the tour I'd barely given the list a second thought. I guess I didn't want to be reminded what a failure I was.

'But you still have it, right? That must mean somewhere, subconsciously, you don't think it's a ridiculous idea.' She tapped my forehead. 'You never know, this could be fun.'

I went inside my hut, pulled out the creased sheet of paper and showed it to Shelley, who chewed her lip as I explained my failures.

Go skinny dipping in the moonlit ocean – Nope.

Dance all night under the stars – Nope.

Taste incredible exotic food – Done! You can't get more exotic than cockroaches.

Ride an elephant – Nope.

Visit historic temples – Nope.

Explore new beliefs – Nope.

Climb a mountain – Nope.

Make friends with different nationalities – Nope.

Listen to the advice of a wise soul – Nope.

Do something wild – Nipple piercing was wild but I've left it in only because I'm too scared to touch it in case I do myself some proper damage.

'That tour you were part of – you said it was awful?' Shelley asked, looking at the list.

'Like you cannot believe. I ate cockroaches, jumped through a ring of fire and nearly drowned going scuba diving, not to mention the drama within the group that was going on.'

She chewed her bottom lip. 'And would you have done these things otherwise?'

'No, of course not.'

'Were you forced to do these things?'

I shook my head slowly. 'Well… No.'

'So you could say you chose to do them. I know peer pressure can suck but in certain situations it makes you push yourself outside your comfort zone,' she said with a sly smile. 'Plus, what great stories they make when you go back home. But don't you realise, you've experienced more than just what's written here? And, your trip isn't over yet.'

I shrugged. 'I guess.'

'Oh and you can tick off "Make friends with different nationalities".' She let out a throaty laugh, pulling me into a hug. And with that we headed off arm-in-arm to the main street to hail a tuk tuk to tick off 'Visit temples' from my list.

On the other side of the island was a small, golden Buddhist temple. Mother of pearl decorated the wat doors, black and gold lacquer lined ornate windows and its entrance was surrounded with frangipani trees. It was jaw-droppingly beautiful. We left our flip-flops at the bottom of the stone steps before heading inside.

'Wow,' I breathed.

'Pretty awesome, right?' Shelley said in hushed tones.

Before us sat an enormous Buddha, which dazzled, even in the dim light. Flowers, candles and smaller decorations lay at his feet, and two older Westerners sat cross-legged in silent meditation on the deep, red carpet. The sense of calm and peace was overwhelming; I felt my eyes prick with tears.

'You OK?' Shelley murmured, stroking the small of my back.

'This is beautiful,' I whispered getting a grip on my emotions. I wouldn't call myself religious, but entering this space of tranquillity was instantly calming. I watched Shelley gently stoop down to light a candle and found myself thinking about my journey here. If you'd have said to me six months ago that I wouldn't be getting married and instead be contemplating life in the middle of a serene Buddhist temple on a remote Thai island I'd have told you to visit the doctor for whatever brain injury you must have suffered. It felt like I was in a dream, woken from the nightmare after what Alex did and the experiences of Kit's tour to find myself in a strangely reassuring, comfortable new existence.

I was so utterly grateful to Trisha for letting me into the secret of the Blue Butterfly, for giving me the confidence to be bold and move away from what was bringing me down. Thinking about Trisha, Stevie's scrawls popped into my head. Was it madness to be daydreaming about a man I'd never met? Especially after my experiences with Alex and then Dillon. The image I'd built up in my head about him meant he ticked every box of what I wanted in a future boyfriend. Someone who isn't afraid to take risks and have adventures, a man who cares about his family, who is full of ambition and motivation to really squeeze every last drop out of life by exploring this fascinating planet. What was I doing? A man like that didn't exist. This Stevie could be married with two kids and a total bore, for all I knew. You don't really believe that though, a voice in my head piped up.

Shelley came over, breaking my thoughts. 'You ready to go, hun?' I nodded. We padded around the room, taking it all in, before heading back out into the warm sunshine. I smiled, watching Shelley nod hello to a handful of other backpackers walking about, offering to take a photo for a couple and buying us both a bottle of water. She seemed like the type of girl who made friends with strangers on buses or in the queue for the ladies' loo on nights out. I was really enjoying hanging out with her, even the few silences felt comfortable.

'So, are you missing home at all?' I asked her.

She gulped down her drink and shook her head laughing. 'No, well obviously family and friends but, other than that, I'm so happy to be here. My parents have never really travelled. We grew up in a small town three hours' drive from Sydney and that's where they've stayed their entire lives. When I said I was going backpacking my mum almost had a heart attack!' I smiled thinking of the similar reaction my mum had had. 'The thing is I never felt like I belonged back home. I moved to the big city for university and started to make my life there but, after my last relationship, I realised I needed to do more and see more. It's stupid but I find comfort in the sounds of foreign languages, and I've got a good sense of direction but I love getting lost!' She laughed. 'All the guys I've been with have just slowed me down. The ones back home never wanted to leave our town, all the guys I met in Sydney just wanted to waste their money partying. I just knew I wouldn't find the one downing shots in my local bar, as much as my parents hoped I would.'

She stopped talking when in the beautifully-kept courtyard we spotted two monks, dressed in bright-orange loose robes with neatly shaved heads, sat at separate marble tables in the shade. They looked like they were waiting for someone. Shelley nudged me towards them: 'Enough about me. Go talk to them.'

'What? No!'

'It's fine. We're just in time for their monk chat session that they do to encourage foreigners to understand how they live their lives. It's an opportunity to ask them whatever you want. Don't worry, women are welcome.'

'Monk chat? Whatever I want?' I thought back to my list – 'Listen to the advice of a wise soul.' How could I miss this? Shelley confidently sat opposite one monk, so I pulled out the plastic chair facing the other.

'Hello.'

'*Sawasdee Krab*,' he said, dipping his head with his hands in a prayer movement. His voice was deep and soothing.

'My name's Georgia and my friend said we were able to talk with you?' He smiled and nodded.

'OK, well that's very nice of you.'

He smiled and nodded. I panicked: what if he didn't understand me?

'Do *you* speeeeeak English?'

He smiled and nodded. Sheesh. Tough crowd.

'So…erm…this is a lovely temple you have here.' Come on, Georgia! That's almost as bad as talking about the weather. 'Very nice…carvings…' I trailed off. My mind went blank. I was sitting opposite an enlightened soul, a man who had given his life to this peaceful religion dedicated to helping others and I couldn't think of one clever thing to say. I glanced at Shelley, who was waving her hands animatedly explaining whatever it was she was talking about to her monk. OK, Georgia. You can do this. What do you want to know?

I took a deep breath. 'Will I ever find true love?'

He smiled, but didn't nod. Instead, he clasped his hands in front of him and opened his mouth slowly. I edged forward to catch these words of wisdom. My bum was hanging off the edge of the plastic chair in anticipation of the eternal truths I was about to have bestowed upon me.

'Clear your mind. You already have the answer.'

Wait, what? He smiled and nodded.

Then as I thought he was about to clarify what he meant, he slowly lifted himself up from his chair, bowed, and glided off – without a backward glance, or anything.

Shelley had also been left stranded, but was grinning from ear to ear. 'Wow. That was insane.'

'It was definitely something.'

'What a cool guy.' Shelley shook her head in astonishment; I, on the other hand, was left more confused than when we had arrived.

CHAPTER 25

Sidereal (adj.) Determined by or from the stars

'Tonight we'll be embracing the moon in a joyful meditative chanting session.' Our group was standing in a circle with sand between our toes in the near darkness. Little Em and Lou sniggered as Astrid threw them an irritated look.

'I understand not all of you will have taken part in such a session before, but you need to open your hearts and minds in order to reach nirvana. Right – let's all hold hands and take deep breaths in…and out.'

I was standing between Phil, who actually looked interested in the night's unusual event, and Shelley, who had her eyes shut and was gently swaying. I couldn't work out if she was taking the piss, or getting ready to give herself up to the power of the moon.

'OK. Now, I need you to fully relax and concentrate on opening your chakras.'

'Our what?' Lou called out, horrified.

'Chakras, dear. They're energy points inside you and for this to work they need to be fully open.'

'How the hell do I open something I didn't even know I had?'

Astrid sighed. This clearly wasn't going to plan: 'Just try and relax your body and think pure thoughts.' That set the two off giggling again.

'I don't think she's capable of pure thoughts,' Little Em piped up then quickly hid her grin when Astrid glared at her.

'I will now ask Dara to play some music I prepared for this evening. As the music starts, I want you all to close your eyes and move gently to the beat.'

As a riff of calming romantic music started I tuned out, thinking back to the conversation I'd had with Astrid, about Trisha and her travel agency. I just couldn't put this mysterious postcard sender 'Stevie' out of my mind. I'd told Phil, Lou and Little Em about him earlier over a very complicated card game they'd tried to teach me.

'So, this Stevie?' Phil asked, as Lou shuffled the deck of cards.

I straightened up, worried that I'd been thinking aloud: 'Yes?'

'What are you going to do about him?' Lou butted in impatiently. I let out a little laugh, willing them to deal. 'Well, you need to do something,' she persisted.

'Do? What is there to do? I don't even know him, just saw a cute but blurry photo, read some postcards and that's it. There is no me and Stevie,' I laughed.

'Yeah, but there could be.' Phil tilted his head, smiling. 'We just need to help with a plan.'

'Ooh, yes, a plan,' Lou gleefully rubbed her hands.

'No. No plan. No help. Seriously, guys – I don't even know his last name, where he lives. He could be married with kids for all I know.'

'Oh yeah cause someone settled down would really be off volunteering in Cambodia for weeks on end?' Lou said, giving me a look. To be fair, she had a point.

'Ah, he sounds wonderful,' Little Em said, clutching her heart.

'Guys, come on, this is ridiculous. This is like something that happens in a film: a girl sees these mysterious

postcards and falls in love, even though they've never met.'
I scoffed at the stupidity of it, noticing Little Em huff out
of the corner of my eye. I bet she was already working out
who would play her in the movie. 'But life isn't like the
movies, it's never going to happen.'

'Well, you thought it would never happen with you and
Dillon,' Lou teased, and Little Em's eyes flashed. I cringed
at the sound of his name, I still felt so stupid about the
whole Dillon thing. It was as if the Dillon I fell so lustfully
for was a figment of my imagination. I had been so naïve
and gullible, again.

'Yes, and look how that ended up. Honestly, hot guys
don't choose girls like me, especially ones that appear to
have a curse when it comes to love.'

'Stop putting yourself down. You're gorgeous. Yeah, so
your track record ain't brilliant but I bet if you tracked this
Stevie down – ask Trisha or put a shout-out on Facebook
or something – you never know where it might lead,' Phil
said, dealing out the cards, as Lou nodded. 'Stranger things
have happened.'

I shook my head, laughing at the ridiculousness of
actually getting in touch with him. I knew that I could try
and track him down but I wanted him to stay as a figment of
my imagination, this perfect man I'd created in my mind.

'Hmm. I'll think about it,' I said, wanting to change
the conversation, turning over my cards to reveal a row of
hearts beaming up at me.

The calming music stopped, bringing me back into the
present. Astrid stepped into the circle and began wafting
freshly lit incense around with her eyes closed, as she
performed some sort of interpretive dance to the clingy-
clangy beat.

'Oh ee, oh ee, oh ee,' she chanted in a warbling voice
that caused me to stifle a laugh. 'Let the moon enter all

of our hearts and fill us with its ancient power, helping to lift us out of the darkness and into the future, filled with warmth and happiness.'

The giggling stopped and the atmosphere changed from one of awkwardness and mockery to – well, we weren't entirely on board with the moon worship, but we definitely all wanted a future filled with warmth and happiness.

'Please, special moon, gift us with your powers and let us all move into the new phase with your blessing. Aid those who need specific care and show others who are ready and willing to let you, and the magic of love, back into their world.' She paused. 'Now, I would like to invite you all to spend a few minutes thinking about what it is you're asking the moon gods and goddesses for.'

Silence descended again and my mind whirred: what did I want to ask for from this yellow ball that I took for granted every day of my life? Maybe I should apologise for ignoring it for all these years. I settled on: 'Please give me the strength to find what I'm looking for', which I thought wasn't half bad. The music continued to roll past as Astrid began bowing in adoration to the inky sky. My hands were getting clammy. The rest of the group appeared to be focused on their own thoughts. I was surprised that Shelley, who I'd pegged for a bit of a cynic, seemed to be buying this hippy dippy event. The song died down and Astrid was back on her feet, smiling serenely.

'OK. You can now unclasp your hands and join me in a short dance to say "thank you" for what we have witnessed tonight.' Astrid then reverted to her imaginatively expressive dance routine and encouraged everyone to join in.

As candles flickered around the small circle, people hopped, kicked and flailed around without a worry in the world, laughing with each other, not caring how idiotic we all must have looked to any newcomers on the beach. After a couple of minutes and some energetic Spice Girl high kicks, Astrid called everyone back into a circle.

'Thank you all for joining me this evening. I appreciate your respect and understanding at such an important ceremony.' Her cheeks were flushed and her eyes sparkling.

'Now, let's go get a drink. I'm gasping!' Lou called out as everyone laughed, padding back to the bar.

Shelley was by my side within seconds, linking my arm: 'So, what did you think about that?'

'Well, I was pretty sceptical to start with. It's not really my sort of thing, but I don't know, I do feel a bit different,' I said truthfully. I felt calmer and lighter, but I'd put that down to some pretty energetic dance moves.

'Me too!' she exclaimed. 'Don't tell Astrid though, I don't want her thinking we're a pair of converts.' She threw back her head and let out a signature husky laugh: 'Hey. I just thought – you can tick another thing off your list, "Explore new beliefs".'

I smiled: 'Yeah, I guess I can.'

'Plus, at the temple you listened to the advice of a monk, so that can get a big fat tick too.' She seemed more into completing my list than I was.

'Yeah. Although I'm not too sure how reliable that advice was. It didn't feel very personal.'

She shrugged. 'Well, we'll see, I guess.' The others had trailed off to the bar, but Shelley held me back in the centre of the candle-lit circle. 'There's another to-do thing that you can scrub off your list tonight.'

'What's that?'

She nodded her head towards the jet-black waves lapping behind us. I realised which one Shelley meant: 'Go skinny dipping in the moonlit ocean.'

'Oh no!'

'Oh yes!'

So, to end one of the most random days of my life, and with as much gusto as I could muster, I stripped off and ran screaming into the dark waters, feeling exhilarated and totally alive. And more than a little cold. Shelley called for the others to join us and before I knew it, my eyes were trying to focus on anything other than pert white bums, dangly willies and floating mammaries. I splashed around, looking up at the net of stars, fully enjoying the weightlessness and risqué feeling of swimming with my bits out. I should be making wedding memory scrapbooks and getting the leaking shower fixed, not gallivanting in the nude on the other side of the world with people who, technically, should never have crossed my path. Now these strangers had come into my life I didn't know what I would do without them.

CHAPTER 26

Atiose (adj.) Being at leisure

'Georgia!' Shelley called over to me. 'Come and meet the new guests. They're from England too.'

I was lazily walking back from a morning meditation class that Astrid had organised with some of the locals from the next village. Since the moon chanting event a few days ago, I'd been more open to getting involved in other weird and wonderful holistic therapies that Astrid organised on the island. Under large drooping palm trees I'd sat cross-legged ignoring the pins and needles biting at my ankles and tried to clear my mind. According to that mysterious monk it was the thing I needed to do to find my path to true love. Although, I kept cheating and peeking through half-closed eyes, catching sight of Dara and Chef, sat side by side, their tanned faces relaxed into blissed-out smiles. Instead of focusing on my own heartbeat and regulated breathing, I wondered if they were together as from their body language you could tell there was definitely something going on between them.

As soon as the class finished Dara had leapt up as if she'd forgotten something urgent she needed to do. Chef's gaze had followed her shadows on the sand as she disappeared back to the Blue Butterfly huts. He placed his palms together and bowed at the group before leaving in the opposite direction, shooting wistful glances over his shoulder in the direction that Dara had gone.

Astrid had gone straight for a dip in the ocean, so I had slowly worked my way along the shore back to the huts, feeling serene and floaty. Shelley's cries had pulled me from the daydream I was having where I'd started to receive these mysterious postcards to my hut. Every day a new dog-eared card would turn up from a far-flung destination, with a simple message scrawled on the back: 'Come find me, S.' I blamed Little Em and her over-active imagination for this.

'So guys, I'd like you to meet Georgia. She is the bravest one of us all, travelling here by herself and eating cockroaches!' Shelley grimaced before half pulling me onto a large cushion amongst the group.

'Oh, hi.' I blushed as my bum slapped the fabric. On the cushions opposite were two guys I hadn't seen before. One had short spiky bleach-blond hair and bulging veins on his extremely muscular arms and the other had messy dark brown curls and hazelnut-coloured eyes.

'Hey, how you doing?' The brown-haired one said nodding. 'I'm Ben, and this is Jimmy.'

Jimmy raised his beer bottle at me in a salute. 'All right!' He flashed a cheeky schoolboy grin.

Shelley leaned closer to me. 'They've just arrived and are staying for a few days.' She raised her eyebrows as if this information should mean something to me.

'Oh great, well, erm, welcome,' I said, getting up to leave. I wanted to walk into the small village nearby to pick up some bits and bobs – strangely I had a sudden urge to send some postcards home as well as finally get my laundry done.

Shelley's hand grabbed my arm and pulled me back down. 'So, Ben was just telling us all about his job, it sounds really interesting.' She raised her eyebrows at me, and seemed to be mouthing something. Her neck was twitching uncomfortably, flicking over to her right.

'Oh,' I said slowly, trying to catch what she was telepathically trying to tell me.

'Ben, why don't you tell Georgia what it is you do? I'm sure she would love to know more.' Shelley now had his tanned arm and was gently pulling him off his cushion to sit next to me on mine. As soon as his bum had left the ground she plopped herself down next to Jimmy.

Ben awkwardly sat down by me. 'This seat's not taken, is it?'

I smiled, shaking my head. What was Shelley like?!

'Ah great.' He cleared his throat. 'Do you really want to talk about my job?'

What I wanted was to find a launderette to wash my stinking clothes and buy a pen so I could send my postcards, but not wanting to hurt his feelings and trying to be a good wing woman to Shelley I said: 'Um, sure. What is it you do?'

'I work for Water Care. It's a charity all about providing the world with cleaner, safer water.' He paused, as if judging by my expression whether he should carry on. 'I was just telling the others about the things that I do in my job. Every so often we get sent out to check on new projects with wells in villages, see everything is up to scratch, listen to any concerns from the families etcetera.'

'Wow, that must be so rewarding.' That was a pretty cool job, to be honest.

'Yeah, it's fantastic. Although this trip is slightly bittersweet because I've just handed in my notice.' He ran his hand through his dark brown waves, a frown knitting his brow. 'Once I get back I'm going to be moving up north to start a new job actually.'

'Oh, you don't sound too keen?'

He scrunched up his nose. 'Well, you know, it's not my dream job. I absolutely love what I do now, but I kind of owe my new boss. There might still be travel involved so I'm sure it'll be OK. I'm just not that good at staying put for too long,' he laughed. 'I currently rent a place in East London but it'll be cool to get a taste of northern life.'

'Whereabouts up north are you heading to?'

He closed his eyes, thinking for a second. 'Manchester.'

'That's where I live! Well lived. Well –' I stopped myself. Where did I call home now?

'No way,' he smiled. 'Well then, if we happen to cross paths again I'll be reserving you as my unofficial tour guide.'

'You're on,' I nodded. As he was talking I had this strange feeling of déjà-vu. His welcoming face, with freckles on his nose and his broad smile, looked so familiar. He was super cute too. 'So have you been working on this island?'

He shook his head. 'No, not in Thailand, I just flew over here to meet Jimmy. He's been out working in Australia for the past year, so we thought we'd meet halfway before jetting back home together. He's actually moving up north with me too. So, you'll have two of us on the unofficial Georgia tour of Manchustarrrr,' His accent was appalling, but kind of cute too.

I shook my head. 'Ha ha! What was that!'

He kicked his heel into the sand and blushed slightly. 'Yeah, accents aren't really my strong point. So when did you get here?'

It had only been a few weeks but it seemed like a lifetime ago that I was waving a sad goodbye to my parents back at the airport. So much had happened, I felt like a different girl from the one boarding that first flight.

I gave him the short version of Kit's tour from hell and my journey over to Koh Lanta. He listened intently; his dark eyes were inky brown pools that never left my face as I talked. I swear I'd met him before, although I'm sure I would have remembered as he was pretty fit. Not in an obvious way like Dillon was, but in a way that you could imagine him growing old and keeping his good looks, a natural masculine sexiness. Maybe he looked like someone famous – a cross between that guy who sings in Maroon 5 and the one who was in that *Fifty Shades of Grey* film perhaps. Yep that must be it.

'All right, Benny Boy?!' Jimmy hollered over, interrupting our chat. 'When you've stopped chatting that poor girl's ear off, we've all decided that we're going to grab some lunch. You in?'

Ben rolled his eyes at his mate before looking at me. 'You hungry, Georgia?'

I was peckish and as much as I was enjoying our chat I did need to get some chores done, plus I could feel my barriers were up just talking to another cute guy. As gorgeous as Ben was, there was no way I was going to let this go any further than friendly small talk.

'Oh, well actually…' I started then stopped, spotting Shelley flashing me her best puppy dog eyes. I slowly nodded my head. 'Yep, count me in.' The postcards and laundry would have to wait.

The four of us walked into town. The word "town" was probably a bit grand for the dusty strip of road that contained one shop selling mostly beach clothes and flip-flops, a launderette, a closed down travel agency and a minimart with stacks of fresh fruit and vegetables piled high on wooden tables. We'd followed a shortcut that Dara had explained to us and thankfully saved so much time. Shelley and Jimmy lagged at the back, her giggling at nearly everything he said meaning I was up front trying to figure out our way with Ben at my side. Food was the main topic of our easy-going conversation.

'You must have been away from home for ages? Do you never get homesick?' I asked, watching my step on some rocks.

'Nah, not that much any more. Used to when I first started my job but the strange thing is it's usually the small everyday things that you miss the most, apart from family and friends obviously,' he grinned.

'Oh yeah, like what?'

'Well, let me tell you about the nights I've been lying under some tarpaulin in the middle of nowhere dreaming about stuffing my face with battered cod and fat chippy chips,' he said laughing. 'I swear, food's the number one thing you crave no matter where you are in the world. For example, I spent some time in China. You could get pretty much anything and everything you wanted to eat over there but still I'd be hankering for a scotch egg or a slice of chocolate fudge cake that my mum used to make when I was a kid.'

'I'm so glad I'm not the only one! I normally don't even like prawn cocktail crisps but since being here I just want to buy a multi-pack and gorge myself on the things.'

'I get it, just be careful when you do end up going back home that you don't do what I normally do, by eating so much of what I've missed that I can never eat it again.' He smiled. He had such a genuine smile, one that made his eyes crinkle and light up. 'God, all this talk about food's making me hungry.'

I looked down at the instructions Dara had given us. 'Well, judging by these we just need to walk past the shops and further down the road on our left should be the restaurant.'

'Perfect.'

I was expecting to be greeted with amazing spicy smells hanging on the warm breeze tickling my nostrils, but I couldn't smell anything at all. What if it was going to be a restaurant like the one Dillon took me to? My stomach clenched at the memory.

'Ah man, whose idea was this?' Jimmy grumbled, holding his head in his hands.

'What's wrong?' I asked. Shelley pointed to the sign next to the door of the restaurant that Jimmy had been blocking with his tree-trunk thighs. Koh Lanta Cooking Course. No wonder I couldn't smell anything cooking, we were the ones making it!

'I promised my mum I'd never go near an oven after nearly blowing up my school in Home Ec classes.' Jimmy bit his bottom lip. 'I'm the worst chef you're ever gonna meet, ain't that right, Ben?'

'Yup. Sorry ladies, but if you're after burnt water then Jimmy here's your man.' Jimmy huffed then nodded his head in agreement with Ben.

'I didn't know we were gonna be cooking,' Jimmy said, rereading the sign. Shelley gave me a knowing nod. She had clearly known all along what we were going to be doing.

'Ah come on, my cooking skills are non-existent too, this will be fun! We can both learn how to cook a decent meal without killing ourselves,' Shelley said. Jimmy immediately changed his face once he realised that she was excited to get involved.

'Yeah, I guess I can't get any worse.'

Lila, our teacher, was one of the happiest women I'd ever met and she welcomed us like we'd known each other for years. She passed out bright red aprons and asked us to sit cross-legged on the floor around a low wooden table as she showed us the ingredients. 'OK, I hope you're hungry! So today we'll be cooking Thai green curry. Yummy! It's one of my favourite meals and it will make you master of the kitchen in front of all your friends, even girlfriends.' She winked, looking at the four of us. One guy for one girl. I felt myself blushing.

'OK, so chefs, are you ready?' She cried out like John Fashanu off *Gladiators*. Our response wasn't good enough for her so she bellowed, 'I said, chefs are *you* readyyyyyy?'

'Yes, Chef!' we called back in unison.

'Well, what are you waiting for, follow me!' She chuckled and walked over to the perfectly kitted-out kitchen set up for small groups. I was paired up with Ben, and didn't complain. He seemed to be confident of his kitchen skills, chopping an onion with super-speedy, chefy knife technique. Jimmy on the other hand was in danger of losing a fingertip the way he was hacking at it.

'Careful!' Shelley cried, wiping the tears from her eyes. 'I've no idea where the hospital is on this island!'

'Sorry, my fingers weren't made for this sort of thing,' Jimmy said, waving his sharp knife in the air.

'OK, maybe the ladies could team up instead?' Lila said, nervously looking at Jimmy. He was nearly double the size of her.

'It's fine, I'll do the chopping,' Shelley said quickly, not wanting to be separated from Jimmy.

'OK,' Lila said slowly, releasing a sigh of relief when Shelley took the knife from Jimmy and established control of the partnership. 'Now guys, when it comes to adding flavour to your dishes remember….' She wagged a chubby finger in the air. 'Spicy's sexy!'

'I doubt the morning after eating a vindaloo she'd be saying that,' Ben whispered to me, making me laugh.

'So, come on guys, spice it up! Let's get spicy in here!' She then danced around the kitchen to her own beat adding a dash of red sauce and a sprinkle of black herbs to our simmering pans.

'I'm not the best when it comes to spicy food,' I admitted to Ben.

'Don't worry, if it tastes rank then I'll grab us something from the minimarket on our way back.'

'OK. So now you should have something that looks thick and creamy bubbling away in front of you?' Lila called out, rearranging her apron. I peered down at mine and Ben's pan. Something was bubbling away but it looked more grey than creamy.

'Have we missed a step out or something?' He shrugged, glancing down at the recipe instructions Lila had told us to follow.

'Oh no.'

'What?'

Ben couldn't keep a straight face. 'Yep, I don't think we'll be eating this.'

'Why? What's happened?' I tried to move past him to look at the recipe, a shiver passing through me at being so close to him in this steamy room.

'Err, you know when I said we needed 400ml of fish sauce and two teaspoons of coconut milk?' I nodded. 'Well, there was a smudge on the paper. We actually needed it the other way round. This is more Thai grey fish curry.' He winced.

'Oh no! I'm so sorry!'

'Hey, don't apologise, it's my fault for not reading it properly. I know, such a man thing to do. I get that from my dad, refusing to follow the rules. Don't even get me started on putting up Ikea flat pack furniture.' He laughed, poking the boiling mess with a wooden spoon as if it was an unexploded bomb.

'So, guys, how's it going?' Lila had reappeared. Her cheerful grinning face changed to confusion and revulsion on spotting our creation. 'Oh.'

'Yeah, it's my fault I–'

'I screwed up,' Ben jumped in, sticking up for me.

'Oh, Ben! I was so sure you were going to get it spot on. You were going to be my star couple,' Lila said disappointedly. She walked over to Shelley and Jimmy's cooking area and peered into their pan. 'Wow. It looks like star couple goes to these two! It looks great, guys!'

I glanced at Ben and mouthed 'thank you' to him; he just shrugged bashfully and headed to see what all the fuss was about. Lila was spooning Shelley and Jimmy's dish onto a bed of soft rice, oohing and ahhing as she did. I had to admit it looked exactly like the photo we'd been shown at the start.

'Now, this is how you make Thai green curry! It tastes incredible! Excellent work, team.'

Jimmy was grinning proudly before winding Ben up that he had kicked his arse in the MasterChef challenge. I raised my eyebrow at Shelley, who blushed and pointed to her beach bag. I stared at it, confused. She nodded at me to come to the washing up area with her.

'Well done, hun! I didn't know you could cook,' I said.

'Shhh. I can't.' Shelley blushed. 'I knew that we were coming here today so I asked Chef at the Blue Butterfly to whip me up a quick curry. When Jimmy was putting on another plaster and Lila was chatting to you I binned the crap that we'd been making and swapped it over!'

I gawped at her before laughing. 'You cheeky minx!'

'Sorry to be so sneaky but my cooking is probably as bad as Jimmy's and I wanted to impress him.'

I put my arm around my friend. 'I don't think you needed fancy culinary skills to do that, hun.'

CHAPTER 27

Astraphobia (n.) An abnormal fear of thunder and lightning

A few days later, I was sitting on my veranda and enjoying some quiet time reading a slushy romantic paperback Little Em had loaned me. Since the two guys had arrived it had been a never-ending party full of stitch-in-my-side belly laughs – so much for playing the cool-and-distant card with Ben. Both he and Jimmy had settled into the group seamlessly. Little Em and Lou gave as good as they got with winding up Jimmy, Astrid had roped them in for a palm reading, Phil was pleased to have some male company for a while and Shelley was just a real-life version of the heart-eyed emoji.

We'd been swimming in the sea, rented stand-up paddle boards that I sucked at, played beach football with some of the local school children and helped Dara at the noisy market haggling for cut-price leafy vegetables and mushrooms shaped like elephant ears.

'Worth the dodgy driving skills?' Ben had asked as we'd all set off on an adventure driving a long tail boat out to sea one morning. Shelley and Jimmy were sat at the other end of the narrow boat, their bursts of laughter piercing the salty warm breeze every so often. Ben removed his damp T-shirt in one smooth move, giving me a few seconds of pure, shameless ogling. I took in his ripped – but not over the top – muscular stomach, where a trail of light-brown hair ran from his belly button into his shorts. He tilted his head, waiting for a reply to his previous question and I quickly dragged my eyes back to his face.

'Yep…you…er, this is *incredible*!' I blushed, my tongue suddenly too big for my mouth.

I suddenly felt very self-conscious at the thought of stripping off in front of him. Even though I'd developed an even, bronzed tan, had toned up a little *and* was wearing a matching bikini, it felt very sexual to be stripping off when I was feeling this chemistry between us. Did he feel it too? He didn't give me much time to stress about this before his shorts came off, just a pair of purple board shorts remained and he expertly dived into the crystal-clear water.

I quickly followed and splashed in with the elegance of my mum hunting down a bargain in TKMaxx, elbows and shins everywhere. I released a huge sigh before opening my eyes to find Ben staring intently at me. 'What? Have I got something on my face?' I rubbed my cheeks and splashed about, hoping I didn't have any food stuck between my teeth.

'No, nothing,' he smiled, looking as if he was about to say something else.

But that moment was over as soon as Jimmy had raced up behind us and dive-bombed into the peaceful waters.

In the evenings Jimmy would play the guitar serenading Shelley, who he'd quite obviously taken a shine to and tried – badly – to hide it. She hadn't stopped smiling since they'd arrived, probably mirroring my own expression whenever Ben was around. Each evening, after a few drinks, we would let off Chinese lanterns into the inky black sky, making promises and wishes that floated away on the balmy night air.

After my disastrous relationship with Dillon, if you could even call it that, my head firmly instructed me not to flirt with Ben, no matter how much my heart begged me too. They were only staying for a couple more days before they went to Nepal to do some trekking, so for now I was happy to keep it as friendly banter, even if I felt this spark between us. We had so much in common, laughing at the same things and glancing at each other at the same time, sharing silent in-jokes when Jimmy said something ridiculous. I never did get round to sending any postcards home.

A breeze rustled the pages of my book. The sky had turned an ominous grey colour. The others had warned me that the storms here didn't announce their arrival; instead, the rain fell thick and fast, drenching you, forcing you to hide undercover and wait it out. A deafening crash of wild black waves thrashed onto the shore, feet from my hut, bringing with it the first warm drops of rain. The air was heavy with moisture; I almost stuck my head out from under the reed-roofed veranda, wanting to taste it. The other huts were in darkness; everyone must have been in the main bar area, probably sheltering with drinks and card games. I was debating whether to chance it and go and join them, when a deep roll of thunder, followed by a fork of silvery bright lightning, pierced the sky, making my decision for me.

Birds squawked loudly. I zipped up my jacket, placing my feet on the chair opposite and rubbed my hands together for some heat. The rain was really coming down strongly now; it was truly incredible – my small roof was keeping all the water out. Another loud crack of lightning made me jump. I could hardly see a thing in this dusky night sky; the moon was obscured by heavy clouds letting just a fraction of light peek through.

Then everything went black.

The pretty strings of lights around my hut went out as well as the table lamp in my room. Even the bar was plunged into darkness, as laughter and girly screams, followed by mwah-ha-ha-type scary noises floated through the moist air. I fumbled my way inside to find the wind-up torch that Marie had bought me, banging my elbow and knee in the process and stubbing my toe on the edge of the bed.

'Shit!' I yelped, squeezing my foot, clenching my jaw at the searing pain. I scrabbled my way to my backpack, where I had packed the torch in a side pocket and rapidly whirred the handle, creating a small tunnel of light. Pushing open the door to go back to the veranda, I heard someone else cry out.

'Shit!'

Shocked, I screamed and pressed the buzzer on the rape alarm that my dad had attached to the end of the torch. An ear-piercing siren filled the air. I flicked the pathetic beam of light at the assailant's face. It took a second for my eyes to adjust; my ears burned from the noise, but as I slowly looked up, I was met with a very wet, grimacing Ben with his hands pressed alternately to his ears and his shins.

'Oh my God! Are you OK?' I shouted over the deafening wail of the rape alarm. He was rubbing his shins where I'd kicked out, fearing for my life. 'I thought you were some sort of storm rapist. Why are you not in the bar?' I said breathlessly.

A booming roar of thunder made us both jump. The sky seemed to be having steel drum lessons as heavy booms cracked through the thick clouds.

'Sorry! Ow, jeez have you been taking self-defence lessons or something? That's quite a kick you have there,' he said, trying not to smile. 'Here, pass me that thing.' He took the alarm, instantly silencing it, and flicked a switch on the torch, allowing more light to pass through. 'I honestly didn't mean to scare you. I just came to check you were OK. We've just come back from helping Chef at the wholesalers, the others were waiting for you in the bar, so I said I'd come and see if you wanted to join us.' His wet curls looked jet-black in the near darkness.

'I was just about to go over, but then the power cut out. I'm the least co-ordinated person in full daylight, so I just knew I'd cause some sort of injury if I headed out in the dark.' I looked down at his shins, and caught a glimpse of his shorts clinging to his muscular thighs from the rain. 'Sorry, looks like I can cause damage without leaving my hut too,' I blushed.

He laughed. 'Don't worry about it. If there is ever a zombie apocalypse at least I know who to hide out with.'

Adrenalin was coursing through my body from his surprise visit. We hadn't properly been alone just the two of us since he'd arrived. I tried my hardest to shush the butterflies prancing in my empty stomach.

'So you want to make a run for it?' He peered out to where the restaurant usually was, but it was too hard to make out through the sheets of rain still lashing down.

I chewed my bottom lip. 'We could sit it out instead? I'm sure it will be over soon.'

He smiled at that suggestion. 'Yeah, OK. If you don't mind.'

'I don't mind,' I said shyly.

Ben used my torch to rummage through the bathroom cabinet, where he was sure he'd seen candles and matches in his own hut. 'Bingo. They must be used to power cuts out here,' he said, thrusting a large church candle in the air. We sat on the veranda – I'd given him a towel to dry himself – and in the flickering light he told me about the places he'd travelled to.

We spoke about everything and nothing, any silences that fell in between conversations were comfortable. An hour felt like minutes as we sat inhaling the fresh storm-cleansed air, under the sky which was changing from deep grey to dark blue. The air seemed clearer now, the rain had stopped, leaving fat raindrops to gently tumble off the dark leaves of the palm trees around us.

'So...are you seeing anyone back home?' he asked slowly, picking the dried wax off the table, avoiding my eye.

Before I could answer, a voice called out from the near darkness: 'Hey, you! When you getting that peachy bum over here?' Little Em was jogging from the main bar, waving animatedly at us. She laughed, then stopped abruptly, taking in the romantic scene, our bodies close together on the small veranda around the flickering candle. 'Oh, sorry! I thought you were camping out alone. Anyway, er...Chef has managed to concoct something over the fire and we're about to start tucking in, if you, erm, want to get food, after...I mean *later*.' She looked down at the wet rain-pocked sand sheepishly.

'You hungry?' Ben asked, a slight pink colour flushing his cheeks.

'Starving.' I needed something substantial in my stomach to stop it from dancing about nervously.

The bar area looked amazing. Soft, glowing tea-lights in small jars were hanging on wooden beams; a large fire that doubled up as a barbecue roared in the corner and flaming torches marked the entrance. Chef and Dara beckoned us over to a long table bearing plates, cutlery and an assortment of papaya salads, handmade bread and glassy rice noodles.

'We don't know when the power will be back on, so I figured we'd have a storm feast,' Dara said excitedly, proud of her spread and thrusting plates towards us.

Ben laughed. 'That's as good an excuse as any. Here you go, Georgia, ladies first.' He passed a knife and fork to me, both of us getting an electric shock. Our eyes met and a frisson of emotion passed between us.

'Over here!' Lou called out, breaking the spell. The others, including Phil and Astrid, were sat at tables that had been pushed together on the damp sand. Large, flickering lanterns lit a path from the bar to the romantic set up. It could have been straight from a film set.

'Looks like we're the last ones to arrive,' Ben said, as we strolled down the candlelit trail to the table closest to the sea. It was much calmer than just a few hours ago; the white froth of the tide glistened against the dark sky as hundreds of stars blinked down at us.

'Oi oi, what've you two been up to? Not seen you for bloody ages!' Jimmy's wide grin seemed to be even larger in the candlelight. Ben fidgeted on his seat; I was sure he was blushing.

'We've been, erm, putting the world to rights, haven't we, Georgia?'

'Mhmhm,' I replied around a mouthful of food. I spotted Shelley giving me a thumbs up behind Jimmy's broad back.

'Ah, is that what they call it nowadays?' Jimmy roared with laughter.

Ben caught my eye and winked before chucking a half-eaten dumpling in Jimmy's direction, which failed and fell into Little Em's drink. 'Whoops, sorry Em!'

That only caused Jimmy to laugh louder. 'Don't worry, Georgia, I'm sure he's got better aim than that usually,' Jimmy winked, chucking a handful of pistachio nut shells at Ben. The tiny missiles landed in his hair and in his drink.

'Right, that's it,' Ben cried, jumping to his feet, brushing himself down. 'You want to play? Well, you're on.' He marched over to Chef and Dara who were starting to pack the food away. We watched him whisper something in Dara's ear, her hand clapping her mouth as she giggled.

'What's he doin'?' Jimmy asked the question we were all wondering.

The puzzled look on our faces must have intensified when a loud riff of the eighties classic *Born To Be Alive*, boomed out of some hidden speakers. Ben strode over to us all, a steely look in his narrowed eyes and a playful smile desperate to show on his lips.

'Dance off. You and me.' He pointed from his chest to Jimmy's. I heard Little Em gasp. For a moment Jimmy just sat there staring Ben out. Not moving or smiling. For a split second I felt a tinge of embarrassment for Ben. Maybe this was a bad idea. Then suddenly Jimmy nodded, kissed his teeth and slowly stood up.

'Yer on.'

The two men circled each other like vultures swarming around their prey. The beat intensified. The mood too. As the chorus rose to the crescendo the pair of them snapped from serious cage fighters ready to pounce on one another to lovable clowns. They stamped their feet in sync, their hands clapping in perfect rhythm and their hips all Patrick Swayze-like.

This wasn't an aggressive dance off. This was a pre-rehearsed dance routine.

Our table erupted into roars of laughter and encouragement. It was like watching those first dance wedding videos on YouTube, the ones where the bride and groom surprise all their guests by busting out some synchronised brilliant routine. Shaking their bums, turning in circles and flicking their elbows, the lads were trying their best to remain straight-faced. I was crying with laughter at the sight of them.

'Come on, girls, let's show them how it's really done,' Shelley said, comically pushing the sleeves up on her colourful chiffon top and grabbing my hand, leading me to the makeshift dance floor.

All of a sudden chairs got pushed back, flip-flops were kicked off and bodies entwined as we laughed and danced under the watchful eye of the bright moon. I looked over at my new friends, throwing shapes like they were on stage at a Miley Cyrus gig, twerking as if their life depended on it, my heart bursting with happiness.

Shelley was creased over watching Jimmy butcher the delicate swaying moves that Astrid was trying to teach him. Lou and Little Em were clapping and laughing with Phil. To my right, Dara and Chef were slow dancing, lost in their own special world. Wet sand clumped in between my toes, my cheeks hurt from smiling but I felt so alive. I didn't realise my experience on this little island could be made even better but, looking up into Ben's creased eyes, his strong hand pressing the small of my back leading the way to steps I didn't know, it turns out it could.

CHAPTER 28

Lachrymose (adj.) Given to shedding tears readily; tearful

I'd left a very energetic late afternoon game of beach volleyball, girls versus boys, to get us all some bottles of water. Astrid was our referee, lazily watching us from her padded sun lounger, although she wasn't the best score keeper as she kept nodding off and losing track of the points, which brought out the competitive streak in the men. Jimmy was throwing himself on the floor football-player style at every hint of foul play, causing good-natured faux-aggressive banter between the teams.

I walked past reception, wiping off the sweat dripping down my flushed face when Dara called out to me. 'Oh Georgia, I was just coming to get you, there's a phone call for you.'

I stopped in my tracks. A phone call. For me? She dipped her eyes to the ground. 'It's your mum.' I jogged over to where she was holding the phone outstretched. Her usually cheerful face was drawn and pale.

'Hello?' I said breathlessly, taking the receiver. Dara shuffled off, biting her bottom lip nervously.

'Oh Georgia! It's so good to finally speak to you.' My mum's voice sounded bright but strained.

'Mum, is everything OK?'

'No, well not really.' My mum's voice broke. 'You have to come home, Georgia. It's your dad. He…he…he's been in a car accident.' I stared at the creamy foam of the surf hitting the shore as my mum's words shattered around me. I felt like I'd been punched in the gut, everything in my vision was shifting, like a kaleidoscope. I clutched onto a gnarled wooden stump that had been sanded into a stool, needing it to support my wobbling legs.

'What?'

'It happened so quickly. One minute he was off to the chemist to pick up his prescription for his back, the next I get a call from some woman who'd seen the crash and called the ambulance.' She blew her nose. 'He was rushed to the hospital but he's now in a coma. Georgia, Georgia are you there, love?'

I nodded, then realised she couldn't see me. 'Yep. I'm here.' My voice was distorted, matching my blurry vision. I felt like I might throw up or faint, or both.

My dad was in a coma.

'Oh love, I'm so sorry to tell you this way.' She was quietly sobbing. I could picture her gripping a shredded tissue in her trembling hands. 'But we need you back.'

'OK.' I swallowed the sting of bile that had risen from my stomach and cleared my throat. 'I'm on my way.'

'Oh, thank goodness.' She let out a sigh of relief. 'OK. Well, I need to get off the line just in case the hospital are trying to get through. Take care, darling. I love you.'

'I love you too, Mum,' I whispered and hung up. Cheers from the volleyball match drifted through the air, I could hear Jimmy's booming voice arguing over a foul. I staggered to the toilets at the back of reception and threw up.

No, this couldn't be happening. My mum would call me back and tell me it was a mistake, the doctors had got it wrong, it was another Mr Green that they were looking after. Wiping my mouth, I held onto the thin bamboo walls, trying to take deep breaths. My stomach lurched and I doubled over, unable to stop the tide of vomit burning my throat. Once there was nothing left to bring back up I wiped my mouth and pushed open the toilet door, forcing my legs to work.

'Georgia? Ah, there you are,' Ben called out, the volleyball under his arm. 'Thought you might need a hand with carrying the bottles of water?'

I couldn't look at him, couldn't reply. I willed my feet to move faster in the sand which, in flip-flops, wasn't easy.

'Georgia? Are you OK?' His tone had changed from relaxed to concerned.

I eventually stopped as my legs gave way, forcing me to land heavily in an awkward heap on the sand. Ben ran over to see what was going on. I picked up a handful of soft, white grains and let them fall through my shaking fingertips: 'It's my dad. My mum's just called. I have to go home,' I said, my voice barely audible.

He sat next to me, the ball making a thud on the sand. 'What?'

His warm hand was rubbing my back, confusion and worry etched on his face. 'I need to go home, there's been a car accident. It's my dad,' I said, as snot and tears streaked down my face. Suddenly, Thailand felt a very long way from Manchester.

'Shit, oh my God.'

I sniffed loudly, trying to breathe and calm down. 'I can't believe it.'

'I'm not even going to ask if you're OK as clearly you're not, but can I do anything?'

'I need to leave now. Right now.'

He looked anxiously at his watch. 'It's too late to get a boat off the island tonight, but I promise as soon as light breaks, I can help book your trip home. Do you want me to get Shelley or one of the other girls for you?'

I shook my head. 'I need to pack. I just want to sleep and wake up to find none of this is true.' I started crying again. He gently placed his warm arm around my lower back, making soothing noises. 'You've got to keep strong, Georgia. I know that's the hardest thing in the world but your dad needs you to be strong for him.' I nodded, letting him pick me up from the floor and circle his arm around my waist to lean on. 'Come on, let me help.'

'Thank you,' I whispered, trembling in the balmy evening.

CHAPTER 29

Disquietude (n.) The state of disquiet; uneasiness

I'd sobbed in Ben's arms until the shock and exhaustion had knocked me out, but suddenly I woke drenched in sweat and disbelief. Normally mornings here were my favourite time of day. There was none of that misty drizzle I was used to waking up to back in Manchester; here the beams of sunlight nudged you awake, willing you to make the most of every moment of the day. Apart from today, when all I wanted was to be anywhere but here.

The medical words my mum had used yesterday didn't fit with my dad; my kind, lovable dad. Knowing how much he hated needles, I couldn't imagine him being prodded and poked in such a sterile, alien environment, without his only child beside him. I opened my tired, scratchy eyes and it hit me all over again. Today I was really leaving this place: my haven, my sanctuary.

Shelley, Lou and Little Em had helped me pack my bags last night as I'd sat numbly watching them, unable to do even the smallest of tasks without losing it. Astrid had brought me a bowl of soup that Chef had made specially and watched over me until I finished the entire bowl. 'You need to keep your strength up for the journey ahead,' she'd said, stroking my hair.

Ben took my bags out to a waiting tuk tuk; I had a long day of travelling ahead, including a ferry and three connecting flights that he'd booked as soon as dawn had broken. All of my new friends lined up, bleary-eyed and helpless in the bar. Dara passed over a plentiful packed lunch and Astrid wrapped a beaded charm bracelet over my trembling wrist. It felt surreal to be hugging and holding onto these people who, until recently, were perfect strangers. Now I felt like I was saying goodbye to my best friends; kindred spirits, fellow members of the Lonely Hearts Travel Club.

'You all put me back together again. I will never forget you,' I sobbed into Shelley's arms.

'I guess we all just needed each other,' she replied, stroking my back, roughly wiping the tears from her own eyes.

'As soon as you get back, you tell us if there is *anything* we can do to help. We are all thinking of you, my love. You're not going through this alone.' Astrid stuck out her chin, as if her stiff upper lip could overcome anything.

'Thank you. I'll miss you all so much.'

'This isn't a goodbye, but a "see you soon",' Little Em said, squeezing me. Phil and Jimmy nodded fervently, their hands in their pockets, unsure of what to say or do.

I turned to Ben. 'Thank you so much for helping me sort my flights back home and, you know, being there last night.' Neither of us had said a thing when he slipped out of my hut after spending the night curled up, wrapped up in each other's body heat. Obviously nothing remotely sexual had gone on, I was way too emotional – not to mention a pale, snotty mess – for that, but there was something powerful about the way he'd just held me in his arms, not saying a word.

He kicked the ground with his foot. 'It's nothing, I'm just gutted we have to say goodbye like this.' I nodded. There were so many things I wanted to say to him, ask him, to know but I kept quiet. My heart contracted – surely this wasn't how our story was meant to end? 'Like I said, we'll try and meet again in Manchester.'

I smiled weakly, knowing full well that I'd never see him again. You said these things to people, made promises, but life always got in the way. Lou handed me a tissue to dry my eyes and streaming nose. I had to practically peel my arms from her waist, so that I didn't miss my connection home. I wasn't ready for this all to be over, but I needed to see my dad and face the facts that my brain wasn't allowing to settle in. The rest of the day went by in a zombie-like blur. I slept most of the way on the empty early-morning ferry from sheer exhaustion. I felt as if I'd failed as a daughter, gallivanting through Thailand, being so wrapped up in my own problems out here, not knowing about the chaos playing out back home.

After catching a taxi through the manic streets of Bangkok, I arrived at the large Suvarnabhumi Airport with plenty of time to kill before boarding my flight home. I remembered walking through Arrivals like a lost sheep, blinking in the bright sunlight that had warmed my milk-white skin. Everything had been possible back then, but all that lay ahead now was uncertainty, sadness and fear. What if my dad didn't wake up? What if he did but he had changed forever? An icy chill flashed up my spine. I hurriedly went to find a bank of payphones, depositing all my remaining change to call my mum.

'Hello?' she answered immediately.

'Mum, it's me,' I cried, letting tears roll down my blotchy face. 'I'm on my way back. My flight leaves in a few hours and I'll get a taxi to you as soon as I land. How's Dad?'

'Oh, thank goodness, I can't wait to see you. They're running more tests on him. I only popped back to get a clean change of clothes, so it's lucky you got hold of me.'

I felt sick and let out the breath I'd been holding: 'Oh Mum, I'll be back as soon as I can. I'm so sorry you've had to deal with this alone.'

'I'm not alone; I've got your dad. He's been the real fighter in all of this. Just get back safely, OK?' We said our 'goodbyes' and, crying, I hung up the phone.

Nearby a family scanned the Departures board as their two young children ran around, hiding behind their oversized suitcases, laughing hysterically when the father pretended to wonder where they had disappeared to, then with a quick 'boo!' caught their squirming, giggling bodies.

'I'll be back soon, Dad,' I murmured to myself, playing with my St Christopher necklace between my trembling fingers.

On the busy flight home I was squished next to an overweight man who kept farting and looking around at the other passengers in disgust. Pulling my hoodie right up to my nose to block out the flatulence fumes, I leant my head against the window and closed my eyes. I couldn't concentrate on any of the films or TV shows that were playing on the small screen in front of me. When the super-smiley air hostess with cherry lipstick on her teeth asked me if I wanted meat or vegetarian option for the free meal my brain turned to mush. 'Erm, err, erm,' I babbled, feeling the fat man's eyes on me, wanting me to hurry up and make the simple decision so he could tuck into his grub. 'Erm, sorry. Meat please.' The air hostess passed me the tray filled with mini portions all neatly wrapped, looking at me sympathetically.

'You not a good flyer, hun?' she asked, still not getting my travel companion his dinner. She needed to be careful – he looked like he was about to eat her if she didn't hurry up.

'Oh no, I mean, yeah, I don't mind flying. It's just...' I couldn't finish my sentence before dabbing my eyes on my already soaked sleeve. 'The meat dish is fine, thanks.'

I picked at the food, realising I must have left my appetite back at the Blue Butterfly. I wondered what they were doing right now, what Ben was thinking about our night spent together, but not together, if you know what I mean. Whether I'd ever see any of them again. Admitting defeat on my barely touched tray of food I offered it to Mr Farty Pants, whose piggy eyes lit up. At least someone was happy.

Putting my tray table back up I closed my eyes, still unable to comprehend that I was en route back home. Back to Manchester, back to my dad lying unconscious in hospital. My big adventure was completely over. So much had happened in the relatively short time that I'd been in Thailand. I knew it was such a cliché but I honestly felt like I was a different person because of everything I'd been through. I mean, how could I not be? From Kit's shambolic tour, getting my nipple pierced, meeting Dillon, almost drowning going scuba diving, losing my phone, surviving the ring of fire, giving Amelie her comeuppance with the elephant gloop, to leaving that all behind and journeying to the Blue Butterfly. From the emotional experience on the fishing boat, meeting my Lonely Hearts Travel Club friends, going skinny dipping under the midnight sky, hanging out with a cryptic monk, to meeting Jimmy and Ben. Things had gone from the lowest of lows to the highest of highs.

I thought about my travel wish-list, written out on a beach in Turkey without the faintest idea of how, or really if, it would ever become a reality. Thanks to Shelley's determined plan to complete it, I was almost there.

Go skinny dipping in the moonlit ocean – DONE
Dance all night under the stars – DONE
Taste incredible exotic food – DONE
Ride an elephant – WOULDN'T WANT TO
Visit historic temples – DONE
Explore new beliefs – DONE
Climb a mountain – NOT YET
Make friends with different nationalities – DONE
Listen to the advice of a wise soul – DONE
Do something wild – DONE

There was me thinking I had all the time in the world to tick everything off. But, even though I couldn't complete my mission, I'd achieved more than I'd ever thought possible.

Manchester welcomed me back in the way it knew best, with dark grey skies and a drizzle of cold rain. Peering outside the aeroplane window I felt the colour instantly drain from my cheeks. I stepped out of the taxi that had pulled up outside of my parents' house and into a puddle, splashing the sand off my feet. With my backpack on I forced myself to trudge up the crazy-paving path, up to the reality that lay just behind the red door, between the two hanging baskets and well-pruned hydrangea bushes. Hearing the doorbell, my mum clomped down the stairs in her slippers to open the door with the security catch on. Her hand flew to her open mouth:

'Georgia!'

'Mum!'

'Oh Georgie, you're here.' She closed the door for a second to take the chain off and reopened it wide, pulling me in for an awkward hug around my bulky backpack. 'We've missed you so much.' She let the tears run down her pale, drawn face. She wasn't wearing any make-up, her comfy sweat pants and plain M&S t-shirt hung off her thinner frame and her hair was peppered with grey. The vision of my usually immaculate mother looking so unkempt shocked me.

'Me too.'

'Come in, come in. You look so different, so... travellery.' She picked up a blonder strand of my hair and let it fall between her fingers in amazement. 'You certainly had some good weather then. What was it, twenty-five degrees each day?'

'Mum, I didn't come all this way to talk about the weather,' I said gently, dumping my bag in the hall and heading to the kitchen.

'No, of course not. Now let me get the kettle on and we can have a good chat.'

'Mum,' I stopped her, 'how's dad?'

She turned to face me. 'Same as yesterday, I'm afraid. But he's getting the best care, the doctors and nurses have been simply wonderful. For all the bad things you hear about the NHS, I have nothing but positives to say about the staff in there.' She pottered around in the kitchen, flicking on the kettle and preparing two matching cups.

'I just can't believe it. So what exactly happened?' I asked, absentmindedly picking at the corner of a Jammie Dodger. At least my mum's tea service was still up to her impeccable standards. With steaming cups of tea we wandered into the lounge. The fussy, floral wallpaper that always gave me headaches was still bright and busy; the pale-green leather sofa still had its familiar sag marks where we would each take up our usual positions; the carriage clock still sat proudly on the cluttered mantelpiece, giving me comfort, showing that some things had stayed comfortingly the same.

'Well, like I said, he'd just nipped out to pick up his prescription. The doctors had finally given him some special painkillers for his back and he'd been feeling a whole lot better – I was watching *Deal or No Deal* and about to put tea on when the phone rang. It was this woman, Sandra or Susan or something, I don't even think she left a name. Anyway she'd found your dad's phone and called home. The poor woman was beside herself having to tell me she'd just witnessed the crash.' Mum paused to take a breath. 'He was driving along Allington Street, you know the one that backs onto that large car showroom? Anyway, the police reckon two lads had just robbed a car, as they slammed into your dad and drove off. This woman had been walking her dog and seen it all. She tried getting their reg plate but it all happened so fast. Thank goodness she was there.' Mum shook her head, her eyes tearing up, looking at the ceiling. 'She called the ambulance.'

'So have the police found them?' I clenched my fists at the thought of the scrotes who'd done this to my dad.

My mum shook her head. 'Not yet, I can't even think about getting justice at the moment, all I want is for Len to wake up.' She sighed. 'Marie's been calling every day, asking if we had any news. She'll be so pleased you're back.'

'I can't wait to see her too. Listen, I'm so sorry for not keeping in contact more, Mum.' I wiped a tear from my cheek.

'Oh it's all right, you weren't to know.'

'I just can't believe it.' I shook my head. 'How've you been?'

'Oh not brilliant, but you know me and your dad, we'll get through this.' She sipped her tea and sighed. 'I guess it's shown me what my priorities are in life and that doesn't mean arguing with Viv from number twenty-three over who has the best hanging baskets.'

'Yours are looking bloody great, though,' I winked.

She frowned at my use of language, before a weak smile crossed her thin, cracked lips. 'I'm so happy you're back, darling.' She leant over and patted my hand, her thin skin almost translucent next to my tanned arm. She knocked a teaspoon onto the carpet, interrupting this moment of rare affection, causing her to pull herself back and plaster on a fake smile. She adjusted her T-shirt as realisation set in for the first time at how she was dressed; a flash of embarrassment at her relaxed attire crossed her face as she collected our empty cups.

'Why don't you go and take a shower? You must be exhausted from that journey. Then we'll go and see your dad. He'll be thrilled you came back so quickly,' she said, busying out of the lounge.

*

'Mrs Green to room two, Doctor Khan's office please,' a nasally voice called out. We shuffled our way down the mint-green corridor of the hospital. I couldn't believe I was here. Just twenty-four hours ago I had been in the bubble of Bangkok; it didn't feel real. The few steps to the doctor's office were taken with reluctance and unease. The frightening statistics of weeks, even yearlong comas, possible brain-damaging fluids, paralysis and even vegetative states swum in my paranoid mind. I was terrified of the diagnosis we were about to be told. I was desperate to escape and go and find my dad but my mum, who looked petrified, explained that we had to find out the latest from the doctor first.

'Come in,' a cheerful voice called as my mum knocked on the oak door. Inside the well-lit room, Doctor Khan, an attractive middle-aged Asian woman with long jet-black hair pulled into a low bun and wearing large, round glasses, welcomed us. After the introductions and formal handshakes she motioned for us to sit on the chairs opposite her immaculate desk. A photo of her teenaged children looked out from a dark brown frame, certificates were proudly displayed on the cream walls and a well-cared-for pot plant sat on the window sill. She shuffled some papers on her desk and cleared her throat:

'So, Mrs Green, I've got some good news. Your husband has started breathing for himself.' My mum squeaked. I held my breath waiting for the doctor to finish with a 'but'. 'Which is a very positive sign.'

'But…' I added, unable to contain myself.

Doctor Khan smiled at me gently. 'But, we are still trying to work out why he is not waking up. The test results so far have shown no abnormal brain activity. We will, of course, continue to run more tests, but until we get a full picture of what's keeping your husband in his current condition we're not out of the woods yet.'

I let my breath out. 'OK, well that's a good thing, he's improving at least?'

Doctor Khan nodded. 'Yes, the signs are positive. All you can do is hope and wait and be patient.'

My mum's eyes welled up as she tightly squeezed my hand: 'Oh, don't you worry. We're not giving up on him. He *is* going to wake up and things will be fine. You'll see.'

'Can we go and see him?' I asked, itching to get out of this room and find my dad.

Doctor Khan nodded. 'Of course, now Georgia it may come as a shock to you seeing him lying there, especially with all the wires and tubes attached. But they are just monitoring him, so it's nothing to be alarmed by. He was in quite a bad way when he was brought in here and may look a little swollen and bruised, so please try and prepare yourself as best you can.' I nodded my understanding, my fears heightened tenfold by her worrying words. 'Right, if you'd like to follow me.'

I could hear people in the ward coughing as we made our way up the corridor; deep, throaty, phlegmy, coughs that seemed to rattle off the bare walls. Mum had her thin arm tight around my waist – or was I gripping onto her? I couldn't tell. I held my breath and walked into the room. The smell hit me first, a sort of antiseptic, tangy odour. I looked over at the body wrapped up in covers, despite the small room being quite warm.

My dad just looked like he was sleeping. He needed a shave; grey spiky stubble shadowed his slightly swollen cheeks and chin. It seemed so alien for a man who prided himself on being as fit as a fiddle to look so helpless. He had almost been dragged into retirement by my mum, reluctant to admit his age.

'Hello, Mr Green, I've got some special visitors with me today who I know are desperate to have a good chat with you.' Doctor Khan winked as she checked the numbers on one of the beeping monitors. My dad just lay there motionless. 'You can talk to him, if you want. It's good for him to hear your voice and might help us get a response from him,' the doctor encouraged.

I walked gingerly to the side of his bed, gripping onto the sides for support. 'Dad, it's me, Georgia.' I gulped back the lump in my throat. My voice sounded distorted and weirdly pitched.

He looked as if he'd aged ten years, his dark brown hair was now dusty, thin and grey. His usually sparkling eyes were sunken and deep purple bags marked the territory where laughter lines used to take pride of place. A nasty bruise dented his forehead and he had tiny nicks across the bridge of his nose.

'They're just superficial wounds from the accident. They will heal in time,' the soft voice of the doctor explained.

'Come on now, Len, wakey wakey time.' My mum was busying herself with tucking in a stray corner of the blanket that had come untucked. She was trying so hard to stay in control of her emotions.

It felt like we were a pair of awful actors in some uncomfortable hospital drama, with the lead actor forgetting his lines and blanking us. Neither of us were sure of what to say or where to put ourselves. The room was full of regular beeping, hi-tech machines and foreign instruments, all keeping my dad alive. Thinking about this, I felt the air get sucked out of me. I couldn't keep my calm composure for much longer.

'I'm back, Dad, it's OK. It's all going to be OK,' I whispered, gently stroking his hand, trying to convince both of us.

'You hear that, Len? Georgia's come back to see you.' My mum raised her voice like she did when she spoke to her partially deaf neighbour. She turned to face the doctor, who seemed to be the only one of us totally at ease in this bizarre set up. 'She's just come back from Thailand. Been backpacking round the world, haven't you, Georgia?' It was close enough; I nodded.

'Wow, well another reason you need to wake up then, Mr Green.' The doctor smiled gently at me, then turned to my unresponsive dad. 'You need to see your daughter's lovely golden tan and hear all her stories.'

'Oh, Len was so proud of her going off by herself,' my mum told the doctor. 'We both were.' Her voice cracked slightly before she cleared her throat. I'd never heard her say that she was proud of me before. I thought she thought me going off was a load of nonsense. 'So he can't miss hearing about all the things she's been up to.'

'Oh Mum,' I blinked back tears at her bravery, at the fight we all still had ahead of us. 'He has to get better, doesn't he?'

'Your dad's not going to leave us now, not like this.' Her voice broke and tears rolled down her cheeks.

CHAPTER 30

Counterveil (v.) To act or avail against with equal power, force, or effect; counteract

The next afternoon Marie popped in; she'd almost sent me flying to the hall carpet with an enormous hug, nearly crushing the lasagne and box of fruit that she had in her arms. We sat in the small conservatory, the one that my mum had my dad build to be just like the Raineses at number thirty-seven, drinking tea and picking at Twiglets as my mum entertained Cole, pleased to have something to keep her mind occupied. I eventually brought Marie up to speed on everything I'd been up to, with much apologising for not having stayed in touch more and promising that she hadn't lost her place as my 'bestie'. Losing my phone had been as hard on the people I'd left behind as it had been on me.

Marie told me all about the urban *Jane Eyre* show she had finished filming and described how the director had tried it on with her one night, snaking his fat hand up her skirt. She'd quit, after defacing the tiny caravan they'd put her up in.

'Since then my agent hasn't had too many offers pouring in, but I've had loads more respect from the other actors who are putting in a good word for me,' Marie said, stuffing a handful of crisps into her mouth. 'So, how's it been, being back?' She nodded towards a faded photo of my dad hanging on the wall. 'I'm so sorry, hun.'

'Well, you know, it's not great, but I'm sure he's looking stronger each day.' I didn't tell her about how I'd been sleeping in the same bed with my mum, wanting to be able to smell my dad's aftershave on the sheets; how I'd found my mum sobbing over the dishes; how I'd been having the time of my life just days earlier and now had no job, no money, no home and a very sick father.

'So, this Ben you met?' Marie looked at me playfully, wanting to lighten the mood.

'Yeah, Ben.' I dipped my eyes, smiling.

'You like him, don't you? What's going on there? First you tell me about some guy called Stevie, then you send me an email gushing all about some Dillon fella, and now there's a Ben. I have to say, I'm liking this new Georgia.'

I smiled. 'That makes me sound terrible! Stevie was a figment of my imagination, Dillon turned out to be a lying, cheating thief, and Ben was this really cool guy I met at the Blue Butterfly, but it was way too early days to say if anything would have happened there.' My stomach flickered at his name. As much as I'd tried to play it cool between us, I had really got to like him. 'It's not like I'm ever going to see him again.'

'Never say never, Miss Green.' She slurped her tea. 'So what are you going to do now you're back? Are you going to jet off again once your dad is…better?' Her bottom lip trembled slightly.

I shook my head. 'No. I'm here to stay, either way.' We sat in silence, neither of us alluding to what that might mean.

Marie looked sheepishly into her mug. 'Oh well, that's good, for me. So you going to be looking for work?'

I sighed. 'Yep. I've avoided checking my bank statements. I can't face finding out how far into my overdraft I am, but I'll need to find a job soonish.' To be honest, I couldn't seem to focus on even the smallest day-to-day tasks, so hitting the job market filled me with fear.

'Hmm, what about getting in touch with that Trisha woman, you seemed to really get on with her. Maybe she could do with a spare pair of hands?'

'You know what? I hadn't even thought about that.' It would be great to see her again. I still needed to thank her for sorting me out at the Blue Butterfly.

'And that way you can do some more research into this mysterious Stevie.' Marie winked, throwing her arms around me excitedly, then pulled back. 'Not that you have time to even contemplate that, with all this going on. I still can't believe it.'

'Me neither,' I said, shaking my head. I was slowly regaining control over my tear ducts but that was probably because they were all dried out. 'So, what about you? Any men on the scene I need to know about?'

Marie placed her mug on the coffee table and hitched her legs underneath herself, suddenly avoiding my question.

'Marie?'

'Well…there is one guy.'

'Just the one?' I teased. She looked upset for a moment. 'Hey, it was just a joke, hun.'

Marie sniffed and brushed a strand of hair from her flushed face. 'I know but I'm sick of being seen as the village bike.'

'I didn't mean it like that!' I was embarrassed that she thought I'd ever think that about her. Yeah, she liked men but she wasn't a complete slapper. I knew that with her it was more talk than action.

'I know you didn't, but I know that other people do.' She sighed. 'I guess seeing you go off and do your own thing, especially after what happened to you, has inspired me to take a long hard look at my own life.'

'Wow. Well, that's a good thing, isn't it?'

'Yeah. And, I've been thinking…' she trailed off, picking one of her nails '…that I'm going to ask Mike on a date.' I was stunned but oh so happy for her. 'Don't even think about saying I told you so,' she mumbled.

I laughed. For the first time since being back home. 'I wouldn't dare. So, tell me everything. What're you going to say to him?'

She hid her face in her hands. 'I don't know! I've never been the one to ask a guy out. I just had this moment, like an epiphany or something, when he came to pick up Cole the other day and I didn't want him to leave,' she admitted honestly, and painfully. 'He said he couldn't watch Cole at the weekend as he's got plans.' I raised my eyebrow. 'So, I spoke to his mum, who said that he's apparently got a date with someone. I felt like I'd been punched in the stomach. And that's when I realised that I wanted to be the girl he was on a date with, not some stranger who he might fall in love with, and I'll never get that chance again.'

'Finally!'

'I know, I know. But now, I need to find the courage to ask him out.'

'You've got this. I know you have.' I leant over and gave her a hug.

As if on cue, a grinning Cole bounded in and we changed the conversation subject to what I'd missed on Corrie.

The next few days passed in a blur of sleepless nights and hospital visits. When we weren't keeping bedside vigils my mum and I cleaned the house so many times it was in danger of being bleached away, each of us repeating tasks needlessly, just for something to do to keep our minds off the situation. Astrid was right when she talked about that strange feeling backpackers got from leaving paradise and returning home. I regressed into myself, not wanting to leave my parents' house, apart from restocking the supply of tea bags, milk and Mr Muscle.

Marie had asked if I could babysit Cole as she and Mike were going for dinner. When she dropped him off at my mum's I'd never seen her so nervous.

'Are you sure you don't mind watching him? I promise I won't be out all night. I'm not even going to drink so I can keep a clear head,' she'd babbled, handing over a bag of nappies and baby wipes.

'It's fine. Like I said, it'll help fill our evening and keep our minds off Dad. We're just sitting here torturing ourselves in silence half the time. My mum's excited to have Cole and I'm just so happy that you've got this chance with Mike.

'OK, if you're sure.' I nodded. 'Right, well, I love you so much and the emergency dummy is in this bag. Call me if there're any problems. Right. Wish me luck!' She'd left in a whirlwind of kisses, hugs and deep breaths.

Four hours later and she was back, hand in hand with Mike, both of them looking like the cats that got the cream. As Mike chatted with my mum and picked up a sleeping Cole in his arms, I'd pulled Marie to one side.

'So?'

'It was amazing!' she gushed, glancing over at him like a love-struck One Direction fan. 'He was in shock at first when I told him I didn't invite him out to talk about potty training and baby food. I tried to stay calm, explain how I felt and asked him if he wanted to try and start dating.' She did a little dance. 'He said he'd been waiting for me to say this for as long as he could remember.'

'Ah, that's fab. I'm so made up for you both.'

'Thank you. We're going to take it slow but I'm so happy, Georgia.' I gave her a big hug before they left, thanking my mum profusely for helping them out.

The days seemed to blur and merge together, I couldn't even tell what day it was most of the time. We'd returned home from another hospital visit, another day with no change in my dad's condition, and I was quietly washing the dishes when my mum burst into the kitchen, her eyes red and nose streaming.

'Mum, you OK?' I asked, placing a soapy plate onto the drying rack.

'Am I OK? Am I OK? No I'm not bloody OK.' She never swore. 'I can't do this much longer, Georgia. I swear I can't.' Her hands were shaking as she tried to get a glass out of the cupboard.

'Oh Mum, it's so hard but you need to be strong, for Dad–' my words of encouragement were cut off by the sound of breaking glass. The glass had slipped from my mum's trembling hands, smashing on the lino.

'Everything is going wrong!' she wailed. My eyes widened at the sight of her.

'Mum, don't worry, it's just a glass, I'll clean it up.' I bent down, carefully picking up the large shards of glass.

'I'm so sorry,' she kept repeating as I found the dustpan and brush. 'I'm so sorry. I should be the one keeping it together, looking after you. When did you get to be so strong?' she asked through gulps of tears.

I smiled sorrowfully at her. 'I got it from you and Dad.' Leaving the mess on the floor I bent down and hugged her. 'But I need you to be strong with me. Dad needs us both.'

She clasped my face in her hands. 'You're right. He does.' As if a switch had been flicked, she shook herself down, picked up the broken glass and chucked it in the bin. 'Georgia, just because your father insists on taking an impromptu holiday without us, sleeping all day and lazing around, it doesn't mean we have to stand for it.'

'Mum, that wasn't quite what I meant.'

'No, no Georgia, don't you see? With us here acting like meek little women, your dad will never come back to us. We need to show him that he has to wake up and come home because we want him to, not because we need him to. So, I'm going to my church committee meeting and you're going to go and find yourself a job.'

The steely glint in her eye was hard to avoid. I nodded: 'OK.'

CHAPTER 31

Gainsay (v.) To deny; dispute or contradict

I pulled my jacket tighter around me as an icy wind swept down the street; I still hadn't adjusted to the cold autumn weather. A light drizzle clung to my sleeves as I edged down the high street, stepping over oily puddles and dog mess in the dull light. There was no one else around. Who else would be stupid enough to venture out on an afternoon like this? I rubbed my hands together for heat. After her motivational pep talk my mum had bustled about, done a big food shop, chucked out the mound of takeaway boxes we'd been surviving on and almost kicked me out the front door telling me to do my part in getting our lives back on track.

I'd nipped into the nearest phone shop to buy a replacement mobile; I still needed to sort out claiming for my old one, which was currently somewhere on the sea bed, thanks to the snotty, tattooed scuba diver – but until now I just hadn't had the motivation. Picking up a cheap handset was the first step on my mission. Step two was going to be a little trickier.

After Marie's visit I couldn't get her suggestion of helping Trisha out of my mind, so armed with my CV and as much energy as I could summon I marched into her shop, the bell tinkling my arrival.

'Hello, how's things?' I asked, making Trisha jump.

'Georgia! What are you doing back?' She walked around her desk to hug me. Her perfume filled my nose; it smelled like Christmas. 'How was the tour? It's not meant to be over for another few weeks is it?'

I winced. 'Yeah, it was…erm…interesting.'

She frowned at me. 'Oh, well, that wasn't the reaction I'd hoped for. Sit down, sit down, tell me all about it. I'll put the kettle on.'

Over steaming cups of tea I filled her in on what had happened with Kit, watching her wrinkled face turn from horror and confusion to embarrassment. 'So what are you doing back?'

I chewed my lip, trying to figure out how to begin. 'My dad erm – ' I paused, clearing my throat, desperate to keep it together. 'My dad's not been very well, so I've come back to help out.'

The light from her face dimmed. 'Oh, I am so sorry.' She took my hand in hers. 'If there's anything I can do.'

'Well, there was something I wanted to ask you.' I took a deep breath. 'I wondered if you were hiring?' She didn't quite seem to catch what I was saying. 'If you had any jobs going?' I nodded to the mound of unopened letters, papers and nearly overflowing wastepaper bin.

Trisha quickly pulled her hand away from mine and covered her mouth. Her whole body straightened up. 'Oh, well…I–' she stuttered, standing up and brushing down her burnt-orange woollen skirt.

'Trisha, is everything OK?' I frowned.

She turned away as if to gather her thoughts. 'Oh yes, fine, fine, dear.' She was fiddling with her small black-and-gold earrings.

'Is something the matter with the business?' I said, my tone growing firmer.

Trisha eventually turned around to face me, her watery grey eyes almost translucent, and nodded. 'You could say that, yes.'

My heart started beating rapidly. 'What's going on?' I gently took her hand and we sat down on the squishy sofa together.

She wafted me away lightly. 'Oh, no. You've got enough on your plate to worry about me and my troubles,' she sniffed.

I pulled a tissue from my coat pocket; I had a constant stash of them close to hand now. 'Don't be silly, if anything I'm looking for something to take my mind off things happening at home. Come on, you can tell me.'

Trisha sighed. 'I'm afraid I can't offer you a job – as much as I would love to – because I'm having to close the shop.'

I could feel my pulse in my ears. No, this was her baby, her life, her passion. 'Are you sure?'

She dabbed the tissue at her eyes. 'I guess I'm just not modern enough, not like the competition.' I thought of the chimps down the road at Totally Awesome Adventours and seethed. 'People don't seem to need travel agents any more, unless they are full of bells and whistles. It's all online, with apps, apples, eye clouds and other words I don't understand. I can't compete with that.'

'But I thought you said you had a family member coming to help you out? Stevie?' Back then I thought she'd meant he would help with admin and odd jobs, not the survival of the business.

'Yes, my godson Stevie. He was meant to be, but after an awful meeting with the bank last week I had to make the heart-breaking decision to sell the company. Stevie will deal with all the paperwork; he's much better at that kind of thing than I am.' She laughed weakly. 'He's as gutted as I am but there isn't another way around it. So, sadly it's going to the auction house next week.'

'No! You can't, there must be something we can do.'

'It's too late, Georgia. Your tour was the last one I booked from here and look at how that turned out.' She was full-on crying now, and I patted her shoulder gingerly.

'No.'

She peered up at me. 'What do you mean, no?'

'I mean, we can fight this. I'll help you.' I couldn't help my dad, but I could help this woman who had given me so much. 'And that tour you booked me on, OK it wasn't what I'd imagined but that was only because you didn't realise it had changed owners. Plus it was thanks to your advice that I went to the Blue Butterfly, a place that I'll never forget, where I met people who helped put me back together again. You can still do this, Trisha, if you want to?'

She looked up at me, so frail, the fight completely gone from her. 'Georgia, it's too late.'

*

I left Trisha's, frustrated that she'd admitted defeat and caught the bus home. Mum's bright idea for us to carry on like everything was normal was not going to plan. As I turned the key in my parents' front door I heard my mum talking to someone. I hurried through the porch into the lounge, stupidly hoping to see my dad sat on the sofa. But in his seat, looking extremely out of place, wasn't my dad but Alex's mum Ruth.

'Oh Georgia, look who's paid us a visit.' My mum jumped to her feet as I entered, a tight smile on her pale face.

'Hello, Georgia,' Ruth said quietly, placing her cup onto the coffee table. I noticed that my mum had found and dusted off the best china, a gift from my parents' wedding that never came out of the cupboard.

'Oh, hi,' I said shrugging my jacket off, the heat of the electric fire burning my cheeks. 'What are you doing here?' I eyed her cautiously. She was perched on the sofa, her legs crossed under her tight pencil skirt. She had never visited this house before; I'd always been too embarrassed about my parents' small maisonette, their old-fashioned decorating style and mismatched furniture. Now I was ashamed of myself for that.

'Mrs Doherty has just popped in to have a quick chat with you,' my mum said, still standing up, looking like she didn't know where to put herself. She said 'popping in' as if we were friendly neighbours on *Coronation Street* and nipping over for a quick brew was something she did all the time. 'I'll...leave you to it, go and arrange us some biscuits.' She slipped out of the room, looking relieved to have made her escape.

'So.' Ruth took a deep breath looking me up and down. 'You've been on holiday?'

I stared at her. What on earth was this woman doing in our house? Then I remembered that email she had sent me back when I was boarding my flight in Dubai, the one I'd never replied to. 'Backpacking,' I said bluntly.

She nodded, not knowing what else to add to that, then cleared her throat. 'I need to talk to you, Georgia. Won't you sit down?' She wafted a slender arm towards the chair opposite, her collection of expensive bracelets jangling as she moved. Her voice was measured and calm, but there was something hidden behind her strict demeanour, something almost vulnerable. I did as she said, noticing that the label on her Jaeger blouse was sticking out as I shuffled past.

'Thank you.' She cleared her throat again and folded her hands across her skirt. 'I want to apologise.' Thank goodness I'd been sitting down otherwise I would have ended up face-planting the mantelpiece.

'What? Sorry, pardon?'

She fiddled with a loose thread, running her tongue over her teeth, thinking through whatever speech she'd prepared in her mind. 'Yes. I wanted to apologise for doubting you as an appropriate wife for Alex.'

'Oh. Right.' Whatever point she wanted to make I hoped she'd hurry up and put us both out of this discomfort. My mum was taking a long time with those biscuits; I suspected she was pressed up against the kitchen door listening to every word.

'I have been made aware of some very embarrassing home truths recently, and I wanted to visit you to make amends. To ask you to come back.' She audibly let out her breath. Her pale neck had flushed to a deep crimson.

'To come back?' I stuttered. Had she been overdosing on delusional pills? She hated me, was always siding with perfect Francesca and taking any opportunity to belittle me. What truths was she talking about?

'Yes. Alex has acted like a silly boy but the spell that bunny boiler Stephanie put on him has finally been broken.' She said her name as if someone had just farted. 'It's over between them; I don't think it ever really started. Alex wanted to come here to tell you, to beg for you to come back to him – he has finally realised just what he lost for the sake of a little fun,' she scoffed. Fun wasn't a word Ruth was used to.

I rubbed my face. 'So, why didn't he? Come here today, I mean?'

She blinked quickly. 'He was too worried about your reaction. I offered to try to patch things up between you first.'

Alex wanted us to get back together? Seeing his mum, her eyes just like his, made my stomach tense. Was this really happening?

'If I am completely honest with you, Georgia, I too realised that I had taken you for granted. That actually, despite certain social faux pas, you would be an excellent daughter-in-law. All this just adds to your charms.' She waved her hand around the room.

'Wait – what about the baby?' I couldn't believe I'd not even thought of this huge elephant in the room until now.

Ruth tensed up and went extremely pale. 'The baby doesn't exist. It never did,' she added sharply.

Talk about a bloody bombshell! So had my dad got it wrong when he saw them in Morrison's? I was sure I had spied a slight bump on Stephanie that time when I bumped into them during the shameful bin-vom episode. Had I imagined it? I was stunned into silence.

'I have also been talking to some very close friends of mine who work for *Elle* magazine in London. You mentioned once that you wanted to be a journalist?' I gawped at her, amazed she'd remembered. 'Well, they are looking to take on a new columnist, a sort of "Northern Girl Living in the City" writer. They will train you up, fully paid, and because of my connections the salary is very reasonable.' She smiled tightly, her botoxed forehead remaining impassive.

'Wait…' I arched my fingers to my temples, trying to get my head around all of this. 'You're offering me a job – in London? Alex wants me back? And there is no baby?' I stuttered.

She gave a quick nod. 'Exactly. You can come back to your old life, Georgia. But this time I promise it will be better than ever. Move to London with Alex, have a fresh start, just the two of you. Lots of people have blips in their relationship and this was just that. A small blip, nothing in the grand scheme of things.'

I stared at her, shaking my head incredulously. 'Ruth, this wasn't a blip! He left me, jilted me right before my wedding day. He lied to me, developed feelings for someone else and humiliated me in front of everyone I know.'

Ruth let out a trilled laugh. 'Well, boys will be boys, and it wasn't like it was at the altar, was it?'

I glared at her, my hands scrunching into tight fists by my side.

She fidgeted on the seat cushion, her tone softer. 'Who knows, maybe it was a good thing for you too? It meant you could go off gallivanting and getting this travel bug out of your system. Now you can come back, work things out and have a fresh start in a brand-new exciting city and really concentrate on your career. I don't think I need to remind you, but you're not getting any younger, Georgia.'

I was grinding my teeth, an angry heat flushed through my tense body. 'I wasn't gallivanting anywhere.'

'Oh please, so you're telling me that you went abroad and what – found yourself?' She air-quoted that last part and pursed her lips in mirth. 'Georgia, you've had your fun but think about what you're throwing away here. Do you really want to stay on this social rung forever?' She wrinkled her nose at my parents' front room, brushing off some invisible fluff from the cushion next to her.

That was it. I stood up, my heart beating so hard I thought it might leap out of my mouth.

'Ruth. You're right, I did get a lucky escape, an escape from you and your sneering, snobby family. You're a ghastly old bat who's always looked down on me and my parents. Did you even know that my dad is in hospital? Did it even occur to you to ask why I came back home early? It certainly wasn't to run back into the arms of your cheating, lying son.' She gawped at me. I'd never stood up to her before.

Yes. This was it. The confrontation I'd tried so long to perfect, I was on a roll. I was going to nail this.

'You pick on the imperfections and vulnerabilities of others around you to protect yourself. You're petrified that your "perfect" life is going to be exposed for what it actually is: nothing more than a vacuous, superficial farce. You have no real friends; your daughters-in-law only put up with you because they're scared of you; your sons think you're weak and pathetic for staying with your husband – who everyone knows is over-friendly with the waitresses in the golf club–' Where was this even coming from? Alex had mentioned his father's indiscretions a few years ago and since then it had become apparent to me just how much of a ladies' man he was. 'Well, I'm not scared of you any more! I could have taken revenge for what your son did to me, but I'll let karma take care of that. You're like a large spot on my bum cheek that needs to be popped.' OK, I was losing the high ground here.

'I beg your pardon?' She sat back outraged. 'How dare you? I will not stand for this.' Hastily she picked up her handbag, moving towards the front door.

Just then my mum emerged from the kitchen, a rolled up copy of *The Daily Mail* in her hand, waving it like some light sabre. 'And you can stick this load of codswallop where the sun don't shine!' my mum shouted after her, watching as she scuttled away up the crazy paving. 'All right, Viv?' Mum cheerfully waved at the neighbour who'd stuck her head out of her front door, wondering what all the commotion was about.

It had worked. I'd finally said what I wanted to say without the words getting mixed up. I felt alive with adrenalin. Mum raced back indoors, convinced she could hear the phone ringing. I took one look back up the street and saw Ruth pull away in her supersized Range Rover, slightly scuffing the kerb. I'd made the right decision, I knew it.

Walking back into the lounge, my legs shaking from the emotional drama, I took one look at my mum's face. The previous cheery glow had been replaced by a tight look.

'Georgia. That was the hospital. They've got some news about your dad.'

CHAPTER 32

Agog (adj.) Highly excited by eagerness; curiosity or anticipation

We grabbed our handbags, locked the door and jumped into my mum's car; always a supremely careful driver, I'd never heard her grate the gears in her trusty Punto before.

'Mum, be careful!' I cried as she came within a hair's breadth of a cyclist. 'Dad needs us there in one piece.'

'Sorry, love. I just have to get us there right away. They didn't say what the news was, apparently they weren't at liberty to say on the phone.' She clenched her jaw, her hands white from gripping the steering wheel so tightly. 'Get out of the way!' she cried at a bus blocking the road.

It was rush hour, something I'd not missed when I was away, and it seemed the whole world was determined to slow us down.

'Don't they know we're in a rush!' my mum fumed, honking her horn.

'Please mum, remember to breathe. OK, take a left, then your next right.' I'd explained the shortcut that Marie had told me about when she went into labour with Cole. Twenty minutes later – with every likelihood that a speeding fine would be winging its way to us shortly – she screeched into the hospital car park. Her small body was pressed up against the steering wheel as she craned her neck to find a space.

We raced through the corridors, neither of us speaking. Ruth's visit was blotted from my mind. All I could think about was my dad. I didn't even know if what we were sprinting into was going to be good or bad.

'Mum, down here,' I called. She was trailing behind, trying to go as fast as her Marks & Spencer court shoes would take her.

'I'm here to see Mr Green. We're his family,' I said breathlessly to the young male nurse on the reception desk. He yawned, looking through the papers in front of him, every second feeling like a lifetime. Hurry up. Hurry up!

'Ms Green?' The soft voice of Doctor Khan called out, her perfectly made-up face not giving anything away. My mum caught up with me, panting and red-faced. She was wearing an old power suit that used to mean business. The slight ladder snaking up her right ankle was the only indication that standards had slipped.

'Doctor!' she said.

'You got here fast,' Doctor Khan said with a smile developing on her lips. 'I have some very good news for you.' She paused as if about to read out the winner of the public vote on *X Factor*. 'Your husband is awake.'

We stared at her in shock. Those words, the words we had longed to hear, were the best thing I had ever heard.

'No! Oh my goodness. But, but how is he?' My mum clutched at her chest.

Doctor Khan put the clipboard she had been holding on the desk. 'Miraculously, everything appears intact. No abnormal swellings or side effects. He just woke up, as if he had been in a really long, dreamless sleep, and asked for you two.'

I pulled my mum into the biggest, tightest cuddle.

'He is still groggy from the painkillers we have him on and I want him kept in for a few more days for observations, but honestly I have never seen a recovery like it.' She shook her head, smiling, her pearly teeth glinting under the bright lights. 'Whatever you did worked.'

My mum's eyes welled up as she squeezed my hand: 'Oh, thank the Lord!'

'Now, if you would like to follow me, your very brave and strong husband is waiting for you.' She led the way to my dad's room. My heart thumped in my chest, unable to believe what was happening.

Dad was lying in bed; he had barely moved but his eyes were finally open. His mouth cracked into a broad smile at the sight of us.

'Oh Len!' My mum flung her arms around him; he winced at the pressure she was putting on his frail body. 'I can't believe it!'

'Hello, love. Did you miss me?' he croaked, wiping the tears of joy streaming down my mum's face.

'Never do that to me ever again. You hear me?' my mum scolded him before squeezing him tight once more.

He nodded his head, smiling weakly before patting her hand gently. 'I promise. Georgia! You're back.' He reached out a hand to touch my face, gently stroking my tanned cheek, letting his tears fall unchecked. It was the first time I'd ever seen my dad cry.

'Dad, I've missed you so much. We both have.' My throat was clogged with emotion. I tried to take deep breaths, forcing myself to calm down from the euphoria of him waking up. 'How are you feeling? The doctor says you're going to be OK,' I squeaked, itching to do cartwheels.

He nodded slowly. 'I'm sorry to have caused so much fuss,' he croaked.

'Don't you worry about that,' I grinned before turning to Doctor Khan. 'Thank you so, so much.' My face ached from smiling.

'You've got one brave fighter here, ladies.' She smiled kindly at my dad.

'Don't be telling him that, we'll never hear the last of it!' my mum joked, rolling her eyes. I'd never seen her so happy. After thirty years together the love between them hadn't faded. This was what I wanted from a husband: unconditional love and support through thick and thin, something that Alex had never given me and never would again. No matter how keen Ruth was for us to get back together, I knew I'd never be able to trust him. I was over him. I felt like I'd grieved the ending of our relationship, those moments together that meant so much, now just mementos of my former life. Pebbles on the path that lay behind me. Seeing close-up what real love was like had showed me that Alex and I would never have had that.

After ten minutes of tears and cuddles Doctor Khan asked us to leave my dad to rest; he still had a way to go until he would be back on his feet. Telling him we would see him tomorrow morning and thanking the doctor once more, Mum and I stumbled out into the harsh strip lighting of the corridor, dazed from what had just happened. My dad was going to be all right! Mum gathered me into her arms with a renewed burst of vigour: 'My girl!' She was kissing my head and trying to walk down the narrow corridor with her arms around me. 'I don't know what I'd do without you.'

After one of the best sleeps of my life, and another hospital visit the next morning to double check we hadn't dreamt the good news, my mum announced that she wanted to take me for a celebratory coffee. We settled into Kendal's and neither of us could stop grinning. It felt so strange to me to be sitting back where it had all started, where I'd discovered the news about Alex and the baby – the baby that apparently had never existed, I reminded myself. I shook my head. Back then, I'd still had my job, travel was just a silly list tucked in my suitcase, I didn't know Dillon, hadn't met Trisha, hadn't helped to found the Lonely Hearts Travel Club…and I'd never laid eyes on Ben. At the thought of his name my heart fluttered, and I wondered what he was up to right now.

'Just nipping to the toilet, Mum,' I said as she wiped happy tears from her eyes. Walking into the cool air of the ladies' room I slipped past two women washing their hands at the sink and into one of the free stalls.

'I just don't know what to do,' I overheard one of the women complain loudly.

The other one replied: 'You can do better than him. You know that.'

'But I don't know how to be without him,' the first woman said, her voice cracking as if she was crying. Her friend warned her that she would smudge her non-waterproof mascara.

'Oh what does that matter any more? Maybe I'll just run off to some foreign country, escape all of this. Wear what I want, do what I want and be who I want.' I felt a lump rise in my throat. My mind was whirring at a mile a minute. This could be the answer to Trisha's problems!

Washing my hands, the girls nowhere to be seen, I quickly raced back to our table and drained my latte. 'I just need to run a few errands whilst we're in town, is that all right? I won't be long.'

'Take your time, love. I think I'm going to sit here a while,' my mum said, busy scrolling through her phonebook, tapping out the good news to all their friends and relations. My dad was going to be OK, the thought danced about my head like a Pharrell Williams song.

*

'Morning,' I said brightly, walking into Making Memories. My eyes widened at how chaotic the room looked. Cardboard boxes, gaffer tape and unusual objects were unsteadily piled upon every available surface. Hidden in the midst of it all was a slightly sweaty Trisha. So, she really was getting ready to sell this place.

'Ah, hello you,' she said warmly, putting down a strip of tape from in between her teeth. 'Oh, I've got some news for you.'

I looked at her world being packed away. 'Oh yeah? Well I've got some news for you too!'

Trisha jumped. 'Oh my gosh – your dad! How is he?'

I think my grin gave it away. 'He's going to be fine.'

'Oh thank goodness.' She gripped my hand. 'Well, my news isn't anywhere near as exciting as that. After you told me just how horrendous your tour had been I was straight onto Kit, giving him a piece of my mind. He actually apologised! I think he realised that he was never going to make a success of it, like his family had done. I told him I would never be using his services again, but unfortunately that was a bit of an empty threat.' She cast her eyes over the mess around her.

'Well, at least you told him straight,' I smiled weakly. 'Wow, Trisha, look at some of this stuff. It's incredible.'

Amongst boxes filled to bursting with glittering trinkets, souvenirs and rare antiques from around the world, I spotted the globe that used to stand proudly under the window wrapped in a beautiful scarf. 'My Fred brought me that in India, haggled with the stall owner for ages,' Trisha said, nodding at the material fondly. She seemed to be holding it together today, as if she was resolved to say goodbye with dignity before locking the doors for one final time.

'It's incredible,' I breathed, running the silky cashmere through my fingers. 'What are you going to do with all this stuff?'

'Oh, well I guess a lot of it will end up at the charity shop or chucked in the bin.' She looked heartbroken at the thought. 'My flat is very small and already bursting with too much stuff,' she sighed. 'I was never very good with abstaining from shopping as I travelled.'

'You can't throw these things away!' I cried, aghast at the idea. We must have been surrounded by thousands of pounds' worth of valuable artefacts. A thought suddenly came to me. 'Trisha, stop packing up. Soon you're going to have to unpack everything.'

'Georgia, love, it's so sweet that you want to help me but, like I've said, it's too late.'

'But you still have the keys? You haven't sold your business yet?'

'No, but it's going to be put up for auction. Stevie's arriving soon to sort the paperwork for me.' My heart fluttered at the idea of finally meeting this guy in the flesh. 'I told you, dear, I just don't have the money to keep Making Memories going.'

I shook my head. 'Nu-uh. Please, just hear me out before you sign anything.' This was a week of firsts for me: with Ruth, then with Trisha, but for very different reasons. My heart was pumping and the adrenalin coursed through me as I prepared to speak. I took a deep breath, right, here goes: 'I don't have everything mapped out yet, but I want us to go into business together.'

'What?' She took a step back, puzzled.

'When my best friend suggested I write a list of what I wanted to do after being jilted, my deeply hidden desire was to travel, but with my low self-confidence and non-existent

self-esteem getting knocked down by those obnoxious jerks
in that travel agency down the road, plus the scepticism
of some people, it nearly didn't happen.' Trisha nodded,
listening to every word, giving me the space to continue.
'Obviously, getting the sack and chance meetings with some
wise souls,' I paused to nod at her, 'pushed me to make
my travel wish-list a reality. But what if there was a way to
encourage others to make changes in their lives and follow
their travel dreams without the drama I went through? We
could create bespoke packages that let people experience
the countries they've always wanted to visit, with a mix of
adventurous challenges, all cushioned with the advice and
support of other like-minded people. They would be trips
where travellers were encouraged to talk about their broken
relationships, to help them realise they're not alone; they can
survive and come out even stronger than before.' I paused,
taking a deep breath. 'It would be kind of like a Lonely
Hearts Travel Club.'

The idea had hit me after overhearing those girls in
the toilets: broken-hearted, confused women, just like I'd
been, weighing up the risk of escaping their old life against
embracing freedom, but terrified and with no idea how to
actually go about it. The confidence and strength I had
taken from spending time at the Blue Butterfly, surrounded
by perfect strangers who just 'got me', had instantly
helped clear my mind and put a smile back on my face.
I'd realised that I wasn't alone. What if I could help others
too? What if every broken-hearted backpacker could share
the same positive heart-mending experience?

I paused, waiting for her reaction, wringing my hands
together. Please don't laugh, please don't laugh.

Trisha stared at me so intensely I could practically see
the cogs in her head whirring. 'I love the idea, but...I just
don't have any money left in the pot to make it a reality.'

I raised my finger in the air. 'I have some cash, the money from my half of the house I owned with my ex has come through. It's only a few thousand pounds, but it could keep the shop open for another few months as we give it everything we've got.'

Trisha shook her head so vehemently I thought it might spin off into the wastepaper bin. 'No. Not a chance, Georgia. That's your money and I couldn't possibly take it.'

'I thought you might say that, which is why I could put in the cash I've got,' she raised her hand to protest. 'Wait, hear me out. You could sell these amazing things, either on eBay or through an auctioneers. Well, the ones you can bear to be parted from. I bet we're sitting on a goldmine.'

She looked as if she was ready to argue back, then paused. 'It would clear out a lot of room,' she pondered. 'Fred never liked most of the things I carted back with us anyway.' I bit my bottom lip, nervously excited. 'But, Georgia, what if it doesn't work?'

'But, what if it does?' I grinned. 'If I've learnt anything in the last six months, it's that you need to take risks, try new things and give it everything. If it doesn't work out then we just pick ourselves back up, but at least we'll know we tried.'

Trisha nodded along slowly. 'If my Fred were here now, he'd be saying the same thing to you that I'm about to.' A relaxed smile appeared on her lips. 'I think it's a marvellous idea. Why should I go out with a whimper and not a bang!'

Oh wow. She actually liked my idea.

'But, there's still the chance it might not work,' I said, backtracking slightly now she was taking me seriously. No one had ever taken my ideas seriously before.

'I understand that, but like you said, if it doesn't work then at least we tried. You can't go through life being scared of making changes, choosing the easy route every time. Fred always said to me, "Choose the bigger life, the one that when everything comes to an end you'll be proud that you were brave and bold enough to live, that way you can't regret a 'thing.'" She dabbed her eyes. 'Oh Georgia, I don't have the words to tell you how pleased I am that you want to help me. You're right, let's do this. Fred would never have stood for those idiots down the road winning, with their loud music and zany clothes. No, we need to give this one last fight.'

'Really?' I let out the breath I'd been holding.

She suddenly pulled herself together, looked around the packed-up room. 'The only thing is we need to let Stevie know our change of plan,' she said, chewing her bottom lip. 'I feel awful that I've made him return from his travels just to help me out and now I don't really need him.'

'I can explain it all to him,' I said fearlessly, even though I would be faced with meeting this man who I'd built up to be Mr Perfect. Just the fact that he was leaving his current trip to fly back to Manchester to help his godmother made my crush for him deepen even more. 'I'll prepare a detailed business plan, with costs and bar charts and everything, to make him love this idea as much as we do. You never know, he might want to get on board!' I'd never written a business plan in my life, but I figured it couldn't be that difficult. Chumps on *Dragons' Den* did them all the time. 'We could probably do with another set of hands helping shift this stuff anyway,' I added, wafting my arm around the many boxes in the small room.

Trisha stepped around a carton full of tribal masks and we shook hands. 'You're on.'

CHAPTER 33

Maudlin (adj.) Foolishly sentimental

I'd spent the past week glued to my laptop, my mind churning with ideas and inspiration. For the first time in a very long while, I felt an excitement about the future… along with stress over creating a professional-looking business plan. I must have read as many websites and 'how-to' business books on drafting a ruddy robust, detailed and targeted proposal as a university business graduate does. From the moment I woke to the moment my scratchy eyes closed I was writing, stressing, planning, calculating, despairing, drafting, grinning and hoping this would actually work.

Trisha had been unearthing other interesting items to sell from her flat, scouring the internet for how much things could fetch, then calling me excitedly with the incredible results. She had full, pristine collections that buyers were desperate to bid big bucks for just gathering dust in a tea chest next to her sofa, rare exotic pieces that she and Fred had paid next to nothing for but were now worth a small fortune. Obviously, the things that held the most memories for her were too priceless to get rid of, but she'd been strict in her impromptu spring clean.

Finally, when the ideas in my head were sufficiently organised on paper, I printed out my hard work, placed it in my handbag and went to meet Stevie, desperately hoping I could convince him of my plan.

I'd told Trisha I'd be waiting in Kendal's café at three. It was the poshest place I could think of for such an important event. I'd got there early, a mix of nerves and excitement swirling in my empty stomach. Sitting at a free table I pulled out my folder full of ideas to show him. If I could combine my PA experience of organising, my limited but authentic experience of travel, my heartbreak at being a jilted bride with Trisha's business know-how, then surely we could create something to help others go from feeling lost to wanderlust? We could expand online and build on the idea of the club, maybe even invent an app. Waiting for him to show I tried to keep my emotions in check, but I felt so damn excited.

'Georgia?' A deep voice startled me. I quickly brushed cherry Bakewell crumbs from my smart trousers and looked up from my notes.

'What are you doing here?' I gasped. It was Ben. And he was standing in front of me, a confused look on his tanned face. Butterflies were fluttering around my stomach at seeing him again.

'Hey, I thought it was you! I didn't recognise you out of a bikini,' he laughed. 'I'm just meeting someone.' He leant down and gave me a peck on the cheek, he smelt spicy and fresh. My mind instantly flooded with images of a glamourous girlfriend he was taking out for coffee before nipping down to the lingerie section. Focus, Georgia. 'How's your dad?'

I sighed, amazed that he'd remembered. 'Ah, he's fantastic thanks. Coming out of hospital soon, and we can't wait to have him back. I don't know if I properly got to thank you for sorting my flights home and everything, so, well, thanks.' The image of us entwined around each other on my last night at the Blue Butterfly sprang into my mind. I blushed slightly and cleared my throat. 'So, when did you get back?'

'Just last week. Jimmy's already found a contract as a personal trainer and we've just sorted out a flat.' He brushed his hand through his dark waves. 'Been pretty much non-stop to be honest. Anyway, I'll let you get on.' He nodded at the folders on the table. 'Can I give you my number? We'll have to go out for a beer and catch up properly. Book in that tour of the city you promised us.'

I hurriedly passed him my new phone. 'Great, yeah.' After typing his number in he headed over to the counter to order a drink.

Shaking my head I tried to focus on the speech cards in front of me, but my sweaty hands were smudging the ink. I know it might have been a bit over the top but since I was going to do this, I was going to do it properly. The nerves really began to kick in: not only did I have to sell our business idea to Stevie, but now I had Ben as an audience. God he looked good! Maroon chinos fitted snugly around his peachy bum and the thick navy-blue jumper only highlighted how defined his back was. He looked as good in normal clothes as he did in trunks.

Checking my watch, I saw it was twenty past three. Maybe Stevie had got lost? I decided to dial the number Trisha had given me for him, taking a sip of lukewarm tea to sort out my dry mouth. All of a sudden Ben's phone rang.

'Hello?' Ben said, looking at his mobile.

I waved over. 'Oh God, sorry! Think I called your number by mistake,' I blushed. He laughed and turned back to the smiling cashier.

What an idiot. What an absolute idiot. OK, focus, Georgia. This is really important. This time I made sure I pressed

Stevie's number. It was ringing… Again, Ben's mobile chirruped to life. What was going on with this new phone?

'Hello?' Ben said, turning to face me.

'Sorry, I – '

I was just about to leap into a beetroot-faced apology when it suddenly dawned on me…and judging by the look on Ben's face he had put two and two together as well.

'You're Stevie!' I gasped down the line.

He walked over with his cup of coffee, hanging up the phone. 'You're the woman wanting to save my godmother's shop?'

I nodded, pointing to the files. He started shaking his head. 'No way!'

My hands were shaking, my cheeks flamed. Just great. Not only did I have a crush on this guy, I now had to convince him that our possibly crazy scheme for saving the business was a good idea. One day we could even be working together. I thought back to the postcards – they were all sent from places that he'd been working with that water charity. He was the cute guy at the Empire State Building in the photo that I'd caught a quick glance of in Trisha's shop. That was why Ben had seemed so familiar. In Thailand he'd said he had quit his job to move up north but I hadn't put two and two together, not thinking for a moment that he was the mysterious Stevie, the perfect man I'd had a strange crush on.

'Wait. Are you Ben or Stevie?'

'I'm Ben, Ben Stevens. Trisha has always called me Stevie.'

I shook my head slowly. 'But, in Thailand you said you'd quit your job? The one you loved so much?' Trisha didn't mention that. Why would he do such a thing when originally all she needed help with was the paperwork?

'I may have told a slight fib there.' He bit his bottom lip. 'I got fired from my job,' he winced. 'I just didn't want to admit it. It probably hadn't sunk in as it happened just before I met you. I was in Thailand as I'd just left the place I was working in the Philippines.'

'What happened?' He'd seemed so passionate about the work that he did.

'I had a few problems with my manager. He was more concerned with cutting back costs and crunching numbers rather than the projects on the ground, you know, getting out there and helping people. When he told me one day just to pretend we'd visited this one town, who I knew were in desperate need of our help, and say they weren't suitable for an aid project just because it wouldn't be profitable from our end, I knew I couldn't stay working for him. So, I ignored him and made the trip out to this town by myself. We had a company rule that there always needed to be at least two people working in the field for safety reasons; luckily everything went fine but when he found out that I'd broken the rule – and disobeyed his orders – he hit the roof and sacked me, citing breach of contract. Technically he was right, since I had knowingly broken company policy, so I had no comeback.'

'What a tosser,' I said.

He laughed. 'Yeah, he was. So, anyway, out of the blue, a few days later Trisha called me explaining what she was going through. Although she'd asked me to help her prepare the papers to sell the business, I was unsure about whether this was the right thing to do. Not that I told her that, of course,' he laughed. 'But I just didn't have a good enough idea to keep the business going, as I'd looked at her figures and they seemed pretty dire.'

'Well, that's where I might be able to help,' I smiled.

Ben stood by the table awkwardly. 'So, I guess I'd better sit down then.'

I nodded, realising I hadn't yet closed my mouth from the shock. 'Is this going to be too weird?' Just wait till I told Marie about this! As soon as I saw him again I'd felt that same instant connection; what I didn't know was whether this chemistry was one-sided or if he felt it too.

He burst out laughing and scratched his head. 'Only one way to find out. So tell me about the Lonely Hearts Travel Club.'

CHAPTER 34

Beatify (v.) To make blissfully happy

Ben, or rather, Stevie – I still didn't know what to call him – had loved my idea, despite my nervous pitch. He totally got what I was hoping to create and was more than happy to get stuck in with bringing it all to life. I'd reminded him of the fact that back in Thailand he'd not seemed too keen to move to Manchester.

Chewing his lip, he admitted he was wrong. 'I love Trish, but I'd just thought it would be a dull nine-to-five job sorting out coach trips for moaning retired people, people with too much time on their hands. After working for Water Care and seeing real problems in the world I knew I wouldn't have the patience or politeness to sort out disgruntled tourists' problems.' He grinned. 'But I reckon we're onto something with your idea. Being able to make people happy plus getting to talk about travel every day is something I couldn't get bored of.'

So nearly one month later, we were ready to officially launch the Lonely Hearts Travel Club.

I'd never worked so hard on anything before, managing the early starts and business meetings, staying up late to work in my bedroom and having my phone practically surgically attached to my ear. It had been a whirlwind of drumming up business, getting our name out to airlines, hotels and tour operators as well as building new relationships with bona fide tour guides; needless to say, Kit hadn't made the grade. We were starting small to begin with, especially as we had such a tight budget, but thanks to the money Trisha had generated from her antique travel souvenirs, we had an emergency backup fund to tide us over while we got things up and running.

Trisha kept repeating how happy she was that we were working together. She always seemed to find a way to dodge answering my questions about whether she had intentionally tried to set me up with Stevie by sending us to the Blue Butterfly at the same time. 'Just a happy coincidence,' she would repeat, smiling coyly.

Ben had pulled in a few favours with previous contacts and mates back home and had a dead professional website created for free. I'd already had loads of emails from women – and men – telling us that this was just what they needed to get out of their rut, to challenge themselves to move on.

My dad was out of hospital, had put on weight and my mum was back to her old self, clucking around him; their excitement for my business was palpable. The callous thugs who'd crashed into him had been picked up thanks to evidence left at the scene and were due to be sentenced soon. I was back living with Marie and Cole, as it was a shorter commute to work every day than from my parents' – plus I thought that my mum and dad needed some alone time. I didn't want to think about what that entailed. However, I was scoping out a rental place of my own, for when we had a more stable income. As much as I loved Marie and Cole, there was only so much *CBeebies* a childless woman could take.

Marie thought Ben and I were crazy for starting this business together when, according to her, 'there was so much freakin' sexual chemistry between us'. After the initial weirdness of the whole Ben/Stevie thing and the excitement of seeing his gorgeous face every day, we'd settled into a relationship of friendly but professional colleagues. I did have to stop myself from licking his face a few times when he leant over my desk to show me some important email, his aftershave tickling my nose and making my ovaries do the 'YMCA'. Of course, he acted none the wiser to my seemingly unrequited affections. I guess whatever we'd had was destined to stay in Thailand, sadly.

'You nearly ready, hun?' Marie bellowed from outside the bathroom door. 'You can't be late for your own party!'

'Yep, nearly!' I called back, quickly getting dressed in the steamy room. Pulling on a pair of opaque black tights, being careful not to snag them, and fiddling with my bra strap I caught a glimpse of my glinting nipple piercing. I'd left it in. To be fair, I'd got used to seeing a flash of silver every time I showered or changed, reminding me of the 'something wild' I'd ticked off my travel wish-list. It was something the old Georgia would never have dared to get done.

Slipping on a new dress, that I'd actually found on eBay when I was typing up the description of a vintage Cuban cigar holder for Trisha, and dabbing on some make-up, I was ready to go. Ready to start this next chapter, however it might turn out.

'Woohoo' Marie wolf-whistled, making Cole laugh, as I spun out of the bathroom. 'You look bloody gorgeous! Ben's not going to be able to keep his hands off you.'

I laughed and stroked the ruby-red dress; it was a vintage knee-length prom dress with a sticky-outy, puffy skirt and beautiful hand-sewn gold beads on the delicate straps. 'Thank you, you look lovely too. Nothing's going to happen with Ben. I get the distinct impression he just wants to stay as friends and try and make the business work. Nothing more.'

Marie scoffed. 'Whatevs. When he sees you in that dress he won't even remember his own name let alone this friendly co-workers act you've got going on.'

'Taxi's ready!' Mike called out, picking up Cole and telling us how nice we both looked. It seemed so normal seeing the three of them as a family.

'Right let's go!' Marie squeaked, rubbing my arms excitedly as we all walked out into the cold blustery air.

Trisha's shop shone like a Christmas decoration; tartan bunting had been strung in the window along with a large hand-painted banner letting people know that tomorrow we would reopen for business. Trisha was still going to be selling 'Making Memories' tours to her loyal clients with my Lonely Hearts Travel Club as an exciting extra.

'Wow,' Ben breathed, as we strolled inside. Marie was right. This dress was working for me. 'Don't you scrub up well?'

I blushed. 'Thanks. You look very dapper too.' He was wearing a skinny-fit navy suit, crisp white shirt and had styled his gorgeous curls into a sort of quiff.

'Can't be letting the side down now, can I?' He grinned and went to say hello to Mike and Marie. Marie peered round his back when he wasn't looking, gave me a thumbs up and pulled a smoochy face.

Ignoring her I turned to face Ben. 'Anything I can do?' Even though we were still a little early, the shop was set up for a party with tea light lanterns glowing around the room, music playing and stacks of plastic glasses on the far table. Trisha hadn't sold all of her travel souvenirs, leaving us some pieces artfully dotted around. We'd given the walls a lick of paint, a soothing pale-blue colour, and replaced the sagging couch for a comfortable pebble-grey one instead making the shop now feel fresher and bigger.

Ben bent down and picked up a case of Cava I hadn't noticed at my feet. 'I don't think so, I'll go and put this in the fridge in the back office,' Ben said, his muscles straining under the weight of the box. 'Oh, wait! I forgot to buy crisps. Trisha won't be back from the hairdresser's in time to grab them.'

'Don't worry, I can pop out for some,' I said, shrugging on my winter coat.

'Are you sure you don't mind?'

I shook my head. 'I'll be back in a minute.' I picked up my purse and walked out into the chilled air.

Standing in the queue at Tesco feeling very over-dressed with my arms laden with Walker's Finest, the lady in front jostled a pram and dropped a tin of beans from her over-spilling basket. I bent down to pass it to her but caught my breath as she turned around. It was Stephanie, the girl Alex had cheated on me with – basically, the whole reason for my very different life. I'd been so preoccupied since Ruth's unexpected visit that I hadn't given a thought to what she'd said. What was she doing pushing a pram? I thought Ruth had said there was no baby!

'Oh hi.' Stephanie's pale skin had broken broke out in angry red blotches.

'Hi,' I said calmly, passing her the dented tin. If I could get over being jilted, having backpacked with the worst tour in history and my dad being in a coma, then I could get over pleasantries with my ex-fiancé's supposedly-fake baby mama. Wow, that was complicated.

'I thought you'd gone travelling?' she asked, warily twisting a strand of blonde hair and looking me up and down. Bit of a difference from the humiliated bin lady look she'd seen me in last time we'd met.

'Yeah, I did. I'm back now – just about to open my own business, actually,' I replied, not caring how smug I sounded. I deserved to be smug tonight of all nights. 'So, you've had the baby?' I was so confused.

'Yep.' Stephanie smiled down at the pram, looking tired but enamoured with the tiny bundle inside. 'Listen, I'm so sorry for what happened.' She chewed on a chipped fuchsia fingernail. 'I feel really bad about what Alex did to you. Especially as now we're not even on speaking terms.' She nodded her head at the pram.

Underneath the covers lay a sleeping, tiny, contented baby that couldn't have been more than a few weeks old. Judging from the blue Babygro and matching mittens, I guessed it was a boy. I peered closer and felt even more confused. He was quite obviously not Alex's baby, not with such dark olive skin and jet-black hair. Was this what Ruth had tried to explain to me when she came by so unexpectedly? There was a baby all along, it just wasn't Alex's. Stephanie had fooled everyone. I had a sudden urge to laugh.

'Oh right. Well, actually, I'm better than I've ever been. If you do see Alex, please say thank you to him from me,' I said genuinely.

Stephanie looked gobsmacked and moved aside to let me pay for my things: 'Um, yeah, sure. OK.'

'Well, good luck with it all.'

'Yeah, you too,' Stephanie said.

Without the shock of what Alex did causing me to take a long, hard look at my life, I wouldn't have realised just how deeply unhappy I'd become and that I'd merely papered over the cracks, kidding myself everything was OK. Being thrust down a new path had forced me to be honest with myself and to discover what I really wanted out of life. I'd experienced more in the last few months than I had in the last twenty-eight years and I couldn't be happier. Grabbing my bulging carrier bags, I sauntered back to the shop. To *our* shop. I stopped a few feet away to take in the throng of guests inside, all sipping cheap champagne and admiring what we'd done to the place.

The bell announced my arrival as friendly faces passed on their congratulations, and returned to talking about what tours they'd like to go on. Marie was with my parents, who were proudly watching Cole roar in hysterics at Mike spinning the large globe in the corner.

Ben wandered over with a cheesy grin on his face, taking the heavy shopping bags from me. 'OK, I need you to close your eyes,' he said, and clasped a warm palm over my eyes.

'What are you doing?' I giggled.

He leaned in close so that I could smell his natural scent, almost forgetting that we had guests standing just a few feet away. 'We didn't actually need any more crisps. I just had to get you out of the shop for a while as I've arranged a small surprise.'

Before I could ask any questions, I was aware of bodies moving around me, perfume filling my nose and the sound of hushed laughter. Ben took his hand away. Standing in front of me were Lou, Little Em, Astrid and Shelley. They all screamed and pulled me into a group hug; I couldn't close my mouth from the shock at seeing their smiling faces here, in the shop, in Manchester!

'How the –? What the –? Oh my God, this is amazing,' I squealed.

'When you emailed us telling us about your new business, we knew we needed to do more than just send some flowers, so Ben here has been secretly planning our surprise visit,' Lou said excitedly. 'Little Em and I returned a few weeks after you left and are already saving to go travelling again, although this time we're thinking India for one of those spiritual yoga tours I've seen on your website. Mmm, sexy, bendy yoga men.'

Little Em poked her: 'It's not some tantric sex tour she's selling.'

'Listen, if love or a bit of loving comes with it, then that's just a bonus, right?!' Lou laughed.

Wearing a plum-coloured velvet dress and chiffon scarf with embroidered smiling moons, Astrid stepped forward and clutched my hand: 'We are all so proud of you, Georgia, for creating this place where soul sisters and brothers can find themselves together. Plus, once I knew the date of your opening, I quickly calculated the astrological benefits and luckily for you, Jupiter is aligned.'

'At least it isn't Uranus!' Lou and Little Em sniggered.

Seeing my blank face and ignoring those two she continued, 'It's the perfect time to start new ventures; I foresee good luck and happiness. This planetary manoeuvre doesn't happen very often. It's a sign!' The rest of the girls feigned yawning noises as Astrid gently rolled her eyes. 'You'll see,' she chortled before dashing off to catch up with Trisha.

Shelley pulled me to one side, a sly smile on her red lips. 'I've got something for you,' she sang, excitedly rummaging in her brown leather bag. She pulled out a tatty purse and handed me £200 in cash. 'What's rightfully yours, thanks to Dillon.'

'What!'

'I know you weren't up for revenge, but after you left, Lou and Little Em weren't far behind you. Jimmy and Ben went off to Nepal, Phil met up with his wife – oh, he's going to Skype us later – and Astrid booked onto some yoga mindfulness retreat. I decided the island just wasn't the same without our gang, so I *might* have popped over to Koh Pa Sai. I kept thinking about what had happened to you and wanted to put things right, not just for you, but for every woman who's been lied to. So I found Nige, which wasn't too difficult armed with your description – him being the only Rasta Brummie on the island. He immediately remembered you as "the girl that almost died". I explained about Dillon being married and about him stealing your money and probably that of many other girls, as well.'

'Well technically, I *lent* him that money.' *Why was I sticking up for him?*

'Yes, you *lent* it to him and he took it, knowing he had no plans to pay you back - which in my book is called stealing.' She had a point.

'But, how…what?'

'Nige offered to help me, so that night he met up with Dillon in a bar. As if we'd planned it, and like some pied piper, a small Thai man led in a group of pasty-skinned fresh-off-the-boat backpackers. Instantly, Dillon left Nige and started to work his charms on the *ahem*…ugly duckling of the group.'

I was speechless, but willing her to continue, checking that no one around us could hear.

'Soon, Dillon was so preoccupied with making out with this girl, he hadn't noticed Nige take his wallet, which was stuffed with notes, from his back pocket. Apparently, before Nige found *one love* he was a petty thief back in Birmingham. I flicked through his ID cards, which were hiding a photo of him and his wife on their wedding day, then marched up to Dillon, who was practically dry humping this poor girl, and took a photo. As soon as the flash went off he glared at me: "Hello, Dillon Dungworth," I said calmly. Ha! That threw him.'

'His name's Dillon Dungworth?!'

'I know. What a passion killer. Anyway, I said: "I'm Shelley and I'm here to right your wrongs. Unless you hand back the money you stole from my friend Georgia, with interest, this photo will soon be winging its way to your wife." He looked as if he might cry. "We know all about your little con with Kit, wooing new backpackers, then you shag them and then steal from them while your wife waits at home for you," I said. He had the cheek to deny it, before he realised that we had his wallet.'

She paused to calmly take a sip of her drink as I gaped at her.

'You should've seen Nige go. He said, "Don't even think about using me as a ploy for the perfect scuba diving date again." Then he pulled out fistfuls of notes. "This is to pay back what you owe and the rest is a sweetener, otherwise you'd be leaving this island right now." Dillon seemed genuinely scared of him. It was awesome! The best bit was when his new love interest screamed at him: "You promised me you'd take me there tomorrow. Liar!" as she threw her drink all over him and cheers erupted over the bar. He was practically begging Nige not to tell his wife before the bouncers escorted him out. That Kit fella suddenly vanished too. You should have seen it, Georgia!'

'So did you? Tell his wife, I mean?' I asked, in utter shock.

'Not yet. I thought about it, but I couldn't be the one to wreck a marriage. I did, however, send her a cryptic message on Facebook from a fake account telling her to watch out. She immediately replied saying I must be confused as her husband was away working in Kuwait.'

'Wow, Shelley.' I didn't think it was possible to like this girl even more.

'So that's your cash rightfully returned. We took slightly more, but that was spent on celebratory drinks – I hope you don't mind?' she apologised as I laughed. 'Nige took his "sweetener" and painted his boat. He says "Hi", by the way. Apparently, there'd been this rumour that he came from a family of Midlands gangsters and was living life on the run, so no wonder Dillon was terrified of him. The next day he told me that Dillon had left Thailand.'

'I can't believe it.'

'Oh and that's not all, as soon as I knew his name I hit google and guess what?'

I gawped at her.

'That dead brother story he'd told you was all lies!'

'No!'

'Yep. His older, and fitter brother, Mathew, has just celebrated his tenth anniversary working for some law firm in London. Guess who was side by side with him on the press photos? Only our lying pig Dillon.' She looked like she wanted to spit into her empty champagne glass.

'What a pathological liar!' I fumed, then caught sight of Ben chatting to my parents and remembered where I was and what I'd luckily left behind. 'Anyway, enough about him, what about the rest of your travels? Manchester is a very long way from home.'

'Well, when Ben got in touch and told me about your special day, I realised I'd always fancied a little jaunt through Europe.' She nodded over at Jimmy, stuffing himself with crisps. 'Got any good tours going?' she beamed, as I hugged her.

Leaving the gang to help themselves to a glass of fizz and handfuls of crisps, I turned to face Ben. 'Thank you. For everything. This is the best surprise.'

'You're most welcome,' he said, dipping his head. 'It's great to see everyone back together again. Dara and Chef wanted to join us too but couldn't get the time off.'

A knife clinked the side of a glass and the volume on the tribal music that Trisha had insisted we play for good luck was lowered.

'Speech!' someone shouted from the back of the room. Ben nudged me forward to an open space in the packed room.

Help! I hadn't prepared anything but I cleared my throat: 'Hello, erm good evening ladies and gentlemen. I'll keep this brief.' Was it hot in here or just me? 'Thank you so much for being here to support the launch of the Lonely Hearts Travels Club. Those of you who know me will know the adventure I've been on that has brought me here to be standing in front of you today. There's a certain group of people who I met on my travels that sparked the idea of the club and I'll be forever grateful for their help and many late-night talks over cocktails. Shelley over there makes a mean mojito.' I pointed; she took an overly dramatic bow, laughing.

'Thank you to my parents for putting up with me, Trisha for believing in me and Ben for supporting me.' I smiled gratefully at him and took a deep breath. 'During my time away, I learnt that sometimes you need a stranger to show you who you are and who you want to be. We'll be back out on the road soon, testing out trips and making sure we can offer the best service for all of our tours. I can't shake off this travel bug just yet! But before then, enjoy the rest of your night and don't forget to "like" us on Facebook. Oh, – and tell all your friends!'

Everyone cheered and clapped, and Ben squeezed my hand, telling me I was a natural as we posed for pictures for the local press that had turned up. I'd never seen my parents look so proud of me, plus now my mum was back to her old self the newspaper cutting would no doubt be thrust into the face of anyone and everyone she knew. Having Ben's strong arms round my waist as the journalist told us to move in closer felt natural, easy, a good fit. With Alex it had felt forced and clunky, as if we were trying to be the version of us we thought we were meant to be. With Dillon I'd lost all sense of myself as I tried to be what I thought he deserved but with Ben it was different. I just wondered if he felt the same.

A few hours later I threw another plastic glass into a bin bag, smiling at the crumbs on the floor. Ben had already called me twice, insisting that I leave the mess and come and join everyone waiting in the pub on the corner, as we planned to celebrate long into the night.

Well that was a success, I thought, trying to ignore the untidiness of this beautiful room. As I went to switch off the lights my laptop dinged. Quickly flipping it open, I expected to see Phil, who had planned to Skype in with his wife; it wasn't a missed call, but my personal emails that had pinged.

From: Clare Lefebvre
Subject: Help!
Hi Georgia,
How are you?
We didn't get to say goodbye when you left Thailand. I saw on Facebook that you've started your own business and I think I might need your services. Pierre and I broke up! I realised he wasn't the one for me, so this time I want to get back out travelling and do what I want to do. Any suggestions?
C xx

I smiled and typed back fast, thinking I had *just* the thing.

Look out for Georgia's next adventure in
The Lonely Hearts Travel Club: Destination India
Out March 2016

Let yourself go...

Georgia Green is about to board a plane to India, alone –
again. Things were supposed to be different this time, but
Georgia backpacked solo to Thailand and survived, what
could possibly go wrong?

Only she is about to find out that when in India the country
calls the shots – not you.

**Join Georgia Green for her next big adventure
in Bollywood!**

ACKNOWLEDGEMENTS

When life gives you lemons you take 'em and run because . . .free lemons. Seriously though, sometimes you don't realise how far you've come until you look back. This is for you, Past Katy, I told you it would all work out.

I have been overwhelmed, humbled and inspired by the many messages of support from all over the world. You will never know how much it has meant to realise that I am not alone in this adventure. I hope both mine and Georgia's journey will prove that it is possible to find happiness after heartache. Mistakes will be made; lessons will be learnt but you will come out of it stronger. I promise.

Huge gigantic thanks to my noisy, fun and ruddy inspiring family. Mum and Dad — you never doubted me and gave me the courage to be brave, say yes and always try my very best. I hope I have made you proud.

A special shout out to Paula Stokes an intelligent and insightful lady with a keen eye for detail. Your ongoing support would make my grandparents proud.

To Gregoire Pruvost for feeding me cake and chatting over ideas in another language. To John Siddle for being a ray of sunshine during the most bizarre of times. To my wonderful friends, old and new including my bezzo Jen Brown, a true diamond. My life is better because you are in it.

To Victoria Oundjian and Lydia Mason for your priceless editing expertise in polishing this book so that it gleams. Also a huge thanks to everyone at Carina UK for believing in me and to the other Carina authors for welcoming me into this new family with virtual hugs and enthusiastic support.

I probably wouldn't be writing this if it wasn't for Rosie Blake and Kerry Hudson. Because of the WoMentoring Project I got to meet two kick-ass women who encouraged me to pour my soul into this wild journey.

Thank you to my writing gang Holly Martin, Kat Black, Helen Redfern, Rachael Lucas, Cesca Major and Emily Kerr, I never knew hot tubs in a powercut and villagers chasing us with jam could be so much fun.

I am forever grateful to the awesome people I've met along my travels. Special thanks to the following individuals who truly inspired both mine and Georgia's journey: Jenny Silkstone, Rachel Bryant, Laura Hughes, Lars Hognestad, Adam Whitley, Desiree McCaffrey, Mary Wade, Brent Alexander, Ryan Harrison and Zoe Collie.

To my social media friends, super lovely book and travel bloggers and supporters of NotWedorDead.com, huge thanks for tirelessly cheering me on, we may have never met IRL but that doesn't mean you don't rock my world.

And finally, a squishy big thanks to you, lovely reader, for buying, reading, sharing and reviewing. If you enjoyed my little book then please tell all your friends, I'm sure they are just as awesome as you.